TITANIC, 1912

TITANIC, 1912

THE SYMBIONT TIME TRAVEL ADVENTURES SERIES, BOOK FIVE

T.L.B. WOOD

Book and cover design by eBook Prep
www.ebookprep.com

January, 2019
ISBN: 978-1-947833-47-0

ePublishing Works!
644 Shrewsbury Commons Ave
Ste 249
Shrewsbury PA 17361
United States of America

www.epublishingworks.com
Phone: 866-846-5123

For Lydia Brook

All fordone and forgot;
And like clouds in the height of the sky,
Our hearts stood still in the hush
Of an age gone by.

— *WALTER DE LA MARE*

CHAPTER 1

"And remind me again whose idea was this?" Kipp asked, craning his big dog-like head around to stare at me, eyes unblinking, for a second. Our footsteps made no sound against the hard packed earthen floor of the cellar; the passageway was not particularly narrow, but it felt claustrophobic, nonetheless. It took little imagination to detect the rancid odor of sweat born from fear, a lingering trace from the past horrors of that place. Not normally given to flights of fancy or unreasonable fears, I pulled my elbows closer, tucking them tightly at my waist. The cloying, musty smell of old, settled dirt swirled around our small party as we navigated the dimly lit passageway; I suppressed a sneeze with a little hiccup.

Our human guide was willing to let us wander, since she had no fondness for the place we traversed. It was understandable she might think I was one of her kind, given my appearance, but I was not. I am a symbiont, and my looks are meant to deceive people so that I can move surreptitiously amongst their midst. And Kipp, despite his canine appearance, was definitely no dog. Together we form a synergistic bond that allows us to travel back in time. Looking for mysteries to solve was my usual trade, and unfortunately our current assignment didn't involve time travel or even a riddle about which I could wrap my interest. We found ourselves mired in a contemporary engagement that I could blame completely upon the unique abilities of Kipp if I felt mean spirited. After all, if he weren't so remarkable, possessing talents only known to our ancient ancestors, we wouldn't be pretending to be ghost hunters on that particular day. And who would have thought that Technicorps, our employer, would be interested in using telepaths to communicate with ghosts, spirits and the undead?

Reaching out, I ran my hand down Kipp's broad back to smooth his fur, which was raised in a narrow strip from his neck to his tail. The rich auburn ruddiness of his pelt, which turned to molten copper in sunlight, faded to dullness in the low lighting. Thick muscles rippled under my light touch; he was at his prime, powerful, elemental and a pretty solid ship to navigate any storm imaginable. He wagged his plumed tail for a moment, signaling me that he was still game, despite his protestations. Being connected telepaths was a joy as well as a natural part of our selves.

The other half of our party almost ran into Kipp and me when we paused, since those two youngsters were busy checking all the nooks and crannies for possible hiding places for ghosts, specters, and other things unseen by the naked eye. I wasn't quite certain how I'd been convinced to bring them along, since this assignment really called for Kipp's skills and the rest of us were just window dressing. But we'd been given the responsibility to tutor and train a novice pair of time travelers in the art of our species, and even though our current work did not require movement through the ages, Elani and Peter were told to accompany us, making what was typically a duo become a quartet.

It was good that our contemporary rules of engagement prohibited Elani or Peter from eavesdropping on my less than charitable thoughts. We were all telepaths and could exchange ideas with a fluidity that mimicked the effortless flight of a bird, but unfortunately our cultural mores kept us earth bound and politely conversant... except, of course, for Kipp and me. We shared complete and unfettered access to one another's thoughts, no matter how private, at all times. That was the natural way of our kind before becoming civilized–if, indeed, that is the correct word to use for the evolution of my species—and I was finding I enjoyed it more and more as my relationship with Kipp expanded over the years.

"I heard what you said," Kipp remarked privately to me, giggling.

"What?" I asked, feigning innocence of any alleged transgressions.

"You said that if Peter and Elani needed a mystery to solve, perhaps they could go figure out if it was Colonel Mustard in the conservatory with the candlestick." Kipp giggled again.

"Why don't you just stick to your business and this job?" I asked, trying to sound stern and not laugh.

Of course, all our mental chat was not heard by either Peter or Elani, both of whom were good students and quite excellent symbionts. Their only problem was that they were young and inexperienced, and Peter was more than a little headstrong. Despite my better judgment and stern reminders to myself to not become attached, I'd grown very fond of them. On our first significant trip together, Peter had managed to put us all in danger as result of a tendency towards unchecked impulsivity that is not a good trait for a telepathic time traveler who can influence the timeline of history. Since he was not ready to fly solo with Elani in search of past mysteries to investigate, the two of them would tag along with me and Kipp for the foreseeable future.

"I'm here, doing my job, and am willing to explore this cellar, but I still refuse to go into the basement of the Farnsworth House," Kipp replied, pursing his lips in a charming, dog-like pout. "I knew what I'd encounter, and the idea of going down that narrow staircase beneath the floor of the house was more than I was willing to do."

"You can walk your dogs back that way." Sandra, our guide, hovered at the base of the staircase, her hand touching the wooden railing, not wishing to walk with us into the darker area of the cellar of the Soldier's National Museum in Gettysburg, Pennsylvania. Along with past ghost hunters, we'd been given leave to explore, and the feeble story of examining the effect of psychic phenomenon on canines had got us past the door. Little did she know that the minds of our canine-appearing companions were as deeply complex as were any humans' coupled with the instinctual gifts of a genuine canine. Kipp's intelligence and sensitivity was greater than that of any member of our collective. His connection to me was an ongoing gift, and I'd been forced to become a more serious practitioner of our craft as result.

I was the elder of the group at a little over four hundred years of age, although humans might think me to be in my late twenties or maybe thirty after a sleepless night. It was placed upon me the responsibility to make certain that my younger cohorts matured in the way of our kind and learned the ethics and role of our trade. The fact we had the ability to travel through time was carefully concealed since humans could easily corrupt and misuse the information gathered from beings who could move effortlessly between centuries.

Kipp was brimming with confidence, and why not, I wondered? After I was stranded during a time shift in a desolate and dangerous place before recorded history, he found me and formed the bond needed between lupine and humanoid for time travel. His origins made him, uh, natural and unencumbered by centuries of procreation with a limited gene pool as well as way too many arbitrary rules from my way of thinking. Without a moment of hesitation, he left his home to travel to the future with me, and that very fact captured the essence of Kipp. Our collective respected Kipp's abilities which, untouched by the passage of time, mimicked what was normal for our kind and allowed gentle guidance to let him bloom, so to speak. I protected him like a mother bear and stepped in when I felt the collective might use him...just because they could and the fact he was unprecedented and fascinating. Love was not a big enough word to describe our feelings for one another.

Kipp paused as his lips curled into an involuntary snarl. Sandra saw his expression and hesitated for a moment. Due to his remarkable size and power, Kipp was intimidating to most humans through no effort on his own.

"He's probably picking up on something," I said, smiling broadly to calm her fears. "Would it be acceptable to just let us wander down here by ourselves for a few minutes?" Tilting my head slightly, I tried to give a plausible reason. "Kipp might react to your anxiety since he's unaccustomed to you."

Sandra replied in the affirmative, her sense of relief flooding the old cellar. We could hear her heavy steps thudding as she climbed up the narrow wooden staircase to the first floor landing, where the aged floorboards overhead creaked and shuddered.

"I'm glad she's gone," Elani remarked, shaking her head. "Her anxiety was getting in the way of my focus." Despite the inadequate lighting in the cellar, her fur had a shimmery, ethereal glow due to long blond hairs woven throughout her thick gray pelt, making one wonder if fairies had cast pixie dust at her birth. Elani was an attractive female lupine by any measurable standard with a feminine, girlie face and brown eyes the color of a tantalizing nugget of dark Dove chocolate that would melt any heart. Well, almost any. Kipp, knowing of her attraction to him, maintained his boundaries. In his rigidly ethical manner, he thought of her as a kid and he as her instructor; his moral core stopped any romantic speculation right there. I'd learned to not tease him about it since the usually good humored Kipp found nothing at all amusing about the situation.

Technicorps initially had chosen Kipp and me for this particular exercise since Kipp had demonstrated an unusual degree of sensitivity when exposed to what might be thought of as ghosts at a local graveyard as well as having a similar experience at a Civil War battlefield. In the eternally curious nature of my species, our boss—and my close friend—Philo had sent us to Gettysburg in search of haunted places and wandering spirits. It was truly off the mark for us, and I felt as lost as anyone who has started a new job with limited skills. It seemed, however, Kipp and I were primarily being used as mentors for the next generation, which included Peter and Elani. Well, work was work, after all, and there was a stack of bills at home on my desk in need of immediate attention.

"So what was it at the Farnsworth House that was so disturbing, Kipp?" Peter asked, as we paused. Obviously, he'd been chewing on Kipp's remark, waiting for an explanation. Usually tidy, one of his shirt buttons was unfastened, and the tail of his shirt had pulled free of his waistband; wisely, I stayed my hand from reaching out to correct either.

The basement we were currently exploring stretched underneath what had once been the Homestead Orphanage which was opened after the Civil War to help accommodate children left without family. It had long been rumored to be the site of hauntings, disturbing ones, and we were looking for places with high densities of reported sightings. Gettysburg, in general, fit the bill. The dirt floor upon which we walked was dry, but the area, as with most cellars, smelled dank. The air was thick and moist with humidity that felt as if it had been collecting for the past century. The walls flanking the narrow passage were formed of rock set in a rough, uneven pattern. The current pathway ended, just up ahead, with a small door that led even deeper into the basement. It was in that dark area it was rumored some of the worst abuses of the poor children had occurred.

"The Farnsworth House was used as a hospital during the war," I replied to Peter's question when Kipp paused.

"It was upsetting," Kipp responded in a taciturn manner that was not typical of him.

My telepathic bond with Kipp enabled me to follow his thoughts which involved the horrifying results of the field surgeries, and his impressions were terrifying, his reactions visceral. I understood why he didn't want to detail them to Elani, for whom he held a gentleman's tenderness. My Kipp has always been quaintly old fashioned.

Kipp paused to shake himself hard, the sound filling the tight space. "I just didn't want to go inside," he muttered. His head drooped, and the energy I normally felt within him dissipated like a deflated balloon. After a moment he seemed to recover and his tail wagged feebly. "I was thinking of being home again," he said softly. The ability to self sooth is not one to lightly dismiss, in my opinion.

"I wonder why the rest of us can't see these things," Elani mused.

"Well, you know, Kipp has abilities the rest of us don't share," I replied, before one look from my partner made me dry up as fast as a lonely watering hole in the midst of the desert. It had only taken my few words highlighting Kipp's wondrous talents for Elani's eyes to glow with the depth of her attraction to him.

"Sorry, buddy," I murmured to Kipp alone.

"I've told you about that," he replied, his eyes blazing as if they were on fire.

The orphanage had been initiated with good intentions in that the care of children left without parents was felt to be a priority after the war. But somehow, under the management of Rosa Carmichael, the noble vision became dark and twisted, and the children were subjected to harsh punishment as well as outright abuse and torture. The story was that some of the children even died during her tenure, their bodies never to be found. After the orphanage closed in 1877, Rosa disappeared from the pages of history. Later, the building was converted into the Soldier's National Museum. Sadly, the quaint museum lost its allure in competition with other exhibits in the midst of a modern world where the internet and all things quick, bright and shiny seemed to rule. The upstairs echoed in hollow emptiness, the footsteps of occasional ghost hunters being the only sound heard. We passed a low table where a collection of toys had been left as gifts for the supposed spirits of children who lingered, unable to move forward into the afterlife. Noting a series of blocks, I spelled out "hello" before we moved on.

"Maybe we'll set a positive tone," I said hopefully, raising an eyebrow at the others.

Peter and I were forced to bend slightly, so that our heads would clear the exposed flooring and conduits overhead. Reaching out with my hand, I let it drag along the irregular surface of the rock wall, wondering if the tactile stimulation would help me to connect with any lingering souls. All I got was a fist full of dust; wiping my hand on my pants, I figured I was already sweaty and dirty so a little more didn't really matter. As we proceeded into the deepest area, Kipp, who was to my left, paused again, and I heard him growl. At first the sound was a soft rumbling, but it quickly escalated into a rolling sound that reverberated in the close space. Inhaling deeply, I almost could taste the grit of old dirt in the back of my throat. I realized Kipp was blocking me telepathically so that I could not access his thoughts and experiences. He possessed an unprecedented ability with that particular skill, and it had come in quite handy in the past. But there was no way I'd let him take the brunt of this moment without my connection to him.

"Let me in, Kipp," I ordered firmly. Behind me, Peter and Elani were left in the dark since they were waiting for Kipp to issue an invitation to them to share his impressions. My bonded symbiont turned to look at me, his eyes sad. I'd always thought them the most beautiful I'd ever seen, the color of aged whiskey caught in a ray of lingering sunlight on a lazy afternoon. The dark fur encircling his eyes only served to enhance their amber glow, as if someone had used a stick of kohl liner to give emphasis to his expression. After briefly hesitating, he nodded, his ears flat against his head, and allowed me access.

The experience was overwhelming. I blinked my eyes before managing to adjust to the sudden onset of thoughts and feelings. Through Kipp, I could clearly see the figure of a young boy slumped along the far wall, held captive by heavy iron shackles on his thin wrists. Shaking my head, I took a deep breath to clear my mind before I looked again. The little boy stared up at me, his face shimmering in the dimness of the room; his dark eyes rested in deep hollows, but somehow I could see their expression of despair and fear. His mouth opened, and I shuddered as his words tried to form, but all I could hear, through Kipp, was a high pitched wail. As quickly as the moment began, it stopped as Kipp slammed the door on the telepathic transmission.

"There's no need for you to see this," Kipp said, his sides heaving as he shifted his posture slightly.

"Kipp, let me back in," I demanded with my most nonsense voice. Over my four hundred plus years on earth, I'd been subjected to more horrors than I could list. Just poking inside the minds of reprobates, sociopaths and killers had been sufficient to jade me on the baser human instincts. But also, I'd been privy to the thoughts of some of the most noble and gentle of mankind. That memory caused me to recall my dear William Harrow, a man encountered during a past time shift; my hand reached up to my throat where the tiny strand of delicate pearls he'd given me lay hidden, cool and smooth against my flesh, beneath the thin fabric of my shirt.

"What's going on?" Peter asked. He crowded up behind me, as did Elani, and the four of us formed a tight wedge deep underground in that basement of horrors.

"Kipp and I are having a disagreement," I replied. "He wants to protect me."

"Well, Elani and I need to see, too," Peter said, trying to keep his tone from sounding petulant. He tossed his head slightly to rid his field of vision of the heavy curtain of hair that normally fell carelessly along his brow but would occasionally dip over an eye. "I know we're young, but we need to start learning what it's like to really dig into the meat of this kind of stuff."

Kipp sat, breathing hard, while he managed to control the onset of impressions. I realized he was trying to gather and organize one singular moment that he could share. Giving Peter and Elani access to the many would instantly overwhelm them with the intensity of the experience.

Peter gasped as Kipp's vision became his, the sound soft and sibilant in the confines of the room. He'd just thought he was ready to see the world of horror through Kipp's eyes. Elani took a step back before pressing her shoulder against Peter's thigh.

"Will he speak with you, Kipp?" Peter asked, his voice a whisper.

"I'll try," my partner replied.

We stood in the dimness for a good sixty seconds while Kipp readied himself. Anyone who has huddled in a dark room while waiting for the quietness to be broken, understands the tension that builds. I tried to hold my breath since even that soft sound was loud and harsh to my ears; the walls seemed to vibrate, while the wood above us creaked and moaned, despite the fact we knew Sandra had gone outside for a surreptitious cigarette out back.

"Who are you?" Kipp finally asked.

Through his mind, we could see the boy's pale face as it turned towards Kipp. The mouth opened, and although the lips didn't appear to move, words came out of the void. I realized the apparition spoke through conveyed emotion or thought without the use of language.

"Timmy," the boy replied.

"Why are you here?" Kipp walked closer and sat in front of the vision only he could truly see.

"Jeremy put me here for being bad," Timmy said, his head drooping on a thin, pale neck that seemed too fragile to support the weight.

I glanced at Elani and Peter, both of whom were staring at for them what was a blank, stone wall. They could only share Kipp's vision, as could I, but the experience was nonetheless powerful. Peter's hand dropped down to gently smooth Elani's fur; her tail wagged slowly in response. I realized they drew comfort from the physical connection with one another, as did Kipp and I.

"Who's Jeremy?" Kipp persisted. He'd broken past his tentativeness to calmly conduct an interview just as if we'd sat down across a table from someone at Technicorps. His big head tilted slightly to one side as he waited for Timmy's reply.

"He's bigger than me, and Miss Rosa tells him to punish us when we're bad." Timmy glanced up. "He's here somewhere." The boy seemed to cower and shudder at the notion; he made a snuffling sound and rubbed at his moist eyes with a thin, balled up fist.

Kipp turned to me, and it was clear he was unsure what to do next. With Kipp's ability to handle several things at once and compartmentalize them all, he blocked off Timmy from me so I could focus on his words.

"What do I do, Petra?" Kipp asked. "I've never encountered anything like this and don't know."

"What do your instincts tell you?" I replied, leaning forward to place my hands on the top of his broad head. The fur radiated the warmth from his body; I enjoyed the sensation, since the air in the cellar was cool despite the fact it was late August outside, and the summer had been unusually hot.

"That I should try and help him release his connection to this place and go to the afterlife," Kipp replied with certainty.

I glanced at Peter who shrugged his shoulders; if Elani had been physically able, she would have done the same. None of us had been in this situation before and were perplexed as to what our involvement should be. Symbionts functioned under one overarching tenant which dictated we must not interfere with human history. I was pretty sure there was no rule book on this type of experience. After another few seconds of deliberation, I made a decision.

"Let's put a halt today, grab some food, return to the hotel and call Fitzhugh. He'll know what to do. And I'm so hungry, I can't think straight."

If I'd been totally honest, I might have added that the environment of the haunted cellar was oppressive and, personally, I wanted a break from it. Kipp knew my thoughts and was in partial agreement. In a single file line, we threaded our way back down the narrow passageway and up the wooden staircase. As we made our way out into the liberating sun, all of the clinging darkness fell away, and I momentarily considered skipping merrily to the SUV as the hot waves of sunlight beat heavily on my head. Peter managed to convince Sandra that our initial findings were so profound, we needed to return the next day, and after packing the lupines in the back of the vehicle, we started towards the hotel.

"There's a Chic-fil-A nearby, and I know they have good salads," Peter remarked, his comment designed to tempt me as the only confirmed vegetarian in the vehicle.

"Leave the salad to Petra, I'm all in for chicken," Kipp remarked.

"You like everything," I said, trying to joke a little and relieve the tension.

"And don't forget the waffle fries," Elani chimed in, laughing, her mouth dropping open.

Yes, food, rest and consultation seemed to be the next logical move.

CHAPTER 2

"Fitzhugh, what do you think we should do?" I asked.

Telephone contact was essentially unpleasant for symbionts since, with our telepathy, we experienced communication in a much more complex manner. There was rarely miscommunication amongst us because context and content were immediately available and a part of our flowing music of language. But we were in Gettysburg, and Fitzhugh was at my home in North Carolina with Juno, an aged lupine who was considered a valued elder. I could almost imagine Fitzhugh's frown, his bottom lip sticking out just a tiny bit, as I disrupted his late afternoon hot tea ritual, where the kitchen would be filled with the scent of bergamot as he stirred his cup of Earl Grey.

Once upon a time, we'd been adversaries of a sort, with his unbending rigidity a constant irritant rubbing against me in my younger days when I was willing to be a little less disciplined than current age and experience had brought me. I reminded myself of how it was to be an unbridled youth when dealing critically with Elani and, especially, Peter. I think Peter made me recall my own mishaps much too often when I'd been considered to be occasionally rash and more than a little obstinate. But Fitzhugh had developed a fondness for me that placed me squarely in his tiny inner circle. Once there, he was solidly on the side of those for whom he had respect, and, yes, even love.

Fitzhugh was the keeper of our adventures, mishaps and memories and maintained a collection of the history of our species. He supervised the research library at Technicorps, and at somewhere past the age of 1380, he was still as sharp as ever and limited only by a nagging cardiac issue, since he'd had two heart attacks. It was the latter big event that led to his cohabitation with me, bringing along Juno and Lily, a little tiger-striped cat who managed to disrupt my typically dull household on a daily basis.

"So, you want to know if it is unethical for Kipp to try and communicate with a ghost...or what appears to be a ghost." Fitzhugh's voice sounded across the distance. "I hate using these things," he added, meaning the phone. "I have to say it to you, and then Kipp, Peter and Elani have to plumb your mind to get my words." He sighed. "I don't know how humans manage it. Where is the nuance and fluidity of communication?"

I realized he was just expressing frustration and no response was required. So, I waited, rolling my eyes at Kipp who bared his teeth in a mock grimace.

"If our only dictate is to not affect the timeline of human history, a ghost would be a part of past events and no longer living. A ghost cannot have offspring or in any way alter the progression of humanity. The only thing that might change would be the experience of humans if the ghost, uh, goes away, or changes his presentation." Fitzhugh was quiet for a minute as he sipped his tea. "I would say that Kipp attempting to talk with a specter is not a violation and, by all means, forge ahead. He has a special ability and sensitivity here, so I think it falls upon him to push it as far as he can. That is, as long as he wants to."

I heard a faint crash in the background as Fitzhugh fumbled with the phone. "What happened?" I asked.

"I think Lily knocked over something in your bedroom. I must go," Fitzhugh said hurriedly as he hung up the phone before I could interrogate him.

We spent the rest of the evening playing Clue, since that game, as well as Monopoly, had become a welcomed traveling partner. Kipp typically outplayed us all, and I routinely accused him of cheating, although I knew he wouldn't. He had the ability to dig into our minds, as well as those of humans, without our having awareness he'd done so and possessed the natural talent to cheat at an unprecedented level. But Kipp was too principled and moral to do such a thing just to win a board game. And I knew he always was happy on the rare occasions when I won, such was his love for me.

After Peter and Elani drifted off to their rooms, I took a quick shower and climbed into bed. The hotel mattress was soft, and I felt my spine curve as the surface beneath me sagged. Kipp, gauging the distance, hopped up and curled next to me–after staggering a little on the spongy surface—his large head finding its resting place on my breast bone. We lay there, quiet, listening to the sounds of a television in a nearby room. Outside, a car door slammed as a new occupant arrived for the night. It wasn't that I was uncomfortable; I just preferred my own home and wasn't that keen on staying in a different place every night…an odd admission for someone who traveled for a living to make.

"It's different," Kipp offered. "When you're on a time shift, there is excitement and anticipation."

"Yes," I answered dully.

"You dreamed about him again," Kipp reminded me, pushing his chin against my chest even harder. "Let me help," he added, with the knowledge he could actively manipulate my dreams as easily as he read my mind.

"No, Kipp, but thanks," I replied, reaching up to scratch between his large upright ears. "It'll get better with time, so I think I'll handle it the old fashioned way." Even as I said it, I wondered how long my grief would last over an ill advised love I harbored for a human man, William Harrow, who I met when traveling to London in 1888. Kipp took a deep breath, his sides heaving, as he exhaled from his nose. The airflow tickled my flesh, and I laughed softly. Lightly running my fingers though his pelt, I gently finger combed him while listening to his soft breathing which filled the dark room.

"I'll make it, buddy. Millions and millions of sentient beings have made it before me, so I'll make it, too."

"If you won't talk about Harrow, then tell me why you like being Professor Plum or Colonel Mustard when we play Clue?" Kipp turned to gaze at me in the twilight of the room's interior. "There are Miss Scarlet and Mrs. Peacock..." his thoughts drifted off as he tried to distract me from my angst by being silly and irreverent.

"If you explain your fascination for Mr. Green...it's a two way street, my friend."

Early the next morning, our little group found itself at the entrance of the museum waiting for Sandra. It was that time of day in the summer when the weather promised to be hot, bringing an expectant stillness before the heat truly broke. Close by, a blue jay cawed noisily, scolding us for whatever bird reasons he had concealed beneath the sassy Mohawk of feathers that jutted up in a spike on top of his handsome head. Kipp had the ability to read the notions of many earth bound creatures but birds stumped him. I saw him eyeing the proud blue fellow and recognized Kipp's need to keep trying, forever if needed, to overcome that obstacle.

A small gray car with a mangled front bumper arrived in a flourish of dust and scattered gravel. Sandra emerged, explaining she had to unlock for us before racing off again to get to the bank when it opened. Privately, I was happy for our isolation because we could avoid having to sift out her stray thoughts as we dealt with the horrors of the basement. The wooden floor of the main level creaked and popped as we walked towards the stairs to the cellar; in the relative emptiness of the room, the sounds echoed and rolled off of the bare walls. The oddest thing happened, however, as we began to descend the narrow staircase into the basement. A pungent smell, much like that of raw sulfur, penetrated the small space to the degree it almost irritated the back of my throat. Trying not to cough, I narrowed my eyes and shook my head at Kipp, whose ears went flat.

"Well, that's pleasant," Peter remarked, his eyes watering, trying to make light of the moment. But it was clear that whatever noxious spirits inhabited the museum were giving us a full display of their displeasure at our presence by unleashing a stink bomb. Peter's hand drifted down to squeeze the back of Elani's neck; her tail wagged in response. She may have been anxious, but she was still game, uncomplaining, and ready to go forward. As we passed the table where old toys had been left as presents, Elani, who had learned to read English while a student in Kipp's classes for young lupines, gave a startled little bark.

"Look!" she exclaimed, exhaling with a huffing sound.

On the low, battered wooden table, a set of blocks had been arranged to spell out the name Tim, sitting next to my previous day's "Hello". I might have thought one of my party was playing a joke but knew the truth, since our kind, with few exceptions, finds it difficult to be deceptive with other symbionts. With humans, there was a different set of ethics and other rules of engagement applied. Looking down, I saw that the hair on my arms was standing on end. Kipp looked up at me, and I nodded. It was time to move into the back passage where the children had been tortured, suffering in the darkness.

It took a moment for our eyes to adjust to the dimly lit area; the apparition of Timmy remained, huddled in a miserable glowing heap on the dirt floor. This we could see through Kipp actively sharing his impressions. Kipp walked forward, but before he could reach the specter, another form moved from out of a shadowed corner to cross the room. It appeared to be an older boy dressed in woolen dungarees with a worn and patched plaid shirt tucked in at the waist. The boy carried a thick stick which he held in one hand, while he softly struck the palm of his other hand with the object. I found it remarkable that I could hear the soft thud of the stick against his nonexistent flesh. At first his head was tilted downward, so his face was not visible, but slowly, as if pulled by strings, his chin tilted up and revealed a pale face split by a demonic grin and red eyes glowing beneath straight, heavy brows. Kipp took a step back for a moment but stopped when the older boy moved towards us. It was clear he wanted to chase us from the space. Timmy looked up; his ghostly face was wet with tears which glistened unnaturally, almost like diamonds caught by the light.

"Are you the one who hurts Timmy?" Kipp asked.

"Yes, this is my place, and I do as I please," the boy responded.

"Miss Rosa says so." He crossed over to Timmy and, using the stick, struck a cowering Timmy across the shoulders.

I glanced at Peter, whose mouth gaped open. We were definitely in uncharted waters, and I was unsure how to craft an intervention with an abusive, toxic spirit. Quietly, I prompted Kipp to go with his gut.

"We're going to release Timmy from this place, and you will be left alone with no one to hurt," Kipp calmly replied, folding his haunches and taking seat on the cold floor. Thankfully, the sulfur smell had dissipated, replaced by the familiar dankness. From above, we heard the front door shut, signaling the return of Sandra; the wooden floor creaked with her steps across the room. Timmy stopped crying as he heard Kipp's confrontation and something akin to hope crossed his thin face.

The boy with the stick made a growling sound and drew back his arm to throw the stick at Kipp, who remained unperturbed. As the stick, which had no form but was an ethereal construct, flew towards Kipp, he managed to catch it in his mouth. When he did so, the glowing object made a popping noise and disappeared; the stick boy's face contorted with rage. Kipp rose, ignoring the boy, and walked to Timmy, who was sitting on the unyielding floor, his back propped against the rough stone wall. With his nose, Kipp manipulated the manacles, which fell free from the specter's thin wrists. Kipp lay down next to him and invited Timmy to touch him. Walking closer, I could see Kipp's fur ruffle as an unseen hand rubbed the thick pelt of auburn hair.

"Your time is past, Timmy. You need to leave this place and go to the afterlife where all is good, and you will be welcomed and loved." Kipp looked up at me, asking for more words of comfort and direction.

"Tell him to go to the light," Peter whispered. "That's what they always say in movies."

"And this isn't a movie, so let's not pull a line out of *Poltergeist*, please," I hissed. "Let Kipp handle it."

"I don't like it here," Timmy whined.

"And you can leave," Kipp answered. "Walk with us and leave him behind," he said, returning stick boy's glare with narrowed eyes and bared teeth.

Reluctantly, because he feared another beating, Timmy rose, placing a shaking hand on Kipp's broad back. Peter's eyes opened wider, as did mine. We could clearly see the imprint of a small hand tangled in the thick fur. Ignoring the hostile taunts of stick boy, we left that innermost room and began traversing the rock lined corridor that led to the stairway. I walked behind Kipp and the ghost, which I could only see through Kipp's view, resisting the urge to reach out and touch the little boy.

"Go ahead," Kipp urged. "He thinks you're pretty and would like you to pet his head."

Looking through Kipp's eyes, I gauged the appropriate place to rest my hand and attempted to gently tousle the little boy's hair. I heard him laugh, the sound bright and tinkling like a tiny bell being rung. Pausing, I stared at my finger tips which tingled slightly after the caress.

"I wanna go home." Timmy's voice was plaintive in the narrow passageway.

"We are taking you home," Kipp assured him.

Sandra stared at our odd convoy as we slowly walked across the room until we reached the front door. Hearing a hissing sound, I turned and noticed that stick boy had followed us into the main room and was growling again, the sound rolling like soft thunder across the room. For a brief, terrifying moment, his teeth resembled those of a predator.

"Ignore him," Kipp said, his words directed at Timmy as well as the rest of us. "He works off of fear, so we will give him nothing."

Peter darted ahead to open the front door and stood aside as Kipp led Timmy to the threshold. The little boy's head rotated on his thin neck as he scanned the environment; he hesitated, his body still inside the interior of the building where he'd been trapped for so many years.

"I've not been outside in a long time," he said, his voice soft in our minds. The ghostly child was filled with eagerness as well as apprehension.

"Go now, play, run, skip...and don't come back here. You're free," Kipp said.

It is difficult to describe what happened next, but the form of what Timmy was–or what was left of him on earth–walked forward into the bright sunlight of day. I saw a smile on his face as he tilted his head back and let the sunlight touch what once had been corporeal flesh. A shimmering glow surrounded him, a circle of light that became brighter and brighter, and then it popped like a balloon over-inflated with too much air. Kipp stared at me, but I had nothing to say.

"Since we aren't ghost busters, I have no idea if we did the right thing, but it felt right," I finally stammered. As the elder of the group, it fell to me to try and define our actions in a positive light.

"As Timmy, uh, popped, he felt happy and safe," Kipp said. "I guess that is our best judge."

A car drove by, giving a toot on the horn to remind us gaping tourists to get off of the road. We stepped back onto the grassy verge and took shade beneath an ancient oak with a heavy canopy of green, summer leaves. The heat of the day as well as our ghost encounter had made me break out into a sweat; using the back of my hand, I wiped beads of moisture from my forehead.

"So, do we go back and rescue stick boy?" Elani asked.

"I don't think he wants to be rescued. He likes the hidden corners of the cellar," Kipp said. "I don't know how to help him. There was something dark about him that's frightening."

"Since we're not really in the business of rehabilitating lost souls and don't know what we're dealing with, I'd opt for staying clear." Peter was the voice of reason on that particular day.

Privately, I felt some despair at leaving the museum with the knowledge that angry, disturbed child lingered there like some sort of demon lurking in a place of sad memories and darkness. We had no knowledge of Jeremy's journey in life and what had led him to such circumstances. Perhaps he'd been terribly abused, too, at some point causing him to follow a grim path. But Peter was right, and it was with sadness mixed with joy that we drove away.

"What's next, boss?" Kipp asked, as he poked his big head in between the front seats. Curling my arm up around his neck, I pulled him close to me.

"We'll head towards the battlefield park and check in with the rangers. Philo submitted a request for us to have access for reasons of research. I guess we'll start at the Devil's Den."

The air conditioner kicked in, and I closed my eyes against the breeze. I didn't formally object to this current assignment but none of this was really in my wheelhouse, and I preferred a time shift to a place in history where a true mystery lurked. And if I had to drag Peter and Elani along, I'd reconciled myself to the fact that was okay, too. Peter, who was driving, turned to glance at me, a big smile on his face.

"What?" I asked.

"That was pretty cool," he replied in the manner of youth.

"We met ghosts, confronted an evil specter, and sent one off to the afterlife." I sighed. "I'm not sure that cool is a big enough word." Trying to return his smile, I added, "Just another day in the life of a quartet of symbionts."

CHAPTER 3

Normally, dogs are not allowed to roam the battlefields of any national park, including Gettysburg. Technicorps had applied for an exception since we were on a research venture. It had taken some convincing and, if Philo was to be believed, the arm twisting of a congressman or two. Philo was the reluctant head of our collective and my oldest friend. We were more like brother and sister than anything else and could argue and disagree with the passion and certainty of solid friends. In terms of the lupines being admitted to the fields at Gettysburg, we had been told, more than once, to curb them elsewhere and not on hallowed grounds.

"I really find that pretty darn insulting," Kipp began, rolling his eyes at me as we walked along a grassy span in our approach to Devil's Den. "The fact they think we would relieve ourselves out in the middle of what is basically a shrine to the fallen and a massive graveyard is just too much."

"Okay, dial it back," I replied. "Kipp, you are always the research hog, so what do you know about Devil's Den?" I asked, trying to divert him from his irritability and get him back on track.

Kipp was still a bit huffy over the park ranger's last instruction to us, and he plodded along, head down, tail slowly wagging as he sniffed at the grass, eyes staring ahead for a moment. The grass on the field had not been mowed recently and was dry from the late summer heat; there was still green but the blades were withered and brown on the tips. Since Kipp hesitated, Peter, who was always the eager student in the back of the class room who would frantically waive his arm to get the attention of the teacher, volunteered.

"We all know that the battle of Gettysburg was the most significant in terms of loss of life of any American battle. And the moment came together accidentally and was not really the culmination of a definitive plan by the combatants. Around sixty thousand men died and countless others were seriously wounded or maimed.

"The history of Devil's Den precedes Gettysburg, going back to the 1700's when the American Indians who occupied this land regarded it as a place of evil, and the landscape has been associated with a sense of foreboding since that time." Peter used his hand to sweep outward in a display. "Some people speculate there's a convergence of the topography and other elements that have made Devil's Den a place of sensitivity for the cosmic world." He glanced at us, obviously pleased with his recitation. All he needed was a mortarboard hat and tassel, a pointer stick, and he'd be good to go.

Elani stared at him, her jaw dropping open as she began to pant in the hot weather. I caught her attention and slowly closed one eye in a conspiratorial wink. Peter was the kid who tried too hard and always knew just a little more than everyone else. It was good that he was basically likeable, since he could have just managed to be annoying. But Elani had grown attached to him, in the manner of our kind, and felt the loyalty of all good, bonded symbionts to her partner. With that thought in mind, she trotted over to walk next to him, her furry side brushing against his leg.

Kipp, too, was an effortless brain. Since he'd learned to read English, he read almost constantly...even more so since I got him a Kindle and a stylus he could grip between his teeth. Peter downloaded volumes of books for him on the American Civil War...as well as every other conceivable topic. And all I know is that anyone who read Shelby Foote's comprehensive trilogy of the war from cover to cover had my admiration.

"I keep telling Petra she needs to study more before we take an assignment, but she just likes to ride on my coattails," Kipp remarked, pausing to snap at a honey bee lazily buzzing around his big head. He had no intention of harming the little bee, which was enjoying the warmth of the day, but a gentle warning was in order, nonetheless.

His sarcastic comment told me he'd located his previous good humor, and we were back on track. No one likes being accused of not knowing where one should relieve oneself, and Kipp was no exception.

To be honest, there was something unsettling about the rock strewn hillside we approached; massive slabs of ancient rock hovered, gray and oddly threatening, against a background of blue sky left barren and cloudless. The tactical advantage of having possession of this place from which to fire on the advancing enemies was immediately apparent. The area was southwest of Gettysburg proper and just to the north lay what had been called "The Wheatfield", another historical killing field. We'd passed that area, which was flat and unremarkable except for the scattering of monuments to those who'd fallen; the gleaming hunks of granite and marble stood out like tombstones beneath the glaring sun. Unsettled spirits were said to walk along The Wheatfield, but on that day, as the unrelenting sun beat down on our heads, we passed unmolested. Closing my eyes, I tried to imagine the topography of the surrounding landscape before the war left behind its devastation. This had been farmland, rolling and fertile, with groves of trees standing like islands on a sea of grass which grew to mid thigh before being cut. When the wind blew, the fields would ripple like unsettled water before a storm. There would have been fruit trees with limbs bent from the heavy weight of ripe peaches and apples. Yes, I could clearly see it in my mind's eye.

"On July 2, 1863, there was intense fighting here." Kipp interrupted my reverie as we began to thread our way through the natural maze of upright boulders. "The Confederates, under Hood's division, controlled this ground." He paused, and I saw the hair rise on the back of his neck. "Uh, the ground underneath us was running with blood and bodies fell in these crevasses, some never to be recovered." Kipp paused again, turning his head; the sunlight fell on his bright, copper colored coat, and the heat was threading through his dense pelt to his skin. Despite his naturally cooling double coat, he began to pant, as might a dog, to refresh himself. "Do you guys see it, too?"

Well, this time I did without the assist of Kipp, and so did Elani. There was a well documented apparition of a man who many thought was a Texas soldier from his appearance. And this particular ghost had been seen by folks who were not particularly sensitive to paranormal phenomena. Why Peter didn't see it when the rest of us did, I don't know...maybe he was trying too hard. About ten feet ahead, the figure of a man dressed in ragged clothes made of brown, homespun cloth, barefoot, with a floppy, big brimmed hat and stringy, lank hair that fell past his shoulders, stood. He turned to look at us, and his face was clearly visible. After a moment, he pointed, turning towards the southeast.

"What you're lookin' for is over there," the man drawled, his voice clear in the stillness on the hillside. His sun weathered face wore an expression of consternation...a perpetual scowl of worry on his furrowed brow.

Curious and feeling no fear, I walked closer, extending my hand. The apparition held none of the malignance of Jeremy, the stick boy from the basement of the Soldier's Museum as well as lacking the terrified desperation of little Timmy. I wasn't surprised when my hand floated through the ethereal body of the man. After a moment, he repeated his phrase, turning to point again, directing us. Since we were researching Kipp's ability to communicate with ghosts, or whatever these encounters were, I asked him to query the man on a few specifics.

"Are you from Texas?" Kipp asked.

The specter paused before turning to point again, but this time he was silent.

"Answer me, soldier...are you from Texas?" Kipp persisted, his tone more authoritative and with a ring of command.

"Yes," the figure answered. We had joined in Kipp's experience and could hear the replies.

"Are you part of the 4th Texas Volunteer Infantry?"

"Yes, I am."

"Why do you linger here? The battle is done," Kipp asked.

After a pause, the figure replied, "I was told to not leave my post."

Kipp looked at me, confusion on his face. "I don't know what to do, Petra. Yes, we intervened with Timmy, but do we do the same with all we encounter?"

A flock of sparrows whirred overhead, their grey and black bodies twisting in the air, and somewhere in the distance I heard a motor start up; the smell of fresh cut grass tickled my throat. Around us, the sunlight became tangled in the matrix of the towering rocks, which appeared to move in the shimmering rays of light. Shading my eyes, I tried to focus and command the rocks to be still, but they kept up their dance. Soft laugher came to us from the pathway we'd just trod; another group of visitors was beginning to thread its way through the maze of rocks, and our peace was about to be disrupted.

"What do you guys think?" I asked, glancing at Peter and Elani.

"I'm uncomfortable with this," Elani replied, her voice definitive. "Yes, Fitzhugh saw no problem in it, but do we "manage" all the ghosts we encounter? We really have no idea what the ramifications are of such actions." She paused, breathing hard. "I think we need to record what Kipp experiences and take the information back with us."

Peter, who lacked Elani's cautious filter, agreed. Actually, I did, too. This was uncharted and definitely out of our field of expertise.

"And the next thing you know," Elani persisted, "Technicorps will have you and Kipp running all over the world to act like ghost busters, just because it is novel and no other collective will have a Kipp to do such a thing." She huffed in agitation."I fear we will set things in motion for Kipp to be used."

Well, I thought, the fascination of the youth of the world with their rebellious notions of the establishment...and she was probably right. I may have been older than she, but I had been a mover and shaker of the establishment most of my career. Age and the responsibilities of being Kipp's partner as well as a mentor for Peter and Elani had made me more cautious and thoughtful of my actions.

I knew Kipp was relieved by our decision and support of him. Intervening with the spirit world was taxing, and he really wished no interactive part of it. But we would dutifully continue our inspection of Gettysburg without changing the continuum of some of the folks who were unable to leave this place for whatever spiritual reasons we didn't comprehend.

Despite the heat and stillness of the air, we trudged up to the summit of Little Round Top where the Maine volunteers found fame when they were ordered to hold that critical position no matter what. There was a well known sighting that stretched back to the actual war itself. The soldiers claimed to have seen a man, mounted on a white horse, riding ahead and beckoning the soldiers to follow him. The figure was described as wearing a Tricorn hat such as would have been popular in revolutionary times. It was said the man's face was that of George Washington. That particular figure had often been seen since the war but stayed in hiding on the day of our visit. Maybe he was wisely avoiding the withering heat.

"I almost wonder if these apparitions are caught in a feedback loop," Peter suggested. "It would explain why they are seen occasionally but not consistently." He sat on a large boulder, signaling it was time to take a break. His face was reddened from the exertion of the climb, the collar of his shirt damp with sweat and soiled from the accumulated dust and dirt acquired during our walk.

Personally, I was fine with a breather. I was glad I'd brought a hat lest my face get burned from the persistent sun overhead. The overheated lupines were happy to find a resting place on some trampled leaves beneath a shade tree. With a soft thud, they dropped to the ground, their panting the only sound on the isolated hillside.

"If Kipp, with his exquisite sensitivity, can't see the man on the white horse when so many others have, it would make you wonder about such," I replied. "Or do those who are in that in-between place between life and the afterlife chose what they do and when they do it?"

There had been tales of another vision associated with Little Round Top, so, taking our chances, we began to work our way down the western slope. Maybe it was just good fortune for a quartet of novice ghost hunters, because it was not long before Kipp's head lifted with interest, and he encouraged us to once again view the world from his eyes. Ahead, picking its way with care down the rock strewn slope was a horse. Of course, the animal was not living, and I knew if I tried to run my hand along its sweaty, trembling flank that there would be no substance. At one point, the animal turned its head towards us, nostrils flaring as if it was trying to take in our scent. The horse's eyes had an unnatural, dull red glow, and even though I perceived no threat, the hair raised involuntarily on the back of my arms. Astride the horse was a man, dressed in a nondescript uniform, whose head was missing. The man's neck, a pale, shimmering stump, ended in a mass of torn flesh. Despite being headless, the body of the man turned towards us, and I felt a jolt of anxious horror as I expected him to guide the beast he road towards our party. But after a moment's hesitation, he nudged the horse, using his knees, his hands lightly holding the reins, on down the slope. Peter's mouth fell open, forming a perfect "O" of astonishment.

"What did you get, Kipp?" Elani asked, trying to act casual, but in reality she was as shocked as the rest of us.

"Not much, since I didn't really get a chance to have contact. Quite simply, the man is looking for his lost head." Kipp looked at me, his eyes bright, plumed tail waving slightly in the almost nonexistent wind. For a moment, I thought he'd made an attempt at clever humor before deciding he spoke the truth.

The afternoon was getting away from us, and I admit I was hot, tired and feeling lost. The thin shirt I wore was plastered to my body from sweat, and grit covered all other exposed skin surfaces. With plans to revisit another site the next day, which would be our last, we returned to our hotel. The rooms were clean but furnished with the typical items found in most low to moderate budget hotels. Techni-corps didn't offer first class accommodations to its travelers, but since I'd spent many a night on the floor of a cave—as well as a memorable week in a shed with only a partial roof and a sagging rear wall—the room seemed pretty sweet. I noticed that some of the faux veneer made to look like wood paneling was peeling off the side of the cabinet. Overhead, a light bulb had blown, leaving its lonely companion the job of providing illumination to the dim room. After hot showers, we gathered in Peter and Elani's room where a delivery boy had brought a box lid full of Chinese takeout containers. Kipp sniffed with care, the whites of his eyes showing, as I spooned out a large portion of beef and broccoli on a bed of white rice. After one careful lick, he began to almost inhale the food.

"I can now assume you like Chinese food?" I asked, laughing.

He nodded, too busy to answer as he started on a plate of lo mein. Elani wasn't far behind as she polished off two containers full of chicken with vegetables. She found the baby corn to be particularly fascinating as it crunched between her teeth.

"So, what did your mom have to say?" I asked Peter as I relaxed in a chair, my appetite satiated for the moment.

He darted a look at me as he set his plate aside. We were all too tired to concentrate on Clue or Monopoly, and it was nice to just eat and have little else to consume our normally busy minds. Peter was wearing his horn rimmed glasses which made him look older and wiser. He was, in actuality, a bright young symbiont who happened to be lacking in judgment department. I still struggled with the notion that I was given the job to teach him such a quality...one barely managed by myself. His brown eyes met mine as he swung the heavy forelock of hair to the side.

"She said the things all mothers say, I guess. She misses me, wants to know if I'm okay, if I'm eating enough, am I getting enough sleep... you know the routine." His voice sounded dull.

"Yes, I had a mother, too," I replied. "What's bugging you?"

He paused, reaching down to push a half eaten egg roll to one side of the paper plate. Peter was typically pretty animated and energetic but at that moment looked like a balloon that was slowly losing air.

"I want to be a traveling symbiont," he said. "I want to time shift with Elani and research the past." He stood, running his hand through his thick hair. "But here we are," he remarked with an exaggerated hand gesture, "looking for ghosts, which seems to be a ridiculous waste of time. I can't help but think this is just a way Philo and the Twelve have to punish me for my inadequacies and poor decision making during our first real trip together." If he had been about eight years of age, he might have pouted, too.

I looked at Kipp, who had exited from his comfortably predictable spot in the back of my mind. He did that, from time to time, when he wanted me to sort things out on my own. Elani had stopped eating, finally, and was delicately licking some white sauce from her paw.

"Peter, if you think this assignment is about you, then you are more egocentric than I thought," I said, ignoring his raised eyebrows. "I assure you, the Twelve do nothing to punish or to make a point. Their directions to us are larger than that and with bigger consequences for humanity. If we screw up, we get pulled off until we can prove we will function as per expectations."

It was difficult for me to take the side of reason, since I had my own issues with the Twelve. Just thinking about the control that body exerted over my actions and the choices I made caused my shoulders to knot with tension; rolling my head, I took a deep breath and tried to dispel the feeling. Maybe it was always easy to criticize the ones who held the reins of power, especially when I had no desire to hold them myself. Being a routine player in the collective of symbionts was enough for me. Did I lack ambition? Probably. Or maybe I was just content with life in general. Best guess was that it was a little of both.

"So while many things may be about you, this is not one of them," I picked back up with Peter, who seemed to need a mild correction. "You messed up during our *General* trip, and you need to consider yourself fortunate that the Twelve didn't ground you permanently." I knew I sounded harsh, but heck, he was a grown up and I wasn't his mother. Kipp opened his eyes wide as he looked at me; Elani avoided eye contact all together and stared at an invisible spot on the carpet.

Peter's face reddened, and he started to reply but obviously thought better of it and walked over to gaze out the window of his room. We were on the second floor which afforded us a nice view of the countryside of that part of Pennsylvania, which was picturesque with its gently curving land that dipped into low valleys where pale mist would linger until mid morning. Sunset loomed; the shadowed disc of a once important sun was now an afterthought as it hung, diminished, behind lavender and coral cloud banks that spilled unevenly across the horizon. The sky was filled with soft color that must have been designed to soothe the beasts of the earth as twilight fell.

Kipp rose, signaling our departure. I knew he thought I'd given

Peter enough of a sermon for the day, and it was time to reel me in. We walked back to our room, dodging a family who had just arrived and approached us on the narrow walkway. The father gripped the hand of his daughter tightly upon spying the massive Kipp who began to wag his tail to signal no harm would come from him. Once back in our room, I plopped in a chair and returned Kipp's stare.

"So, what was bugging you?" he asked, shamelessly borrowing the question I'd thrown at Peter. Folding his haunches, he sat opposite me, his eyes almost level with mine.

"I'm not sure. I'll apologize to Peter in the morning." I sighed, closing my eyes.

"He's doing a good job, and you know it," Kipp persisted.

It was rare I was aggravated with my best friend and bonded partner, but he was getting annoying, and he, of course, knew it.

"I never wanted to be a mentor for young symbionts," I began. There was an unpleasant whine in my tone. "And here we are, looking for ghosts in Pennsylvania, when there are other things you and I could be doing. I wonder if this assignment had more to do with giving Peter a break, considering his mistakes during our last trip out, than evaluating your talents at ghost communication." Raising my eyebrows, I added, "Maybe Peter is right, and it's all about him." Leaning forward, I began to unlace my athletic shoes; the feelings of discouragement and uncertainty returned with a vengeance. "I used to know what I wanted to do and my place in the general scheme of things."

Kipp almost bounced forward and gave me a big, sloppy, wet lupine kiss on my cheek. Once there, he nuzzled close, the stiff whiskers on his muzzle tickling my flesh.

"Petra, if the Twelve had wanted to restrict Peter and Elani, they would have just done it. None of this has to do with us. And, yes, I think they are genuinely curious as to my abilities. And, no, I don't care for it either. All of this is uncomfortable." He'd sat again, his face close to mine. "And when we get back, I intend upon telling them I won't be ghost hunting anymore."

"What if they insist?" I asked.

"I'll still say no, and they can't force me."

A determined Kipp was something to be reckoned with. And with his ability to conceal parts of his mind from me, I would never be sure if he was just telling me what he thought I wanted to hear or if it accurately reflected his thoughts and feelings. In any case, he had made up his mind and nothing, short of a miracle, would change him.

I started to pick up the phone before deciding I would just knock on Peter's telepathic mind and ask to speak. In a moment, I did just that, giving an apology for my rude and abrupt behavior with him, as our thoughts traveled back and forth between the thin walls of our rooms.

"Oh, it's okay, Petra. I wasn't offended...well, I was at first but I got over it. Maybe you're right. We have to be able to take direction, and that is just the way this works." He pushed some cheerfulness in his thoughts. "I plan on getting a really good night sleep and tackle the next obstacle at the college, tomorrow."

He really was a good kid. I hoped I wouldn't ruin him with my irritable self.

CHAPTER 4

Peter was behind the wheel the next morning; he liked to drive and being an observant passenger suited me just fine. Although this current assignment had some loose objectives, we could leave whenever we desired, and that would be today, if I had my druthers. Peter maneuvered the SUV up the winding, scenic drive that led to Gettysburg College. Our timing involved visiting when the school was between terms, and only a few scattered cars littered the parking lots. The school, especially Pennsylvania Hall, was replete with tales of specters and ghostly sightings. Technicorps had obtained the necessary permission for us to bring the lupines on campus to thread our way through the corridors of what was now an administrative building but had been once known as "Old Dorm". The large white building stood out prominently in the early morning sunlight. We'd been blessed with good weather, but it seemed the forecast was changing with the promise of storms by early evening.

We parked beneath the welcomed shade of a massive oak with the hope our vehicle's interior would not become as hot as the interior of a blast furnace. Craning my neck, I tilted my head back and squinted against the glare of the sun as I gazed at the famous cupola crowning "Old Dorm", which was said to be the home of soldiers, ghostly ones, who would point into the distance as if to attract the attention of a superior. That particular morning, the circular wood construct was empty, save for a solitary crow perching nonchalantly upon one of the timbered sides before taking flight with an iridescent flash of blue black wings.

"Maybe the ghost is on a smoke break," Kipp quipped, pressing his heavy body against my legs.

Peter jogged ahead to let the staff know we'd be wandering through the building, with a particular focus on the basement. Thanks to the careful pre-arrangements, there was no explanation needed. As we waited for him to return, I realized that Kipp was carefully guarding his thoughts, and I edged up to him to lightly touch his upright ears.

"What's up?" I asked, my query for him only and not audible to Elani, who was caught in mid-yawn.

"Petra, I don't want to go in there," Kipp replied, his amber eyes meeting mine. "I think I know what I'll see, and it will be worse than anything before." He exhaled slowly. "I don't want to do it."

I realized the admission was difficult for him, since he typically was happy to take on all adventures. As I scratched between Kipp's ears, I watched Peter walk back towards us, swinging his arms and whistling.

"Peter, I've changed my mind," I said, noting the cloud of disappointment cross his brow. "I don't think this is a good idea, and we have proven what we came here to prove, and that is Kipp can communicate telepathically with spirits." As Peter stared at me, I added, "I've heard about the elevator that drops to the basement, even when you don't want to go there, and it frightens me. Period." I hoped my point wasn't made too lightly.

We desperately needed some type of diversion, at least I knew Peter did, since his plans had been dashed by me. He probably thought I was bossy, which I could be at times, and I was at that moment. There was a green field to the right of the building where two young men were tossing a Frisbee back and forth, their laughter challenging the somber mood of four, lost symbionts. I will never be sure, but I think Elani figured out what had happened with Kipp, and before we knew it, she teased him out onto the field, much to the delight of the two men, who began to fling the disc higher and farther, watching Elani and Kipp chase the soaring object. Kipp only thought he was faster than Elani, but along with his muscles came bulk and the more streamlined Elani flew across the grass like winged Pegasus, her gossamer fur stretching over her lean body. Kipp became more and more frustrated as she out maneuvered him time and time again. As the humans played with what they thought to be two dogs, I turned my attention to Peter, who was brooding.

"I'm sorry," I began. "I know you are disappointed."

"The only thing that disappoints me is that you weren't really honest," he replied, staring at me. "This was obviously about Kipp and not you, and you could have said so."

What can one say to such directness? As I let him simmer, the thought came to me that he had matured greatly since the time I first met him working at the library under the stern eye of Fitzhugh. That job had not been a good fit for a young, eager symbiont who wanted to travel. And he'd even gone against the wishes of his protective, hovering mother who had planned for him to marry and fill her holidays with screaming grandchildren. I had to smile.

"What?" he asked, his eyes darkening that I would find his comments humorous.

"I like you," I replied, linking my arms with his. "I thought I did before, but now I'm sure of it. And, yes, I wanted to protect Kipp, and it was wrong of me to lie." I blinked in the sun as the light was a little too bright, and I'd left my sunglasses in the SUV where they did me absolutely no good at all. Lifting my hand, I used it as a shade as my eyes followed the antics of the two racing lupines.

"Well, I like you, too, Petra. But just don't treat me like a kid," he said.

I was proud I managed to not fire back one of my zingers, such as 'then don't act like one'. It took a fair amount of self control on my part.

The original plans for our trip included a visit to the Hummelbaugh House, where the ghost of a confederate general and his eternally loyal dog lingered. But we'd lost our zest for anything else and simultaneously made the decision to head for home. Even the perpetually energetic and curious Peter had enough of haunted places. To the west, the clouds, which were dark and swollen with the threat of rain, were moving in quickly, and the looming change in weather seemed prophetic, almost giving a nod to our collective decision to leave.

"It's a six hour drive," Peter remarked. "If we start now, we can get home by late today or even stop if the weather breaks."

With nods of agreement all around, we returned to our hotel, packed up our meager belongings —there is something to be said for traveling light—and checked out. By the time we left Gettysburg, the wind whistled and moaned as it spun through the groves of trees, and the sky, which had been bright and cheerful, became overcast and dark, blocking the sun from view. I had a fanciful notion that the ghosts of Gettysburg were happy to see us leave. Peter managed to quickly pick up the interstate, and we'd only traveled about two hours when the navigation device warned of a traffic snarl ahead. Fortunately an exit was near, and Peter swung off before we became entangled in a jam that was the result of an unfortunate accident. By that time, the clouds were almost black overhead, accompanied by the soft, rolling rumble of thunder; the smell of rain filled the air. After three attempts, we found a motel that accepted pets, and we were checked in and in our rooms, which were side by side, in less than twenty minutes.

"Let's get cleaned up," I suggested. The hot day and sticky, oppressive weather had left me feeling damp and gritty. "Then let's order pizza and start a Monopoly tournament." I spoke with more cheer than I actually felt. There was a part of me that wished we'd never started the ghost exploration, mostly due to the fact it was stressful for Kipp. But another part of me—that suspicious part with occasional trust issues—wondered if Elani was correct, and Kipp could be easily used by Technicorps, almost as if he was a novelty act about whom they could brag to other collectives.

In less than an hour, we had a couple of hot pizzas on the table and were setting up the Monopoly set on the floor. We'd spread out a blanket, and Peter, in his compulsive way, was sorting the money by denominations as well as herding the tiny green houses and red hotels into neat piles. The lupines, especially Kipp, loved the game but needed help with handling the money and moving the tokens. Having to work with paws was a minor constraint for our dog-like brethren.

Kipp began to munch on a slice of cheese pizza. Peter had ordered the thin, hand tossed style that Kipp preferred. "Glad you left off the onions and green peppers," Kipp remarked between mouthfuls. "I get indigestion and have bad dreams."

Peter laughed as he handed me a slice balanced on a napkin. "Well, we wouldn't want that, Kipp. If you have tortured dreams, the rest of us will suffer."

Kipp was eyeing me closely, his amber gaze half shuttered as I poked among the little playing tokens. The game was a genuine vintage set with tokens that became obsolete as time marched forward. There are advantages to having a long life span and being able to carry some choice items with you through the years.

"Where is my top hat?" I cried, unable to find my favorite piece. I always took the top hat, and I'm not embarrassed to admit I'd become a little superstitious about that particular token. A soft roll of thunder echoed from outside; I could feel the slight tremor in the floor beneath me.

"I hid it," Kipp replied, as he finished the pizza crust, the crunching sound echoing loudly against the thin walls of the room.

"Why on earth would you do that, Kipp?" I was annoyed that he'd taken such liberties, and my thoughts quickly spiraled to agitation.

"You are too comfortable...too set in your ways. I think it's good for you to break out and do something different." He rose and walked over to me, nuzzling the side of my face. "You need to get a little crazy and unpredictable from time to time," he added, as if he thought I was incapable of getting his point.

"So you took my top hat! I hope you didn't lose it." I was close to tears and didn't know why.

"Your little top hat is safe and sound. Pick something else. You might as well," he added. "You've had a consistent losing streak with the top hat."

I started to have a tantrum and refuse to play, given his high handed behavior. But, reason was maintained, as well as my temper, and I decided to take the thimble, which was a sentimental second choice to the cherished top hat. Kipp, always the aggressor, took the battleship, while Peter chose the race car—an appropriate choice—and Elani the iron.

"Okay, now that I've committed myself to the thimble, where is my top hat so I can put it back in the box?" I didn't want it lost, given my longevity with the set.

"It is in the side pocket of your duffle, goof. You know I wouldn't lose it." Kipp yawned, his mouth opening to alligator-like proportions, all his teeth exposed.

Peter, good naturedly, rose and crossed over to where my duffle was crumpled in a swaybacked chair that had suffered the weight of way too many fannies over the years. He reached in the deep side pocket and, with a smile, lifted out the metal top hat, displaying it with a little flourish. In retrospect, perhaps my relinquishing my nostalgic control of the top hat was well advised, because I won the game, something that hadn't happened in a long time. Hotels on all the green and red properties had given me a distinct edge. And I'd left the playing field owning Marvin Gardens, my favorite piece of real estate on the board.

"Now didn't that feel good?" Kipp asked, raising a furry eyebrow. "You're finally not a loser."

I rolled my eyes at him. The game had been long, as Monopoly can run, and we were tired. After carefully repacking the pieces, Peter and Elani retired to their room, leaving me and Kipp alone. The closed curtain allowed some softly filtered light into the room, the shape of the windows highlighted on the far wall. A rumble of thunder sounded, followed by a crack of lightening that flashed bright against the backside of the thin curtains. The rain intensified; the room felt cozy and safe in the midst of the storm outside. Kipp snuggled closer, his chin upon my chest, my fingers gently caressing the back of his neck.

"Mmm…that feels good," he murmured, his eyes half closed.

"Before we get home—and now that we are alone—what are your honest thoughts about this ghost business?" I asked. Shifting slightly, I moved my leg since I had a cramp in my left calf. Outside the room, we heard a couple of people laughing as they raced by in the rain and thunder, trying to get to their room as the wind slapped the driving rain against their fleeing bodies. A minute later, we heard a door slam.

"I never mind trying anything new, Petra." Kipp took a deep breath and sighed. "But honestly, I didn't care for the ghost gig in general. I wouldn't mind exploring distinct episodes of paranormal events but just to be thrown, as we were, in the midst of so much activity was unpleasant. I have no true interest in doing that sort of thing again." He paused and shifted his heavy weight to his left side. "There were experiences that I didn't even share."

"Like what?" I asked, turning towards him in the dark, his profile a graceful silhouette against the occasional flashes of light from outside.

"When we were in the Triangular Field, I saw a pit where bodies would have been thrown to be buried in a mass grave. Some of the men were crawling, their hands digging in the dirt on the sides of the pit, trying to get out. I could hear them moaning in pain." I felt his shiver resonate on the bed. Reaching out, I scratched the top of his head and heard his sigh of approval. "Do you think what Elani said is true? Will Technicorps attempt to use me?" he asked.

It had happened before–or at least would have happened, had I not intervened. A totally despicable character named Max Stone had plotted to clone Kipp in the hopes of manufacturing an army of advanced symbionts for what end, no one knew. I didn't trust the entire governing body of the Twelve, but I did trust Philo implicitly. And Juno, a long term member, was without deception and was as close to a pure spirit as came.

"Philo won't, and since he is in charge, I wouldn't worry about it. And you know, Kipp, I've told you before, if you ever are pressured to evolve into something you despise, you and I can just disappear into the past and never be found."

He turned slightly to gaze at me. "You'd give up everything for me...your home that you love, your friendships, security...all of it." He swallowed. "I knew my mother loved me...and you love me. That's enough for me."

Pulling him closer, I listened to the rain fall. The occasional sound of thunder was oddly comforting and almost acted as a sedative, helping us nod off to sleep. At some point, I awakened during that time of early morning when all is still and the world seems to be holding its breath in wonder of what might happen next. Kipp's thoughts were restless as his dreams became mine. Resting my hand along his chest, I felt the heavy thud of his heart as it beat, his mind consumed with the ghosts he'd encountered as they pursued him, unrelentingly. Taking a deep breath, I timed my interventions and one by one dismissed the specters which plagued the memories of my friend. With a satisfied smile, I watched the last one pop into oblivion. Kipp awoke suddenly, startled; the sound of the pop had reverberated in his head. After a second, he regained his bearings and glanced at me.

"Thanks."

"It was nothing," I replied. "Just don't take my top hat again," I added wryly, trying to inject some mild humor. Thirsty, as result of too much pizza, I walked to the bathroom to get a cup of water. Clicking on the overhead light, I blinked at my unflattering reflection in the harsh glare of the too bright bulb; my dark hair, which fell past my shoulders, was in disarray. The pizza consumption had left my face slightly puffy, and there were unbecoming dark circles beneath my hazel colored eyes. The days in Gettysburg had caused my freckles to pop; they stood out vividly in a haphazard pattern across my nose that was too large for conventional standards of female beauty. Leaning forward, I splashed a little cold water on my face, hoping it would help with the swelling that gave me a Humpty Dumpty look. Hearing the soft pad of feet, I turned. Kipp left our comfortable nest and came to stand behind me.

"I'm glad pizza doesn't make my face swell up like yours," he began, trying to get a rise out of me. "You look awful."

"Thanks," I replied drily.

"You need to stick to salads for a few days and try to detoxify." He sat, cocking his big head to one side.

"Okay," I said.

"Petra?"

"Yes?"

"Thanks for what you said. I know you'll always be on guard for me, and it sort of goes without saying. But it's nice, all the same, to hear you say it again." Kipp's mouth fell open to expose gleaming teeth in a bizarre, grimace of a smile.

I walked past him to the window, pausing long enough to pull back the curtain and gaze outside. It was still raining but the torrential downpour had slowed, and it was more of a drizzle. The pitiful halo of wavering yellow from the nearby street light gave off enough illumination to reveal a fog bank that had settled across the hillsides like a blanket of soft down.

"There must be a cold front behind this mess," I remarked. "Peter will have to drive slowly tomorrow, and that will aggravate him, no doubt." Turning, I smiled at Kipp. "I'm looking forward to getting home."

"Me, too," he answered. "I can't wait to see what Lily managed to break in your room."

CHAPTER 5

M y house rested comfortably on a quiet, tree-lined street where
the sidewalks were uneven and broken from the stubborn
roots of old trees that didn't know when to stop growing. Some
symbionts—and people—enjoy a dwelling that is spare of belongings
and perhaps appeals to the esoteric side of nature. But my home
reflected my long life, and for reasons that perhaps only an analyst
would understand, I carried pieces of history with me to the present. I
had filled most of the walls with pieces of art work found in obscure
corners of antique shops or at estate sales. On my battered table tops,
which I refused to refinish, bits and pieces of what some might classify as junk were displayed in all their dusty glory. Such clutter and
lack of a decorative theme might not be for everyone, but it suited me
quite nicely.

As Peter slowed and pulled to the curb, I noticed, critically, that
the iron porch rails, as well as the front door, were begging for a fresh
coat of paint. It was Saturday, so Fitzhugh, my one time reluctant
roommate, would be home. In any case, the front door was open, and
I could see Lily sitting inside, on the other side of the storm door,
watching our arrival. The minute Kipp hopped out of the SUV, Lily
began to weave back and forth, dragging her furry feline sides across

the glass leaving a smear of tabby hair to mark her progress. Kipp had found her abandoned in a grassy field, and she imprinted upon him, if such a thing is possible with cats, and loved him like he was her mother. Despite a mild level of embarrassment over her attachment, he tried to humor her, with his natural compassion for all the abandoned of the world.

We'd left the bad weather up north, and it was a typical late summer day in North Carolina. A robin that had reared her young the previous spring in a nest in a large hickory tree to the right of my yard greeted me. It seemed there were a few more robins present than usual, making me wonder if her kids were loathe to leave home. Well, that seemed to be the current state of affairs for many human parents, too. Peter, who obviously felt the need to act as my cavalier, brought my duffle, which I was completely able to handle, to the door.

Reaching out, I lightly touched his arm. "Come back tonight so we can debrief with Fitzhugh. I'll pull something together for dinner."

With a little salute, he grinned and ran back to the idling SUV. He had to return the vehicle to Technicorps and retrieve his own smaller car so he and Elani could go to his apartment. As I watched him drive away, I wondered if he had any social life at all before recalling when I was his age I, too, was single-minded about one thing—and that was to become a traveling symbiont.

"Hi, honey, I'm home," I called out cheerfully as the door swung open, hoping to irritate Fitzhugh with the mock familiarity.

After all our time together, he still exited his bedroom covered from neck to ankles with pajamas and a robe. If I were ever to see a bare chest, I might faint dead away with the vapors. Fitzhugh appeared, tall and lanky, in the kitchen doorway, a teapot in his hand. I must have caught him in an extra casual moment, because he was wearing stretched out sweat pants and a tattered shirt with long tails that trailed over his concave backside.

"Hi, sweetheart!" he replied with a smile, launching his own broadside in response. "Just getting the tea going," he added. Juno stuck her grizzled muzzle around the corner; I could hear her thumping tail hitting the drywall as Kipp went forward to touch her nose with his, dragging Lily behind him as she determinedly clung to his hind leg with her forepaws. At some point, she bit his leg; in response to Kipp's growl, Lily detached and ran down the hallway, her feet pounding the worn wood floor. I knew she was laughing in the manner of rambunctious cats.

I took a moment to dump the contents of the duffle into the washer–I wasn't one for sorting clothes–and added some soap. With a turn of the knob, another chore was done. Since I'd been born in 1604, I knew all about doing such things as laundry the old fashioned way–from beating clothes on rocks to using a scrub board. Of course back then, hygiene was a totally different matter, and daily ablutions were an activity that was frowned upon. Some of that history had to explain why the advent of indoor plumbing and hot water accessible by the turn of a handle were two of my favorite human achievements.

Taking a seat, I begged for all the recent gossip from Technicorps. When I was not traveling, I assisted Fitzhugh in his beloved library and worked to translate old scripts into modern English. The originals, many of which were deteriorating, were scanned into the computer so a visual record remained. My translations accompanied them so that our kind maintained a running historical record of our activities. We had divisions at Technicorps where we worked side by side with humans who had no idea of our origins and merely thought of us as people oddly attached to our canine companions.

Fitzhugh sat down opposite of me at the battered dinette set I'd found in an obscure junk store many years before. Fondly, I ran my hand over a burn mark that marred the surface of the table; it was comforting to know some things didn't change and familiarity bred comfort. The fragrance of the Earl Grey steeping in Fitzhugh's antique tea pot filled the confines of the small kitchen. The sun angling in from the rear of the house created a cheerful checkerboard light pattern on the wooden floor and highlighted some dust and cat hair that had escaped my less than optimal cleaning routine. Kipp waited for Juno to situate her arthritic body in the golden patch of sunlight before circling to lie next to her; he was too much of a gentleman to hog the prime space, in deference to her advanced years. Lily, not needing an invitation, crawled up his body to sprawl across his back at the base of his neck. Her little paws began to knead the thick pelt of fur, her eyes squinting almost shut, such was her joy that her beloved one had returned.

"Philo has introduced an assistant for me," Fitzhugh remarked. "He kept it a secret, I think, fearful I'd refuse to break in a new worker after having watched Margaret Shelton come and go so quickly." His thick gray brows drew together. "I don't like change, as you well know." The old symbiont took a sip of tea. Rather delicately, I thought, he dabbed at his mustache to make certain no droplets quivered from the adornment.

My mouth compressed in a hidden smile. His comment was the understatement of the year—Fitzhugh was known for his unbending rigidity. I still found it remarkable that he had decided to let me become a confidant and, yes, friend. Fitzhugh, when he was younger, had a bonded symbiont and traveled, as did I, in search of information, truths and mysteries to be solved. Some of our kind, however, never bonded with a lupine and took, instead, a same type mate for purposes of marriage or partnership. Philo fell into the group that had never experienced time travel. At least when I talked to Fitzhugh, he had an understanding of the demands of being a traveler. I'd had the indulgence of both: a bonded lupine as well as a beloved marriage partner and little family. But the latter was a long time ago, and I chose to not linger in those bittersweet memories.

"So who is she?" I asked. Reaching forward, I poured a smidgen more tea into the fragile cup. Fitzhugh had named the pattern of the fine bone English china, but the title eluded me at the moment. Feeling decadent, I added some honey to the steaming brew.

"She is a he," Fitzhugh replied. "And apparently a very desirable he. Suzanne seems to find new reasons to visit the library as well as a covey of other females." He raised his eyebrows. "I'm just relegated to the junk pile."

I knew the latter comment was made in jest but reached out to touch his forearm, nonetheless. "You're top of my heap," I said.

"Better wait until you meet him. He seems to have some type of hypnotic effect..." Fitzhugh's voice drifted off, indicating he was bored with the subject.

"And the name of this Adonis?" I asked, daring to look at Kipp, who was amused with the novel concept of a male babe magnet.

"Mark Elliot," Fitzhugh replied.

Deciding to change the topic, since I was uninterested in Mr. Elliot, I told Fitzhugh that I was going to run to the store to buy something to throw in the crockpot. Peter and Elani were coming later so that Fitzhugh could debrief us—unofficially, of course. After getting Fitzhugh's consent to add Philo to the small gathering, I called him at home to make the invite.

"This will be officially off the record," I began.

"So, even though I'm the leader of the Twelve, you are going to tell me things you don't necessarily want me to share. Right?" he asked, his voice sounding rather flat and expressionless over the phone. I could imagine the look of displeasure crossing his face.

"I'm not always sure you like your job," I remarked.

"Not always. I'll be there at seven," he replied gruffly before hanging up.

I managed to create a meatless Creole-style red beans and rice, leaving it to simmer in the crockpot, which was my favorite cooking method as it required the least amount of effort and more than a little promise to deliver something edible. Kipp was anxious to run, as was I, pacing the kitchen floor impatiently while I rinsed off a sauce pan. It was mid afternoon when we set out, taking a familiar route. I always kept a slip lead wrapped around my waist in case a vigilant police officer stopped to remind me of the local leash law, but such events were few in the quiet neighborhood. Kipp began to dance in circles around me, barking softly, trying to nudge me to go faster.

"Show off," I complained. "You have four wheel drive, and I'm just using two feet, so don't press me."

Kipp laughed as he feigned a move at a squirrel that showed us his bushy backside as he scampered up the pretty, decorative bark of a thin dogwood tree tilting with an unfortunate lean over the curb. A car was approaching, so Kipp quickly returned to my side, acting the part of the obedient canine. We didn't need a complaint lodged. Though the summer had begun with more than enough moisture to ward off a drought, August had promised little in regards to rain; alongside the road, dirt had become caked like fine powder. Inhaling deeply, I felt the heat spread through my body as my feet thudded out a soft rhythm on the roadway. Kipp's mind was relaxed, without the usual laser focus that characterized his state of robust energy, and his elusive thoughts drifted in and out of my mind just enough to be tantalizing without hooking me. We completed a pleasant loop and returned home, where the enticing fragrance of Creole spices met me at the front door.

With a wave at Fitzhugh, who was sitting in front of the television—a rarity for him—watching a documentary on the sinking of the *Titanic*, I trotted down the hallway to my room. I didn't think my dinner guests would care for my sweat covered body. Kipp followed and lay on the bath mat. He found the need of my side of the symbiont family tree to take baths both amusing and inconvenient. He lazily licked his forepaws as I was toweling off.

"We can run faster; our senses of hearing, smell and vision are superior, and we don't have to take baths...aren't you jealous?" Kipp asked, tilting his large, auburn head at me. His ears rotated forward to show off his natural talents.

"Well, if I had ears as big as satellite dishes, I might hear better, too," I laughed as I threatened to snap my wet towel at him.

A casual evening called for comfortable clothes, which meant almost threadbare blue jeans that had lost their blue color, evolving into an odd, one dimensional gray shade, and a t-shirt that was stretched out at the neck. Fitzhugh met me in the kitchen, raising an eyebrow.

"I see you have dressed for dinner," he remarked, blinking his eyes in feigned innocence at the barb.

"What was your interest in the *Titanic*?" I asked, ignoring his comment. I was at the kitchen counter chopping up some boiled chicken for Kipp and Juno. As I mixed it with rice in their bowls, Juno looked up, hopefully. I winked at her. "So, Fitzhugh, did you not feed this poor girl while I was gone? I swear I see her ribs sticking out."

"I take umbrage at that accusation," he replied, exhaling forcefully through his mustache and beard. A second later he realized I was joking with him. Smiling, he said, "I'll admit a Pop Tart tastes better when you fix it." He took a seat at the dinette. "I, as did you, lived through the loss of the *Titanic*. Some recent dialog has reasserted itself at Technicorps about the sinking, but I'll wait until Philo and I can meet with you."

"A time shift?" I asked, turning to look at him.

"What is the *Titanic*?" Kipp asked.

Technically, Kipp was older than all of us combined. His origins in prehistoric times made for some unique experiences from his point of view. But then he sort of jumped over thousands of years when he made the time shift to contemporary times with me. As result of his rapid progression through the ages, he'd missed all the important historical markers that we older symbionts had experienced.

"The *Titanic* was an ocean liner," Fitzhugh explained. "She was the most luxurious ship ever built with amenities to lure the wealthy to travel in the highest style available. She was widely touted to be unsinkable but hit an iceberg on her maiden voyage. The *Titanic* sank in less than three hours with an enormous loss of life."

"I understand the horror over losing so many people," Kipp said. "But why would that one disaster stand out among so many others?"

Fitzhugh rested his thin arms on the table top. While he'd been talking with Kipp, I prepared a pot of tea, using my battered old stoneware teapot and placed it on the table top with a mug. I'd leave the niceties of fine china to Fitzhugh. Looking at me, he smiled and nodded, oddly pleased at the informality. "Kipp, it was a product of the times. There was a surge in people acquiring wealth, and there were many super rich in the world. Societies were strongly divided by class and money, and the times were referred to as the Gilded Age. Somehow, the *Titanic* pulled together all the opulence as well as the hopes and aspirations of people of lesser means who were traveling to America for a chance at a better life."

Kipp glanced at me. "Sounds interesting. I'm gonna get Peter to download some books about it on my Kindle." Kipp had the most curious, multi-faceted mind of any symbiont I'd ever known. When he set his sights towards gaining knowledge of an event, there was no end to his pursuit of facts as well as conjecture.

The four of us felt the common stirring that signaled other

symbionts were nearby. I recognized the familiar flow of thoughts of my friend, Philo, as well as the more chaotic, youthful ones of Peter and Elani. Kipp darted to the front door to act as greeter while I checked on the crockpot fare. That plus a salad and bread was all I had planned. As an extra delightful bonus, while I was jogging, Fitzhugh tried his hand at brownies; the pan was cooling on a rack on my chipped tile counter top.

Philo breezed in, his graying hair mussed as usual. Leaning down, he kissed me on top of my head with easy familiarity before joining Fitzhugh at the dinette. Philo was some two hundred years older than I and was my closest friend. We'd known one another for countless years. Fitzhugh was now included in that small covey of special symbionts, having pushed past his role as chief inquisitor and critical analyst of all I did. Peter, showing a surprising level of comfort, walked by and gave my arm a brief squeeze. I wondered if he considered bestowing a kiss upon my dark hair but thought better of it. I guess he didn't want to be omitted from the friends of Petra club. Kipp inquired as to Elani's needs since he'd eaten, and she assured him she was fine, except she could smell brownies.

"You know I love chocolate," she said, looking at me, her tail wagging. Lupines didn't share canines' issues with chocolate.

"We will have dessert, and you can have as many as you like, sweetheart," I replied. Reaching down, I caressed the dome of her head which, unlike Kipp's rounded noggin, had a funny little point at the crest.

We enjoyed a leisurely meal while Philo and Fitzhugh plied us with countless questions. Kipp took the lead, since it was primarily he who had experienced the odd phenomena associated with the ghostly specters. The rest of us filled in gaps with our perceptions of the days spent in Gettysburg.

"Our main issue, Philo, aside from the fact the images were emotionally disturbing, was that we didn't know what to do with the situations we encountered. Kipp was able to communicate with them telepathically, but then what?" I laid down my fork, my meal unfinished. "And I didn't see the need for Kipp to continue exposing himself to such pain without an end goal that seemed to benefit our kind." I, as always, felt intensely protective of my friend and would go down in a blaze of glory, if needed, to keep him safe. It was meant to be that way amongst bonded symbionts but was even truer between me and Kipp.

"I'm confident there is no documentation of such activities–other than the experiences of some who might be more sensitive to paranormal experiences—in our collective record," Fitzhugh remarked, his heavy brows drawing together in a frown as he pulled from his memories. "I am glad that Kipp did attempt communication, and it adds to knowledge that we previously would not have had." He reached forward to crumble one of the brownies he'd baked. For a first attempt, I admit he did well. They had the requisite crusty exterior and a gooey, fudgy middle...perfect.

"But, Philo, I have concerns," Fitzhugh said. "I don't think any of this should be shared." At Philo's raised eyebrows, he continued. "I fear that others would want to push the experience and try and force Kipp to replicate this again and again since it is novel, and, well, it highlights our collective as being unique." He shrugged his thin shoulders. "Humans are not the only species with maladaptive egos. And the most important factor is that it is emotionally difficult on Kipp. In addition, we have no idea as to the long term consequences brought on by meddling with something we don't fully understand."

I gazed at Fitzhugh, my eyes opened wide. He caught the expression before I ducked my head. Philo was accustomed to my taking the role as a defender of Kipp. I'd tilted at more than one windmill over the past few years when a notion tossed Kipp's way threatened to stretch ethical boundaries. I realized, as did Fitzhugh, that he had just put Philo in a terribly compromising position. As the leader of the Twelve, Philo had a responsibility to not free wheel and make decisions on his own; he was bound to bring information to the governing body for deliberation and determination.

"Would you like another brownie?" I asked, glancing down at Elani, who wagged her tail hopefully. As I rose to get the treat for her, I looked at Peter, who had remained quiet and avoided interjecting his opinions on the matters at hand. His brown eyes, partially hidden behind the horn rimmed glasses that made him seem older, met mine.

Philo pushed back from the table and stood; he walked to the kitchen door that led out into my back yard. Shoving his hands deep in the pockets of his pants, he began to rock slightly on his heels. The sun had disappeared beneath the far horizon, and the darkened back yard seemed to stretch into oblivion. I'd opened the windows, and on the other side of the screens, we could hear crickets and cicadas as they chirped and clicked; the constant hum of nature swelled into the kitchen. The cultures and exploits of humans had changed greatly in my lifetime, but those sounds of insects and creatures milling in the darkness never did and remained timeless. A mild breeze had kicked up in anticipation of storms later that evening, and the leaves softly rustled in the black void as trees gently swayed beyond our field of vision.

"I don't like being put in this position," Philo finally said. "When I became leader of the Twelve, I assumed responsibility for decisions that are sometimes difficult." He sighed deeply, his back to us. "But, I agree. Kipp would be used if the others found out about the degree of his sensitivity." Philo turned to us. "As far as I'm concerned, Kipp's trip was a failure, and he has no more skills than the ordinary paranormal human expert." He smiled, but the expression didn't make it to his eyes. "Let's never talk about it again."

Kipp was on his feet, his eyes meeting Philo's. "Thank you," he said, exhaling forcefully.

Standing, I rushed to Philo and grabbed him in as tight a hug as I could manage without breaking bones. Fitzhugh, along with Juno, nodded in tacit approval. Sometimes friends just keep secrets forever, it seems.

CHAPTER 6

He was tall, well built and sufficiently handsome that I was forced to swallow twice before I could speak. But I was uninterested, and that was a fact. If the truth were told, I was still in love–and deeply so–with William Harrow. And while Mark Elliott's nose might be a little more classical in shape and form, and the sweep of his hair more dramatic–and his eyes were a remarkable shade of azure blue instead of the color of Harrow's eyes, which matched the blue gray color of the storm-tossed Atlantic Ocean—Harrow would always be more beautiful in my biased view that was one of the lovelorn. I had many flaws, and still do, but being fickle in matters of the heart was not one of them. Once my allegiance was set, it was unshakable. That quality, in part, explained my relationship with Kipp. All things being considered, Mark Elliott seemed bright, pleasant and with a natural charisma that some humans, as well as symbionts, just possess through no fault of their own. But, as I said, I was uninterested. Suzanne and all the other females who previously had spent little time in the library, could hang out in the corner reading nooks all day long, as far as I was concerned.

I could tell that Fitzhugh was slightly amused by my polite but distant attitude towards the new addition to the library. Although I was technically a traveler, my base of operations was the library, and there I labored in between more exciting jobs appearing in irregular bursts from direction of the Twelve. Peter, who had once been Fitzhugh's reluctant assistant, still helped out but was consumed with furthering his bond with Elani. The two of them were busy studying the history of our species as well as past trips–some of which were monumental successes, while others were catastrophic failures.

"So, Petra, how long have you worked with Fitzhugh?" Mark Elliott's baritone voice almost purred. He walked to my desk and parked his lovely body, uninvited, in the chair nearby. I observed he was careful to pluck at the crease in his trousers to maintain its knife-like perfection. As I noticed his white teeth, I figured it was a pretty sure bet I still had some spinach lodged between mine following my lunch salad. Fitzhugh had stepped out to meet with Philo, leaving Mark and me alone. Kipp was upstairs with the young lupines; he taught English, and now he was challenged with an ethics class, too. I was privately amused at his disdain at having developed a bit of a cult following amongst the youngsters.

"A long time," I replied curtly. Glancing over at him, I took note of his blue eyes, exemplary features and hair the color of summer wheat cut in the latest style. He obviously had used a little product to hold it in place. I tried not to frown. I was busy and had no time for idle chat.

"Well, you and Kipp have an amazing history together," he continued, obviously not put off by my brevity. "Your journey was unprecedented."

I looked at him again. "Yes, that's true." Bending my head forward, I nudged my chair closer to my desk. The manuscript was written in German idiomatic expressions specific to a certain region, and I needed to concentrate.

"Can I help?" Mark asked.

"You can quit talking and let me work," I blurted out before I could stop myself. Yes, we were both telepaths, but Mark was of the civilized variety and would not intrude in my thoughts without an invitation… and he wouldn't be getting that. I have to give him credit for being cool and composed. My rude remark seemed to fly right over his lovely head, and he laughed in response.

"Okay," he said, holding up his manicured hands in mock surrender. "I'm gonna fix some coffee, would you like some?"

I did but lied and said no. Please, just leave me alone, I silently pleaded. It was enough that my research work was tedious to the extreme. I had no desire for fun, verbal jousting, or playful exchanges with this new symbiont. He finally left me, and a short time later Kipp appeared, his big head resting on the corner of my desk. I couldn't see his back end but knew his tail was wagging from the swaying of the visible parts of his body.

"Tough day?" he asked, pausing to yawn and blink his eyes. His sleep the previous night had been disturbed by dreams of the haunted places we'd visited in Gettysburg.

"Just tired of Mark Elliott being overly friendly," I replied.

"He likes you," Kipp said.

"Stop it, or I might get irritated at you, too." I added a little growl in the back of my throat for extra emphasis.

As we walked home that evening, I slowed my steps, enjoying the feel of twilight with its falling temperatures and the simplicity that accompanies impending nightfall. Against the black wall of a stand of trees, the deep throated chuckling of a barred owl echoed in the darkness, the sound primitive, almost alien. A moment later the caterwauling began, as the owl sang its song to a hidden companion. In the distance, I made out a brief flash of pale wing color as the owl sought another perch. Walking slowly on the sidewalk, since I was in no hurry, we passed a hillock that stood guard over a little boggy pond, the shimmering edges of which were lost in the low light of evening; the bellow of an agitated bull frog abruptly rang out. Reaching down, I ran my hand along Kipp's back, enjoying the feel of his thick pelt beneath my fingers. At his direction, I scratched an itchy place on his spine.

"You know, Petra, holding a lamp for Will Harrow isn't healthy," Kipp began, his words a surprise, since I'd not been thinking about Harrow. Kipp assumed a wise tone, which seemed inappropriate for one who'd never experienced romantic love.

"You mean, holding a torch?" I asked, trying not to laugh.

"You know what I mean, so don't be obtuse," he replied. Tilting his head back, he gazed at a brown bat that was circling and darting in its pursuit of a fleeing insect. His ears rotated forward; he could hear the bat's trilling series of echo locations that were inaudible to me.

"I'm not ready to give up those feelings," I said. "It will take me a long time...I'm grieving, Kipp."

He nudged closer, ducking his big head under my hand. To comfort me, he pushed his bushy body next to my leg, his touch a physical reminder of his permanence in my life. As we approached my house, I noted the lights were on inside which meant Fitzhugh had beat me home. Knowing my preference to walk to work, he had arranged a complicated grid of rides to get him and Juno to and fro... unless it was raining when I took my car. I dreaded the day Mark would be on the schedule, since I figured he'd want to come inside and view my private nest. He was way too busy in regards to me.

"No, Fitzhugh knows how you feel and won't ask Mark," Kipp replied, addressing my unspoken worries. "Although he is a very nice guy," Kipp added unnecessarily.

The evening was uneventful; Kipp was already sleepy so we went to bed early. He curled up next to me and was breathing heavily in a rumbling lupine snore within five minutes. I picked up his Kindle and began perusing one of his downloaded books on the *Titanic*. Yes, I'd lived through those times, and the sinking still stood out vividly as a monumental event that lingered as an exquisitely bad memory. Such a hopeful and exciting moment in history was forever marked as a disaster affecting so many innocent people. I'd skimmed past the first few days and was about to launch into the day of the accident when Kipp's dreams reached my thoughts. Once again, he dreamt of the ghosts and spirits that he'd recently encountered in Gettysburg. Jeremy, the demonic stick boy who lurked in the dark corners of the cellar, was prominently featured. Gently, so as not to awaken him, I entered Kipp's thoughts and began to manipulate the dreams to have good outcomes; his breathing slowed as he relaxed next to me. The fact that Kipp's subconscious continued to be plagued by things encountered in the spirit world provided me with even more resolve to avoid any more ghost hunting; the toll on Kipp was too great. The rest of the night passed with him in a state of happy oblivion. I, on the other hand, dreamt of Harrow and eyes that were neither blue nor gray but somewhere in between, a not too subtle reminder of the Atlantic Ocean and all its hidden dangers.

"Why is Philo calling us to his office?" Peter asked. He was wearing his glasses and looked handsomely owlish. Tossing his head, he swung the dark curtain of bangs away from his eyes. I wondered when he might outgrow that juvenile adornment.

"No idea," I responded curtly. Had anyone ever been called to the principal's office or that of a supervisor without thinking something bad was about to drop? Kipp and Elani were walking behind us, side by side, chatting over some issues with the young lupines with whom Kipp worked. Elani had once been a member of that particular class but was now considered to be in the big league, since she had actually time shifted several times with Peter. The younger lupines, hopeful travelers all, now watched her pass, eyes rounded, breath held. Yes, she'd reached celebrity status.

The secretary who monitored Philo's office and allowed visitors based upon her changeable moods was absent from her desk, so we eased past her vacant spot and tapped on Philo's door before barging in. He was standing, gazing out the large window overlooking the garden below. I was happy some forward thinking landscaper had added crepe myrtles since they stubbornly retained their blooms throughout the latter half of summer. A few of the white ones had recently shed some blossoms, making the ground below appear as if it was dusted with snow. Philo gestured for us to sit, while Kipp and Elani circled and plopped on the carpet.

"Fitzhugh got word of something interesting, and I wanted to run it past you," Philo said, pulling up a chair to sit close by. He knew I hated it when he sat behind his desk, making me think of a stern, disapproving teacher about to leap up and whack my hand with a ruler.

"He didn't say anything," I remarked.

"You know Fitzhugh. He wanted to do some research on his own before presenting it." Philo smiled. "He's not much of a gossip," he added. "Fitzhugh has a friend who lives over in Winston-Salem. His friend happened to be visiting at Technicorps while you guys were busy in Gettysburg. They were talking, and the friend told Fitzhugh he'd run into a man whose father was alleged to be a survivor of the sinking of the *Titanic*. Apparently, the man made comments that were, well, very suspicious and would impact the knowledge we have about the facts of the accident."

There was a soft tap on the door, and Fitzhugh stuck his head around the corner. With a nod, he entered the room, chose a chair and took a seat. For a moment I wondered why he hadn't mentioned any of this, since we cohabited, but then I realized Philo was correct–Fitzhugh had been busy collecting information before he brought anything forward.

"My friend lives at a retirement, uh, village with elderly humans," Fitzhugh began. "He's not quite my age but decided to slow down years ago due to some nagging health issues. Simon and I worked together in the past in a setting similar to this," he said, spreading his hands. "He has developed a friendship with one of the men there and has been privy to some interesting information."

I am an unabashed hog for any vague reference at a mystery–maybe it's genetic–and found myself sitting forward, my mouth dropping open in anticipation. Catching Philo's glance of amusement, I managed to close my mouth and scoot back in my chair.

"This man," Fitzhugh continued, "has some degree of dementia and therefore his recall is suspect. He, in the words of professionals, confabulates when there are gaps in his memories. Some things are corroborated by the staff while others are not."

"Such as?" Peter asked, turning slightly to smile at me. Yes, it was evident he had acquired the addiction that lead symbiont teams to either unravel puzzles or find themselves broken by their inability to succeed.

"It seems validated that this man's father was on the *Titanic* and was a survivor. But what he says about his father is unusual. He states his father was an anarchist who remained highly political until his death. His father was aboard the *Titanic* with the intent to plant a bomb and sink the ship as a stab at the British Empire and class division in general." Fitzhugh paused to let us register what he'd said.

Outside the window, there was a little gray Phoebe perching on the limb of the towering tulip poplar. The bird craned his head, peering through the window as if he was eavesdropping on our conversations. He glanced upward, as if startled, launched into the air and soared out of sight. I privately hoped no hawk was circling overhead, watching for the solitary bird. I'd always had a fondness for the Phoebe who lacked the colorful flash of other birds but displayed an admirable work ethic and stubborn nature when it came to nest building. Once I'd had a pair of Phoebes start a family outside my bedroom window, the nest lodged under the crook of a gutter. After the eggs hatched, something–probably an owl or hawk–managed to swoop down and take the nest and the baby birds. I watched the Phoebes look for the missing nest and their family for days before they began building again, in a slightly different location. Tough little guys, I thought.

"As you who lived through those times may recall, there was great unrest in the world around the end of the nineteenth century and the beginning of the twentieth," Fitzhugh continued. "There were social upheavals due to discontent brought on by countless years of stratified societies, poverty and lack of social mobility. Even the strict class system aboard the *Titanic* was symbolic of the age. There was a first class area and certain first class amenities that the rest of the ship did not share. Combine that fact with political unrest due to rebellion against power held in the hands of few, and it was a perfect storm for agitation. Consider the assassination of William McKinley...his killer was an anarchist. At that time, there was some degree of social discontent in America due to the extreme wealth of some compared to the relative poverty of many, but the issues were more intense in Europe, where there was a more radical philosophy that grew out of social unrest as well as a rejection of any type of governmental authority. Several European leaders had been assassinated, including the president of France and the king of Italy."

"I was living in France during those times," I remarked. "Although I stayed out of the political issues affecting humanity, I was an observer and the times were difficult. The common worker suffered under the inability to progress, for the most part. One's class at birth defined an entire lifetime. That was pretty much how it was everywhere."

"According to Simon, he has spent a lot of time with this man, who, in the way of people with dementia, recalls past events with clarity." Fitzhugh paused to clear his throat. "The staff just discards his remarks as the rambling of an addled mind. But Simon, with his telepathy, has a greater ability and has come to the conclusion he thinks the thoughts are based on reality."

"And what do you need from us?" Kipp asked, tilting his large head up. His jaw opened in a lupine smile as if he predicted the answer.

"We, Simon and I, want you, Kipp, to go and meet this man. Only you have the ability to push through his present thoughts back to the place where his memories were set down originally. You can determine what his father actually told him; no one else of our kind has your talents." Fitzhugh smiled at him.

"And why does any of this matter?" Elani asked. She was resting in a patch of sunlight that spread across the floor like a pool of liquid gold. Her gray pelt looked invitingly soft and warm as it absorbed the rays. For a moment, I toyed with the idea of stretching out on the floor next to her, letting my head rest upon her furry side as the sun lulled me to sleep. With effort, I suppressed a yawn.

"If this man's memories are correct, then it could mean the sinking of the *Titanic* might have been related to a bomb explosion. It would change the entire view of the tragedy," Philo answered. He'd been remarkably quiet during all the exchanges. I glanced at him, and he returned the stare, his expression neutral.

"And...?" I asked, feeling more cautious than usual. It was part of my trade to take risks and plunge headlong into any place in history, no matter what.

"Then a trip to the *Titanic* might be in order so that the events around the sinking can be re-examined." Philo crossed his arms and gazed at the window again. From the office view of the skyline, it was evident that the onset of evening might bring with it stormy weather. I'd not brought my car that day and had no enthusiasm for walking home in the rain.

When the purpose of the meeting became obvious, I felt myself detaching from the dialog. As I studied the dark clouds gathering on the horizon, I darted a glance at a passing dog, who was ambling across an expanse of neatly cut grass that was part of the landscaping. He looked well fed, happy…a big brown brute with a white patch covering half his face. His head was up as he enjoyed his walk; unexpectedly, he dropped to the ground and began rolling, squirming his back into the grass, all four legs kicking enthusiastically. That dog was happier than was I.

"Hey, the weather is looking like it might break soon. I'd rather get home and not dodge lightning bolts, if you don't mind, so let's wrap this up," I said, shaking myself into action. My voice was brusque and no nonsense, and I hoped my tone and attitude would push things along.

Fitzhugh wore a puzzled look on his aged face. He, too, had been a traveler, and was consumed with endless curiosity as was typical of our species.

"Petra, I thought you'd be all over this," he said, frowning slightly.

"Well, then I guess you don't know me too well," I answered, my tone abrupt, rude and unfortunately flippant. "The sinking of the *Titanic* was a terrible tragedy. The desperation of all those people as it was sinking…can you imagine what it would be like to time shift into the middle of that hysteria and horror? It would be emotionally difficult to watch and not intervene to save people. Such a moment would tear at our, uh, humanity." I paused to close my eyes for a moment and take a deep breath. "I don't see why we would subject ourselves to such an intense moment just to find out if a bomb hastened the sinking of a doomed ship."

Kipp was staring at me, and in the manner of our private dialog with one another, he asked, "What is wrong with you? This is what we do, right?"

"We also have the responsibility to protect ourselves from stupid time shifts with no other purpose than to satisfy morbid curiosity," I replied, feeling my face go rigid. The others knew Kipp and I were conversing in our typically enmeshed manner and remained quiet.

"Listen to what you are saying," he said. "Curiosity drives us, most of the time. If we don't go back in time to change the arc of history, then all we ever do is to gather information. And can you tell me that when we were in the presence of Jack the Ripper, it wasn't difficult to know who he was and not keep him from taking lives of innocent women? Were their lives less valuable than the ones aboard the *Titanic*?" Kipp was getting hot, no mistake about it.

"Whatever," I replied, using the annoying slang expression that I disliked. I even waved my hand dismissively which really set Kipp off.

"Don't whatever me," he said. His head lifted, amber eyes back lit with a disturbing glow. If he could have trembled with indignation, he might have done so, but lupines didn't manage that well. "We will do what we always do and analyze this situation and make a rational decision unaffected by emotion."

Ducking my head, I started to reply with a "whatever, boss" but changed that to a meek "okay, boss". Kipp had limited experiences traveling in comparison to me. He really had not encountered a situation where the emotions of a mass of humans were roiling and agitated...but I had on more than one occasion. It was draining and even aging. I'm certain I'd lost several years of my naturally long life from a couple of time shifts that left me empty and wondering about my career choice.

"We don't even know yet that a trip to the *Titanic* is in order or even appropriate," Fitzhugh said, as he smoothed his long beard with a thin hand. I realized he was trying to soothe me, too. "It would be interesting for Kipp to be exposed to this man and determine if his memories are true versus some type of confabulation."

I caught myself just before saying "whatever" again. Maybe I'd had too much exposure to popular human culture as of late? Philo was staring at me, a slight frown on his face. He might have been a good friend, but I felt no need to explain my position. Couldn't I just have an opinion without having to defend it, I thought, whining to myself. Peter was carefully studying his shoes while Elani remained quiet and patient. Glancing out the window again, I noted with relief that the big brown dog was gone; I hoped he'd get to a secure location before the storm broke.

We were released from that meeting, much to my relief, and Kipp and I began our walk home. Peter offered to drive Fitzhugh and Juno; they passed us, as we trudged along, giving a little toot on the horn as they did so. The storm was behind us. Part of me looked forward to the coziness of being within my safe place at home while the rain beat down impotently on the roof. Even though it was still late summer, I thought hot cocoa might be in order. Obviously a part of my soul was seeking comfort.

"I'd really like to talk to the guy." Kipp lifted his head to look at me, as he gauged my reaction to his words. "And I'm not pushing doing anything more than that," he added to mollify me.

"Kipp, it's exquisitely painful to be in the midst of a major event where there is massive loss of life that you can prevent," I said, attempting to explain my reluctance. "If one of us advises the lookout or bridge that there is an iceberg ahead, and Murdock orders the turn a few seconds earlier, the entire event would be avoided." I reached down to touch Kipp's broad back. "It's always tempting."

"Maybe that's why God created us to work in pairs," Kipp replied. "We act as each other's conscience."

Kipp was, and still is, much wiser than I.

CHAPTER 7

The journey to Winston Salem was less than a hundred miles from my home in the Piedmont. For Peter, who loved to drive, it wasn't long enough to pose an interesting challenge to his skills. Other things had taken priority, and the trip was delayed until the end of September. Personally, I wish we could have waited until mid-October and added on a little side excursion to the Smokies, but Philo wouldn't approve any vacation for me and Kipp anyway, so it didn't matter. The SUV beat an uncomplicated path along Interstate 40, and we arrived in the town, which is situated pretty much in the center of the state, by mid-morning. The lupines took turns shoving their heads in between us, as well as sticking their massive noggins out of the half lowered windows in the back. They looked most like canines when doing the latter as the wind flattened their ears and made their jowls flap noisily in the breeze. With effort, I avoided making amusing remarks since it would have taken the joy from them. Peter was relying upon a GPS that bleated out instructions in a bored, female, mechanical tone. Personally, I missed the old, fold up paper maps one could pick up at a gas station along with a big gulp drink and a bag of Fritos. It had always been more fun to trace one's route with a hesitant finger tip trailing along the surface of the map than to be ordered about by a harsh, no nonsense voice. My transition into the modern age was not without personal angst.

The retirement village, which offered different levels of care, was situated on the north end of town. Peter waited with the lupines in the SUV while I inquired at a main reception desk for Simon. Since we had the lupines with us, all meetings would be outdoors. This was one time that I was glad I had a more than adequate font of knowledge about the subject matter. On my first consequential time shift with Peter and Elani, they, plus Kipp, knew much more about the Great Locomotive Chase than did I. But in terms of the *Titanic*, I was well informed and had in my possession many details that escaped my observant peers. With a self-satisfied sigh, I looked around the foyer while waiting for Simon. The walls were covered in patterned wallpaper upon which prissy little flowers were harassed by pastel butterflies...for some reason I found the scene mildly annoying. Brightly colored window boxes were filled with plastic flowers covered with a thin coating of dust. The designer, undoubtedly, was going for a cheerful look, but the end result was it appeared forced, as if the message was that people were expected to be happy, by golly, no matter what. It was only a minute later when I felt the tingling of a telepathic mind, one that was curious, alert and friendly. Simon may have chosen retirement, but there was no diminishment in his agility and activity level. Apparently, he just wanted to do something different for a change. I suppose all life choices don't have to involve complicated equations; some choices are simple. A short male approached me, his head lifting as he smiled in recognition of a member of his species. His head was adorned with a bushy top knot of white hair that looked as if it hadn't been combed in a while; curved, narrow shoulders were drawn up to his neck, his knees angled in towards each other as he walked.

"I'm Simon," he said, nodding at me. His eyes reminded me of those of a bird, as did his alert, quick manner. To my delight, he bent over my hand and bestowed a kiss to my flesh, his lips dry and almost scratchy as they made contact. There were some aspects of old courtesies that I did miss, and a gentleman was a gentleman, no matter the species or the age.

"Petra Goodgame," I replied, returning his caress of my hand by pressing his lightly between mine in an old school response. "Kipp, Elani and Peter are out in the car...with the air conditioner going," I added with a smile. Simon would appreciate the need to keep the lupines from overheating in a closed vehicle.

"Since I understand Kipp is the one who's crucial to this meeting, let's walk outside and talk before I go and bring my friend," Simon suggested.

The grounds of the retirement facility were neatly maintained with sloping lawns covered in thick green grass which appeared suspiciously free of weeds. Not a perfectionist by nature, I think I would have welcomed some crabgrass or even a late dandelion. Due to the proximity to autumn, the overnight hours were starting to cool down, but the vibrancy of the grass was yet unaffected. There were azaleas strategically planted in thickly bunched groupings with some of the late blooming variety adding unexpected splashes of pink and coral color to the scenery. One could sense from the air that a turn of the seasons was right around the corner, bringing with it a flood of fall colors.

"My friend is Nicholas Little," Simon began, as we stopped to talk in a pretty wooden gazebo angled in a shaded nook. A rock paved trail wound around some plants and trees to find its way to the round construct. "His story has been consistent for years that his father was a survivor of the sinking of the *Titanic*." The old symbiont glanced up and watched, a smile crossing his face, as an elderly couple walked by, holding hands, their fingers woven together in a firm embrace. "Lately, however, he has been telling some of us that his father planted a bomb on the *Titanic* in order to sink her." He raised his eyebrows, which were not well groomed, the stiff hairs tangled. "The staff tells us his memory is slipping, and he is confabulating as humans do when they get dementia. But there's something in his recollection that rings true, and I have wondered if he is retrieving an actual memory, one he'd been counseled to keep private for all these years."

"Was there anyone by that name rescued?" Elani asked.

"I'm not sure, and it doesn't matter, since there was a fair amount of confusion amongst the survivors. The other impression I got is that

Little was an, uh, Americanized name or at least it got changed some- how, and that his father went by another surname. But I–along with any other symbiont I've known—lack the ability to dig into his hidden thoughts and pull that information loose." He smiled at Kipp, who wagged his tail in response. "That's where you come in, Kipp."

"So, you happened to be speaking with Fitzhugh when this topic came up, and he told you of Kipp, right?" I asked.

"Yes. Fitzhugh and I are old friends–and I do mean old. We and our symbionts began traveling at about the same time and crossed paths more than a few times. Things were more haphazard in the earlier days than now, when everything is put on a grid and carefully scheduled." His lips turned down in a frown as his blue eyes darkened a shade.

"So you disapprove of the current methods?" Peter asked. I narrowed my eyes at him, since Peter, of all symbionts I knew, needed control and restrictions. I'd just thought I was a free wheeler...Peter would put me to shame if allowed to wander, led by his own whims.

"Not exactly. I do understand the world is more complex, and that fact affects how we interface with humanity. But there was something exciting about time shifting when there was less planning and more spontaneity." Simon shrugged his thin shoulders. "But things change."

I didn't inquire about his lupine partner whom he'd obviously outlived. And I didn't ask why he chose to spend his later years in a retirement village for aging humans versus being with his own kind.

"Simon, if Kipp does conclude that Nicholas's memories are valid and he believes his father planted a bomb on the *Titanic*, why would it matter for symbionts to have that knowledge?" I asked. He glanced at me and smiled. It had been a while since a younger female symbiont had visited him, and I could tell he'd been a bit of a flirt when a young, dashing fellow. The tender kiss planted on the back of my hand had betrayed the romantic side of his nature.

"There have been a few trips which to my knowledge, symbionts have avoided," I continued, trying to draw him out. "The *Titanic* is one since the acquisition of knowledge would only serve the purpose to alleviate curiosity at this point in time. After the ship sank, there were recommendations made leading to changes in design that added to safety on ocean liners. For a pair of symbionts to be on board that ship while it was sinking and have to endure the anguish of so many humans dying would be difficult, to say the least. No one, as far as I know, has wanted to go."

"Would you want to go now, if you had a significant clue that the sinking might have been the direct result of something other than a collision with an iceberg?" Peter asked the old symbiont, carefully avoiding looking at me, since I knew he had ulterior motives for the query. Peter was trying, not too subtly, to make a point.

"Yes, as difficult as the experience would be," Simon replied. His expression was serious as he spoke.

As he went to retrieve his friend, Nicholas, we waited in the wooden gazebo and reflected upon what he'd said. A small breeze spun around the circular enclosure–an errant wind devil captured within the framework—blowing my hair across my face. Annoyed I'd not confined it in a braid, I tried to tame the dark mass that fell to mid back. Peter dug in his pocket and found a rubber band which he handed to me.

"So, do you usually carry office supplies with you?" I asked, raising an eyebrow. "I might need a stapler or ruler." He grinned in response. "And you don't need to be so carefully subtle about your questions," I added grumpily. "I'm not totally stupid and got your meaning." The smile fell from Peter's face at my brusque remark.

"Petra, you need to switch to decaf," Kipp said, opening his jaws in a bored yawn. He'd obviously had enough of my being difficult. "After all, we're just collecting information at this point. No one has committed to anything."

I frowned. It wasn't that I minded being alone on my journey of intransigence, since I'd been there before, but it felt uncomfortable to not have Kipp trotting happily along by my side. Internally, I chastised myself for the very thought as I felt Kipp politely remove himself from my brain so that I could figure things out on my own. Kipp was fully a partner now, not a novice, and it was presumptuous of me to think that he had to follow my lead. I glanced down to where he was resting on the weathered boards of the gazebo floor. He thumped his tail and squeezed his eyes shut, a subtle love kiss much like the one the feline Lily would bestow upon him. Well, friendship involves loving one another despite faults, and I think Kipp was continually challenged to love me in the face of my less than stellar personality characteristics.

It was a short time later that Simon returned, slowly walking along the stone pathway, his arm linked with that of a very old man, who moved his feet in short, shuffling steps. The man's back was curved so that his head was tilted downward, staring at the stones which, due to their uneven texture, posed a bit of a challenge to navigate. But he was obviously game as a patient Simon took time to let him find his footing.

Respectfully, Peter and I stood, as Nicholas got settled. Automatically, the lupines stood, too, before resuming their places on the wooden planks of the floor. The rigidity in Nicholas's neck forced him to turn his body slightly sideways to peer up at us. I resisted the urge to duck a little lower since the movement of his neck looked painful due to the arthritis that had almost immobilized his joints and prevented any fluidity of motion. His eyes appeared blurry due to a gray opaqueness covering the irises, which were lost behind the cover of glasses as well as cataracts. There was no way to know if he shaved himself or had assistance, but there was a fuzz of uneven razor stubble on his chin and above his upper lip. I noticed a hearing aid in his right ear, and he tended to turn his left ear, his good one, towards us when we were talking.

"Nicholas, these are my friends Petra and Peter and their dogs, Elani and Kipp," Simon began, lightly touching his friend's shoulder. I couldn't help but notice he introduced the ladies, me and Elani, first. What an old dear.

"I'm happy to meet you," Nicholas replied, trying to nod his head which was on the end of his stiff, immobile neck. "How nice that Simon gets a visit from young people."

At this point, obviously all four of us were pouring through his thoughts, since such plunder of human minds was natural to us and not a violation of symbiont boundaries. But Peter, Elani and I could only really access his current notions and feeling tones. It would take Kipp to push through those and get into the repressed and hidden memories that humans kept in their brains for lifetimes. He'd done this before with the man known as Jack the Ripper to determine the psychological aspects of his early life to help explain his aberrant behaviors.

"And what handsome dogs," Nicholas added. "Some of the people here have pets, but I don't have any interest in putting up with the mess."

"Mess? What mess?" Kipp was clearly offended. He narrowed his amber eyes and glanced up at me.

"Not about you, Kipp. He's talking about curbing a poodle or scooping out a cat box," I replied. "You're on autopilot."

"I'm 95 years old," Nicholas was saying. "And I've been living here," he said with a gesture, "for seventy years." His voice was soft and monotone with a trembling waver.

Of course, he had his timing wrong, and as he chatted, it was clear that he did suffer from some moderate cognitive impairment that seemed to affect the context in which he framed his thoughts and memories. But he was a generally pleasant, cheerful old gentleman, and all of us, as we monitored his thoughts, found him to be an honest broker.

"You were telling me a story about your father the other day," Simon said, gently prompting him. "About why he was on board the *Titanic*..."

After a moment of hesitation, Nicholas made a quick visual survey to make certain no one else was nearby and within listening range. Leaning forward, he said, "Well, I'd rather this not get out." After we all nodded vigorously and almost symbolically crossed our hearts and hoped to die, he continued. "My father was a survivor of the sinking of the *Titanic*." He glanced at me, smiling. "You know what that was, don't you? Most young people don't have a good grip on history anymore."

I smiled and nodded. "Yes, I'm familiar with the name." Nicholas would be startled to learn I was over four hundred years old, but there was no reason to give the old gentleman a heart attack.

"His name was Anthony Littleton–he changed it to Little after he arrived in America." For a moment, he rambled off on another topic, easily distracted by a grounds worker who pushed a loudly squeaking wheelbarrow past our location. I noticed that when Nicholas's attention wavered, his hands began shaking with a fine tremor, possibly from some type of palsy. Simon gently redirected the conversation to get him back on track. "He never spoke of his early life until he was dying. As I sat with him, he said he needed to unburden his soul and told me he'd planted a bomb on board the *Titanic* in order to cause her to sink."

"Why would that be important to him?" Peter asked. He leaned forward and pushed his glasses, which had slid down, back up to perch on the bridge of his nose.

"He was from England and had become increasingly agitated over the social inequities in the system at the turn of the century. His parents were middle class, so he didn't suffer in his upbringing as did the poor and lower classes who, no matter how hard they worked, couldn't advance in society." Nicholas's voice was soft, his projection rather weak, so it was easy to see how humans might just listen to certain points and direct their attention elsewhere, nodding as if they were actually paying attention. None of this was an obstacle for telepaths, since we followed his thoughts, spoken or not. "The notion that so much money would be spent on building those wondrous ships such as the *Oceanic* and then the *Titanic* just, well, got under his skin." He reached out with a thin hand to brush an imaginary piece of lint from his trousers. "Over time, he became covertly involved in groups promoting anarchism. His first wife became ill with consumption, and she died before their first child was born. I think that is what sent him over the edge, so to speak."

His attention began to wander again as the arrival of a bright yellow minivan rolling along the circular drive caught his notice. He frowned, and his thoughts betrayed his worries that he was supposed to be on board that van, en route to destinations unknown.

"Nicholas, the van is taking some folks to appointments. You don't have anything scheduled today," Simon said, with a gentle reminder. With a little prodding, Nicholas was off again, unwinding his story as one might pull thread from a spool.

"My mother was his second wife; he met her here," he said,

meaning America. "But he developed a terrible problem with the bottle and began to drink heavily. Most people assumed it was the trauma he experienced as the ship was sinking which led to his problem. I think it was the whiskey that finally killed him." Nicholas took a glance around at our odd party before letting his lips part in a tremulous smile. "I guess it's safe to tell you all," he finally concluded. "One night, after he'd been told that his days were numbered, he told me the truth about his trip on the *Titanic*." It was clear Nicholas's memory had meandered again, and he'd forgotten he'd just told us those facts. "He spoke of his mission, as he termed it, and that he took a quantity of gun cotton concealed in a steamer trunk on board to do the damage."

Nicholas abruptly stopped speaking, and his eyes began to blink rapidly. When his speech stopped, the hand tremors returned and were more severe than previously. Simon leaned in to him, his face creased with worry. It was clear that Nicholas needed assistance, and Peter raced to the front desk to get help. I edged closer to Nicholas, so that I was on one side and Simon was on the other. Kipp and Elani both stood, concerned, but unable to assist. Reaching out, I took Nicholas's hand, which was cool and dry; he didn't look at me but his grip tightened around my fingers. In less than a minute, two staff members dressed in bright blue scrub uniforms darted towards us, pushing a wheelchair. They were discrete, of course, but it was evident from their unexpressed thoughts that Nicholas had suffered from similar spells before...a type of mild seizure it seemed. Simon, after a hurried goodbye, trailed after his friend.

There was no need for us to wait since the staff had things in hand, and Simon had departed to be with his friend, so I herded our small party back to the SUV. As Peter swung the vehicle into traffic, I half turned in my seat despite the constraint of the seat belt.

"Kipp, what impressions did you get?" I asked. He'd been conspicuously quiet during the interview, but I realized he had been intensely concentrating and had tuned me out for the duration.

He poked his head in between me and Peter; a moment later, Elani joined him and we made a sight as we drove along, with our four heads lined up in a row across the front seats of the vehicle. Kipp drew close and pressed the side of his face to my cheek. It was then I was aware how taxing his deep dive into the thoughts of Nicholas Little had been. After a pause, he let out a sigh.

"Well, I have no doubt that Nicholas believes what he was telling us. I was able to go back to his memory of what his father disclosed and recall the moment as his father told him of his efforts to sink the *Titanic*." Kipp pulled back since he was acutely aware of his close physical proximity to Elani. Proper gent that he was, he never liked leading her on in any manner since he knew she harbored tender feelings for him. "The issue is that we have no way of knowing if his father was telling him the truth." Kipp paused to yawn. He wasn't sleepy but needed the sudden influx of oxygen to help clear his mind.

"Why on earth would someone lie about that?" Elani asked. "And especially on one's death bed? It doesn't make sense to me."

"There was intense detail in the memories, as you all can see," Kipp remarked, inviting Peter and Elani to share his thoughts. I was already busy canvassing them. "There was an original plan and then, after the ship hit the iceberg, there was a revised plan. If you know anything about the construction of the *Titanic* and what happened to the bulkheads that lead to the sinking, then what Nicholas was told is completely logical and believable."

I watched the road, not speaking, as we clicked off the miles towards home. I wasn't sure what any of the information meant but knew one thing for certain–a trip to the *Titanic* was unprecedented, dangerous and psychologically threatening. This might be one of those times for a wise symbiont pair to walk away from an assignment.

Kipp nuzzled the back of my head, his breath warm against my flesh. Privately he assured me we'd agree together or not at all. My hand drifted up to scratch his chin; there were a few bristly hairs–like those that might grow on the face of an old man—caught up in the soft pelt of fur. I knew I'd feel better when we could talk with Fitzhugh, just Kipp and me.

CHAPTER 8

Previously, I'd enjoyed time spent with Philo. Now it seemed, not so much. Kipp attributed my change in feelings to my natural opposition to authority and, if I was honest, there was some truth to that notion. But it was difficult for two beings who had been as close as us to make the transition to supervisor and employee while maintaining a friendship.

"I think it would be prudent to do some preliminary research on the *Titanic* in order to present a coherent plan to the Twelve," Philo was saying.

I felt my eyebrows scoot so far up my forehead they threatened to disappear into my hairline. "Hold on, there," I began, settling myself in the chair. "I don't think that I said I was interested in going to the *Titanic*." I glanced over at Peter whose face was neutral. At least the kid was letting me take the lead. Kipp looked up at me, his jaw opening as he began to pant. He knew the atmosphere in the room was about to get tense. Elani, bless her, maintained her predictably even keel. I was finding, over time, that she was a wonderfully steady ship to have in any storm.

"What exactly do you think your job is, Petra?" Philo asked. He removed his reading glasses, the way he did when he was trying to delay an emotional response and remain irritatingly patient. Yes, I knew him too well, it seemed. As he exhaled, his lips pursed slightly, and I figured he was counting to ten.

"I know my job, but I also realize I have the right and responsibility to, perhaps, decline a bad choice." I crossed my arms and tilted my head to the side. I cared not for being backed into a corner. "After all, our backsides are on the line, not those of the Twelve."

"There have been many trips to dangerous events," Philo began before I ill advisedly cut him off.

"And you've made none of them, so it's easy for you to say." The minute I said it, I regretted the words which were dismissive and unpleasant. I suppose I felt the way many employees did when the boss would reel off some impossible series of tasks followed up with "you gotta problem with that?". To his credit, his face only reddened slightly before he sighed deeply. Philo glanced over at Fitzhugh, who remained quiet.

"There's a reason we avoid places like Mount Vesuvius and Krakatoa," I said, rolling my eyes as if I was conducting an entry level class on time shifting for novice symbionts.

"Well, actually there was a trip to Krakatoa," Fitzhugh began.

"Did I ask for your help?" I was getting agitated, feeling the heat flush up my neck to stain my cheeks. The chair in which I sat suddenly felt constraining, uncomfortable; I shifted my position, crossing my legs. Glancing towards the window, I felt an almost desperate wave come over me wishing to be outside, free of that room and those inside, despite the fact I loved every one of them. To draw attention away from my red face, I began to swing one of my legs as if I was feeling carefree with no issues on the table.

Philo stood and walked over to the window that overlooked the garden. He was tall, slender–almost thin, those days—and I noticed, for the first time, that his shoulders were beginning to slump. A couple of centuries ahead of me on the timeline, Philo was starting to show a little age in the way he held himself. I was next, I supposed, feeling a frown appear on my face.

"Petra, you should know that Arnie and Tig have retired from traveling." Philo turned, and his face looked tired and lifeless in the harsh, fluorescent lighting of the room. "That leaves Laurel and Devon and you and Kipp as our experienced travelers. Of course, we have high hopes for Peter and Elani," he said, smiling, his gaze darting towards the duo, who sat quietly.

"Sorry to hear about Arnie," I muttered. He'd had some health problems that must have finally taken a toll on his abilities. He'd been good...very good. "But why the *Titanic*?" I asked. "I just don't get that choice."

"The word *Titanic* still resonates with people, over one hundred years after the tragedy. Anything we can discover addressing questions about the voyage and her sinking will add to the history of humans, even if we can't directly share some of those answers." Philo sat on the corner of his desk. "I've really wanted to do this for a long time, but I don't have the ability, as you so aptly pointed out," he added unnecessarily, his mouth curving in a wry smile that didn't quite make it to his eyes. "Haven't you wondered the truth behind how the people in steerage were treated? Was the captain pressed by Bruce Ismay to ignore safety regulations?" He sighed. "There are countless stories within stories. And if there is some possibility that a bomb placed hastened the sinking, it would be invaluable to have that knowledge." Standing, he walked towards me. "What if the bomb was involved in the sinking? If it wasn't and the *Titanic* stayed afloat longer, would the *Carpathia* have arrived in time to rescue more people?"

Kipp looked up at me, his eyes bright. I knew that he was drawn, like a moth to a flame, to anything new; at his essence, he was filled with boundless curiosity. Once I'd been like that, and I wondered where that Petra had gone? I knew for certain that she wasn't present in that room listening to a cockeyed proposal for an ill-advised time shift. Peter and Elani were listening but not contributing. I figured Peter might think any words uttered would fall under attack by me. Smart kid, I thought.

"I don't want to be totally closed-minded," I offered, glancing down at my shoes. The laces were dirty and frayed at the end. I needed some new ones if I could remember to pick them up the next time I was at the market. How could I coordinate a time shift to the *Titanic* when I couldn't even take care of the basics like shoe strings?

"What I'd like is for the four of you to start pulling anything you can find to read about the *Titanic* and then let's get back together in a few weeks and talk again. Is that unreasonable?" Philo was wearing that irritatingly earnest expression that was meant to convince me of his rightness. Of course, he knew his request wasn't unreasonable, which is why he would pose such a question. He was in a safe zone, and I was out on the diving board, perched, ready to fly off into oblivion.

"I guess we can do that, but I'm not promising anything," I grumbled, not meeting his eyes.

"There is always Peter and Elani who can manage if you can't," Philo said unexpectedly.

"You must be joking!"I exclaimed. "They are a couple of kids, and you know they can't safely navigate a risky trip like that." Narrowing my eyes, I stared at Philo. It was unusual for him to be cleverly manipulative, and I didn't care for his trying to force my hand by involving Peter and Elani. "I think your job is changing you in ways I don't like," I finally said, standing. I'd had enough of the office, Philo and most things Technicorps. Kipp hopped up and moved to my side to softly nuzzle my hand. I was truly done and, after a hasty good bye, made my way outside where the air would hopefully cleanse me of my agitated mood.

Despite my irritation, a promise was a promise, and we spent that weekend watching James Cameron's *Titanic* as well as the classic movie, *A Night to Remember*. October began as a rainy month, so we four travelers, plus Fitzhugh, Juno and Lily, of course, hung around my house watching movies, discussing scenes and eating popcorn and grilled cheese sandwiches. During some of the more suggestive scenes in *Titanic*, Kipp edged away from Elani and came over to sit by me.

"Don't want her getting any romantic notions," he intoned privately to my ears only.

"You're a stud muffin, and you know it, Kipp," I whispered back, resting my chin on top of his head.

Over the next few weeks we read all the books we could find. Kipp and I shared his Kindle, falling asleep each night with the device propped upon my chest. I found he became a little lazy and would let me do the reading while he just followed along with his telepathy. Fitzhugh utilized the Technicorps library researching events before and after the sinking, moments in time that defined the Gilded Age and many of the personalities who were already notable for the day and with the amazingly bad luck to book passage on the *Titanic*.

"There were more than 2200 people on board the ship, including passengers and crew members. Only seven hundred plus people survived the sinking. Exact numbers are still a little fuzzy, depending upon the reference," Peter began. "As per what would have been acceptable practice during those times, the classes were separated into first, second and third, or steerage. Parts of the ship were reserved, exclusively, for the different classes, who, with few exceptions, did not mix. The *Titanic* was the second of three mega liners designed and built by Harland and Wolff for the White Star Line, and the *Olympic* was already in service by the time *Titanic* was completed. The White Star Line was in direct competition with Cunard for the choice North Atlantic routes. *Titanic* was conceptualized to be the ultimate in terms of luxury, and Ismay hoped that her magnificence would offset the fact that Cunard had faster liners in service." Peter paused for a sip of water. He enjoyed the role of narrator and had huddled prior to his presentation with Fitzhugh, who watched, nodding, like a proud father, a slight blush staining his thin cheeks.

"The *Titanic* departed Southampton, England on April 10, 1912 and, after stops at Cherbourg, France and Queenstown, Ireland, started her voyage across the Atlantic." Peter pushed his glasses, which had skidded down his nose, back into proper position. "She actually had been scheduled to leave earlier in the season but a coal strike hampered the activities of the big ocean liners, and she was delayed. It's odd to think of the timing…if she'd left on schedule, she'd not have encountered that iceberg on April 14th, and she would have not sunk."

"Life is full of what ifs," I remarked. "Are such things bad luck or predestination?" My rhetorical comment went unanswered. With a sigh, I glanced out the front window; a brisk wind became tangled in the tree tops. Even from my vantage point within my house, I could hear the fall leaves tremble against the cooling breeze surging from the north. It was my favorite time of year.

"And then there was the weather which caused the ice to be more prevalent longer into the season as well as dipping deeper into the North Atlantic shipping lanes. All the ships navigating during that time were aware of the increased danger of flow ice as well as bergs." Peter sat back in his chair and stretched. He'd been hunched over my dinette table all morning reading another book he'd found at the library. With Kindles, Nooks and the internet, I was happy to see people still frequented libraries.

"There were several survivor stories that would seem to indicate that explosions were heard as the *Titanic* went down," Elani remarked. She lay before my fireplace which was dormant. Glancing up at the wooden mantle, I gazed at the little framed picture of my son, George. His toothless, silly grin remained unchanged, frozen in time, over the years since his accidental death. I'd kept the picture boxed up safely out of view until Kipp, in his typically bossy way, determined he knew what was best for me and forced me to bring it to light again. I admit the picture brought both sadness and happiness to me; it was good George's face was back again, clearly in view. Kipp had been right about that.

"Yes, but some people attributed those sounds to other events," Kipp was saying. "The officers and crewmen thought that the boilers and engines detached from their fixtures as the ship tilted at a greater angle when water began to fill the bow. As the angle increased, the heavy equipment broke through bulkheads as they crashed throughout the ship's lower decks."

"The fact is, no one would know for certain if there were explosions or not." Fitzhugh was sitting in his favorite chair, an overstuffed piece that carried the imprint of his narrow backside upon the seat cushion. "But there was testimony as to sounds that could or could not have been explosions. And since you are investigating whether or not there was a bomb on board, the information is important evidence of suspicion."

I felt more than a dart of irritation. Kipp glanced up at me, aware of my thoughts in our manner of sharing. I was tired of others making the assumption that this trip to the *Titanic* was a go and there was no question that we should take the plunge, metaphorically speaking. I must have been wearing my feelings on my face because Fitzhugh commented.

"What's bothering you?" he asked, frowning.

"I don't feel like this is time well spent," I began. "Unless we are definitely going, then this research is a waste of time."

"And maybe Peter and Elani will go without you," Fitzhugh replied. His cheeks reddened slightly as he stared at me. Despite his growing fondness for me, he'd not abandoned his no nonsense approach to our work. Since he'd been a traveler, I couldn't accuse him of asking me to do things of which he had no awareness of the associated risks. "The Twelve are down to few choices, as you well know. Perhaps some of the classes for youth will give us possible candidates who possess the genetic ability to link up for travel." He paused, his face growing sad. "There are no Kipp's left who can do the remarkable, Petra, due to his genetic diversity. We have to work with what we have left of our species."

I, as did most sentient beings, cared little for someone using guilt to force my choices. "Do you want me to feel guilty if I don't go and let Peter and Elani go by themselves?" I finally asked.

"Yes, quite frankly...yes." Fitzhugh crossed his thin arms across his narrow chest.

I had to laugh at his reply which reeked of brutal honesty, but my attention was drawn to Kipp who was watching me closely. "What?" I asked, since he'd closed his thoughts to me. Suddenly, they hit me like a rush of flood water.

"Why is it you make this your decision only, Petra? What if I want to go?" Kipp huffed out an agitated breath. "I thought we were a team." His large ears drooped a little as he finished.

I felt a little startled, since he'd previously indicated he didn't want me to go against my druthers in terms of a time shift to the *Titanic*. It occurred to me at that moment that he'd spoken from a position of love and not intellect or desire. Kipp had given me permission to be selfish and only think of my feelings with no regard to his. Swallowing hard, I scooted off my wing chair and plopped on the floor next to him. Despite lacking the knees of a youngster, I managed to pull my legs up, crosswise, in a sloppy imitation of a yoga pose.

"Kipp, tell me how you feel…and I mean honestly." Reaching out, I touched his fur, threading my fingers down through the hair to comb his thick pelt.

"I don't want to push anything that you don't want to do. But at the same time, there are risks I'm willing to take and ideas that seem exciting. I hesitate to suggest them because I'm afraid you don't want to go." His amber eyes looked up at me. "I don't know what to do."

I pulled him close and pressed my face next to his. "Oh, Kipp! This is one way we can be like humans. When desires and wishes conflict with those of a loved one, it's difficult—maybe impossible—for everyone to be happy. And sometimes, we compromise." I laughed and invited the others to join in what had been a private conversation. After listening for a minute, Peter smiled, having scooted down on the floor to put his arm around Elani, who snuggled close, her tail wagging.

"Elani and I have done that about what to have for dinner," he said, feeling happy he could join in the topic. "She wants chicken and I want steak; we end up eating fish, which neither of us wants, just to keep from pushing something on the other!" Peter laughed at the thought.

"And I love Captain D…they have that great fish with those little bits of fried, crunchy batter that get tossed in the box and the hush puppies…" Kipp glanced at me. "But Petra doesn't eat fish, so we don't go there very much."

I glanced up at Fitzhugh who was definitely amused at the musings of youth.

"Have you come to any conclusions?" he asked, his query directed at me.

"Well, Peter likes steak, Elani prefers chicken, and Kipp wants some hush puppies from Captain D." I sighed as I tried to smile. "I think Kipp and I need to talk in more depth. And we all need to work less on pleasing and protecting one another and focus on honest dialog."

Kipp gave a sharp bark of agreement.

None of us were exempt from having to show up at work, even though the research on the *Titanic* was technically an assignment. On the following Monday, Kipp and I made the pleasant walk to Technicorps. Autumn was fully engaged at that point, with the bright, fiery leaves just past mid-peak; the hues were so vivid they made me think some artist had swept his brush against his palette and flung it to carelessly spatter the colors against the canvas of blue sky. Inhaling deeply, the thick odor of dying foliage hit the back of my throat in a burst of musty, dusty molecules, as I tried to suppress a cough. Kipp's head swiveled as he watched a pair of squirrels dart for safety, their toenails scrabbling loudly as they raced in a spiral up the trunk of a large hickory tree. A couple of intrepid adventurers were out walking their dogs. As we passed the dogs, their heads lifted with interest at the massive Kipp, but once they realized he was no dog, their ears flattened, and they pressed against the legs of their human companions, seeking security in an uncertain world.

Kipp laughed softly, adding a little strut to his walk. "That little one with the shaggy hair over his eyes thought he wanted to rumble with me. Not gonna happen."

We separated at Technicorps as I took the stairs down to the lower level where the research library was located. Fitzhugh and Juno had begged a ride with Peter and arrived earlier than had I. Juno would have made her way to the lupine classroom where she and Kipp worked with the young ones.

"Slacker," Fitzhugh remarked, pointing at his wrist where an imaginary watch resided, making a point as to my arrival time. He looked more tired than usual, and I wondered if he'd slept well the previous night. I could smell coffee, the fragrance tantalizing as it threaded its way through the large room. Arching an eyebrow at Fitzhugh, I tilted my head to the back office.

"So, are you letting Mark Elliott change all the traditions?" I was needling Fitzhugh and he knew it.

"We suffer when we are rigid and not accepting of new ideas," he deftly replied, knowing his comment had a dual meaning and targeted my vulnerability with Kipp.

"I still enjoy the Earl Grey," I replied, yawning. "It's familiar," I added, after struggling for an apt description.

Mark appeared at that moment carrying a tray with a carafe, cups, and containers of cream and sugar. His teeth gleamed when he smiled; his wheat colored hair was a little longer than usual and showed some natural wave rippling through the thick, lovely mass. My hair had not looked that perfectly styled in 400 years.

"I've asked Mark to help with our *Titanic* research," Fitzhugh remarked, his voice bland. "Philo thought it is prudent to explore every possible fact, given the nature of the event."

I smiled, nodding, glad once again that contemporary symbionts didn't read each other's minds since Mark would pick up on my negative thoughts towards him. As he leaned forward to hand me a cup of coffee, I caught a whiff of some expensive fragrance...subtle but pleasant and not overpowering. Probably contained some pheromone laced chemical, I thought darkly, meant to lure unsuspecting females to become entrapped in his web of allure.

"I actually have a remote connection to the event," Mark said. He took a chair in the small gathering of upholstered chairs placed in a comfortable semicircle near my worktable that was currently overflowing with manuscripts. I never thought I'd look longingly at the pile, but I did take a peek.

"Yes?" Fitzhugh prompted.

"One of my very good friends lives in the Atlanta collective. His name is Tristan Taylor, and we grew up together, since our families were very close. You know how it used to be before collectives...we just sort of gathered in small groups and kept on the move most of the time." He looked at me and I nodded. That, too, had been my experience as a youngster.

"Tristan decided to go to school in Germany and there he met John Pierpont Morgan, who later became the steel and railroad magnate of America and one of the world's wealthiest men." Mark leaned forward and warmed up his coffee from the carafe after Fitzhugh and I waved him off. "As you may recall from your readings so far, J.P. Morgan's company, International Mercantile Marine, acquired control of the White Star Line in 1902, I think it was." He raised his eyebrows. "My friend, Tristan, was close to him over the years and knows about him, the times in general, his involvement with the *Titanic* as well as his relationship with Bruce Ismay, who managed the White Star Line." Mark smiled. "Tristan is a helpful person to know."

"How on earth would a symbiont manage to have an ongoing relationship with a human from college days to the man's death at an old age and avoid being conspicuous by not aging?" Fitzhugh asked, sitting forward to replace his coffee cup. I knew he was not a coffee fan and longed for his Earl Grey, carefully brewed in his favorite antique porcelain tea pot, even if he wouldn't admit that fact.

"Well, I've heard him tell, but it probably needs to come directly from him. That in itself is a fascinating story."

"I bet," I remarked.

Our collectives moved us around every so often to keep humans from suspecting our origin, since our lack of aging made us stand out like a crimson colored cardinal in a flock of crows. Yes, it would be worth a drive to Atlanta to meet Tristan Taylor. After Mark walked back to his office to begin work, Fitzhugh looked at me, smiling.

"What?" I asked.

"You're getting interested in this possible time shift, aren't you?" He was wearing the Irish sweater I'd given him at Christmas. Even though it was not winter, the library tended to be on the cool side, and the sweater was buttoned from top to bottom. The walls of the library, at Fitzhugh's insistence, wore a paint motif that hinted at Victorian days, and there were pieces of antique furniture scattered about. All we needed was a carved wooden mantle surrounding a roaring fire to make the scene cozily complete.

"Kipp and I had a talk, and I realized I was driving the car a little too often. Kipp wants more time behind the wheel," I explained lamely.

"It's about time," Fitzhugh snorted. "Now we're in for some adventure!"

CHAPTER 9

"Let's play, for the moment, with the thought that we will make this trip," I began. I felt very pleased with myself that I'd taken the adult, mature route and would systematically be able to demonstrate why a time shift to the *Titanic* would be ill advised. At some point, I believe I even managed a convincing smile during my introduction. With effort, I ignored Kipp who narrowed his eyes at me.

It was after hours, and we–Philo, Fitzhugh, Peter, Elani, Juno, Kipp and me—were huddled in the library long after Mark Elliott had clocked out for the evening, even though the scent of his cologne lingered. Philo ordered a couple of pizzas so no one could whine and complain of an inability to concentrate due to hunger. Peter brought a stack of paper plates from the kitchen along with a roll of paper towels to serve as crude napkins. None of us really stood on ceremony.

"Pizza makes me thirsty," Kipp remarked as he downed his second slice.

"Let's assume that Littleton was on board the *Titanic* with his bomb material," I began, ignoring Kipp's comment, my plan of attack lined up in my head.

"Actually, we don't need to assume that fact anymore," Peter said.

"Littleton's name is on the passenger lists, at least indicating he bought a ticket. I did further research yesterday and found the listing. What had thrown me off was that his name was not on the survivor list, which was where I'd started, but such omissions were not unusual due to the chaos. From what his son told us, he changed his identity and simply disappeared."

"Ha!" Kipp said, smirking that my self-satisfied and logical approach had been shot down so quickly.

"Do we know what class?" Fitzhugh asked.

"First class," Peter replied. "Maybe the group of anarchists helped fund his passage, or he might have paid it himself, thinking it was a one way trip," he speculated. "It would make sense that a first class berth would give Littleton more freedom to move about the ship as well as granting him a private cabin."

"Well, we've run into our first issue, and this threatened to be the problem up front," I said. "If we go on the *Titanic*, I don't know of any way to keep Kipp and Elani close by. There were kennels, and only a few first class passengers could get by with letting their dogs stay in their staterooms. The first class stewards, in order to keep the travelers happy, pretty much kept their mouths shut."

"I am not staying in a kennel," Kipp began.

"Of course not," I said, nodding my head a little too vigorously. "See, the main issue is accessibility."

Philo stared at me. He'd known me too long for me to get by with acting that casual and reasonable. "So what if you all travel first class?" he asked. "I really view this as Peter and Elani's trip with you and Kipp as support." The comment was an unnecessary insert, designed to let me know my place. "You and Peter can travel as brother and sister... unless you want to go as a married couple this time." The latter statement, to which I did not respond, was meant to embarrass me. I merely compressed my lips at Philo while avoiding Peter's gaze. Kipp never helped those moments by giggling hysterically in the back of my head.

"The first class berths were all taken. There is no way for us to get a first class passage," I said. For once, I was happy I'd done the research. A lonely piece of pizza lingered on my plate, begging for my attention. After breaking off the crusty corner, I nibbled on it, savoring the salty tang of tomato paste on my tongue.

"Technically that was true," Kipp remarked. "But there were last minute cancellations and no shows, and the ship's crew was busy moving a few people around after boarding to accommodate their wealthy clientele. But the problem would be on paper; if we just arrive expecting to get a ticket, they will show first class as booked. And if we try to reserve beforehand, we risk bumping someone and changing the timeline of history."

"So, the only way to board the ship and not change history is to show up at the very last minute and book passage when all the other passengers are set." Elani's jaw opened as she began to pant slightly. I hadn't asked her if she wanted to go but figured she'd give an affirmative in the manner of impetuous youth.

Fitzhugh sat back in his chair and stretched his long legs before crossing them at the ankles. As he closed his eyes, his fingers began to rub his jaw as if in contemplation. I noticed the knuckles on his hands were enlarged from arthritis. Even symbionts were not spared the rigors of aging...we just did it slower and perhaps with a little more grace than humans.

"Maybe it is fortuitous that Mark Elliott came here to work," he finally said, his voice soft. "Do you wonder about the timing of events and wonder if such things are happenstance or predestination?" He was mimicking a remark I'd made just a few days earlier.

"Yes, just look at the *Titanic*," I said, glancing at him from the corners of my eyes. What was he about to hatch?

"Mark Elliott told us he has a good friend, Tristan Taylor, an associate of J.P. Morgan, who technically, through his conglomerate International Mercantile Marine, owned the *Titanic*." Fitzhugh took a deep breath. "As I recall, Morgan was scheduled to be on the maiden voyage but only cancelled at the last minute. He'd had some health problems and chose to be in France at his villa to take the waters, as they used to say. He had one of the posh suites on B deck with a private promenade and all the amenities."

"Yes, but Bruce Ismay took those rooms when Morgan cancelled." I had done my reading, too.

T.L.B. WOOD

"Which indicates some last minute shifting around and would prove Ismay had some other place on board the ship that he could use. I don't know if we could determine exactly where, but we know there would have been a room for him." Fitzhugh reached up to smooth his beard, the way he did when he was engaged in serious, methodical thinking.

"Where are you going with this?" I asked. The next moment, I wondered why Fitzhugh and I were the only ones talking. Everyone else was still or munching quietly on pizza. It was clear he had become the voice of promoting the time shift while I took the solid position of reasonable opposition. Or at least I saw myself in that positive light.

"If there was some way to influence J.P. Morgan to give up his suite to your four, you could travel in style, with the lupines at your side. Undoubtedly if Morgan told the ship's staff to let you be, that would happen."

"And how would that be arranged, Fitzhugh?" The entire discussion was making my head spin...and I was feeling my agitation grow in increments. "You're suggesting there is some way for us to time shift, meet up with J.P. Morgan, who doesn't know us from Adam, and get him to influence the crew on the *Titanic* to give us the nicest accommodations on board and let our lupines go to the first class smoking room for some brandy and a cigar." I rolled my eyes.

"Kipp does have the ability to insert thoughts, so yes, that could be one way." Fitzhugh sighed. "But since we find such a manipulation to be, uh, unpleasant, I think it might be prudent to go visit Mark's friend in Atlanta and see if he can help fill in the blanks."

Philo was the one who could make things happen, so it was only two days later when Peter, Elani, Kipp and I were traveling south along the interstate, following an unusually heavy line of traffic towards Atlanta. The SUV was a Technicorps vehicle from their motor pool that we'd used previously.

"Whoever used this last was a slob," Kipp remarked. "There is a bag full of trash back here." His disgust and minor outrage filled the small space. "And I think I found a French fry from the 70's."

"We'll toss it at our next stop," I promised.

Pushing back against my seat, I pulled my fleece jacket closer, turning the collar up against my face. Although it was early November, the weather was unseasonably cold, and it felt more like January, with all its brittle harshness. I glanced longingly over my shoulder at Kipp and Elani, who were playing a lupine mind game with one another to pass the time; their fur looked invitingly thick and warm. We'd left home at daybreak and made it to the outskirts of Atlanta by noon in spite of the normally clogged traffic arteries. The collective was actually just north of the city itself, located in Alpharetta. As we drove up, the first thing catching my attention was that the buildings formed a cluster of poorly maintained structures, unlike the pristine condition of Technicorps. The collective must be on the financial decline, I thought, sharing my notions with Peter. The buildings were set in a heavily wooded area; November had stripped most of the leaves from the limbs, leaving only a few withered remnants to rattle as the wind passed.

"This is an older collective," Peter said. "Fitzhugh knows more about it, of course. While we've stayed competitive and try to change ourselves to adapt to a modern world, this group has not and suffers, as you can see."

Peter rolled down his window to ask a passing symbiont where we might find Tristan Taylor, and after a few minutes spent weaving around some narrow, hedge banked roads, we finally parked in front of a three story brick building topped by a stained, worn roof which had seen better days. The shrubs were overgrown and hovered ominously around the front entrance in a way that almost made a weary traveler think twice before entering. We were met politely, however, and directed to an office on the second floor.

"Come in!" A baritone voice rang out from behind a heavy door scarred by too many close brushes with rolling carts and equipment being shoved without care past the aperture.

As we opened the bruised door, I was amused to see the humanoid male symbiont who greeted us was almost lost behind a large, oak desk which was covered in stacks of papers and books threatening to collapse at any moment. To the right of the desk, a small electric fireplace made to look like a little wood burning stove glowed red as waves of heat radiated out to fill the air that was musty due to inadequate air circulation. With effort, I suppressed a sneeze originating from my toes. Sitting close in front of the heater was a mature lupine, black with some touches of gray on his muzzle.

"I'm Tristan Taylor," the humanoid introduced himself. He was tall and slender, almost to the point of gauntness. As he reached out to shake our hands, his flesh felt soft like that of a young child; it was evident he'd spent years working behind a desk. "I understand you are friends of Mark Elliott." He introduced his symbiont, Meko, and Kipp and Elani touched noses with the older lupine in the traditional nod of respect for his age. Tristan's face was still youthful, despite his hollow cheeks, and from what Mark had told us, Tristan was probably about a hundred years older than me. His mop of brown hair was tinged with gray at the temples and was worn long, the uneven ends touching his collar. His eyes were dark, their expression somewhat guarded behind the thick lenses of rimless glasses. With a sweep of his hands, Tristan invited us to sit.

"We'll get right to the point, if you don't mind," I began. "We are investigating the possibility there was a bomb placed on the *Titanic* that may have contributed to the accident. Mark told us you were close friends with J.P. Morgan, and since you were involved with him, you might be able to help us think through some problems we would encounter should a time shift take place." I sat back in my chair, not aware I'd been sitting on the edge of the wooden seat, which looked like something that might have once been in a classroom, the chair where recalcitrant children were forced to sit due to some minor infraction of the rules. Perhaps I'd picked the most uncomfortable seat in the room as a reflection of my general negativity?

Tristan took a deep breath and exhaled slowly. He walked to the window which was coated in a dewy layer of condensation; the building lacked adequate insulation, and the room was cold, except for the warmth provided by the free standing heater. As he composed his thoughts, I peeked furtively around the room. The walls were finished in dark paneling which, although not in step with contemporary fashion, appealed to me; two of the four walls were covered in ceiling to floor book cases. I was sitting close enough to one to pick out many valuable books, some of which were most likely first editions of classics and tomes that were long out of print. I could bury myself in that room in my guise as researcher and avid reader...just me, the electric heater, a cup of tea, and Kipp, of course.

"I find it difficult to believe a collective would approve of a time shift to the *Titanic*," Tristan began. He turned to look at me, then Peter. Meko's dark head lifted as he glanced at his bonded partner. I was curious if they still traveled or if they were retired from such. As if he impolitely read my notions, Tristan said, "Meko and I haven't shifted in quite a while, but we made many trips back to those times and are very familiar with the days."

"And how would you classify your relationship with J.P. Morgan?" Kipp asked.

"You know, it's kind of funny in retrospect. It is almost impossible for symbionts and humans to be close for any period of time due to our aging differences." Tristan took a seat across from me. He knew I was the more experienced of our group and naturally showed me some deference. "But somehow, J.P. and I managed for most of his life to stay connected." He sighed deeply. "I met him at the University of Gottingen in Germany. He'd been sent there to finish his education, as it was called. He'd already had training in terms of business and finance but went abroad to study French and then German. He attained a degree in art history at the University."

"How did you connect with him?" Kipp was persistent, digging for details.

"I was also at the University, pursuing a degree in art history, so we were in the same classes. Just one of my interests over the many years," he said smiling. "From J.P.'s perspective, we seemed to be about the same age, and he assumed we were from the same social class, although he really didn't care one way or the other. He was a product of American wealth and not European nobility so he wasn't too impressed by lineage." Tristan shrugged slender shoulders. "Quite simply, we liked one another. J.P. was not given easily to trust, but for whatever reasons he trusted me implicitly."

"How long did you maintain this relationship?" Peter asked.

"From the time we attended the University until his death in 1913," Tristan replied.

"So, if your timeline ran concurrent to his, how did you manage your obvious lack of aging?" Kipp rose and moved a yard away from the heater before plopping down with a big sigh. His corner was getting too hot.

Tristan laughed and glanced at Meko who returned his gaze. "It wasn't easy. I took to growing a beard, wearing heavy glasses and would put graying powder in my hair. J.P. would enviously remark upon my health and vigor which I attributed to genetics. I even used a walking stick and affected a slower, arthritic gait during his later years."

"But Meko, how did you explain him?" Elani glanced at the large, black lupine, who, despite his alertness, was letting his head nod, as if made sleepy by the warmth of the heater.

"That was much more difficult. Meko became a succession of dogs, in the sense of Meko, then his son, grandson, etc. I would use some of the graying powder on his face, too, as he supposedly aged. J.P. recognized my affection for my "dog", and we three went everywhere together. As he became rich and powerful, he pretty much could dictate all the rules he wanted."

I confess the dark confines of the room as well as the soothing monotone of Tristan's voice were causing me to become drowsy. Outside, the wind blew in unpredictable bursts, and I watched a flurry of dead leaves fly past the window, scraping the glass as they fell to earth. The sky was gray, overcast...a dreary day made barren by the chill in the air. Oddly, I'd always liked those types of days that seemed straight from the pages of some Victorian novel. If I'd been home, I might have pulled *Jane Eyre* from my bookshelf and nestled, in my favorite chair, in front of the fireplace, listening as the logs broke and fell in a shower of sparks.

"So what do you know of J.P. Morgan closer to the time of the sinking of the *Titanic*?" I asked, urgent to focus the discussion and redirect my attention. It was with effort I suppressed a yawn.

Tristan looked up at the ceiling as he conjured his memories. "He, of course, had acquired control over the White Star Line through his shipping conglomerate, International Mercantile Marine. Prior to the launching of the *Titanic* for her maiden voyage, he was in Rome with Frank Millet to examine plans for the new American Academy of Art." He wrinkled his forehead. "Frank was an interesting, brilliant man who was actually quite friendly despite his occasional act as a crusty curmudgeon. I think that was the second or third day of April, 1912. J.P. planned to be on board the *Titanic* for her first crossing but had some health issues. His physician recommended he not travel, and he finally went to Aix-les-Bain in France to get some rest and recovery."

I noticed that Kipp was focused intently upon Meko, who in turn was staring unblinkingly at Tristan. The elder lupine had unusual pale gray eyes that were brought to prominence by the dark mask of fur on his face. However, Kipp had closed off his thoughts to me; I suspected he was poking into Meko's mind but didn't want me to know. He'd been getting a little too free with that sort of thing, which was unethical by our contemporary standards, save for an emergency.

"Kipp, what are you doing?" I hissed privately. With the toe of my shoe, I gently touched his leg in such a manner that no one else observed the action.

"I'll tell you in a minute," he replied. Yawning, he lazily licked the place on his leg that I'd defaced with my toe.

"We know Morgan reserved one of the parlor suites for his use–B52, 54 and 56," Peter was saying. "There is no approval, of course, for a trip to the *Titanic*, but if we did, we'd have to work out some way to accommodate the lupines."

"And you'd need to travel first class with a special word to the staff of the *Titanic* to let you do as you wished," Tristan finished the thought. "And that would have to come from J.P. Morgan to have any weight behind it."

"Exactly," Peter remarked. He ran a hand up through his thick hair, pushing back the heavy fringe that had settled over his eyes. "Since Morgan didn't use the suite, we thought there might be some way for us to have it."

Tristan took off his glasses and rubbed the bridge of his nose with thumb and forefinger; his chair creaked as he leaned back, staring up at the ceiling while he collected his thoughts. "I recall that Henry Clay

Frick jumped on those rooms when Morgan released them before having to cancel the booking when his wife had an injury. Bruce Ismay took the rooms at the last minute."

"If somehow we could get those rooms, it wouldn't change the timeline of history," Peter persisted. "Morgan didn't make the trip; neither did Henry Frick. And Ismay would have had other rooms already available for him. So he'd just use the rooms he'd already reserved."

"Kipp, what are you doing?" I asked my partner again. Now I was certain that he was privately accessing Meko's thoughts.

"There's more to this story that Tristan is concealing," he replied. "Meko is on the verge of spilling some information that needs to come to light."

"Could you, perhaps, write us a letter of introduction we could present to Morgan, asking him to help us gain passage?" Peter asked.

Tristan glanced at Meko, who continued to gaze at his partner. The unnerving gray eyes of the lupine seemed to grow larger.

"Uh, that could get very complicated," Tristan replied. "And there would be a very fine timeline to make things happen."

"Not if we get to our destination early enough to accommodate any last minute changes," Peter opined. "We have Kipp, who is very good at pinpointing a destination and time frame."

"What are your thoughts, Meko?" Kipp asked, ignoring Peter's "atta boy" comment.

The dark lupine turned his head away from us, gazing instead at the glowing grate of the electric heater. It had the appearance of fake fire but was nonetheless hypnotic with the wavering, flowing colors of red, yellow and orange that rippled and swayed as if blown by an invisible, gentle breeze. He sighed deeply before standing; his eyes met those of Tristan, who shook his head slowly from side to side.

"I think it is time to tell the truth," Meko said.

"Meko, don't!" Tristan's voice rose with agitation, his hands clenched into fists.

"J.P. Morgan died on board the *Titanic* on her maiden voyage. He went down with the ship on April 15, 1912." Meko glanced at Tristan. "I can't sit on these lies anymore and keep what's left of my integrity."

CHAPTER 10

"I didn't push that revelation, in case you wondered," Kipp remarked, his thoughts meant for my ears only. Of course, I trusted him completely, and if he said it, then it was so. "Meko's wanted to unburden his soul for years but didn't out of deference for Taylor."

"What made the difference now?" I asked.

"Taylor is sick, and his time is winding down." Kipp sighed. "He won't live to be old, like Fitzhugh. Meko wants him to leave this earth unencumbered by guilt and pain." Kipp glanced at me, his ears drooping slightly. "There is a lot of sadness as well as love in this room."

"Tristan, why don't you tell us your story?" I requested, sitting forward slightly, hoping I appeared inviting and nonjudgmental. What Tristan shared in terms of his health was his own business, but the rest of the tale was tempting to hear, and I couldn't pretend to be uninterested. This possible story beneath a story had possibilities to pull me in, despite my wavering interest in anything involving the *Titanic*.

"It must stay in this room, at least for now," he replied, his shoulders slumped in resignation.

I glanced at Peter who nodded; a second later, Elani and Kipp signaled their agreement. Outside, a large cloud must have passed between the sun and earth because the room's interior suddenly was cast in dark shadow, and it felt as if a chill settled, in defiance of the work of the resolute heater. It seemed a solid invitation for the telling of secrets.

"As I told you, I was a good friend of Morgan," Tristan began. He sighed deeply and glanced at his hands, which were balled up into fists in his lap. With effort, he relaxed his fingers and exhaled slowly. "Meko, too, loved him as a friend." He smiled at his lupine symbiont who blinked his eyes in response. "On April 10, 1912, we accompanied J.P. on the boat train from Waterloo Station to Southampton, where the *Titanic* was docked." He closed his eyes. "I recall quite clearly, although it has been over one hundred years, the fabulous mahogany wood work on the interior of the train. The upholstery was plush, deep blue in color, carefully piped in a tasteful contrast tone." His dark eyes met mine. "It says something that even the boat train had exclusive cars for the elite of the day.

"Morgan had just arrived in London from his meeting in Italy with Frank Millet, who also was scheduled to be on the *Titanic* on her maiden voyage." Tristan's eyes clouded with a far away expression. "Millet was one of those who died when the *Titanic* sank. I think he was playing bridge with some other men in the lounge up until close to the end. At that point, the deck was tilted to the degree one couldn't have kept a seat, much less stand, without holding on to something.

"I know the stories indicate Morgan went to his villa in France after leaving Italy, but in truth he went to London, and after a day or two of business dealings, he boarded the boat train. He felt it important to be on board the minute the *Titanic* first sailed, and that was from Southampton.

"The last time I saw him, he was walking up the gangplank to enter the Reception Room on D Deck where he registered for the voyage. Morgan had the finest suite of rooms on the ship, more than enough room for him; he was traveling alone. He turned to wave goodbye to me and Meko." Tristan looked up and glanced around the room at each of us in turn. "Well, what I should say is that was supposed to have been the last time I ever saw him."

"But it wasn't," Meko said, his voice soft in the back of our minds. He gave that type of deep, shuddering sigh that only big dogs and lupines can manage. I noted he was curled upon a worn, circular rug woven from wool. At one point in time, it must have been a fine piece, but now was almost a tattered afterthought but something still cherished.

Tristan laughed, the sound dry and mirthless. "The first reports of the tragedy got back to London, and I eagerly scanned the survivor lists. There was no mention of him among the survivors, so my assumption was that he'd gone down with the other first class men who stood around pretending to be unafraid and doing whatever humans think is the right thing to do in the midst of a tragedy." He looked at me. "You know they had to be terrified as they handed off wives and children into the lifeboats."

"The survivor lists weren't accurate for quite some time," Peter pointed out. "What if he'd survived but his name wasn't listed?"

"I thought that improbable since he was a well known figure, quite vocal, and no stranger to telling everyone who he was." Tristan smiled. "He was a dynamic, larger than life sort of man...pushy, energetic, bright and confident."

"I read he was self conscious of having his photograph taken in later years," Elani said. "You would think a man of his importance and wealth would not be so."

"He had rosacea which distorted the shape of his nose. And, yes, he was very aware of how disfiguring it was." Tristan replied. "I was his good friend, so, as is true with people who care for one another, I never noticed it as looking unattractive or unusual."

"So what happened?" I prodded, eager to move past large noses and other useless trivia. Kipp glanced at me and bounced an annoying question mark off my brain. "Ready to get to the story," I murmured to Kipp, hoping he'd leave me alone.

"I knew I had at most a couple of days to intervene in such a way that any disturbances to the timeline or recorded history could be attributed to post *Titanic* frenzy and flawed information flying back and forth across the Atlantic. At that time, the only communication between the two continents was by wireless or letter, so obviously there were delays." The clouds outside suddenly lifted, and the sunlight flashed through the long windows to cast an amber spotlight on the room's interior. As if his chair could not contain him or his story, Tristan stood restlessly and turned to stare at the bare trees which formed a ragged, black outline against the sky. Rocking back on his heels, he thrust his hands deep in the pockets of his trousers and stood there, his back to us, as he gazed out the window.

"Meko and I made a narrowly focused time shift, landing in London a week before Morgan was scheduled to arrive. Instead of accompanying him on the boat train to Southampton, I convinced him that due to his health, he should travel to his villa in France to recover."

"How did he receive that suggestion?" Elani asked. Her tone and attitude was so gentle and without critical judgment, I felt she could effortlessly persuade me to confess my many sins.

"He was hesitant at first, since he greatly wanted to make the voyage. But I finally convinced him by enlisting his physician to have a talk with him, too. Morgan was a little bit of a hypochondriac, so it didn't take much nudging to push him in the needed direction. He sent a telegram to Ismay telling him he was going to France for rest due to illness."

"That was clever of you," Kipp observed. He'd been quiet but obviously was paying attention. "But there's a more important question that nags at me." Tristan stared at him, raising his eyebrows in response. "Why did you do it?"

There was a long pause as Tristan considered his reply. Outside of the office, we heard footsteps and laughter as symbionts passed by on business. The female of the duo had a high pitched, giggling laughter that seemed frivolous against the somber environment of the office. Tristan took a deep breath and bowed his head for a moment. When he raised it again, there were unshed tears in his dark eyes.

"Morgan was an old man, not in good health. He was also afraid of deep water, such as in a lake or the ocean, where he couldn't see the bottom. The idea of my friend at his age and with his fears being thrust into the freezing water to slowly die of exposure just horrified me. I felt I couldn't allow it to happen when I knew the outcome could be manipulated." He looked away for a moment. "He died of natural causes less than a year later." Tristan's dark eyes blazed with defiance as his eyes met mine. "At least he didn't die in the water, struggling, helpless, alone."

"So you changed the timeline?" I asked, knowing the answer but needing to say it regardless.

"Yes, and I guess I don't care anymore who knows about it."

"What about the ethics of such manipulation?" Peter asked after a long, awkward pause, as politely as if he were at high tea and inquiring of the Queen of England her plans for a delightful holiday in the countryside.

Tristan's face was guarded for a moment before he caught Meko's gaze, and then he smiled, but the expression was lopsided, his lips tightly compressed.

"Meko and I teach symbiont ethics," he replied, daring us to laugh. "So, I guess I know something about the issue." Bending his knees a little awkwardly, he dropped heavily into his waiting chair.

The room fell quiet for an uncomfortably long minute. For a moment, I hoped the loud, giggling symbiont would return, just to break the silence. The heater seemed to be on a relentless mission to make us all hope for a window to be cracked to let in some blessed fresh air. A bead of sweat traveled between my shoulder blades down my back as I squirmed in my chair. With a feeling close to desperation, I wanted to be free of that room.

Unexpectedly, Kipp stood and approached Tristan. "I can think of no team better qualified to do such a thing since you have experienced what you teach others to avoid. Only you can understand the issues that have impacted you as a bonded pair due to the choice to change one man's life line."

Tristan's face paled as he placed his hands on his knees. I realized he wanted to touch Kipp but kept from doing so out of respect for boundaries. But Kipp had given him an unequivocal pass of complete understanding. And as I digested what Kipp had said, I realized the value in his perspective and the rightness of it.

"The choice you made put a divide between you and Meko that has never healed." Kipp paused, carefully selecting his words. "Now this is no longer a secret, I hope you can find it in your hearts to forgive one another and trust again."

"The truth is I pushed Meko to do this thing that was wrong by all our measures. I valued my friendship with Morgan more than my bond with Meko. I've asked him to forgive me, and he says he has. But it is still there." Tristan looked away again, his cheeks reddening slightly; it was apparent he was uncomfortable with the self disclosure.

"That's because you haven't forgiven yourself, Tristan," Kipp replied. "To be forgiven, you must forgive."

Peter and Elani appeared spellbound–Peter's mouth fell open in a perfect O—as Kipp acted with the wisdom of a healer. I stole a quick glance at the mantle clock to make certain it was still ticking and time hadn't stopped with the gravity of the moment, and it was with great effort I didn't sigh loudly and roll my eyes. I confess I was irritated with Kipp and impatient, wanting to move on. No, that wasn't noble of me, and I should have been more involved and caring of the general angst in the room. But it was, in the modern way of speak, way too much information, and I wanted to be on with our business. In many aspects, my general negativity about the entire proposed time shift had dampened any displays of compassion. I did care about Tristan and Meko, but we had serious issues on the table. Honestly, the revelation of their emotional rift was embarrassing to me, and I had no wish to observe their distress as they twisted in the proverbial wind.

"Is there any way you can help us to influence Morgan to get us on board the *Titanic* or not?" I asked, my tone abrupt and cold, even to my own ears. I felt my face flush as Kipp glared at me. Wanting to move on, I felt no inclination to explain my tangle of thoughts and feelings.

"What's your hurry?" he hissed privately. "I was trying to help them."

"This is not our problem," I replied airily. "We were sent here to get information, not conduct family therapy."

If I'd made a disparaging remark about Kipp's mama, I don't think

I could have managed to make him angrier with me. He was truly, deeply agitated and assured me that we'd be talking about his feelings again, later that evening.

"Oh, boy. Something fun on the horizon," I replied flatly.

My poorly timed query broke the rhythm of the flow of dialog, so it seemed appropriate to leave Tristan and Meko to do some deep thinking about our dilemma. We quietly left and walked outside...I almost felt like crying with relief as the cool air touched my over-heated skin. It was difficult to ignore Kipp who was glaring at the back of my head, his thoughts shuttered as he processed his irrita-tion with me. Peter and Elani walked quickly ahead to the SUV; it seemed no one wanted to be my best buddy at that particular moment. There were no words spoken or thoughts exchanged amongst us while Peter labored to find a hotel nearby where we could stay the night. I was happy to sit listlessly in the car, offering no help, while fervently wishing to be home eating popcorn and reading a good book.

"So, what was that about, Petra?" Kipp settled in the bed at my side, his muzzle stretched across my chest. Idly, I stroked his long ears; it was always hypnotic and soothing, that caress, for both of us.

"I'm not sure, Kipp. I'm glad only you could hear my thoughts since Peter and Elani might have misinterpreted my intentions."

"Which were what?" Kipp turned his massive head to stare at me, our noses almost touching in the close confines of the bed; the mattress was so hard and unyielding, I expected a series of colorful bruises in the morning. In the room to our left, a television was play-ing—I distinctly heard the theme whistle from *The Andy Griffin Show*—making a pleasant background noise. Peter and Elani's room was to the other side where they were quiet, their thoughts still in the dark-ness. I could feel Kipp's soft breath caress my cheek; his whiskers scraped against my skin as he burrowed his long muzzle against my neck. Andy always seemed to recognize when he'd misjudged Opie and could humble himself with a heartfelt apology. I wished I had more of his common sense wisdom and quality.

"I really felt uncomfortable being a witness to Tristan's flaws and the discord between him and Meko." My hand tightened on the back of Kipp's neck as I gently massaged the muscles which felt bunched up and tense.

"Mmmm…" he muttered. If he'd been a cat, he might have begun to purr.

"I guess if I were in that type of conflict with you, I'd hope we could resolve it privately or at least in the company of good friends. Tristan and Meko are strangers to us." I sighed. "It wasn't that I just didn't care."

"And I never thought that of you, Petra," Kipp replied. "I know you too well, and you have a deep capacity for warmth and love." He paused before saying, "But you hurt my feelings for discounting what I was trying to do."

"I'm sorry, Kipp. Can you forgive me?"

He licked my cheek in response.

"Maybe…I'll think about it while you massage my shoulders some more."

The next day, we returned to the symbiont compound and found our way, unassisted that time, to Tristan and Meko's office. It was clear, upon first sight, that they were more relaxed and the room seemed filled with a new vigor and sense of purpose consuming the space that had been occupied by despair and mistrust. Obviously, Kipp's suggestion had been taken to heart. Bonded symbionts simply could not exist when there was discord with one another.

"Meko and I stayed up half the night trying to figure out how to make this thing happen, in the event you are approved for a trip on the *Titanic*. But why you'd consent to do such, I don't pretend to understand." Tristan breezed on without letting us weigh in on his comments. "We can intervene with Morgan in such a way that he will give you the tickets."

"And how would you do that?" Peter asked. He looked very nicely attired, having taken time to shake the wrinkles out of a tweed sport coat that made him appear at least thirty years older, or at least he hoped so. He glanced at me, frowning, as I struggled to hide the smile on my face. When you are young, you want to look older; then you mature and want to look younger. That dynamic never seemed to change.

"You four will travel to London and meet up with me and Meko during our time shift that was made in 1912. You will explain the situation–what has happened here—and I will take you to Morgan with an introduction that you are, uh, the children of my estranged sister in America. I will ask him if there is some way he can get you aboard the *Titanic* with your lupines. I'm sure he'll do it." Tristan sat forward in his chair as he spoke.

"And since we are traveling back in time to see you as you were in 1912, what is to say that you will believe our story?" I asked. "We will be strangers to you."

"I'll write a letter to myself that you will present to me," he replied. "And after all, we will recognize one another as symbionts amongst all the humanity. With our telepathy, we can be assured of no false intentions in any case."

I felt my mouth drop open with surprise. The suggestion seemed so simple as to be fraught with issues. But maybe that was the beauty of it?

"What was the original timeline?" Elani asked. The room was unexpectedly cool; the free standing heater was obviously on holiday and only working at half strength. She'd angled her body so that she wouldn't block the feeble flow of warmth to the rest of us.

Tristan's eyes rolled towards the ceiling as he visually recalled the memories. We didn't intrude but could feel Meko's hovering presence as the two of them tried to determine the correct answer.

"Morgan and Frank Millet were in Rome on April 3, 1912," Tristan finally said. "They left and went to Florence, and J.P. arrived back in London on April 7th." He leveled his dark eyes at us from behind the thick lenses of his glasses. "The reason the London trip didn't make the top news was because he was involved in a new business dealing that he didn't wish to go public. The parties involved met privately in his London townhouse in Mayfair." With a shrug of his shoulders, he added, "We left his townhouse very early on April 10th to catch the Boat Train at Waterloo."

"And that was the time he boarded the *Titanic* and died when the ship sank." Elani was making a comment, not asking a question. Kipp looked at her with all the pride of a father watching his daughter blossom. She was his brightest student and the most capable of the class of young lupines.

"Yes. After Meko and I realized what had happened, we time shifted to the previous week, to give ourselves the needed wiggle room since such is not an exact art, no matter how talented the pair." We all nodded in agreement...I'd been there myself more than once. "We waited in London until he arrived again, on April 7th. I was ready with my plan to have his physician available to emphasize the need to not travel overseas at that time. Morgan was just recovering from something akin to the flu and would likely suffer a relapse if he was exposed on a boat deck when the weather was still cold." He looked down at his feet for a second...his shoes needed polishing, and the heels were worn from where he walked on the sides of his feet. A frown tugged at the corners of his mouth. "The sinking of the *Titanic* led to hearings in the United States as well as Great Britain. The International Mercantile Marine was not found liable but ran into serious problems a couple of years later due to poor cash flow."

"So, if we time shift with a letter for you and Meko, you believe we can intercept you before you intervene with Morgan, and you can finagle an introduction for us." Kipp laid out the plan. "It seems simple enough, but I'm sure it isn't."

"Nothing we do is simple," Tristan said. "You'd have to go to London early enough to assemble some proper clothes if you plan on staying in first class. And if Morgan gives you his Parlor Suite along with instructions for the crew to let you have your way in terms of the lupines, there is only one thing left."

"And that would be?" I asked.

Tristan's jaw worked for a moment. "For you four to successfully find your bomber, survive the accident and return home to tell the rest of us about it."

CHAPTER 11

Since the Twelve had not been presented with the notion of a time shift to the *Titanic*, we were still free to consider the trip and problem solve free of their noxious meddling. Of course, they were only doing their job, but I was enough of a nonconformist that having to be exceedingly cautious in the words coming out of my mouth was a struggle. Grudgingly, I conceded the need for some external controls since there were those among us with less than sterling motives. But the idea still did not make me happy and some of my best work, historically, had been done when I was freewheeling. Peter and Elani definitely put a damper on my activities, I thought darkly.

The weather remained consistently cool and stark with more than a few gray days; the air had that sense of brittle fragility signaling an exceptionally harsh season. Occasionally, the clouds would darken with moisture and promise snow and ice, but eventually the wetness would come in the form of cold, drizzling rain as if nature was unwilling to commit to anything more drastic. Fitzhugh and I were content to survive off of crockpots full of vegetable soup and meatless chili since those choices seemed to fit the stereotypical dinner choices for the climate. Philo invited himself over for dinner one Saturday and took it upon himself to bring Peter and Elani.

After dinner, we gathered in my front room; I'd laid a fire which was blazing nicely by the time everyone had arrived. Opening one sleepy eye, I stretched my back slightly, sighing, as I watched the light from the fire flicker, animating shadows that crept along the dim walls. When I was a child, I'd found those moving patches of darkness to be frightening and would curl closer to my mother, who would stroke my hair to comfort me. Kipp, always present in my thoughts, glanced up at me and thumped his tail. With age, I'd lost my fear and felt relaxed enough to melt into the fabric of my chair, if such a thing were possible. Juno, being allowed the courtesy shown to an elder, claimed the prime spot close in front of the blazing embers; a log broke and a shower of sparks whooshed up the chimney. Lily, who'd become somewhat fickle with her affections, was tucked in next to Juno, displaying the canny ability of a feline to pick the best place in any room for comfort. Outside, the wind was picking up with another threat of snow flurries, early travelers, it seemed, for that time of year. It was only November, after all.

"I read your brief," Philo began, staring over his reading glasses at Peter. "You did a good job and were very thorough."

Peter's face flushed pink high upon his cheekbones. Clearing his throat, he glanced across the room at me as I tried not to smirk. "Uh, Petra, Elani and Kipp were just as much a part of it as was I," he said. I had to applaud him for his fairness, but he had taken pen to paper... make that finger to keyboard. Peter was a much more patient scribe than I would ever be.

On the front of the house, a loose shutter began to bang against the wall. Fitzhugh frowned at me, his thoughts filled with disapproval over my casual neglect of home and hearth. "I have been busy," I said, eyebrows raised, arms crossed defensively.

"Getting back to business," Philo said, clearing his throat, "let me see if I have all of this in clear sequence." He sat back in his chair, crossed his legs at the ankles and stared up at the ceiling. Following his gaze, I noticed a hairline crack in the finished sheetrock. I hoped Fitzhugh didn't see it, too, since it would further magnify my inadequacies. Kipp giggled hysterically in the back of my mind, which didn't help things one little bit. Sometimes it felt as if my safe nest was in danger of collapsing upon my head.

"You will, after preparation, travel to London a few weeks before the *Titanic* is set to sail. The main objective of the early arrival is to arrange a suitable wardrobe for two people traveling first class." Pausing, he removed his glasses; squinting narrowly, he held them up to the light. After a brief examination, he polished the lenses with the corner of his sweatshirt. "You will meet Tristan and Meko at Paddington Station where they are scheduled to arrive on the 0830 train on April 8. They would have been elsewhere in England about a week before that date, just killing time. Of course, they will recognize fellow symbionts and allow you to approach. After Tristan reads the letter, he recognizes what he's agreed to do and takes you to Morgan's town home for an introduction and subsequent manipulation of his old friend."

As Philo continued to speak, Kipp's mind, which was predictably tangled with mine, began to question if we were less than honorable to not share with him the secret that Tristan changed the human timeline when he saved Morgan from what would have been his natural death aboard the *Titanic*. Peter had managed to craft the story in such a way that the facts were blurred, and Tristan's serious lack of ethics was hidden from view.

"I feel bad, like we are lying to Philo," Kipp said to me.

"We made a promise to Tristan, and his past actions have no bearing on what we do," I replied.

"Am I boring you?" Philo asked, his dark eyes staring at me over his reading glasses.

"Uh, no," I replied with a bright, false smile. "Keep going."

"You and Kipp are free to share your thoughts with the rest of us anytime you wish," he added, glaring at me for a second before continuing. "After you four get on board the *Titanic*, you will plan on mingling as much as possible, considering the presence of the lupines, which understandably makes things a little awkward. Even with Morgan's considerable influence, I would doubt they can go everywhere a humanoid symbiont can go."

"All I know is we are gonna have to work out some reasonable bathroom accommodations," Kipp commented, his eyes opened wide. "There is no way I'm going to use a place called a poop deck to take my, uh, constitutional."

Juno, sensitive dear that she was, tried very hard to not laugh; turning her head away, she stared at the fireplace, pretending to be lost in the dancing flames.

"Is it really called a poop deck?" Elani asked. "I'm with you, Kipp," she snorted, her nostrils flaring just a little...ladylike but still a snort.

"There is a reason it's called that, Kipp," Fitzhugh began before he was interrupted by Philo.

"If I can please get back to this," Philo growled, as he shook the papers in his hand. "You will, of course, look for Littleton who appears to have been traveling in first class. As best you can, you will arrange moments to speak with him and draw him out. You will not interfere in any way with the activities of the other passengers, nor will you do anything that will change the destiny of the *Titanic*. Your only goal is to determine if Littleton had an actual bomb aboard the ship and if he detonated it at some point after the collision with the iceberg." He smiled. "Any side observations about the general, uh, milieu aboard the ship will be valuable, too."

Philo sat back, placing the sheaf of papers on a small table by his chair. He fell quiet and took his turn staring at the fire while the rest of us waited. The nagging wind caught the edge of the loose shutter; the clatter of the shutter and the moan of the wind as it raced around the corner of the house filled the silence.

"It seems like something that can be done," Philo finally spoke, his voice soft. "The valid question is does it need to be done and do you want to take on this job?" He smiled, but the expression didn't make it to his eyes, which held a sober expression. "There is a reason no one has gone to the *Titanic*."

Philo, as he left, asked me and Kipp to meet with him privately. So, after awakening the next morning, I sat nursing a cup of hot coffee at my bruised retro dinette table. It was earlier than usual for us, me and Kipp, to stir; the house, as old houses do, creaked and settled against the cold breeze, which was still vigorous, forcing the walls to complain as the wind whipped up under the eaves and slapped against the asphalt shingles on the roof. Yawning, I rose to cross over to the back door, where Kipp was begging to come back in after his morning constitutional.

"Whew! Pretty brisk out there," he remarked. "How 'bout cutting on this thing?" he asked, pointing with his nose at the infrared heater Fitzhugh had picked up for the kitchen. That room, with its considerable panel of rear windows, tended to be the coldest in the house. I clicked on the device and sat with my chair angled toward the heat source.

"So what's up with Philo?" Kipp was referencing our impending date for that morning. "It's cold as you know what, and he wants to go for a stroll in Duke Forest. The weather doesn't faze me, but you two will be freezing."

Our discourse was interrupted by the sound of Fitzhugh, whose leather scuffs made a loud scraping sound on the wooden floor of the hallway, as he made his way to the kitchen. He appeared in the doorway, his flannel robe cinched tightly around his narrow waist. As he drew closer, I noted the cuffs were frayed, and there was a suspicious worn spot wearing through on his "propping" elbow.

"Now you know what to get him for Christmas this year," Kipp commented to me. Last year I'd surprised the inhabitants of my home with gifts; the Irish sweater I'd given Fitzhugh had been a hit, and it would be difficult to find anything he'd enjoy more than that bundle of soft wool.

"Good morning," Fitzhugh said, waving me away as I made to stand and fetch him coffee. After pouring a steaming cup black into the mug I'd left out for him, he sat across from me. Juno had not appeared, and I could only conclude she was sleeping in. "Why on earth would Philo want to drag you two out in this cold, nasty weather?" he asked.

I shrugged, since the inner workings of Philo's mind were as much a mystery to me as to Fitzhugh. Kipp circled and dropped on the kitchen floor, his back end pointed towards the heater.

"And that was a good purchase," I noted, nodding at the little machine.

"I am sure he wants to get you away from Peter and Elani to

discuss a time shift to the *Titanic*," Fitzhugh persisted, ignoring my applause of his choice of heating appliance. "I would want to do that," he added.

"What do you think we should do?" I asked. In that moment, I was amazed to find that Fitzhugh had become, following Kipp, my closest confidant. Once that had been Philo but his ascension to the leader of the Twelve had naturally caused some distance. And Fitzhugh living in my household had pulled us closer...he felt like a member of my family now. And although he wouldn't admit it, I knew he felt the same...not a fatherly figure, but something special and valuable. It was not Fitzhugh's way to talk in riddles or be indirect, so he didn't surprise me with his bold, decisive answer.

"I think you should go," he replied. Pushing against the back rest of the chair, he sat up a little straighter. His dark eyes, alert and perceptive, met mine. "And I say this as a traveler, which many of the Twelve are most certainly not. Well, there are a couple of them..." He shook his head as if to force himself to not begin to ramble.

"Would you make this trip?" I persisted.

"Yes, I would have gone, me and Lydea, when I was young and full of energy and still believing I had the world by the tail. The *Titanic* is active and alive today, through the memories and human fascination with her. There have been shipwrecks with greater loss of life, but *Titanic* was and always will be special. It is indefinable but true." Despite the heater, the room was still a little cool; Fitzhugh curled his hands around the warmth of the porcelain mug.

"But to be in the midst of such emotion, watching people go to their death and not being able to help..." I shook my head.

"You've been involved in wars," he replied. "I know of several trips you've made to the Civil War, and you became engaged with people who were destined to die on the battlefield. How is this different?"

"I'm not sure," I said, looking over at Kipp, who thumped his tail on the floor.

"And how do you feel, Kipp?" Fitzhugh took a sip of coffee.

"I want to go...Petra and I have talked about it," he replied, his eyes bright. Obviously the heater was too intense because he used his front paws to slow drag himself forward out of the circle of warmth, his soft underbelly of fur serving to ease the friction. "But I don't want Petra to force herself," he added.

"You two love each too much to make a rational decision," Fitzhugh said, smiling. "Lydea and I were close but nothing like you."

"Kipp saved my life," I began before my voice broke. Our connection was deeper and more complex than any other symbiont pair.

"And you saved me, too," Kipp said, standing to come over and put his head in my lap. Leaning forward, I pressed my cheek against the fur on top of his head, enjoying the feel of his auburn pelt made toasty by the warmth of the heater. He licked my face in reply. "Life was hard back home as well as being lonely. Now I've become soft like a cream puff!" I knew he added the latter to soften the emotional tone of the moment.

"There is no doubt that your meeting and subsequent bond is unique," Fitzhugh commented as he sipped the cooling coffee. "Maybe Philo can help you to find the decision you seek."

Duke Forest had long been a favorite of mine, even before Kipp came into my life. Tula, my first symbiont, and I would go out into the woods and walk for miles, sometimes encountering people, many times not, as I searched for paths seldom trod. Smiling, I recalled, in my mind's eye, a particularly lovely day, when the spring wild flowers had pushed through the soil to dot the forest floor with color, and the sky above was perfect, unblemished. The smile left my face as Philo's car jerked between the yellow lines on the road. He was driving with his typical breakneck pace, swerving along curves on tires that had seen better days. After one particularly vicious yank on the steering wheel, Kipp, an intrepid passenger most of the time, was forced to give an opinion.

"Okay, Philo. I'm about to get out and walk if you don't quit slinging me around back here," he complained. "That last move left me with whiplash."

"Sorry," Philo muttered, his apologetic eyes meeting Kipp's accusatory ones in the rear view mirror. Kipp must have been more persuasive than I because there was a noticeable deceleration. I usually just strapped myself in and prayed.

It was cold; the parking area was empty because most people with any kind of common sense had decided to not freeze to death in the midst of the woods, where their rigid bodies would be left, undiscovered, until the following spring thaw. I was wearing my fleece jacket that L.L. Bean promised would keep me warm to twenty below zero. After tugging on my gloves and hat, I trotted to catch up to Philo and Kipp who were walking doggedly ahead, their steps hurried as if to force some modicum of warmth to their extremities. Our feet swooshed through fallen leaves bunched in wind driven piles against the bases of trees and in the hollows, which dipped and curved unpredictably with the lay of the land.

The brilliant colors of autumn were sadly gone; all that remained were brown, withered leaves still attached in ragged patches to the tree limbs. A stubborn wind wound through the forest, the breeze causing the limbs overhead to scrape heavily against one another. As the wind touched a clustered stand of American beeches, the silvered leaves trembled, making a soft sound, adding to the dialog of nature. Their leaves were the most tenacious and would be hanging on until spring when new green growth managed to force the dead debris to fall to the forest floor. None of us spoke as we walked deeper into the woods; Kipp kept his thoughts curiously guarded and closed to me.

We arrived at a rock ledge overlooking a meandering, curving stream. The water mirrored the deep blue color of the sky, making the stream look like flowing turquoise contained between the muddy banks; a ray of sun seemed to be caught in the water, which flashed quicksilver in the light. Philo leaned down to spread out a throw so that the three of us could recline in that barren place.

"I knew it would be cold and have no wish to freeze my butt completely off," he said, his mouth twisting in a smile. "This is good," he said, meaning our time together. "It feels like it used to," he added, his tone slightly wistful.

I didn't respond since I wasn't sure what to say. Kipp caught my eye and twisted his head slightly at an angle, looking surprisingly like a big dog who hoped I might have a squeaky toy in my pocket. Smiling, I gazed at the water and allowed myself to be soothed by the sound of its flow over the smooth rocks of the stream bed.

"I'm not stupid, you know, despite rumors to the contrary," Philo continued. "My becoming the leader of the Twelve has affected our friendship. In fact, I've considered resigning. I don't like the wall that is here," he said, using his hands to create a space between us.

We'd always been the best of friends, and I thought of him as the brother I'd not had. He'd been a sounding board and the one who always had my back and would defend me against all odds.

"I wouldn't want you to do that," I said, continuing to gaze at the water. That was easier than looking at Philo. "You're the best candidate for the job, and it would be ill advised for you to give it up." Finally, I glanced at him. "We can work through this, Philo." After a moment, I changed gears. "How's Claire?" I asked, narrowing my eyes against the bright sunlight.

"Mad at me...which seems to be the typical state of affairs as of late," he replied, as he tossed a small pebble into the water.

"What about?"

"Silas, always Silas." Philo turned to look at me. "I know more happened in London than you and Kipp will tell. And I suspect it wasn't good," he added with a sigh. "I love Silas, of course, since he's my son, but he has some character flaws that disturb me. Claire, of course, can't see anything at all and becomes defensive if the subject is even remotely broached." He took a deep breath and closed his eyes, allowing the breeze to tease his hair that had escaped from beneath the wool cap he wore. When he opened his eyes, I followed his gaze as he stared at a shadowed copse, where the dull brown and gray palate of winter was broken by a bright flash of red as a cardinal flicked its wings to effortlessly land upon a high tree branch.

"Sorry to get sidetracked," Philo said with a lopsided smile. "I brought you and Kipp here to discuss the *Titanic* time shift without Peter and Elani to cloud the issue. I know how they feel, and I think I get Kipp, but the hesitant one is you, Petra. And frankly, given your history of some pretty dangerous doings, I'm surprised you'd not want to make a historic trip."

Kipp's head went up as I listened in on his thoughts. Across the stream in a tightly bunched grove of young hackberry trees, there was movement; several white tail deer were walking, their bodies camouflaged to perfection in the dead underbrush. The twisting witches' brooms of the trees served to hide the deer, which were busy calculating their next move. The deer must have caught our scent because they suddenly wheeled as a group and dashed up the hillside, their white tails flashing as signal flags in retreat.

"Maybe I'm getting older and wiser," I replied, tilting my head back so that the sun could find my upturned face, praying a tiny bit of warmth might be found there. "I feel responsible for Peter and Elani," I added lamely.

"You're neither old nor particularly wise," Philo replied, his mouth twisting in a wry grin.

"Thanks, I think," I said with a laugh. "I talked with Fitzhugh this morning, and he told me he would make the trip if he were able. So, it seems I am the only one acting out of an abundance of caution. Maybe it's an over abundance," I added. "So, I guess I'm in."

Kipp snuggled closer on the throw, his warm body pressed against my thigh. He blocked his thoughts, but I knew he was happy. Neither he nor Peter or Elani had truly experienced horror as result of a time shift, but I had. Perhaps this would be crucial to their maturity as symbionts. Or maybe they would never desire to travel again. One way or the other, *Titanic* could be a deal maker or deal breaker.

CHAPTER 12

Suzanne breezed past me where I sat at a long table that was covered in books filled with clothing styles from centuries past. Even though Suzanne, who created designs for time shifts, had lived over four hundred, it was easier than one might think to lose track of what was popular and when. With that thought in mind, I recalled, somewhat wistfully, a fringed vest I wore during the 1960's that I paired with some faded blue jeans. I think I had a beaded headband, too. After that time, fashion went rapidly downhill in my estimation... there was the 70's era with wide ties and lapels for men, as well as pastel leisure suits with contrast stitching, an unspeakable horror that still resonated. I remembered a powder blue suit that Philo wore...the thought made me grimace. I scooted a bolt of cotton print fabric out of the way so that Suzanne would quit giving me worried glances over the cup of coffee I had placed on the table. Well, she gave it to me, after all. Our number of travelers was diminished of late, so Suzanne also did work for other collectives at times. She was skillful and in demand.

The workroom was crowded; multiple tables were filled to overflowing with fabric being cut to the specifications of a particular client. The air smelt slightly musty, a result of the tangled bolts of fabric that were strewn haphazardly around the room. Suzanne's assistant, a somber faced young female who rarely spoke, hovered nervously in the background. I didn't think Suzanne was an easy taskmaster.

"The *Titanic*," Suzanne remarked. "That's ambitious, and I don't envy you." Her expressive eyes were made even more dramatic by cat eye liner drawn with bigger wings than usual; her dark hair was upswept in a typically chaotic mess. Somewhere in the black strands lurked a pencil that she had stuck for future use. She normally wore bright red lipstick but had opted for a neutral tone; her features seemed pleasantly softened.

"It was good to see you in the library," I said, trying to draw her out for a little fun gossip. "It gets lonely with just Fitzhugh and Mark," I added, knowing she'd have to bite at the comment.

"I don't see how it could ever get lonely with Mark there," she replied, her face flushing prettily. "He's dreamy."

I looked at Kipp and tried to not smile. Calling a male of any species "dreamy" had gone out in the 1950's I thought. Well, it was kind of sweet, and I was happy she was interested in him. Fitzhugh seemed to think that Mark was a little smitten in return, so maybe we'd have a symbiont love match soon. Neither one of them was a traveler, so they would look for a stable relationship for the long term.

"He was asking about you the other day," I remarked, trying to look innocent as I took a sip of coffee. Kipp twisted his head to the side as he glanced at me.

"Really?" Her face grew animated. "What did he say?"

"Oh, just wanted to know if you were involved, that sort of stuff."

She began to hum a tune that was unfamiliar to me for a moment before I realized she was softly singing "People Will Say We're in Love" from *Oklahoma*.

"What is it with you guys that you get completely silly when you're in love?" Kipp asked, his words meant for me alone. "You did it with Harrow…I mean, you could have lost your head and not realized you needed one. And now this behavior," he said, looking at Suzanne, his tone slightly disapproving.

"Oh, Kipp, it's a wonderful feeling. You feel overwhelmed, full of anticipation and slightly dizzy all at once." I sighed.

"Doesn't sound wonderful," he huffed. "Sounds like the plague or influenza."

I had to remind myself that Kipp was still pretty young, after all, and was perhaps at the stage of a youth who was mesmerized by females and the thought of romance for a flash before becoming horrified at the very notion.

"One day, you'll get there and will be all goofy over some lovely lupine...maybe, Elani?" I was teasing him, and he returned my glance, eyes narrowed almost shut.

"No way!" His ears flattened at my playful suggestion.

Suzanne managed to refocus, which was timely, because Peter and Elani chose that moment to make their entrance. Peter struck me as maturing rapidly; his self confidence, having made more than one successful time shift was growing, and the effect showed on his face. Any vestiges of tentativeness or anxiety had dissipated leaving a calm, settled exterior. The end result was good and made him even more attractive. Not that I was interested, of course. He was much too young, and I still pined for Harrow. Where Philo was like a big brother, Peter was becoming a younger one, and I applauded his growth.

"Hi!" Peter said.

His jaw line looked suspiciously shadowed, and I realized he was working on a beard. I ducked my head so he wouldn't see my lips tighten. Yes, he was trying to look older for some reason or the other. Peter was wearing his corduroy jacket that was most becoming, too. I wondered if he had a secret heart throb before reminding myself that his goal was to travel and nothing, at least for the near future, would get in the way of that.

"Thought I'd work on some facial hair since it was popular at the time," he muttered, drawing his hand along his jaw.

"Looks good," I replied, trying to sound upbeat.

Elani wagged her tail in greeting before moving close to Kipp. Her precious heart was open to all...she had a crush on him and nothing would alter that fact. Kipp constantly tried to let her down gently, but she wasn't gonna go without a fight. He looked up at me, amber eyes full of confusion. Despite his unprecedented talents and brilliant mind, he remained perplexed by the notion of romance. Suzanne managed to redirect the bizarre, conflicting energy in the room as she pulled out a large book on fashions that were in style just after the turn of the century. After offering Peter a cup of coffee, she sat next to me.

"Well, of course, the silhouette for women was changing constantly. No hoop skirts," she added, smiling at my soft applause. "The bustle was declining in popularity, and the idea was to enhance an "S" shaped curve to the body. There was a "health corset" which was less of an issue than the old fashioned type that compressed the ribs and abdomen. But, as an advancement for women, the use of a brassiere and chemise was gaining in popularity, and the corset was becoming a thing of the past."

"Sign me up," I said, raising my hand. "You know how I feel about corsets, health or not. I will go the brassier and chemise route on this trip." Peter ducked his head and laughed, his cheeks reddening a little at my remarks concerning ladies underwear. It was difficult, having become accustomed to sweat pants and t-shirts, to think of binding myself into a stiff garment. As I reflected upon my increasingly contrary nature, I wondered what I would be like in about another three hundred years?

"You'll be impossible," Kipp replied in response to my private thoughts. "But I'll still love you, despite that."

Suzanne was frowning at me as if she suspected I'd drifted off from her tutorial. "You will, of course, have to obtain a suitable wardrobe once you get to England. If you plan on going to dinner, it will require formal wear." Her pretty face darkened as her lips compressed into a straight line. "You won't be able to get by with some tattered traveling costume."

"Well, I haven't decided about dinner, since Kipp won't be allowed," I said, nodding at my partner. "But Elani is definitely pushing Peter, so he'll need a tuxedo and all the appropriate accoutrements. Did men wear spats at that time? I can't recall." I darted a wicked glance at Peter, who laughed again. He was so excited over the trip, that my ribbing him was not having the desired effect.

"For you, Petra, I recommend a two piece traveling garment. They were popular then, mostly tweed fabrics, with a shirt waist blouse, jacket and matching skirt. We can have a spare blouse and another skirt to stretch things a few days while you are shopping for other clothes." Suzanne pulled the pencil from her tangle of black hair and began to take notes on a pad. I wondered who actually still used an old fashioned lead pencil that had to be sharpened and realized I'd found that person in Suzanne. "I probably won't be able to convince my boss that we can let you have any antique jewelry, since you lost the stickpin we leant you during you last shift." She stared at me, unblinking. "I got in trouble over that."

"It was an accident!" Kipp rushed to my defense, as Elani nodded vigorously. "We were on a pole car going really fast down a hill when it derailed. Petra must have flown twenty feet before she landed hard, rolling in a patch of grass and mud." Kipp's eyes opened wide. "You should have seen it!"

Suzanne ignored me as well as Kipp and turned towards Peter. "You will be the most mobile character, Peter, since you are male. There will be greater opportunities for you to engage with a fellow male passenger, given the cultural norms of the day."

"Hey, I'm a guy, too," Kipp burst in. He was definitely having fun as a spoiler of Suzanne's serious demeanor. "Maybe if you fix me a bow tie, I can go in the smoking lounge and hob knob with the swells."

Suzanne lifted an arched eyebrow as she pushed on despite Kipp's irreverence. "For traveling, I think a Norfolk jacket, again of tweed, trousers with creased front and back with cuffs turned up..." Suzanne didn't get to finish due to my untimely interruption.

"Hey, there seems to be a lot of tweed. Does that make Peter and me Tweedledee and Tweedledum?" I asked. Despite the expression of fake innocence plastered on my face, Suzanne, who had been pushed a little too far, finally lost patience.

"If you can't settle down, you need to leave," she said, narrowing her pretty eyes at me, before including Kipp in her warning glance.

Crossing her arms, she began to literally tap her foot in annoyance while she waited.

"I'm sorry," I murmured, compressing my lips. In the back of my head, Kipp was giggling as he began composing a mildly ribald limerick that involved all things tweed, which didn't help matters one bit. I took a large sip of the now cold coffee and refrained from inelegantly spitting it back into the mug.

"Both of you will need hats, since men wore bowlers for day wear; women wore large hats during the day and even into formal evening functions." Suzanne managed to keep going despite all odds.

"I like hats," Peter said, nodding his head eagerly, trying to get her to regain her good humor.

"I want a hat, too," Kipp said privately to me. "A cowboy hat might be nice, with a big brim...or maybe a pirate hat." As he began to demonstrate a pirate impression in my head, I completely lost it and had to excuse myself.

Free of the confinement of Suzanne's studio, I began to laugh uncontrollably, followed by Kipp, who was acting innocent, blinking his eyes as if he was confused over what had happened. Suddenly, Technicorps seemed to close in on me, and the two of us made our way through the hallways to the courtyard where an old bench rested beneath the towering tulip poplar which hugged the side of the building. I'd sat there many times over the years, thinking of life, past adventures, and musing about the future.

"Sorry, Petra." Kipp rested his chin on my knees. "She was just so serious that I couldn't stand it anymore."

"Me neither," I replied, leaning over to rub my cheek against the furry warmth of his head.

It was cold in that garden and difficult to imagine the setting in spring when the azaleas were so full of blooms that the stems bowed slightly from the weight. And then, later, the crepe myrtles blossomed; some were quite large, as they had been left unmolested to grow naturally.

"I often think of what it will be like when the collective makes us relocate," Kipp remarked. "I feel I've just gotten settled here and then we'll be moving on," he added with a sigh. "But as long as we're together, it will be okay."

We sat there, in the chilled air, enjoying the solitude of the garden. Beneath my feet, the grass was brittle and stiff, crunching under the soles of my shoes, the ground hard and unyielding. The freeze from the earth bypassed my shoes and socks, making my feet throb and ache; I moved them, trying to wiggle my stiff toes a little. Due to the unpleasant temperature, the grounds of Technicorps were deserted, since anyone with common sense had taken the comfortable route by choosing the warmth of indoors. But, in my estimation, they were missing a beautiful day. The sky was bright blue, unblemished by clouds; the sun was almost directly overhead, managing to bring some blessed rays of warmth that caught in the strands of my hair, which fell in a mussed braid down my back.

"Can I join you two?" Philo had managed to sneak up on me, which was not easy since we were both telepaths. Obviously, I'd been overly immersed in my own thoughts. I scooted over enough to give him room on the bench. "I saw you from my window, and after looking at the stack of papers on my desk, I thought sitting out here with you was preferable."

I glanced at him. He looked tired and not exactly older, but drained. Philo noticed my expression of concern and reached over to squeeze my hand.

"I really wish you would tell me what happened in London with Silas," he said.

I looked away, staring at a wild dogwood tree that had managed to survive the construction of the building and the aggressive landscaping of the grounds. Smiling with satisfaction, I was happy that it was thriving amongst its cultivated neighbors.

"Philo, you really must ask Silas about it. It had to do with ethics and a disagreement we had. It's not my place to tell you." My eyes met his. "Please don't ask me."

He shrugged. "I love him, but some things have happened lately that make me not able to trust him. He's been caught in some, uh, fabrications, that are distressing to me. Vashti has been threatening to leave him, too."

Kipp perked up at news of a fellow lupine. He'd become fond of Vashti and worried her symbiont bond with Silas could be fractured due to a lack of trust. After all, we'd just met Tristan and Meko, who'd suffered for years due to the same.

"You and I will never have that happen to us," Kipp said, glancing at me.

Philo knew Kipp and I were talking privately and paused to give us time. "I sometimes wonder if I made a poor career choice when I was younger," he remarked with a sigh. "There was an opportunity for me to form a bond and travel, but I confess the idea was frightening to me." He looked at me and tried to smile. "I never had your courage... still don't," he added somewhat ruefully.

I edged closer on the bench so that my shoulder grazed his. Reaching out, I took his hand in mine. Yes, we'd always be friends, no matter where our journeys might take us.

"I've been thinking that if the time comes for a transfer from this area, I might try to finagle something so that Fitzhugh, Juno, you, Kipp and I can all be relocated to the same collective. Maybe I'm getting older and just don't want to change and lose the ones who are important to me." He raised an eyebrow, waiting for my reaction.

"And what about Claire?" I asked.

"Claire, too, of course, if she wants to come."

"She will, Philo. You two love one another. It's just that your common love for your son is causing a divide. It can be worked out." I squeezed his hand which felt like a block of ice. "You need some gloves," I chided him.

The cold finally forced us back inside, and I reluctantly returned to Suzanne's workshop where Peter and Elani lingered. Peter, having shown deference to Suzanne and an interest in her craft, had been granted an unusual level of accommodation. I found him going through bolts of cloth, trying to decide which fabrics he found most suitable for his Norfolk jacket and traveling attire. Suzanne had typically not given me such leave. She glanced up from a pattern book and glared at me.

"So, have you managed to compose yourself?" she asked, directing the comment towards me.

"Some of it was Kipp's fault," I replied, pointing at my companion.

"Was not!" he rejoined.

I knew I had to get control and try to pretend to be professional, so I clamped my mouth shut and sent Kipp the notion he needed to keep his crazy thoughts to himself for a few minutes. We managed to pass the remainder of the afternoon in the workroom, surrounded by the thick atmosphere created by fabric, paper, and old, well-thumbed books. I'd probably have a headache from all the dust inhaled. Suzanne lost her bad humor and brought me a fresh cup of coffee while Kipp made a nest on some discarded woolen fabric that had fallen to the floor. After a while, he began to nod off, our soft voices acting to lull him to sleep.

"I like this one for you, Peter," I remarked, my fingers running over the soft texture of a light wool fabric swatch. "It isn't so heavy that you will feel constricted in movement, but the wool will help with warmth. And the color will be good on you."

Peter's dark mop of hair, his brown eyes and even complexion pretty much insured that he would look good in anything, from jeans and t-shirt to formal attire. But the brown fabric with threads of deep navy running throughout would be exceptionally flattering.

"And you can go with a beard and mustache or just a mustache and long sideburns," Suzanne was saying. "The facial hair makes you look older, and if you are trying to mix with the first class male passengers, you will want to seem as if you fit in."

"We're traveling as the niece and nephew of Tristan Taylor, who was a good friend of J.P. Morgan," Peter said. "The story we created with Tristan is that he was long estranged from his family, which is why he never mentioned having any close ties. But recently, he was informed that his sister died in an accident, leaving us—me and Petra —as his sole family. Feeling angst over the rift, he asked to meet us while we were traveling in Europe."

"So how do you come by your money to travel?" Suzanne rarely got the details, and she was enjoying being part of the conspiracy.

"Our father recently inherited some money from his family, so our, uh, situation had changed," Peter said. "Tragically, he and our mother were killed in a boating accident shortly after receiving the inheritance. To recover from the blow, we decided to travel to Europe. Of course, we are accompanied by our faithful canine companions," he added with a grin, glancing at Elani who was reclining on another pile of wadded fabric. Her tail began to wag. "Tristan then connives to get J.P. Morgan to secure our first class passage on the *Titanic*, since we are ready to return home."

"Pretty good story," Suzanne nodded. She took a sip of her coffee, leaving a soft smudge of lipstick on the side of the mug.

Kipp lazily opened one eye. "If Mark Elliott appears with that color lipstick on his cheek, we'll know what's up," he remarked softly to me alone. He was obviously trying very hard to get us sent to the bench in the garden, once again.

CHAPTER 13

Peter's jacket and trousers fit almost perfectly on the first try. My outfit, however, needed some attention.

"Either I measured you wrong, or you've gained fifty pounds since that day," Suzanne opined as she tugged on the front of my jacket, trying to make it meet across my chest. There was a pair of reading glasses perched upon the end of her nose; she squinted slightly as she backed away to give me another appraising glance. "I may have to put in a side gusset," she remarked, lips pursed.

"I'm not going on this trip with side gussets," I said, feeling irritated. Since I wasn't keen on this time shift in the first place, it didn't require much to further sour my mood. "Maybe you have been distracted and wrote down the wrong figures," I suggested, staring at her face which flushed immediately.

"Well, maybe so," she conceded. It was well known that Mark had been courting her, to use an old fashioned term, and it showed in her lack of concentration and silly demeanor.

"You were like that with Harrow, so I don't want to hear any complaints or criticisms," Kipp offered from his vantage point in a corner of the dressing room. He'd resigned himself to the fact he'd have to wear the usual money collar, which he detested but tolerated. The collar, which was a clever design, functioned like a man's money belt and had saved our bacon more than once. While someone might try to steal a reticule I would carry, no one with half a brain would grab for a collar strapped around Kipp's massive neck.

"I'll put in a couple of side panels that will work like princess seaming, and I promise you, they won't look like gussets," Suzanne promised.

"We'll see," I thought darkly.

That evening, Fitzhugh, Juno, Kipp and I settled in the living room after a modest meal of Greek salad that I'd ordered–the lupines stuck to the chicken which came on the side–and waited for TCM to begin its eight o'clock fare. We were in for a rare treat since *Casablanca* was on the line up. Before the arrival of Kipp, who saw no boundaries to his life, lupines couldn't enjoy movies since they didn't comprehend spoken language and depended upon their telepathy to decipher meanings. Given the one dimensional nature of movies and television, there was nothing to comprehend. But since Kipp and Juno had both learned to read and understand spoken language, their appreciation of television had changed.

The movie started after the usual introduction by the host, and I was completely engrossed until I realized that Fitzhugh was distracted. At first it was noticeable by the tapping of his foot against the wooden floor. Then, he began to aimlessly hum some odd tune that seemed vaguely familiar but just out of reach for me. The winter remained unrelentingly brisk and outside of my snug house, the land-scape seemed fragile in the crisp air. I was happy that the fireplace was fully engaged, although my stack of firewood was getting low for the season. There was a man in Creedmoor who supplied me from time to time, and it appeared a phone call was in order in the event the low temperatures lingered into spring.

"What's bothering you?" I finally asked, using the remote to turn the sound down a notch.

"Oh, I'm not sure," he replied with a wan smile. His hair, always worn long, looked mussed and tangled as it straggled down to graze the collar of the new flannel robe I'd given him for Christmas. The holidays had passed quietly in our little home, and I'd just managed to get the Christmas decorations put away the previous day. Looking down, Fitzhugh stared at the left wrist cuff and carefully turned it back so that it matched the one on the right. "I worry that I gave you bad advice now that it appears you will really attempt this trip to the *Titanic*."

"I'm a big girl," I began before he waved me off.

"Yes, I know you have the world by the tail and nothing can get the better of you, but I'm still concerned." He angled his position in the chair so that he gathered more heat from the fireplace. With a sigh, he propped his chin against the palm of his hand. For a moment he shifted his attention to Humphrey Bogart and Ingrid Bergman before glancing at me, since he knew I wouldn't give up quite so easily.

"Philo was talking, theoretically of course, about the need for some of us to move to other collectives at some point. It is the discussion we either greatly anticipate or dread, depending upon where we live and what the experience is like." He laughed softly. "I recall one posting I had in Italy that was so terrible, I finally bribed a leader to let me go. I was sent elsewhere and remained until moving here," he said with a wave of his thin hands. Fitzhugh dared to peek at me. "And now that I'm here, I've been completely happy." It was clear he meant my home–which had become our home.

"Of course, if Kipp and I are relocated, Fitzhugh, you can stay here. I mean, this house is yours," I said, leaning forward towards him.

"I told Philo I'd want to go with you, Juno and me," he said, his face opening in surprising vulnerability. "It feels like family, being here with you and Kipp," he began. "I never had a daughter or son, for that matter, and it's nice to occasionally pretend that you belong to me." His eyes were soft in the shadows of the room, illuminated only by the flickering screen of the television.

I had experienced that moment of total honesty before–which Fitzhugh just expressed—where one feels as if one is hanging on a precipice, terrified that one's words will be rejected or subjected to scorn and ridicule. Glancing at Juno, I let my eyes roam lovingly over her graying face; she was old but vital and a source of wisdom and strength. Her tail thumped at my visual caress.

"We talked about it, Fitzhugh and I, while you were gone to Atlanta," Juno said. "This would no longer be a home if you and Kipp were not here."

Kipp, who was lying close to Juno on her favorite little woolen rug, edged closer and draped his neck across her back, sighing as he closed his eyes. She was as close to a mother figure as he might have.

How did I, a relatively confirmed loner, with the exception of Kipp, end up with an entourage of valued elders who could not do without me? But as I mused, I realized that I felt similarly towards them.

"Well, at the risk of sounding like Scarlett O'Hara, why don't we worry about this issue at a later date? Philo doesn't indicate anything on the near horizon." I was pleased at my practicality and common sense approach, which in truth smacked of careful avoidance. The life of the traveling symbiont was filled with comings and goings, and the well adjusted traveler figured out how to do both effortlessly and with few regrets. Maybe I wasn't as good as I thought I was at managing such things.

Fitzhugh's face relaxed but neither of us could generate any interest in the movie. After muting the volume, we began to speak of other matters.

"It will be up to you and Kipp to keep the youngsters in line," Fitzhugh remarked. "I know Peter can be a bit impulsive, but hopefully he has learned to modify that tendency since his last time shift. This trip will leave no room for error." He crossed his long legs and tilted his head to rest on the chair back. "You will have to remain aboard until the last possible moment and time shift out at a time when human emotions are at their peak in terms of hysteria. It will be difficult."

"I'll probably make Peter and Elani leave a little early, just so I won't worry. Don't you think so, Kipp?"

He nodded his head, although his eyes were blinking sleepily. Juno was snoring softly from her warm place in front of the fire, which had died down; only a few glowing embers still winked at us from the darkness of the hearth.

After gently rousing Juno, all of us went to our respective rooms for the night. I climbed in my bed, dreading the embrace of cold sheets after having enjoyed the fireplace all evening. Kipp hopped up and curled next to me, his muzzle across my chest.

"Petra?"

"Hmmm?"

"Thank you." Kipp pressed closer.

"For what?" I asked, my hand gently kneading the back of his neck, where his fur still held on to the warmth from the fireplace.

"For going on this time shift. I know you have hesitations, but you are doing it, in large part, because I want to go. So, thanks."

"Go to sleep, Kipp," I replied. He needed to quell his busy thoughts.

The next morning, I awoke with the nagging thought I had to prepare for my leaving party. A long run usually worked to dissipate the anxiety, and I was happily outdoors within the hour. Kipp was at my side, holding back since he had four legs compared to my two and was naturally gifted with superior speed. Yellow clusters of daffodils were grouped in uneven patches along the rolling hills where the dead grass of winter was gray and matted. With pleasure, I felt the welcomed burn grow in my legs as I trotted easily along the edge of a seldom used country lane. The sky was filled with dark, scudding clouds, and it seemed rain might set in by late afternoon. The air felt moist and heavy; I preferred lower humidity when running. We startled a covey of doves that rose into the sky, their wings making a heavy, thumping noise against the quiescent hillsides. High above, a circling hawk seemed to be watching the doves with interest, and I could only hope they would find their way to safety. Nature was beautiful as well as breathtakingly brutal. Kipp stayed silent and exited from my mind. He seemed to understand my need to gather my thoughts before tackling the most consequential trip of my lifetime. It was with reluctance I eventually turned for home.

Fitzhugh helped me to prepare for the leaving party, which was a traditional send off for the traveling pair or, in this case, the traveling quartet. Our shift date early in March would give us time to assemble a wardrobe and allow room for error. Time shifting inherently had an element of unpredictability and was not linear in nature, but it helped to keep our internal clocks a little more aligned when we tried to come and go in a time frame that paralleled the natural order. With that in mind, we hoped to arrive in London close to the first of March, 1912. Then we would depart from the decks of the *Titanic* on April 15, 1912 and time shift home. If we were fairly accurate, our personal time lines would be uninterrupted.

I decided upon a vegetable lasagna, salad and brownies for dessert, since I knew Elani was a chocolate addict. Fitzhugh kept me company by supplying some colorful stories of when he and his symbiont, Lydea, traveled. As he chatted, I was amused to have to rethink my notions of him, since he'd obviously been somewhat of prankster himself, a quality he would heartily denounce in others. A rumble of thunder interrupted my thoughts...the rain had arrived earlier than I anticipated from my previous amateur analysis of the sky. From the view outside my kitchen windows, it didn't look as if it was mid after-noon. Rather, it seemed as if twilight was hovering, ready to fall at any moment. It was a good thing that weather, fair or foul, didn't compro-mise a traveler's ability. Kipp's amber eyes watched me from across the room; his head was up, his plumed tail occasionally waving in excitement. I'd wisely allowed my misgivings to be dismissed and surrendered to the general air of anxious anticipation.

"Are you going to try and see him?" Fitzhugh asked. "After all, you'll be in London, and he was still living at that time."

Of course, he meant William Harrow. I'd harbored a secret fantasy to lie in wait outside of the school that Harrow had built, hoping for a sighting of him...from a discrete distance, of course. But I didn't want to seem like a love obsessed teenager, and there was no way I would admit to such thoughts. Kipp, knowing of the sensitivity of the subject, didn't overtly intrude on my notions but delicately pranced around them in his attempt to try and give me some modicum of privacy.

"Don't be ridiculous," I replied, trying to look indignant and irri-tated simultaneously. It didn't work, however, because Fitzhugh ducked his head in an effort to hide the growing smile on his face.

Thankfully, the first of our guests began to arrive, and within the next forty five minutes, we had a room full of friends. To create a cozy space, I kept the artificial lights at a minimum and lit candles set at strategic points around the living room where we gathered. Each time the front door opened or someone walked across the room, the flames would flicker in response, causing soft shadows to ripple across the walls. Philo was present, of course, sans Claire. I raised an eyebrow in query to only be met with a silent shake of his head. Peter and Elani were next, brimming with excitement. Peter's mother drove them, and I was more relaxed greeting her than previously when she made me personally responsible for Peter's safety.

"Hello, Evelyn," I said, embracing the petite female with a polite hug. Her pretty face, brown hair and quick, alert eyes made me think of a Carolina wren.

"Do you remember what I said to you last time?" she asked, a smile touching her trembling lips. "It goes double this time."

"Oh, Mom," Peter began, his voice almost sounding like a whine.

Well, she had cause to worry. This would be an unusual trip. Leaning forward, I whispered, "I'll get him off in time, I promise." Her grip on my forearm relaxed.

Suzanne asked if she could bring Mark Elliot since they were a duo, and I'd reluctantly said yes. Something about him bothered me, but it seemed I was the only one in that category. Even Kipp could not find fault with him. As Mark bent forward to give me a friendly little buzz on my cheek, the cologne he wore enveloped me in a tiny cloud.

"Hai Karate? Aqua Velva...Brut...English Leather? Maybe Old Spice?" Kipp looked up at me, his normally expressive face deadpan.

Suddenly, I thought of Kipp's pirate impression and began to giggle uncontrollably. Almost staggering, I walked through to the kitchen and exited out the back door, where I erupted into boisterous laughter. The door opened behind me, and I turned to see Philo standing on the narrow porch, arms crossed at his chest. We were both sheltered by the overhang which offered respite from the rain. A rumble of thunder caused the concrete beneath my feet to tremble; overhead a gust of wind threaded its way through the tree limbs which were still bare of leaves.

"Are you finished?" He was wearing his manager's serious expression that was making an unwelcomed appearance much too often, it seemed.

Holding up my hands, I brushed past him and re-entered the living room where my guests waited, wondering what had sparked my rude exit.

"It was Kipp..." I began lamely. "He does this pirate impression..." I deliberately didn't finish my remark and everyone seemed relieved to blame Kipp for my unusual behavior.

Leaving parties were typically quite festive with the travelers being subjected to rather humorous and sometimes vicious roasts. But this particular one was different, and everyone seemed subdued. Juno huddled close to me, her gray muzzle resting upon the top of my foot. Finally, the funereal atmosphere bothered me, and I had to remark upon it.

"We are supposed to be having fun," I said. Kipp, in total agreement, lifted his head and wagged his tail. "Peter, Elani, Kipp and I will be back here in a few weeks, and after that there will be another time shift at some point in the future." I looked at Peter's mother. "We're going to be fine. And if someone doesn't come up with a really terrible story to share and embarrass the heck out of me, I'm going to my room to read." Placing my hands on my hips, I tapped my foot in mock agitation.

"You once took a trip and were exposed, as fate would have it, to the King of Spain, as I recall," Fitzhugh said softly. Clearing his throat, he continued. "When I say exposed, that is a literal term. It seems your, uh, undergarments had been misplaced, and when the king entered the room, you tried to curtsey but the hoops in your skirt caused it to fly up in the back. The row of supplicants to your rear viewed your rear, as I was told rather graphically. When one of the involuntary spectators gave an exclamation of surprise, you whirled around and allowed the king his turn to view your, uh, posterior."

Well, no one had ever had the nerve to tell that one before–and I wasn't sure how Fitzhugh knew about it anyway—and I felt my face turn beet red. Peter choked on a carrot stick, while Mark Elliot bent his head forward trying to show good manners as he hid his perfect white smile in a napkin. Philo, on the other hand, felt no such compulsion to be restrained and threw his head back and howled.

"You never told me that one!" he exclaimed, wiping his eyes.

"It made its way rather surreptitiously to my chronicles by a fellow traveler who happened to witness the, uh, exposure." Fitzhugh remarked, using his forefinger to smooth his mustaches.

"You are on my list," I warned him, narrowing my eyes. "And I know who blabbed, and he's on my list, too." Kipp stared at me, his eyes rounded with curiosity. I avoided looking at Evelyn's horrified face; she was, no doubt, wondering what sort of heathen was going off into the sunset with her precious boy in tow.

The evening finally drifted to an end, and after warm goodbyes, including a lingering bear hug by Philo who almost fractured my ribs, Peter and I, supervised by Fitzhugh and Juno, began to clean the kitchen.

"I'm glad it won't disturb you if I just stay quietly in my room while you make your exit," Fitzhugh said. "I'll keep Lily under control, I promise."

"Well, we've jelled as a team, and I think there are fewer exterior distractions that can challenge our concentration at this point. There better not be, or we may have trouble getting off of a sinking ship." I made my remarks while Peter walked outside, accompanied by Kipp and Elani. The rain had finally ceased, and the lupines were restless.

"Petra, you are very skilled, and we know that Kipp is exceptional. I have full confidence that all will be well." Juno was the voice of sober reason and her counsel was valued. Just hearing her calm words helped me to feel better despite the mountain of misgivings I had erected over the time shift. Leaning forward, I kissed the warm top of her furry head. She wagged her tail in response.

"So, I guess I'll be seeing you in about six weeks?" Fitzhugh looked up at me.

"Yep," I replied, smiling at him.

"You promise?"

"Yes, I promise." Walking over to him, I leaned forward and pressed my cheek against the top of his head. "You and Juno need to go on now, and let me get Peter and the lupines situated."

Fitzhugh lifted up his hand to grasp mine with a squeeze that almost caused pain but not quite. Without looking back, he rose and left the kitchen to disappear down the hallway. Juno followed, but she glanced at me over her shoulder, slowly closing one eye.

"I'll take care of him," she said softly.

"You promise?" I asked.

"Yes, I promise."

CHAPTER 14

There are aspects of symbiont, uh, physics, that remain a mystery. For example, we just don't materialize inside objects, in the tops of trees or under water. Also, we almost always land in a place where there are few human obstacles, too. I guess the nearest natural comparison might be flocks of birds or large gatherings of fish that can swim and turn but don't collide with one another. There are obviously some inherent safety mechanisms in our nature that helps us to land safely. But there are hard landings and soft landings, and I'd had some of both. It was nice that this particular landing was soft.

After the time shift, which felt as if one dived off of a shapeless precipice to fall into a dark, bottomless pit, I opened my eyes to find myself sitting in what appeared to be a small flower garden located at the side of a large, red brick house. It was daylight, and I quickly turned my head to see if any human was nearby, watching...horrified to see two humanoids and two lupines appear out of nowhere to sprawl inelegantly in a colorful patch of hyacinths and tulips. After a moment of dullness, I noted that the type of blooming flowers indicated it must be early spring—wherever we were. When traveling to a new location, there was typically a great deal of preparation work to nail the locale as well as appropriate time frame. But London was familiar to both me and Kipp, and he led our quartet effortlessly to what we hoped was the desired landing spot. Kipp licked my face, his tongue harsh and raspy against my flesh, assuring me he was okay. A short distance away, Peter blinked his eyes, his hand automatically reaching for Elani, who was yawning. She, with the exception being Kipp, was the easiest going traveler I'd ever seen. The sound of a door opening broke the early morning quiet, and I scrambled to my feet, indicating we needed to beat a hasty retreat. In a moment, we were on the sidewalk, attempting to get our bearings and assess each other for injury.

Even though it seemed by the angle of the sun—which barely peeked over the eastern rooftops—to be early, the streets were already busy with horse drawn carts delivering food, coal and other necessities. The clatter of hooves on pavement was grounding, somehow, and I gave a silent prayer of thanks. Peter and I paused to give one another a visual check to make certain our clothes were not torn or too mussed, while the lupines shook themselves vigorously to settle their fur. Peter reached out to adjust my hat which had become a bit askew during my flight back in time.

"I feel like I'm wearing a bucket on my head," I grumbled. The hat, although lightweight, was larger than my preference, and I felt like the Mad Hatter.

"It looks good, really," Peter assured me. His brown eyes assessed Suzanne's creation, which had a brim that extended out about four inches; the crown was large, projecting up, almost like a short, fat stovepipe. She'd covered the hat in decorative twists of lace and a taupe grosgrain ribbon encircled the crown.

Peter adjusted his own hat, which was a derby style with a flat brim. Quite honestly, I envied him that conservative hat which I privately coveted...so much simpler than the silly, impractical thing I wore. His facial hair had filled in nicely, aging him by at least five years. He had a full mustache that drooped off either side of his mouth to meet and merge with a short cropped beard.

"That looks like a lot of trouble," I remarked, thinking of the trimming required.

"I finally mastered a straight razor, and it's kind of interesting to use," he said, trying to sound nonchalant but failing. The pride of his accomplishment was clear in his voice.

A seemingly vacant four wheeler had turned the corner and was approaching; Peter threw up his arm to hail the driver. We always began our time shifts by establishing a home base, so to speak. A man's face peered down to us from the carriage box; there was a broad smile across his ruddy flesh, obviously glad for a fare so early in the morning.

"Where to?" he asked.

As he spoke I noticed the fog in the air from his exhaled breath. I must have had the heart of a child at that moment, because the excitement I'd felt had made me immune to the fact it was chilly and damp in London that early in the season. At least I thought it was early based upon the flower bed upon which I'd landed. Until we verified the date, we wouldn't know if we'd made a colossal time shift blunder. Unconsciously, I pulled my traveling jacket a little closer around my body. The driver squinted slightly at our backpacks, which we usually converted to a traveling valise by the time we made our appearance, but we'd rushed from the garden without the opportunity.

"We are travelers from America visiting London for the first time," Peter cleverly responded, so we would get verification that we'd hit our correct target location.

As he spoke, I saw the man's face relax. Yes, we were foreigners, and that would explain our odd backpacks as well as the huge dogs at our sides. There was no accounting for Americans who often acted in strange and unexpected ways.

"We need you to take us to a nice establishment where we can take rooms for a few weeks. Of course, it will have to accommodate our pets," Peter said, adding a smile to his request.

We clambered into the four wheeler, and after a sharp command from the driver to the unenthusiastic horse, the vehicle jerked into motion. Kipp stuck his big head out of the window, barely able to contain his excitement. Draping my arm around him, I snuggled closer, returning Peter's smile as he did the same with Elani. In addition to the chill, the palpable moisture in the air added to the discomfort I felt, and Kipp's body felt good nestled beside me. I'd probably add some type of woolen undergarments to my shopping list. Elani glanced at me and barked softly, giving me some support from the female quarter.

The carriage only traveled a short distance but far enough so that I could easily see the changes in London, comparing 1888 to whatever year we'd snagged in our current travel. I could only hope we'd arrived in 1912. Although horses were the predominant method for travel as well as still widely in use pulling wagons and carriages, cars had made their noisy, coughing presence known. One rumbled past us, honking rudely, the noise causing our carriage horse to flatten her ears and swerve away from the unexpected sound. After a few lurches and stops as we waited our turn behind other contraptions, the four wheeler pulled up in front of a nondescript four story building made of dark brick. Someone had the foresight to paint the entrance door bright red, making it both inviting and cheerful. We opened the carriage door and hopped out, Peter giving me the gentleman's assist, before digging in his pocket for the correct currency.

"And where are we exactly?" Peter asked, as he handed the driver the coin.

"You're in Marylebone," the man replied. "This hotel is small and caters to, uh, out of town folks. I believe the proprietor will accommodate you as well as your doggies." With a tip of his hat, he nudged the horse and rolled away, the wheels of the carriage rattling loudly on the hard pavement.

"Well, here we go," Peter announced, as he tried to sound casual but managing a poor job of camouflaging his excitement. I was comfortable to let him take the lead. In any case, at that time in history, he most likely would be acting in a more dominant role since he appeared to be a human male.

The lobby was small and comfortably cozy from my point of view. Soft colors were put to clever use to offset the size of the room. It was evident that an industrious worker had recently polished all the furniture; the wood surfaces gleamed as the early morning sunlight broke through the windows, and the pungent scent of lemon wafted through the air. A man was hunched over the front desk reading the morning paper, which was spread out to almost cover the desk top. As he looked up at our entourage, I was gratified we were not met with a frown over the lupines, who were larger than the typical dog. The desk man's thoughts were curious but not negative as he carefully collected his paper.

"I am Peter Keaton and this is my sister, Petra," Peter began, tipping the edge of his hat with a courteous finger. "We are Americans on holiday and need rooms while we are in London." Before the man could reply, Peter added, "As you can see, we travel with our dogs and certainly will pay extra for any bother or inconvenience. They are very well behaved," he added. Mischievously, he barked a sharp command. "Kipp, Elani, sit!"

The back ends of the lupines hit the floor so quickly that I thought the china teacup holding the desk man's morning tea trembled on the mahogany countertop. Kipp glanced at me, narrowing his eyes.

"I am not a trained circus elephant," he muttered.

"Me neither, Kipp," Elani chimed in.

"Pipe down, you two," I replied, trying not to laugh. "Peter is making a point, so just play along, please."

"We often have guests who travel with their dogs," the man was saying. It seemed he was not concerned. "Once a lady showed up with her pet goat...that was a little unusual," the man added, his eyes growing large. "But the goat was quite well behaved, and our staff became quite fond of her...Gloria, I think her name was. I'm Mr. Haley," he added, "and I will be glad to see to your needs."

As Peter and Mr. Haley examined the costs and other issues, I took a moment to walk around the room. A wall that was painted the soft yellow color of a lingering sunset featured a series of lovely watercolors, dainty and tasteful, caught in the glow of the early morning sun. Kipp stared after me longingly but didn't think he was free to meander since Peter hadn't formally released him from the sit. I was familiar with this part of London from my past visits, most recently during the Whitechapel trip when I lived in Mayfair. We should be far enough away from Harrow's home that we wouldn't inadvertently run into any past acquaintances who might still be living in the area.

"Petra, today is February 27, 1912!" Peter exclaimed telepathically out of the hearing of the desk clerk. "We couldn't have timed it any better. At the very most, we are off a day or two from our target which was a little fuzzy anyway." He turned and met my eyes, his face flushed slightly from excitement.

A boy, who was maybe seventeen if that, showed us to our rooms. He, like the few others we'd met, looked askance at our backpacks, eyebrows raised, obviously thinking that American culture was odd and not to be understood. He offered to take mine, but I shook him off. The rooms, which were large and well lit due to a series of narrow, long windows stretching from ceiling to floor, were in the rear of the building. They wouldn't have been considered the choice rooms based on location but worked for us due to the rear staircase for the servants that would give quick access for the lupines to visit the grassy area across the back alley behind the hotel, which was named The Dovecote. Why someone would name a hotel after a pigeon coop, I didn't know.

"I worked out the usual deal where we will pay extra for special attention. The manager will have a boy bring food in for the lupines, as well as us, as we request. I told him we'd often be gone but needed to retain these rooms until April 10th." Peter shrugged his shoulders. "He seemed happy enough with the additional money I gave him."

Despite living in a modern world with many conveniences, I missed oil lanterns and candles and the soft, natural light they created. Electricity was widely dispersed in London by 1912, so with a turn of a knob, a bulb flickered to life, feeble at first but then bolder as if it wanted to impress me with its work ethic. There was a water closet close by, and the boy brought fresh pitchers of water to each room. Obviously, the Dovecote's plumbing was still a work in progress. Kipp's eyes followed me as I inspected my room; my fingers ran along the top edge of the water basin, unexpectedly finding a small chip in the smooth porcelain. The mirror above the dresser was surprisingly free of ripples on the surface, and the reflection which gazed back at me was true. Kipp hopped up on the bed to sample its comfort; a satin coverlet made the surface so slippery that he almost slid down before he could brace his feet.

"Not sure I like this cover," he remarked nonchalantly, his nostrils flaring. Since I was constantly in his mind as he was mine, I realized he was slightly embarrassed that Elani had observed him in a clumsy moment. He cared about her impressions of him, despite his statements to the contrary. Ducking my head, I avoided his sharp glance as he dared me to say anything. Wisely, I remained silent.

Since obtaining appropriate clothing was a first necessity, we went out front and hailed another four wheel carriage. "Take us to Park Road," Peter requested, using my suggestion. Kipp wedged his body next to mine on the upholstered bench seat, his head stuck out the window as we breezed along. It made sense to start on a more widely traveled thoroughfare and then use the smaller side streets as needed to shop for vendors to meet our needs. The humidity was beginning to lessen as the rising sun cut through the dissipating fog, and I closed my eyes, daydreaming of the last time I made such a journey.

"We need to go find him," Kipp remarked softly, his nudging words meant only for me. "Even if from a distance. You know you want to."

The cherished pearls Harrow had gifted me hugged my neck, showing at the modest V of my collar. "Let me think about it, Kipp. Don't push me."

Across the carriage, Elani was standing, her large head hanging out the small window, her tail wagging so vigorously that her entire back end shimmied. Peter reached over and ran his hand lightly down her broad back. I didn't intrude but his body language spoke of his pride in her abilities. Had she been familiar with the area, Elani could have driven this time shift and landed us pretty much square on. In that way, she rivaled Kipp's talents, even though it was not a competition. Unlike many humans, we tended to applaud one another's skills and accomplishments without envy or rancor. Strength and talent in one of us benefited the entire community, from our way of thinking. The wheels caught on a patch of uneven pavement, jostling us hard on our seats. The driver's muttered apology drifted back from his perch on the box.

Deposited at our requested location on Park Road, our odd party drew a few looks due to the size of the lupines, who ambled nonchalantly at our sides. We kept close, however, and avoided crowds while managing to make our way to a shop that we spied as we approached a cross street. A well dressed man, wearing a fashionable navy blue blazer over a shirt with a collar so crisp it jutted into the underside of his chin, almost collided with us as we entered. A man whose youth was betrayed by the gentle flush on his cheekbones, as well as a valiant attempt at wispy strands of facial hair, met us under the tinkling bell hanging over the door to the shop. It seemed that the shop only served men, but the fellow was delighted to have his assistant accompany me the short distance to the seamstress shop a mere two blocks away. As I walked with the youth, I realized I glanced back a couple of times; it fell odd to leave Peter and Elani behind.

"You've become attached," Kipp said, pushing his shoulder against my leg to make a point. "And not only with Peter and Elani but also with Fitzhugh and Juno."

"Haven't you?" I asked more than a trifle defensively.

"Always," he replied, nudging his head under my hand.

We were deposited at the seamstress's establishment, which like all such places smelled of musty fabric, candle tallow and old sachets of lavender. Fortunately, the proprietor was a dog lover and seemed happier to see Kipp than me, as she offered him a good size hunk of her biscuit while giving me nothing. Her shop, though small, obviously catered to the more affluent, and with my guise as a traveling American of adequate means, she was delighted to work with me to create a wardrobe that would, at least, help me pass muster while on the *Titanic*. Kipp dropped down in a corner and watched, wagging his tail to approve of a fabric or suggested fashion style, or closing his eyes to things of which he disapproved. Although I didn't think I'd attend a sit down dinner on the *Titanic* since Kipp would be left behind, I, at his encouragement, did allow the seamstress to talk me into one pretty gown that could pass in a pinch for something more formal. She pulled out a length of delicate watered blue silk and held it up beneath my chin as I gazed at my reflection in a full length mirror. It was one of those colors that would be attractive on anyone, and I liked blue, so it was a go. I warned her that I was not wearing a corset and had chosen the very modern brassiere; her lips pursed in disapproval of my libertine attitude but said nothing and nodded her head. It was my preference that she collaborate with a milliner, since I had neither time nor inclination to involve myself in the creation of hats. The lace draped bucket I currently wore on my head would see me through most eventualities, but I'd need something a little fancier for other occasions. Looking up, I saw Peter peering nearsightedly through the front glass of the shop, and, with a promise from the seamstress that she could have my dresses ready for a final fitting in time for our departure date on the *Titanic*, Kipp and I joined the others outside.

With directions given by Peter's tailor, we found a readymade goods shop and enhanced our traveling wardrobe with undergarments as well as a couple of fresh blouses for me and a hat which, thankfully, didn't feel so large and cumbersome. This one had a broader brim and tighter crown and would be more comfortable for our daily excursions while we wasted almost 6 weeks.

"So, what do we do while we wait?" Peter asked as our carriage lurched along carrying us to The Dovecote, our packages stowed neatly in a rear compartment.

"I have a little side trip I'd like to make," Kipp remarked. "If you guys think you can stomach one more ghost encounter," he added unexpectedly.

CHAPTER 15

The train left London early in the morning, as the fog was lifting from the Thames to shroud the rooftops like a damp, white ceiling so dense it blocked the view of the sky. Smoke from countless chimneys combined with the cloying mist to create a seemingly impenetrable wall through which our carriage had pushed on our journey to the train station. Leaving Kings Cross behind, we began the trip towards Suffolk, where the land gently sloped to meet the sea, and the landscape was thick with bogs, marshes and other wetlands.

"Okay, Kipp, what's up?" I asked as my body rocked back and forth with the motion of the train. We had a first class compartment to ourselves, and both Kipp and Elani were craning their enormous heads to view the countryside as we passed. Small villages dotted the mostly level landscape where a few rolling hills were segmented by thick hedgerows gone dormant from the previous winter.

"There's a tale of a spectral dog called Black Shuck which is rumored to haunt the eastern coastal regions." Kipp hopped up on the seat next to me and rested his head in my lap. I was wearing my spare traveling skirt with the matching tweed jacket and a fresh blouse; I'd ditched the bucket hat for the new one I'd purchased. While not as stylish as current trends demanded, I never bothered over minor details involving fashion. Rolling my eyes, I looked at Peter who smiled.

"I thought you'd had enough of ghosts and haints," I replied teasingly, gently tweaking his big ear for good measure. My jest was met with Kipp's amber eyes, serious and unblinking, as he stared back.

"I've had enough of worrying that the Twelve or others might want to use me. This particular trip is to satisfy my curiosity." Kipp adjusted his position on the seat, stretching as he did so.

"Which is what?" I asked. I glanced out of the window as our train sped over an elevated trestle, where a gently flowing stream curved beneath, the sunlight flashing off of the surface of the water. A short distance away, a young boy and girl played at the edge of the water, throwing rocks to watch them splash since the weather was still too cool for wading. Now that we'd cleared the big city, the sky, which was free of soot and smoke, was bright blue, lit by a yellow sun that failed to bring any heat to the chilled earth.

"There's speculation that Arthur Conan Doyle wrote *The Hound of the Baskervilles* after hearing of the tale of Black Shuck. The image of a large, black, spectral hound has been documented for centuries, crossing the marshes and wetlands, terrorizing the inhabitants," Kipp intoned dramatically, half closing his eyes as if he was casting a spell upon us.

Elani darted a quick glance at me, not sure if Kipp was purposely building a tale just to frighten us. Slowly, I closed one eye and smiled at her; she was far too naïve and trusting, a result of her youth. There was a part of me that wished she'd stay just that way but time and experience would change her. Such things were inevitable.

At Kipp's urging, we'd packed our small backpacks, now turned inside out to resemble valises, with a change of underwear and a fresh shirt so that we could stay overnight. Now I understood why—Kipp wanted to go out into the marshland surrounding Blythburgh in search of an encounter with Black Shuck. We'd left London quite early, and the train ride was uneventful but soothing, the motion of the car eventually lulling me into a light sleep. As the train eased to a stop in the small station, Peter reached forward to give my arm a slight nudge. There were times I thought I'd never get fully caught up on my rest. After nodding off on the train, I was ready for a walk and we, with Kipp's guidance and the helpful directions given by a couple of villagers, wound up a hill to where the Holy Trinity Church stood, overlooking the surrounding countryside. The land was filled with promise as grass tried to take hold of the fields left dormant by the harshness of winter. Off to the east, I saw what appeared to be a white cloud break apart before realizing it was a flock of gulls seeking the ocean. The origin of the church was established in medieval times, and the front entrance, which was crafted using stacked rock, was surrounded on either side by graves from past centuries. Leaning forward, I tried to make out the inscription on one only to find, with disappointment, that the name and sentiments had been eroded by weather over the ages. An old man—a caretaker—made his way towards us, taking care not to step on the physical graves.

Smiling, the man put down his rake and half propped upon a rock pillar, squirming his shoulders to find a place of comfort on the cold stone. After a minute of fumbling in his pocket, he pulled out a pipe. "So, you've read of Black Shuck," he said, in response to Peter's query, as he began to fill the pipe with some loose tobacco from a worn leather pouch.

"Well, I really have only heard some vague rumors," Peter replied, pushing his hands in his pockets. "Can you tell us more?"

"Well, we've been told not to gossip about it, since it involves demonic goings on, but I'll tell you what I know if you don't repeat it." The old man squinted up at the sun which was almost directly over-head, obviously happy to have a rapt audience in Peter and me.

"Oh, we won't, sir." Peter's eyes were opened wide, his voice full of earnest cooperation. I was filled with admiration how he could pull off such moments while I, if I tried a similar tact, would be subject to suspicion. Maybe it was that pair of big brown eyes?

"In 1577, there was a service being held in the church. Suddenly, there was a clap of thunder, and this door burst open," the caretaker intoned, gesturing at the front door. "A large black hound entered, raced down the center aisle to the nave and killed a man and boy; as he left, the church steeple collapsed. The hound reared up, putting his feet on the door, leaving scorch marks on the wood." The old man had grown serious; his jaw had a slight tremor as he considered his next words. "They call the marks the Devil's fingerprints."

"Can you open the door for us to see?" Peter was at his best as naïve schoolboy.

The man looked around, almost furtively, as he rubbed a faded kerchief over his face. I followed his thoughts…he knew the church staff were in a back room, deep in a meeting concerning finances, and they'd never know. The old man loved to tell the story and see peoples' expressions of astonishment when the marks on the door were revealed. So, with a little dramatic flourish, he pulled the wooden door back. We peeked at the interior finish, and indeed, there were black marks on the surface of the wood.

"Wow!" Peter exclaimed, wanting to give the caretaker some pleasure by seeming amazed. I added a little drama by grabbing Peter's arm and gently fanning my face with a lace handkerchief.

The old man thought I was going to collapse, so he quickly closed the door and resumed his tilting posture on the rock pillar. His reluctant pipe, by then, was fully engaged, and a cloud of blue smoke encircled his head; the scent of burning tobacco filled the air. "The story was that a local nobleman became enraged at his wife, thinking she was unfaithful to him. He threatened to kill her, and she ran off, crossing the moors. He chased her and finally caught her, stabbing her with a knife. Her dog, which was a large black hound, loved his mistress, and he turned on her killer and savaged him, ripping out his throat." The man sighed. "His master is the Devil, now," he concluded with a shrug of thin shoulders.

I glanced at Kipp who was starring at the marks on the door, his ears flat, posture rigid. Elani was next to him, her furry shoulder almost pressing against his. It was clear the story of the devil had made them both more cautious than usual.

Tugging on Kipp's collar lightly to break the hypnotic spirit of the moment, I asked the man if he knew of anywhere we might stay the night. He suggested a small boarding house and gave directions. We excused ourselves after thanking the man and walked slowly down the hill towards the picturesque village. The one and two story dwellings were separated by tiny gardens which, later in spring and summer, would be filled with flowers. I could imagine larkspur, bluebells and delphinium stalks lined up against the rock and clapboard walls. The scent of the ocean was subtle but suggestive of our proximity to water.

The proprietor of the rooming house was short, barely five feet, with a knot of white hair wound so tightly on the top of her head that I wondered if her smooth complexion was partially due to the pulled strands tugging against the effects of gravity. She answered the door wearing an apron which had the makings of dinner upon it.

"I'm Mrs. Higgins," she answered in a brusque, no-nonsense voice. "And, yes, I have one room available, but I don't usually let my boarders bring pets," she said disapprovingly, her lips pressing together, turning down at the corners at the very thought. As she spoke, a huge yellow cat the color of orange marmalade stalked down the hallway, pausing to glare at Kipp and Elani. Like all animals, the cat could perceive that Kipp and Elani were not dogs, but he couldn't quite make them out. I had to applaud his moxie, watching as he finally plopped his furry backside on the floor, glaring at the huge lupines as he began to clean his face and ears with a large paw. Only a cat could act in such a deliberately casual manner.

"Kipp and Elani are very clean, as you can see, and are completely house trained," Peter began his litany of their wonderful qualities. "We are willing to pay twice your rate for just one night stay."

I think it was the offer of extra currency versus the dissertation about the cleanliness of the lupines that helped her make up her mind. Blythburgh was small, after all, and didn't get many visitors in the off season, when the chilled ocean fueled air brought an unpleasant dampness to the town. Mrs. Higgins ushered us past the threshold and bustled down a narrow hallway crowded with umbrella stands, a towering bookcase and fragile chairs with seat covers decorated in fine needle point, the sort of things one did not use for sitting but more for admiring. Although the house had two stories, she showed us to a ground level room in the back of the house. It was an average sized room with wallpapered walls covered in green tangles of twisting ivy that made me think I was in the midst of a neglected and overgrown garden. After she left, Peter stared at me as Elani gazed at Kipp.

"She really meant one room, didn't she?" Peter asked. He shifted back and forth on his feet.

Over my lifetime, I'd slept in some awkward settings as well as a memorable and uncomfortable cave shared with a tribe of prehistoric people. There had been fire, so that was a bonus at the time. Communal situations were not an issue for me. Peter, however, was definitely new to this aspect of traveling.

"It's fine," I said, to comfort Kipp as much as Peter. "There is a divan over there that will serve me perfectly." As Peter started to offer to take the smaller bed, I added, "I'm shorter than you, and I will take the divan. Kipp will snuggle with me, while you and Elani share the bed." Raising an eyebrow, I smiled. "It is only for one night, guys. I'm sure we can all manage."

Leaving them to stare at each other, I found the kitchen, which was on the far side of the ground floor, and, after knocking politely on the wooden door frame, I entered as Mrs. Higgins nodded to me. Surreptitiously I checked my shoes, since the kitchen had a wonderful floor of bruised and mismatched tiles that appeared to have been mopped that morning; the room was filled with the smell of bread baking. Our proprietress was busy kneading a new loaf on a large, wooden table, her entire body swaying with the motion.

"Mrs. Higgins, we came to Blythburgh to hear the story of Black Shuck," I began, taking a seat out of her way on an elevated stool. She frowned but said nothing and seemed to knead even more vigorously. "Is there some way we can leave here late tonight, if we can find a driver, and go out into the countryside without disturbing you and your household too much?"

She finished the bread, which she had shaped into a perfect loaf, and placed it into the oven. There was a row of finished bread loaves, cooling on the windowsill. Turning to me, she asked if I'd like a cup of tea from the pot she'd brewed just before I interrupted her routine.

She handed me the cup and indicated the small crockery vessels containing cream and sugar.

"That story, some say, is just an old tale passed down by superstitious people who were trying to explain a natural event." She turned to examine her bread loaves, sighing in satisfaction at their perfection. "There was, by all accounts, a bad lightening storm that night. The steeple took a direct hit and collapsed, striking and killing two people. And the burn marks on the door are nothing more than old scorches from candles being held too close."

"I can see you are driven not by superstition but by natural facts," I remarked, hoping my cleverness would gain her support. Kipp was following my thoughts from his perch in our room in the back of the house.

"I am a spiritual woman and know that superstition, itself, is the act of the devil."

I nodded my head, trying to appear big eyed and innocent. We'd only be there one night, but I had no wish to incur her disapproval any more than was necessary. After all, we'd disrupt her routine by coming and going at odd hours. So the lies began.

"My brother, Peter, is actually here on a research project for his university," I began, my mind searching for direction. "Personally, I agree with you, Mrs. Higgins. Neither my brother nor I are superstitious by nature." As I rambled on creating a false narrative, she seemed mollified by my explanation and promised she'd make enquiries of a local who might be persuaded, if the price was right, to drive us around the countryside in the wee hours of the morning.

After I rejoined the others, we decided to stretch our legs and take a stroll around the small community. From behind white picket fences, tiny dogs bravely yapped at Kipp and Elani. One intrepid barker with a furry face that seemed full of teeth was probably no bigger than Kipp's foot, but in the manner of dogs, size mattered not. At the edge of town, we could easily view the countryside, which eventually would join with the sea. Although we couldn't visualize the ocean, the smell of it was in the air, its salty tang biting on the back of my tongue.

Blythburgh was settled near the banks of the River Blyth, in close proximity to the estuary where river and ocean merged. Overhead, a small grouping of ducks flew towards the water, their wings thumping loudly against the damp air. Water birds with curved, long necks and spindly trailing legs hovered, suspended it seemed, as they flew towards the swampy low lands. At some point, the lane upon which we walked became so narrow that the hedgerows seemed to close in, their untrimmed branches snatching greedily at our coat sleeves. A breeze stirred and plucked at my hat, which thankfully was anchored by more than one pin. Gazing upward at the western horizon, I noted some dark clouds and hoped that rain would not interfere with our plans for the late evening excursion to the country.

"Rain, fog, and the like will probably only make the setting more conducive to Black Shuck," Kipp observed, nuzzling my hand. "And no wet dog jokes, please."

The driver was a little greedy to my way of thinking, and his price to be our tour guide seemed excessive, but he was the only game in town, so Peter happily handed over the coins. The driver was a local who owned a battered four wheeler carriage that had seen better days; the fabric seats were split with wear and cotton ticking protruded like cotton bolls threatening to burst. The man, I noted, was heavily dressed, even to a muffler wound around his face. I understood his caution; it was just the first of March, and the weather remained damp, cold and wildly unpredictable.

"I'll take you out to the country," he said, "where the swamps and bogs be." I could see the whites of his eyes as he glanced at us. "People have claimed to see old Shuck in those parts." Canvassing his thoughts, I realized that he was anxious and not just ramping up the excitement to frighten the two goofy Americans, who seemed to have nothing better to do with their time than ride around the desolate countryside in a beat up carriage after darkness had fallen.

I had no expectations of the excursion as we were being jostled roughly out to the middle of nowhere in the chill of the night to satisfy Kipp's curiosity. As we bumped along, I had cause to wonder if the driver was purposefully hitting every rock and rough spot on the unpaved road. After another jolt caused my fanny to come in sharp and unexpected contact with a broken spring diabolically concealed in the worn seat upon which I sat, I almost called it quits. Peeking into the driver's mind, I discovered no ill intent at the rough passage, just happiness that he had thoroughly taken advantage of us in terms of the price of his labor. From his point of view, this was commerce in full gear. We were fortunate there was a full moon hovering overhead, an enormous, amber ball that shed some light on the somber landscape. An occasional lonely strand of wispy cloud drifted across the orb as if a prankster had taken a piece of gauze fabric and draped it to purposely create a spooky atmosphere. Glancing up, I looked over at Elani, who wagged her tail in response. For a young lupine with little experience, she didn't seem to be put off by much that could be tossed her way. I liked her boldness then and still do. The driver pulled up the horse; the carriage slowed and finally rolled to a creaking stop. Peter stuck his head out the carriage window, since it was obvious the driver didn't plan on dismounting from his box. In fairness, I suppose he was no tour guide and was under no compulsion to assist us in disembarking from his vehicle.

"Over there is where some poor farmer lived before my time," the driver's raspy voice announced. He drew our attention to a tumbled down hovel of rocks; there once had been thatch covering the roof, but most had blown away or rotted with time. "Many folk have claimed to see Shuck wandering about this place."

It became clear that the driver wanted to deposit us in the midst of the empty, dismal countryside, while he returned to the village to sit before the warmth of a crackling fire with a pint in hand. I almost refused but another glimpse into the man's thoughts indicated no deception. He fully planned on returning for us, so I nodded at Peter.

"I'm wearing the new wool undergarments I bought, so I'm okay," I offered.

"And Elani and I brought our fur coats, so we're good to go," Kipp quipped.

I'll admit, although I've seen a lot in my life, the countryside was the epitome of desolation, and if one had planned on writing a novel about haunted hounds, the atmosphere and locale were perfect for inspiration. The land was mostly flat, with a few small bumps that might qualify as tiny hills, but we were at the edge of marshland which was bleak and nondescript. Kipp's nose crinkled in distaste as the smell of stagnant water clung to us like a damp, mildewed blanket. Curious, I wandered into the fallen down house of rock and tried to make out the interior, as best I could, led by the illumination cast by the hovering moon. The odor of decaying thatch that had crumpled into black, moldy lumps on the ground only added to the general funk swirling in the air. The romantic side of my nature was in full force as I speculated about who might have once lived there...and died there. What children were born beneath the thatched roof that once protected them from the wind and rain, and what was their destiny? Such past sentimental musings had led to me acquiring large amounts of useless junk in my house. Suddenly, I wheeled around as an eerie sound broke the silence of the marshland. It was still a little early in the season for insects, frogs and other bog dwelling creatures to be giving voice.

"What on earth was that?" Peter asked as I joined him outside.

I shook my head and resisted the impulse to grab his hand, like a child afraid of boogie men lurking in the dark. Kipp and Elani walked forward a few paces, their huge ears pitched forward like radar dishes trying to catch a signal. A leafless tree towered next to the tumbled down house, its branches looking like the hand of a skeleton outlined against the enormous moon; an owl flew overhead, its wings softly beating the air, the feathers flashing pale against the darkness. Could anything have been timelier, I wondered wryly. Then the sound echoed again, and this time I heard it more clearly. It was obviously the voice of a dog or canine of some type, howling, the sound echoing across the eroded hills and winding through the swampy lowlands.

"Kipp?" I asked, since his abilities were greater than my own.

"Sounds like a dog," he replied, "but I'm not picking up on anything living yet." He turned to look at me, and the amber of his eyes flashed, caught in a soft blur of light. "Could be too far away," he added.

Over the next few minutes, we heard the eerie howl three more times. Each time it seemed closer, louder, more intense. Finally, there was a fourth howl. Looking towards where it seemed the sound originated, I saw the large form of what appeared to be a hound, silhouetted against the descending moon. This time I did grab Peter's hand as he reached for mine. He'd seen it as clearly as the rest of us, despite his being challenged with ghost detection in the past.

The dog–whether made of flesh or a construct of spirit–began to move towards us, its head up; the sound of large paws beating heavily against the sandy loam was clearly audible in the otherwise still countryside. Suddenly, Kipp and Elani shot off, racing towards the animal, which was running towards us, as if they planned on intercepting it. I started to warn them to stay, but if it was a ghost, then what was the harm? It was then I noticed that somehow Peter and I had ended up in an embrace and gently removed myself from his arms. Feeling somewhat silly, I realized I'd been caught up in the Black Shuck lore and was afraid. Peter might not confess to the same but it was there, nonetheless. Kipp was blocking his thoughts, for what reasons I didn't know. Perhaps he was trying to protect me, as he did in Gettysburg?

Peter and I waited, breathless, until a few minutes later when Kipp and Elani trotted back to us, leading a large, black dog that was the size of a Great Dane but obviously some type of mix. He was a goofy, friendly fellow who almost knocked me down with a head butt as he begged for attention. The dog had an awkward lankiness that betrayed his youth as he managed to trail a slobbery slime trail down my sleeve with his large tongue. Most dogs were put off by the lupines, but the giant youngster didn't appear bothered and seemed happy to make some new friends at that lonely abandoned farmstead.

"He's a lemon head," Kipp said, playfully batting at the giant with his paws. "In other words, he's kind of dumb." Glancing at me, Kipp added, "He isn't disturbed by us."

I knew then what had happened. Some villager, hearing of our trip through local gossip, brought Marmaduke out to scare us. It was a great jest! I appreciated a good practical joke, and this one would stick with me a long time. The village, which was a quiet one, needed a good stir, so we'd play along and act suitably terrified when we returned.

Finally, the big brute ambled off, wagging his tail as he drifted away, probably towards home and a bowl of Gravy Train. As we watched him fade into the darkness, I took a seat on a partially collapsed rock wall, ignoring the cold chill of stone that attacked my posterior with a vengeance, as we waited for our hired driver to return.

"So, do we think there is a Black Shuck demon dog out there somewhere?" Peter glanced at Kipp.

"Well, this one trial is insufficient. And I know we have other business that takes priority, and we don't have time to run all over England checking out rumored sightings. I guess it was silly of me to think we'd strike gold on one try." Kipp looked deflated, his ears flat against his skull. I knew he was hoping to make a miraculous contact.

"It was a valid attempt, Kipp," I remarked. Reaching out, I scratched the top of his head and was relieved to see his ears perk up, a barometer of his mood. "It, after all, is not like Gettysburg where everything is concentrated in one area." I laughed softly. "And that was one of the best frights I've had in a while. Just think of what we did to boost the morale of that village. They'll be talking about us for years."

Kipp glanced at me as his tail began to wag. His head turned as we heard the clopping of hooves against the earth...it seemed our driver had returned, somewhat mellowed after having spent hours in a local pub while he waited.

"So, did you see the Devil's hound?" he asked, his gravelly voice made more so by the chill in the air. His worry was genuine; his thoughts told us that he'd not been complicit in the jest.

"Why, yes, we actually did see and hear a large hound running along the countryside," Peter replied, eyes big, voice filled with excitement. "My sister," he said, gesturing at me, "was terrified, so I'm glad you returned when you did," he finished with a grateful nod, pinching the back of my arm to stop me from giggling.

"So you saw old Shuck!" The driver's bleary eyes were suddenly clear, and he glanced about, obviously fearful the hound from hell would show up at any moment. I think his horse made the short trip back to town in record time. If we'd been in a car instead of a carriage, we might have heard the sounds of tires squealing in the turns.

In the end, it was sweet Mrs. Higgins who had arranged the fright, although I only knew that from her mischievous thoughts. In her mind, she felt fully vindicated since she was teaching the youngsters a lesson about believing in such silliness. From her point of view, we needed to be in church listening to the word of God instead of pursuing a thread of superstitious nonsense through the bogs and marshes of Suffolk. She was a prankster at heart, camouflaged in a deceptively soft middle-aged body, who had managed to pull off a magnificent jest to help us grow as human beings—or so she thought us to be. I'm just glad I didn't wet my pants.

CHAPTER 16

K ipp lay quietly, tucked into an unobtrusive ball in a corner of
the seamstress's shop. Both Peter and I had gone for our
fittings, and as the seamstress accidently poked me with a straight pin,
I silently wished that I'd been born a lupine.

"All you have to do is shake your fur out really good, put on the
collar–which I know you despise–and you are ready for high tea," I
grumbled, glaring at Kipp while giving him a telepathic piece of
my mind.

He yawned in response and delicately licked his right forepaw,
pretending there was some fuzz or a flake of dirt to mar the pristine
auburn surface. Yes, he was gloating, no doubt about it. Resting his
head on the floor, he closed his eyes and pretended to sleep, but his
mind was active and in full chat mode.

"I like that color on you, Petra," he remarked. His color vision was
as acute as mine, maybe more so. "You need to choose green
more often."

Looking down, I was pleased with the seamstress's choice, since I'd
given her carte blanche. She thought the color would bring out the
green flecks in my hazel eyes. And she was right.

"The gowns will be ready, Miss Keaton, in time for your departure," the seamstress remarked as she stepped back to gaze at her creation with thinly disguised satisfaction. Her voice was tiny, as was her body. But she was obviously a work horse by nature. True, she had one young girl who was an apprentice; the shop stayed busy with a good reputation in the upper crust districts. With a flourish, she produced a hat from a lovely hat box, which was covered in a tastefully understated floral pattern–and I confess I have a weakness for hat boxes–and displayed the creation of a milliner who partnered with her to produce hats to match gowns.

"At your request, she made a hat that is, well, neutral in color, and should be acceptable with most of your clothes." The seamstress's lips pressed together. "Although I might have preferred more diversity in the choices."

I'd asked for a hat in oyster white that would cover less square footage than the current styles. It had the large, boxy crown that was typical of the day with a short, sassy brim. The designer had wrapped some lace netting in a slightly darker shade of ivory held in place by narrow ribbons—matching the various colors of gowns I'd be wearing—that were woven together. With that one, plus the larger bucket that I'd arrived in as well as the smaller one I'd purchased for traveling comfort, I should be set. After all, I was only looking at a five day span. And in any case, what did I care if the other passengers found me to be out of style and lacking in taste?

We four symbionts had found various ways to keep ourselves busy while waiting, and it was now edging into the last week of March. We only had a few days remaining before we would waylay Tristan and Meko at the train station and begin our finesse of J.P. Morgan. It would work or not, but Tristan had seemed extremely confident, based upon his relationship with the old man.

On that particular day, we'd split up. Peter and Elani wanted to travel to Regent's Park, a place I would avoid since I had past relationships who tended to frequent that area of London. True, I had no idea which members of Harrow's household might still be alive, but it was better safe than sorry. Unfortunately, Kipp and I would stand out too prominently, no matter where we went. The only thing we knew for certain was that Harrow and his nephew, Daniel, were still living in London if recorded history was accurate.

"You know you want to go," Kipp said, shoving his head under my hand as we left the shop and threaded a path along the busy sidewalk. People naturally veered when they saw Kipp ahead, despite his sterling behavior.

"I don't know, Kipp. Part of me does and the other part is afraid." I sighed and nodded as a well dressed man tipped his bowler hat. Canvassing his thoughts, I acknowledged he found me attractive and preened inwardly, just a bit, as I smoothed out a nonexistent wrinkle in my jacket. I'm not exceptionally vain, but like any symbiont, I have my moments.

"Let's do it, Petra. We don't have to tell Peter or Elani or, for that matter, anyone else. This will be a good judge of whether time and distance has softened some of your feelings or not. You could be relieved and able to let go of some of these thoughts that have plagued you." Kipp shoved his shoulder against my thigh, giving me a physical nudge for extra emphasis.

A large wagon rumbled past, pulled by a short team of large draft horses. Looking up, I admired their effortless labor, their cropped tails busy slapping their rumps. The man on the box was smoking a long, curved pipe and the aroma of burning tobacco filled the street. The smell of the horses and old dung that had collected against the curb while awaiting a sweeper took me back over my own four hundred year existence to marvel at the trajectory of humanity over a relatively short time. Although the comforts of contemporary life were many, a part of me missed the sound of wagon wheels striking the ground, along with the creak of harness leather and the weary voice of the driver coaxing his team to get a day's work done.

"Okay," I replied simply. Maybe Kipp was right, and I would benefit to see if my attempt to go home again would fail.

Since there was no need to tarry, I hailed a four wheeler driver who eagerly spied a potential fare in me from a block away. The driver hopped down from his box to give me an assist; I knew he did this not from altruism but in the hopes of a greater tip. I would oblige him, much to his delight. As the gently rocking carriage began to pick its way through the congested streets towards Whitechapel, I noticed familiar landmarks from my previous trip. Odd, that was now some twenty four years in the past, but many things seemed fixed in time, unchanged. While some store fronts and buildings seemed shiny and new, others looked old and used. I began to have misgivings, the farther east we traveled.

"It will be okay, Petra," Kipp said, hopping from his perch on the opposite bench to squeeze in next to me. "This may be hard, but you need to face it."

I sighed in response and let my eyelids drift shut. The tiny breeze from the moving carriage caressed my face; although the weather was cool, it seemed overheated in the small confines of the carriage. The deeper we pushed into the more densely populated areas of London, the greater the general sense of energy and chaos, however controlled, grew. Street vendors abounded, and I recalled, smiling, when during my previous trip I had asked my kind driver, John Parks, to stop and buy a vendor's entire supply of pots and pans. Kipp laughed softly in the back of my mind.

"That was a good day," he agreed, nudging his head up under the crook of my arm. "I wonder what happened to that street vendor and his poor family." Kipp had a gentle nature, a degree of thoughtfulness that was beyond the ordinary.

Scratching the back of his neck, I said, "I think your mama did a good job."

He glanced up at me, his ears swiveling for a moment, before he uttered my often remarked statement, "Ditto."

We finally arrived at Whitechapel Road, and I called out to the driver to slow and stop his carriage a half a block from the building that housed William Harrow's dream of a school for orphaned and wayward lads. The carriage was parked in such a way that I had a good view of the front. I instructed the driver I needed to wait for a while, and that I would pay him well for any missed fares. He seemed content to sit and doze, comfortably, on his box. The horse was happy, too, and after bobbing his head a little, settled down to wait.

"He has built on and made improvements since we were here," Kipp noted. He tilted his head, which hung out of the carriage's window. A young man walked by, his small terrier on a leash. The dog took note of Kipp and started to bark before his voice trembled off into a whimper as he managed to get himself tangled in his master's legs. Dogs, with the exception of the Black Shuck wannabe, were typically wary of the lupines or, at the minimum, pretended a false aloofness that fooled no one.

Over the next hour, people arrived and left from the school, but there was no sight of Harrow or anyone else I might recognize from my 1888 time shift. I'd even hoped to see McNish, Harrow's friend and former war comrade. Of course, he'd married, and there was no telling if he was even in London anymore. As the day stretched on, I became sleepy and felt my head nod, from time to time, only to jerk up with a start every time a heavily loaded lorry would rumble past or the laughter from a child would ring out.

"Petra, wake up," Kipp's urgent voice knocked on the back of my mind, rousing me from some bizarre dream where I was being chased by Black Shuck across a patch of sticky mud that kept sucking at my feet, trying to pull me underground. In the way of dreams, I realized that underground led to a nether world where red eyed demons dwelt. It was terrifying, and I knew I needed to awaken and leave that bad place.

Blinking my eyes, I sat up, my hand massaging my neck which was stretched at an unnatural angle while I dozed. As my eyes focused, I stared at the front door of the school and felt my heart push up into my throat as it became difficult to swallow. On the front steps stood my William Harrow! On his timeline, twenty four years had passed since he'd told me goodbye and watched me leave, wondering if I'd come back to him. Yes, he finally recognized the odd reality that I was a time traveler, but his mind would only allow for some type of means of mechanized travel such as conceived by the agile mind of H.G. Wells. The concept of my being of a different species would have stretched the boundaries of imagination and tolerance too far, I feared. Kipp pushed even closer to me, his head crowding in the window as he sought to get a better view.

"He looks good; maybe his hair has some gray, but other than that, he looks the same," Kipp remarked. "And that has to be Daniel next to him, all grown up now."

Yes, the handsome, dark haired man standing to the left of Harrow had to be his nephew. I recalled the night Harrow and I jointly put Daniel to bed, when he was a young and fearful lad, and as Harrow's eyes met mine, I realized the depth of his growing love for me. I took a deep breath, my trembling fingers becoming lost in Kipp's fur.

As Harrow and Daniel began to walk along the sidewalk, I noticed, fondly, Harrow's slight limp, a relic from his days serving England in the Afghanistan war. He kept his horrors private and didn't share those days, but of course, I knew his thoughts and understood his pain. I suppose one can think of my ability to read his mind as either an unfair advantage or a gift. I chose to think of it as the latter.

"We better move," Kipp said, nudging me out of my stupor. Harrow and Daniel were coming close.

With a soft call to the driver, I asked him to move on; he prodded the horse, and the carriage lurched forward. As we passed Harrow, I pushed back in the carriage as far as I could, turning my head away from the window. From the corner of my eye, I saw his head go up with interest at the passing vehicle. Harrow thought for a minute that he'd seen Kipp but then internally chided himself, knowing it was impossible for a dog to have lived that long. As his thoughts turned towards his memories of me, I was startled when Kipp threw up a mental block so that I could not access Harrow's mind.

"You don't need to go there," Kipp said firmly. "It was enough to see him and register how you feel at this point in time." He put his head in my lap and waited.

It took me a while to answer. "I feel just as I did the day I left him. It took all my control to not jump out of the carriage and run to him. I would leave everything and everyone, except for you, behind and stay here to live with a human, until the end of his days." I didn't realize, until Kipp's fur became wet, that I was crying as I blurted out my feelings.

I was glad that it took some time to make our way back to The Dovecote since I needed to compose myself and let my puffy, red eyes recover to an extent. The traffic on the streets was thick, and the carriage was forced to stop several times to accommodate over-crowded trams as well as horse drawn drays and the occasional gas propelled passenger car. I made certain my driver was happy with the abundant tip I gave him for wasting much of his day and losing other potential fares.

"How did you two spend your day?" Peter asked. He and Elani were in their room, which was similar to ours except for the festive wallpaper and a worn stuffed chair covered in a faded toile pattern. We'd joined them so Peter could show off some of his new wardrobe. He'd also purchased a couple of trunks to carry our stuff and opened mine to show me all the compartments as well as the cloth lining. He carefully chose a cheerful coral shade for the lining of mine, thinking I'd like it. I did and it was thoughtful of him, which I acknowledged as his cheeks flushed.

"We just messed around," Kipp replied, answering before I could. We'd jointly decided to keep our side excursion private.

"Are you okay, Petra?" Elani asked. Her pretty face tilted up towards me with concern. "You seem weary."

"I think I am just a little tired. Kipp and I walked too much today," I lied, blocking my other thoughts of distress from her, even though I knew she was too well civilized to pry beneath the surface.

"You know, I wish now that we'd spent another couple of days in Blythburgh," Kipp said. He stretched on his back in a patch of sunlight that cast a dappled pattern on the large rug occupying the majority of the floor; he craned his head to stare at me, his jowls hanging loosely from the angle of the position. It was not his best look, but I didn't have the heart to tell him so. "I'm not certain the Black Shuck legend is all local folklore and would have liked to determine for myself if such a creature exists."

"There was no way to continue that experiment, since the locals decided to have some fun at our expense," Peter remarked. "I have to admit, when you and Elani showed up with that big dog, I almost had a heart attack."

If there was one thing I liked about Peter, it was his honesty. Many would not confess to having been duped to such a great degree and still find it humorous. But, it had been a great gag, all things considered. And Mrs. Higgins was understandably proud of her instrumental role and would no doubt repeat the story over and over for many years, how she played a magnificent joke on the naive Americans.

The boy who had been seeing to our needs arrived, bringing dinner. The savory smell of steak filled the room, and I thought Kipp was going to yank the piece of meat out of the boy's hand. I was pleased to see some peas and carrots nestled up to tiny roasted potatoes on my plate; I'd not eaten since the previous evening and was hungry. Although the day had started bright, with a cheerful sun hanging lazily overhead, the sky had become congested with dark, water filled clouds that rushed in, crowding the far horizon. A distant rumble of thunder caused a porcelain plate resting on a table top to tremble and rattle against the wood surface. As we ate, I decided to outline our plan of action.

"We have been going pretty fast and furious for several weeks now. Since we're about to move into high gear once we get on board the *Titanic*, I think we need to go into hibernation mode for a few days. We are supposed to meet Tristan and Meko on April 8th, and today is April 5th. So, let's jointly agree to chill out until that time." I could have just done that for myself, but as the elder knew it fell to me to rein in the youngsters who knew no boundaries to their energy and capabilities.

My species has a very slow metabolism that helps us survive times of starvation as well as other stressors. We also can put ourselves into a voluntary state of hibernation where we sleep for long periods, require no food and lapse in and out of somnolence. It is a good way to regenerate, especially following a time shift, since the very act of time travel wreaks havoc on our bodies as well as our minds. I was mildly surprised when Peter agreed with my plan and excused himself to speak to the desk manager to ask we not be disturbed.

As the rain began to fall, Kipp and I retired to our room. Moving to the window, I pulled the heavy brocade drapes closed and began to remove my traveling skirt and blouse. Hanging them carefully, I inspected the fabric and saw no sign of obvious soiling and figured they could air out for a couple of days. That left me in my chemise which was comfortable for sleeping. Unwinding my hair from the braid that had been secured to the crown of my head with a thousand hair pins, I ran a brush through the dark mass, enjoying the feel of the bristles as they scraped against my scalp. Kipp watched with a critical eye, his head tilted to one side.

"I'm sorry I suggested you see Harrow. I pushed you too much." His face wore a contrite expression.

"It's okay, Kipp. I did need to see him, I think. And after we hibernate, I'll feel strong again." I turned towards him, putting the brush down on the vanity dresser. "We've had a lot of traveling and the stress on us–me–has built." I smiled wanly. "Actually, I was glad to see him. It was exciting and made me happy as well as despairing, all at once." I climbed into bed, pulling the covers up to my chin, enjoying the snug, safe feeling that must have originated in childhood as my mother tucked me in for the night. Kipp hopped up, circled and lay next to me, his heavy warmth like a security blanket. "Love is often like that, you know."

He rested his jaw on my breast bone and sighed deeply. I recall he fell asleep before I did, his breathing deep and even. As I lay in the dark room, the sound of rain outside helped me to finally drift off to the land of nod. It would be a long time before I awoke again.

CHAPTER 17

The chaos in Paddington Station was predictable. Early trains were arriving from the countryside depositing people coming to the city for reasons of business or pleasure; men in conservative business attire were just as busy departing to parts unknown. We hadn't bothered to get specifics about Tristan Taylor's arrival, only that he should disembark at approximately 8:30 in the morning. We were telepaths, and he and Meko would conveniently ping on our symbiont radar, so there was no question that we could find them.

"Beg pardon," Peter murmured to a very large man who rudely and unnecessarily almost elbowed him out of the way. Elani growled involuntarily, deep in the back of her throat. The large man, hearing the sound, turned with a startled expression on his face. Seeing Elani's fixed gaze, he tipped his hat, which seemed undersized in consideration of his massive head, in manner of an excuse and hurried away. Kipp couldn't help himself and giggled over the exchange.

"You go, girl," he said to a beaming Elani, who wagged her tail, pleased, as always, to gain a nugget of approval from Kipp.

"Kipp, you simply have to let go of the current slang," I playfully chided him, while gently tugging on his left ear.

"But it just gets to the point so nicely," he whined.

Vendors were hawking their goods, hoping to snag easy sales of food and other traveling paraphernalia. A teenage girl caught my eye and smiled beguilingly. Just because I couldn't resist her compelling glance, I walked over to see what she had for sale or trade. Kipp trailed after me, his head swiveling as he noted the latest train to arrive, as the station continued to fill with noise and steam.

"Here's a lovely little something, Miss," the girl said, holding out a tiny purse that was completely impractical unless one was only carrying a lipstick and a scrap of a handkerchief. The bag was a lovely example of petit point with little flowers and birds mingling in the midst of a blooming garden. The work was skillful and told of a patient heart and steady hand. I couldn't stop myself and held out the coin—and a little extra—as I tucked the bag under my arm.

"You are such a soft touch," Kipp commented, staring up at me. "But it is pretty," he conceded grudgingly.

"I'm glad you like it since I bought it for you to carry," I quipped in response.

A second later, his head snapped around, as did Elani's. The lupines were just a second faster than Peter and I...a symbiont duo was in the station! It was not long before we spied the tall, slender figure of Tristan Taylor with Meko at his side. They, in return, could feel our presence and stopped a short distance away, their eyes meeting ours in confusion across the crowded station, as people pushed past us to be on their way. Automatically, Tristan reached up to remove his felt bowler, a gesture of courtesy that Peter mimicked.

"Do we know you?" Tristan asked, referring to him and Meko as a joined entity.

"Yes, you do," Peter responded. Lowering his voice, he added, "We met you in the future and traveled back to specifically intercept you in this place and time. I have a letter," he added, pulling it from an inner jacket pocket.

The four of us let down our guards enough so that they could see we had no ill intent. With a puzzled look on his face, Tristan followed us out of the station, walking until we came to a small city park, where a few large trees loomed over a scattering of benches made of rough cut oak. I privately surmised that more than one fanny had left those benches impaled with wooden splinters. Meko fell into step next to Kipp, sizing him up as the more dominant of the two lupines. The two touched noses for a second before trotting to catch up.

Tristan adjusted his glasses on the bridge of his nose. It was interesting to note than in over one hundred years, nothing much had changed except he would eventually have a few more wrinkles and some authentic gray hair. Meko was jet black, his pale gray eyes peering out from the dark mask of his face. As Tristan read the letter he'd written to himself, his face tightened; his jaw began to work as he realized we already knew of his plans to change the timeline of history to save J.P. Morgan. A slight flush began at his neck and traveled upwards to his face. He finally put the letter on the bench, placing his hand over it to keep it from taking flight in the cool breeze that curved through the little park. A couple of working class women bustled past, their hands anchoring their hats, giggling at some private conversation.

"So, you already know my plans and have no wish to stop me?" Tristan asked. "That would, after all, be the ethical thing to do." His voice sounded slightly sarcastic in tone.

"We aren't here to judge you," I replied. "We just want you to help us get on board the *Titanic* so we can go about our investigation."

"Maybe you should judge me," Tristan said, tilting his head slightly, a slight challenge to his tone. "Meko has been trying to talk me out of my rash action, but I don't listen to him. He thinks I'm selfish, and he's correct." He removed his glasses and held them in his hand, his brown eyes unveiled and unguarded. After a moment, he polished the lenses on the corner of his jacket and carefully replaced them, centering them on the bridge of his nose.

"Would you listen to us if we tried?" Kipp asked, his voice a whisper in the back of our minds.

Tristan sighed deeply and looked up, closing his eyes for a minute against the flush of soft early morning light. "No, I suspect I wouldn't. I am compelled to do this thing that violates our code. And, yes, I can help you with J.P. Morgan," he added, his voice becoming brisk as he shook off his emotions. Fumbling slightly, he reached for the pocket watch attached by a golden chain that stretched across his dark woolen vest. Tristan was nicely attired but not in the fashion of a wealthy human male. He passed for middle class in Edwardian society.

"We've been traveling while waiting for this day, visiting the coast of Cornwall." He blindly stared out at the street, not seeing the teeming rush of people who passed, busy to be about their day. "It's rugged, somewhat bleak along that coastline where the Atlantic Ocean breaks against the rocks and sand. It seems everything there is gray...the sea, the rocks, even the sky. He smiled, looking down at Meko, who wagged his tail. "Meko wanted to visit Tintagel, and we traveled there, too."

"I always wanted to time shift to Tintagel at its peak of activity, but I didn't get that assignment," I remarked with a sigh. "And no one would even approve it as a vacation spot due to the fragility of that time and the worry we might change the arc of history." Even as I said the words, I regretted them. Tristan's face darkened in response, but he quickly rallied, clearing his throat.

"I am scheduled to visit J.P. today," he said. "My task, at which I will succeed, is to convince him to not travel on the *Titanic*. I will mention that I'm entertaining my nephew and niece in London and will allow him to ask to meet you two, which he will. I'll be vague, just mentioning a sister from whom I was alienated. He will be naturally curious, and I will tell him that I never spoke of my family due to the painful nature of the parting. It will be up to you to figure out a sympathetic story." He stood, indicating our time together was over. We arranged for him to meet us at our hotel the next day, April 9th. That would only give us less than one day to prepare to board the *Titanic*, if all went well.

My excitement grew so that I was unable to sleep that night but then neither could Kipp. We lay together in the bed, his chin resting upon my chest, waiting until daylight began to glimmer behind the thickness of the floor length curtains in the room. The hotel lad who catered to our whims brought a light breakfast, and after we finished our meal, we were simply waiting when a card was delivered to Peter —Tristan Taylor was waiting for us in the lobby downstairs. I would like to recall that his eyes lit up at our arrival, but he merely looked tired and somewhat resigned. Meko, however, was courteous to Kipp and Elani. I noticed that Tristan and Meko had assumed their aging disguises for their meeting with Morgan. Tristan's hair was highlighted with touches of gray from powder applied at strategic locations; he acquired a slight limp as he handled a walking stick. He'd obviously treated Meko with some of the same powder as the lupine's muzzle was now almost white. Walking outside, we found Tristan hired a larger carriage that could accommodate three humanoids and our large traveling companions.

"J.P. is most curious to meet you," Tristan remarked, his voice flat and toneless, as he stared out the window at the passing scenery. We were headed towards Cavendish Square which was on the northeast boundary of Mayfair. Although the atmosphere in London was generally thick with smoke and humidity, on that morning the air felt fresh and cool; the usual odors drifting from the Thames and the distant tanneries that were situated in the east end of London were minimal at that. A flock of crows flew overhead headed inland, their voices loud and echoing along the street. "I told him I'd let you share your story." Turning to glance at me, his face reddened slightly as he dropped his gaze.

"He's embarrassed over the fact we all know of his violation of ethics," Kipp murmured in the back of my mind. I reached out and pulled Kipp close as I recalled having been so unkind to him when he tried to broker a healing moment between Tristan and Meko. Kipp licked my face in response...no words were needed, no grudges held.

Instead of my traveling outfit, I'd chosen a dress more suitable for an afternoon tea visit, or at least I hoped it was suitable. My time living in the future had spoiled me, and I'd conveniently forgotten some of the etiquette of the day. If the truth were told, I really didn't care too much about such things any more. Having lived through it once in real time was enough. Peter was nattily attired in a blue blazer that was in style and all the rage among young gentlemen.

"So what's Morgan like?" Kipp asked, glancing at Tristan and Meko.

Meko, who typically chose to say little, answered. "He is an interesting combination of generosity, ruthlessness, good humor and serious, single-mindedness all rolled into one." He smiled, his jaw dropping open in a pant. "He latched on to Tristan in college, and once he's your friend, he is steadfast forever as long as you're genuine with him" he added.

"J.P. is no fool and realizes many people gravitate towards him due to his enormous wealth. He often feels used and has trouble trusting people in general," Tristan remarked.

"And he trusts you when you are not a "people"," Elani commented.

"Ironic, isn't it?" Tristan raised his dark eyebrows before resuming his watchful stare from the window of the carriage.

As we rolled along, I realized I missed the earthy, fundamental, busy part of town that made up Whitechapel and Spittlefields. The area of Mayfair through which we traveled was well manicured, controlled and devoid of the tangled bustle of transit and trade that defined other areas of London. We passed a street that I knew led, eventually, to Harrow's neighborhood. Involuntarily, I sighed; Kipp pushed closer, if that were possible.

We rocked to a halt in front of a large, white townhouse that was bordered on either side by equally impressive homes. There was a tasteful garden out front with only scattered patches of color due to the early season. A wrought iron fence encircled the garden with an ornate gate spanning a carefully rocked pathway leading to the front of the house. There was little porch to speak of, and by the time we got to the door, it swung back to reveal a well dressed butler who bowed neatly from his trim waist.

"Mr. Taylor, so good to see you again," the man said, beaming.

"And you, Headley," Tristan replied.

"What, no Jeeves?" Kipp asked me, twisting his head to look up at me with that innocent look I knew too well.

"Can it, Kipp," I hissed.

As Headley secured the men's hats, Tristan took the lead in a familiar way and led us along a polished floor to a sitting room that was just off the main hallway in the front of the house.

"J.P.!" he called out, swinging back the door.

"Tristan!"

I was struck by J.P. Morgan who was a paradox; his sense of confidence and powerfulness was tempered by a natural reticence that he'd learned to master. Here was a man, one of the wealthiest in the world, who had made his fortune in ways that sometimes destroyed others... but he would have been just as happy to have worked in a mercantile store selling canned peaches. He had become this man as result of many forces. I found it endearing that he was self conscious of his large nose. Morgan stepped forward to shake Peter's hand before reaching out to take mine between the two of his and gently pressing against my flesh. As he bent forward over my hand, I caught a whiff of his cologne, which had the subtle fragrance of woodlands and grassy fields baking under a warm sun. I noticed his finger nails were neatly trimmed and buffed to a subtle shine. With a little flourish, he motioned us to be seated as Headley saw to tea.

"I see the love of dogs extends to all members of your family," Morgan said, smiling. He had a pair of very intense eyes set beneath heavy brows that were dark, even though his hair was flecked with gray and white. I could only imagine what it would be like to be on the other side of that gaze when he was percolating with anger.

"Oh yes, sir," Peter replied. "Our mother told us that she and Uncle Tristan grew up in a house filled with all sorts of dogs." He paused to gravely introduce Elani and Kipp, who dutifully wagged their tails.

"We've been through several generations of Meko dogs," Morgan said, laughing. "Tristan keeps getting a puppy of the previous Meko, and so we move on towards the future with our trio happily intact." Morgan leaned forward, smiling at me. "I know you, young lady, will tell me the family secrets that Tristan guards like a vault of gold."

I was grateful Headley arrived at that moment, pushing a mahogany cart carrying an ornate tea service of the most exclusive china decorated with gold leaf.

"My dear, would it be an imposition to ask you to pour?" Morgan asked, a smile tugging at his mouth. Yes, he was being an old chauvinist, but I had to remember the times and not act put out or irritated. For a moment, I tried to pretend I was at home with Fitzhugh who managed all things associated with tea with understated elegance. The serving of tea was definitely a weak spot in my repertoire. With Kipp silently prodding me in the back of my head, I managed to fill all the cups and balance them nicely on the saucers without tripping and spilling the hot brew in Morgan's lap. Kipp, my ever faithful cheerleader, applauded my success.

"Well, Mr. Morgan, my mother was terribly fond of Uncle Tristan," I began, having rehearsed the story in my head. "But my uncle's disapproval of her marriage to my father caused a terrible rift, and they never spoke again after that." I looked at Tristan, my lips trembling slightly. "I can only imagine the terrible heartache given how close they'd been."

Tristan glanced at me and purposely took a sip of tea to delay as he considered his remarks. As with all our kind, he could fabricate on the fly, and in a moment he was up and running. "Yes, J.P., it was one of those things that gets blown up out of proportion and then people say things they can't take back. I never spoke to her again and had no contact until I was notified that she and her husband had died in an accident." He shook his head. "Pride is a terrible flaw."

Surreptitiously, I glanced around the room. It was decorated in excellent taste, with just the right amount of art work and decorative touches combined with furniture upholstered in bright, cleverly textured fabrics. I wondered how much of the planning and execution had been done by Morgan, or did he just hire a professional? My guess was the latter. On the far wall, a large fireplace stood dormant; the mantle featured ornate carvings of hunting dogs chasing nonexistent prey over the rolling countryside. On the top of the mantle, a large clock ticked, the sound unexpectedly loud in the room which had fallen quiet after Tristan's painful, fabricated admission.

"But we must try and move past all that now, Uncle, most certainly," Peter chimed in, his voice cheerful. "I know Mother never stopped loving you, and she would be glad we're here and can be family again." Peter's earnest attitude combined with his big brown eyes contributed to his ability to lie with a shockingly convincing ease. He was better at that than was I…and I was no slouch.

Morgan reached for the tea caddy and retrieved a little frosted cake which he nibbled, trying in vain to keep the icing from clinging to his heavy mustache. He was quiet, thoughtful, as Tristan appeared to gather his thoughts.

"I was telling J.P. that the two of you are eager to return home after touring the continent," he was saying. Obviously, he'd made some tasteful reference to our having inherited some funds upon the death of our parents. We were making our way as middle class, as was he. Turning towards Morgan, Tristan assumed an earnest expression. "J.P., what will be the best way to ensure they can travel and keep their dogs close by?" He smiled. "You know how we are!"

"Yes, we managed on the trip over since we had more funds available and snagged a first class passage on one of the Cunard ships." Peter shook his head. "Believe me when I tell you that was a terrible mistake, and I wish I'd chosen White Star which is known for comfort and passenger satisfaction."

I had nothing to contribute and was pleased with Peter's command of the situation. Yes, his little poke at Cunard helped fuel the fire.

Morgan grinned, enjoying hearing that Cunard, his fierce competitor, had failed to please; he leaned forward, slapping his knee. "Come here, boy," he coaxed to Kipp, who played the role of dog and approached the old man, his tongue hanging out in lopsided smile. As Morgan thumped Kipp's sides vigorously, Kipp turned his head to stare at me. With little effort, he rolled his eyes and managed to cross them as I bit back a laugh. "I've never seen more interesting color on a dog!" Morgan exclaimed. "Puts me in mind of an Irish Setter I once had...stupid dog but a great personality." He offered Kipp a broken off piece of cookie after ensuring Kipp would sit first.

"What am I?" Kipp grumbled as he returned to my side. "A trained seal?"

"Just remember, sweetums, you don't have to dress up and wear big, stupid hats," I reminded him as he dropped down to curl up on the floor next to my feet.

"Well, if you two are anything like your uncle," Morgan said, addressing Peter and me, "you are dog fanatics." He stared up at the ceiling, frowning as he gathered a memory. "I recall we got into quite a bit of trouble once because Meko just had to go with us into an exclusive club. That little escapade cost me some money," he concluded, smiling.

"It's rather urgent we get home to take care of some business," Peter said, hoping his words would prompt the old man.

"You guys seem to forget, I can plant the thought in his head and take care of all this waiting," Kipp reminded us, his jaw resting comfortably on front paws.

"Let's avoid that, Kipp, unless needed." I chimed in to the telepathic dialog that was floating in the room. If I didn't reign in Kipp and Peter from time to time, chaos would ensue. Elani caught my mood and winked at me in agreement.

"I just cancelled my passage on the *Titanic*," Morgan was saying. "I heard another man wanted the rooms, but he had to cancel, too, due to family illness. So they are free at the moment." He paused before adding, "I know Ismay thinks he can use them, but it will do him good to drop down a notch or two and take lesser accommodations." His brows drew together as he remarked upon the latter, his bottom lip jutted out in what might have been thought of as a pout, and I saw the part of him that could be manipulative and unpleasant. For all his joviality with us as we enjoyed his hospitality over tea and little sugar dusted teacakes, he could be a harsh man.

"So, let me send a telegram and tell them I have friends who will need my parlor suite," he was saying. "They are the best accommodations on the *Titanic*."

"J.P., do you see any issue with the dogs?" Tristan asked. His face wore the expression of a total innocent.

"Not if I instruct the captain and crew that I would consider it a personal favor if certain liberties are allowed," Morgan replied. "Of course, I know you won't abuse those privileges, since the dogs can't go into the formal dining room." He laughed again. "Well, they could, but it would be pretty disruptive, and that could only happen if I were there to enjoy the moment."

"Oh, no, sir," Peter was saying, his eyes huge. "We would never take advantage of your good nature and generosity."

Of course we would, and given the ultimate destiny of the *Titanic*, who would worry about a couple of big dogs that had been given a little too much freedom.

CHAPTER 18

The boat train sped towards Southampton, its path taking us past congested, inhabited areas where the sky above was blackened with the smoke from coal fires, as well as rural villages where tired fields lay fallow next to others carpeted in pale, new grass. I could only imagine, when the grass grew high, the rippling waves of color like an ocean of green as the wind stroked the hillsides. We were offered refreshment by the porter, but both Peter and I were too nervous to eat. I did, however, sip on a cup of black coffee that was full of caffeine and hit my brain like a hammer. Kipp and Elani watched the passing scenery that varied from dark brick row houses to timber and thatch dwellings scattered along the gently rolling Surrey countryside. Kipp, as always, was curious but relaxed; his natural self confidence did much to soothe Elani, who had the mild anxiety expected of a youngster. After all, we were doing something that none of our kind had attempted. I confess I felt a touch of anxiety myself, despite my years of experience engaged in the unpredictable and downright dangerous business of traveling.

"The moors," Kipp was saying, "always make me think of Sherlock Holmes and *The Hound of the Baskervilles.*" He sighed. "I realize they're just another land feature, but there is something inherently mysterious about them." Kipp almost seemed moody, an unusual state for him, as he gazed out the window at the desolate, barren expanse where early morning mist rose from the ground to cover the concave valley with a shimmering gray haze that would be burned away as the sun climbed higher in the heavens.

We were passing through the area of Surrey where darkened moors stretched into the distance until they were lost from sight on the far horizon. A harsh winter had paled the deep bronze color of clumps of bracken nestled beneath the curve of a hilltop. It required little effort to imagine the swath of heather that would overtake the land later in the season, turning the ground into a soft carpet of purple. From our vantage point, the land looked bleak and sparsely inhabited, with occasional isolated homesteads punctuating the land-scape; a road twisted, going nowhere, resembling a fresh scar upon the land. Gazing at a far hillside, I saw a thin, wavering line of blue smoke trailing upwards from the chimney of a lonely steading. Some family was living in that small dwelling made of stone, timber and thatch. I wondered how they made do with no farmable land. A cloud must have passed between the sun and earth, because a black shadow chased up that bleak hillside until it was lost from view. As we left the country and passed Winchester, I realized we were close to our desti-nation. Shortly thereafter, we coasted into Southampton and eased to a stop at the train platform specially built on the White Star Line's ocean dock. We couldn't see her yet, but I knew the *Titanic* waited for us, tethered to that dock; for a moment, I held my breath, not real-izing I was doing so. The boat train stopped so gently, that I barely felt the tiny jerk as the compartment shuddered to a halt. A moment later, a porter opened the outside door to our compartment and, with a grand flourish, indicated the direction we should go. Our trunks were already being sent to our suite, he assured us. I guess there was some-thing to be said for being a personal guest of J.P. Morgan.

"How do I look?" Peter asked, his brown eyes grave, his face wearing a much too serious expression.

Reaching up, I straightened his tie. "Perfect," I responded. With a slight adjustment to my smaller traveling hat which I'd worn for comfort on the train, I leaned down to clip a leather lead to Kipp's collar, ignoring his bared teeth. "Chill out, bud," I whispered. "It's something I must do. Why don't you act like Elani?" I asked, gesturing to her as she preened and pranced as Peter hitched the leash to her collar.

"Whatever," Kipp replied. He took a sharp breath before intoning, "There she is!"

Turning my head, I could see the *Titanic*; I felt my pulse quicken. She lay quietly next to the ocean dock, purring as if she were asleep. It seemed almost impossible something of that size, made of metal, could bob so lightly in the dark river water of the Test. The four gold smokestacks towered upward...it seemed surreal, almost as if some hopeful street artist had painted them against a glazed background of azure blue. As people pushed past us, I recognized some elite faces from pictures we'd studied in preparation for the trip. Since Peter and I were unknown to society, we were ignored except for the attention drawn to us by the two huge lupines who walked politely at our sides. The confusion and noise was disconcerting for telepaths, with so many minds roiling with excitement and anxiety. Instinctively, our mental blocks involuntarily popped up in defense. We finally arrived at the gangway that led to D Deck where the Reception Room was located. A young, fresh faced steward started to object to our bringing the lupines, suggesting instead that he promptly take them to the kennels.

"Oh, Mr. Morgan said they could stay with us," I remarked, my face innocent, eyebrows lifted in mock consternation. "We will need to discuss this with the purser," I added, smiling at the man.

"No need for that, ma'am," the fellow replied, his face turning red. Yes, he'd gotten the memo from J.P. Morgan, who'd been good to his promise. The lupines had been cleared from one word from the big man at the top of the food chain. In the past, I'd been forced to fight for such accommodations for my lupine partner—previously Tula, now Kipp—and, for once, it was nice to have the skids greased.

We joined the other first class passengers who trailed up the gang-way, waiting our turn. As fellow voyagers who recognized one another from their place in society began to chat excitedly about the upcoming trip on the most exclusive ship in the world, Peter and I melted into the scenery, only subjected to curious glances since we were strangers and our clothing was not as fine, hinting at our more conservative roots.

"If we were in steerage, we would have been engaged in some friendly chit chat by now, I think," Peter remarked. "Elite society is remarkably insular, isn't it?"

"Try being a dog," Kipp replied drily.

I peeked over the railing of the gangway, looking down at the gray river water which seemed so far below, before glancing up to stare at the ship which loomed overhead. The closer I drew to the actual ship, the more I was struck by her size and the beauty of her lines. I could imagine the pride on the face of her creators as she was first launched to land gently in the water as she tried out her sea legs.

The Reception Room, which led to the First Class Dining Room, was part of a large "U" shaped hallway that opened off the landing where the Grand Stairway wound its way through several levels of the ship. The gleaming walls were white paneled, with arched leaded paned windows that allowed diffuse, gentle lighting into the room. White wicker chairs were positioned strategically around small tables, the entire presentation understated and tastefully elegant. We waited patiently until our turn to meet Hugh McElroy, the purser, who was in charge of registering the upper crust. I knew that history described him as the epitome of discretion, a necessary quality since he dealt with the world's most famous people. He was tall, nice looking, with an open, charismatic face. Yes, I could see why he invited the sharing of secrets.

"I am Peter Keaton," Peter began. Almost immediately, McElroy's face changed, but not in a bad way. He'd appeared curious, since we were unknown to him, but upon hearing Peter's name, he immediately became very effusive in his greeting.

"Oh, yes, Mr. Keaton. You and your sister are the special guests of Mr. Morgan," he purred. "On behalf of the White Star Line, let me welcome you aboard the *Titanic.*"

Kipp looked up at me, smiling, as his jaw dropped open. "This is gonna be sweet."

"Well, not really, Kipp, when you consider the outcome. But, yes, up until the end, it will be fascinating, and we will be well treated." I had to bring him down a notch.

A short distance behind us, the line had thinned, and I saw Kipp twist his head to look towards the entrance. Following his gaze, I saw a short man hesitate as he crossed the threshold. I almost gave a start, since the resemblance was so shocking. It was clear I was staring at Anthony Littleton! All of the information that led to this moment was true, and a man named Anthony Littleton, who was obviously the father of Nicholas Little–if genetics had anything to do with physical similarities–had just entered the Reception Room. I noticed he kept his head down, avoiding contact with the other passengers, who were chirping happily like a busy flock of birds. Yes, he'd be left alone, just as were we, unless he sought the comfort and social exchanges with his fellow passengers. But he wouldn't, given his dark thoughts and terrifying purpose. Kipp stared intently at the man, who was slightly built, with narrow shoulders across which his suit jacket fit poorly; he'd removed his hat which he kept turning in his hands, holding it by the brim.

"It doesn't take a telepath to see he's anxious," Kipp observed. "He doesn't worry so much about dying in an accident as he is about failing in what he thinks is his mission." Kipp's eyes closed as he lifted his head and focused to dig deeper. "He misses his wife and for a moment wondered what it would have been like to have her here with him, enjoying the loveliness of the ship. His hopelessness and grief is almost overwhelming." Kipp's ears flattened for a moment.

"It makes you wonder if he, at his core, wants to damage the ship due to his anarchistic leanings or because he is terribly depressed. Is this an act of self-annihilation?" I glanced at Littleton again, curious about the man.

Littleton looked up at that moment and must have caught my stare, because he turned away, ducking his head even lower on his chest, if that were possible. I linked my arm within Peter's and tried to act as if everything McElroy was saying was the most important in the world, while listening in on the thoughts of Littleton.

McElroy brought us back to the present as he introduced the steward who would be assigned to our suite. Charles was his name, a cheerful lad who appeared to be in his mid twenties; his cheeks shone with a natural ruddiness that deepened as he was introduced. His face was clean shaven and glowing on top of the pristine white tunic he wore. The top button seemed a little too snugly fastened for comfort and one could only hope his head wouldn't pop off. Between the obviously uncomfortable tunic button and his rosy cheeks, I immediately liked him.

"Did he make it?" Elani asked before I brusquely shook off her question.

"We won't do that, Elani," I said curtly, my voice harsh in her mind. "We simply can't look at all these people and worry about what will happen to them in the end." Reaching down, I tousled the hair on top of her head, my finger tips tunneling through the fur to find the funny, now familiar, point on her noggin. "We just can't, sweetheart, and keep our sanity." No one contested my setting down the rules, since they knew I was correct. If there ever was a mission to steel one's heart, this was it.

Although there were elevators, I wanted to experience the Grand Staircase, having seen photos of the one on the *Olympic*, *Titanic's* sister ship. There was no photograph of the one on the *Titanic*, but the two were said to be identical. As we ascended, I ran my hand lightly along the surface of the smooth oak paneling at the landings and paused to examine the ornate wrought iron scrollwork along the banisters. Tipping my head back, I could see, far above on A Deck, the huge skylight that allowed the sun to fall through the levels of the ship to illuminate the Reception Room below on D Deck. I didn't realize I was smiling until I noticed Kipp's curious gaze.

"What?" I asked, innocently.

"The expression on your face," he replied. "You're looking at something you never dreamt you'd see, and the beauty is capturing you." Kipp searched for an analogy. "Maybe like a little girl who gets the bicycle she'd hoped for at Christmas...and it's grander and more beautiful than she imagined."

I laughed softly at his comparison. There hadn't been bikes when I was a child, and the *Titanic* was just a wee bit more spectacular than any bicycle, but it was a pleasant thought, nonetheless.

Charles halted our ascent on B Deck and led us the short distance to the parlor suite—B 52, 54 and 56—which we knew was the most exclusive on the *Titanic*. Bruce Ismay, who jumped on the accommodations when Morgan defected, was relegated to another unused cabin somewhere else on the ship. With a little flourish, Charles opened the door and stood aside, beaming, as he waited to observe our reaction. As we walked into the sitting room, I think I was most struck by the ornate, gold finished fireplace that was surrounded by a carved mantle; on top of the mantle was a clock as well as two vases of fresh cut flowers. The fragrance of roses filled the room, which was paneled in dark mahogany wood that looked as if it had been freshly polished. Across the room, large windows were attractively framed by tasteful curtains, which had been pulled back to afford one a view of the private promenade deck. The door to the deck was open, and a gentle breeze wove through the sitting room as I felt the hair curling at the nape of my neck stir. I could smell the river water as well as coal fired smoke improbably mixed with a pleasant food fragrance drifting up from the galley. Kipp looked up at me, his tail wagging; he was clearly fascinated. All of us had read and studied extensively, and this moment almost felt like we'd lived it before...déjà vu for time travelers. The gimbal lamps, table fan, as well as the beautiful fireplace were just as described in the various literatures.

As Peter and Elani followed Charles down the passage that led past the bathroom, a small servant's room and the two bedrooms, Kipp and I stepped out onto the fifty foot long private promenade. Kipp playfully trotted back and forth a few times, panting in an exaggerated manner as he did so.

"Good place to exercise," he remarked. "I don't want to get too soft with all the fine living and good food," he huffed. "Gotta stay buff," Kipp added, holding his head a little higher.

"Baby, you were born buff," I replied, smiling at his silliness.

The promenade was decorated in mock Tudor style with white panels segmented by dark, half timbering. White wicker chairs gathered around a table where one could enjoy afternoon tea, I figured. Large potted palm plants swayed gently in concert with the air currents that streamed through the row of windows. Walking to one aperture, I peered out to view the dock, which was teeming with people. The noise and chaos was significant, and I was grateful I was a telepath and not forced to shout to make myself heard.

Peter returned, wearing a big, happy grin on his face. The atmosphere of excitement was definitely infectious. "Petra, the last room must be yours," he said. "There's a canopy bed with velvet curtains draping over the frame. The bed coverlet is made of the most amazing deep red brocade fabric, very rich and simply decadent. The wall paneling extends to the wainscoting, which has been hand carved." He paused to take a breath, his face flushed. "I've never seen anything this beautiful."

I knew he was being generous and giving me the more magnificent room. I would have been happy in the servant's room, which was nicer than most places I'd visited in my lifetime. It really mattered not, but I let him make the gesture so that he'd feel he'd given up something nice for me.

Before Charles left, he tilted his head in a conspiratorial way and admitted that the crew had been told to extend every courtesy to us as well as our four legged traveling companions. "You can count on me," he advised. We knew we could but had decided we wouldn't overtly push the envelope, such as showing up with the lupines in the formal dining room on D Deck. Even with the lupines brushed and a pretty bow tied around Elani's neck, their appearance would be beyond the pale. But Peter would definitely visit the men's smoking lounge with an elegant Elani at his side. And I wasn't sure for myself yet but would only go where Kipp could follow.

Unfortunately, the bathroom issue reared its ugly head again. Charles offered to take the lupines to the poop deck as needed for their daily constitutionals. Peter deftly handled that delicate moment by telling him he'd manage to their needs. He did, however, discretely ask for some newspapers and also that Charles dig up a couple of water bowls. The little we'd eat, we planned to do so in our room.

"I figured, guys," Peter said, addressing the lupines, "that we will all use the same bathroom. We'll just put down some paper, and I will go in and take care of it later. And I promise not to tell," he added, crossing his heart symbolically with the forefinger of his right hand.

Kipp was still grumbling until Elani coaxed him out of his mood by engaging him in a game of chase, galloping up and down the promenade and through the line of rooms. She would pose just out of reach, bow her back so that she was on her elbows, butt in the air, teasing him as do dogs during play, before shooting off in an unexpected direction.

It was a given that we wanted to be on an outside deck as the ship left the dock, since so many odd events associated with the actual launch had been documented. So, after I checked the angle of my hat in the mirror, we found our way to the staircase so we could join the other first class passengers on the Boat Deck, where there was a promenade amidships. As we walked along, Peter linked his arm companionably in mine.

"I'll check the registration book later and see where Littleton's room is located. He's traveling first class but probably didn't land one of the more elite, higher cost rooms, such as ours or a stateroom." Peter tipped his hat at a couple of women who passed us. Another woman approached, a huge black Great Dane walking calmly at her side. The woman caught our gaze and smiled, fellow dog lovers, or so she thought. Of course, the Dane was utterly confused by the lupines who were leashed, despite Kipp's annoyance over the constraint. I knew what ultimately happened to the poor dog and his loyal mistress. Hardening my resolve, I pushed down the disturbing thoughts and kept walking.

We found a small vacant area and took up position at the railing. As Peter checked his timepiece—the one belonging to his grandfather—tethered by a fine gold chain that looped across the wool of his weskit, the steam whistle of the *Titanic* blew once, the sound reverberating off of the dock as well as the surrounding buildings. The intensity and strength of the whistle caused the wooden deck to tremble slightly beneath our feet. Kipp's ears went flat as he cringed at the volume of the sound. Then, the whistle blew two more times in quick succession. The massive mooring lines were dropped as the pilot vessels began to push the ship from the dock and nudge it gently down the River Test.

Since we knew what was about to happen, it was no surprise when the displacement of water caused by the enormous bulk of the liner created suction that pulled another smaller ship, the *New York*, from her mooring, causing the tethering lines to snap with sounds that resembled gunfire. Several of the people around us cried out in alarm, not certain what was happening. As the *Titanic* continued to move with the river current, the *New York* swung out into the waterway, uncontrolled and at the mercy of fate; her stern missed hitting the hull of the *Titanic* by no more than three feet. Even though I knew the outcome, I felt my face flush with alarm as I clenched the railing where we stood, observing. Peter glanced at me, trying to suppress the huge smile on his face. Yes, it was all exciting and lovely but ultimately that would change, I thought darkly. A quick thinking tug boat skipper adroitly moved in and prevented the unthinkable by snagging the *New York* and nudging her safely back to her berth.

That singular event would have been enough to make some people leave the ship since there was always superstition associated with water travel and boats in general. But then the moment occurred when a stoker from the boiler room, who obviously had a mischievous streak a mile wide, stuck his head out of the fourth funnel, which was a dummy vent for the kitchen. One woman dropped into the arms of her male companion in an honest to goodness faint, while others were horrified and alarmed at the man's face suddenly appearing out of nowhere, his flesh covered in black soot.

"Good joke!" Kipp giggled, pushing his head up under my hand for a caress.

We turned to walk back along the Boat Deck, eager to explore, when a tall, well built man almost collided with me, his pace fast, head down as if deep in thought. Kipp adroitly jumped out of the way so his feet wouldn't get trounced.

"I beg your pardon!" the man exclaimed, glancing up, his face flushed.

The apologetic man, easily recognized from photographs, was Thomas Andrews, and I paused to wonder about kismet, destiny and just plain old good luck. Without breaking a sweat, we'd managed to meet the ship's designer within our first few moments aboard. Peter, thinking quickly, stuck out his hand and introduced us.

Andrews did the same, his handsome face smiling as he recognized the name of Keaton. "Oh, yes. I recall you are special guests of Mr. Morgan," he said, his voice pleasant but neutral. His thoughts didn't betray any agitation but rather a sense of resignation that those in power would always control pieces of his world. But in his fair minded way, he didn't hold our badge of distinction as friends of Morgan against us.

I immediately liked him, as I thought I would from my reading of his life story. He'd worked hard to get to this point in his life and was well respected by men from all walks. A perfectionist by nature, the *Titanic* was his glory. But because he was a perfectionist, his mind was already swirling with things that needed to be done to improve the ship. There was a sister ship on the drawing board...the *Gigantic*.

"I like him, too," Kipp chimed in.

"What magnificent dogs!" Andrews exclaimed. "I don't think I've ever seen any quite to match." Kipp and Elani responded to his praise by acting dog-like and wagging their tails, showing off a little with a couple of acrobatic spins. "Perhaps, later in the voyage, you can visit my cabin and bring along your furry friends. Tea?"

I didn't know at first if he was just being cordial because of Morgan but immediately recognized that he was just a very nice man. He liked people, we were Americans traveling in an odd manner with our big dogs, and he thought we seemed rather quaint and funny. More than curious, he was hoping we'd like his wonderful ship.

"This is an amazing accomplishment, Mr. Andrews," I gushed, before I realized I'd spoken too soon and was responding to his unspoken thoughts. Andrews face became confused as he tried to figure out how I knew his role in the ship's creation.

"Mr. Morgan mentioned you to us," Peter smoothly inserted as I shot him a glance of gratitude.

With an invitation to join him in his cabin the following day for afternoon tea, Andrews darted away as we continued walking along the deck. I almost forced myself to glance at the lifeboats which hung empty, carefully fastened in place. Any idiot would have clearly seen that there would not be enough seating for all the people aboard the ship. I felt my lips turn down in a frown as I tried to bite back my critical thoughts. The *Titanic* finally cleared the river and was ocean bound to Cherbourg, where more passengers would board. Glancing back, I took a last look at England's coast line, which shimmered prettily in the glare of the bright sun hovering overhead. The ship, with its tragic destiny, was underway.

CHAPTER 19

The weather was brisk but still pleasant, cooler than usual for that time of year. The water was relatively calm, as the huge ocean liner surged effortlessly forward, leaving a surprisingly small footprint in the water in her wake. The size and construction made the ship so stable, that it felt as if one were walking on solid land versus the horizontal planking of a ship. The turning of the three enormous propellers in the water was evidence of underlying immense power and machinery at work; otherwise, all was quiet and still, save for the voices of the people aboard. After taking on passengers in Cherbourg, the ship would head for Queenstown, Ireland. The true elites, Benjamin Guggenheim, accompanied by his mistress, and John Astor with his teenage pregnant wife clinging to his arm, boarded from tenders that shuttled people to and from the port in Cherbourg. A ship the size of *Titanic* could only dock at ports deep enough to handle her massive size, and there were few enough of those, so she was forced to wait in the bay while the smaller tenders served as water taxis. Along with people, the tenders delivered huge bundles of mail to be taken to New York. Margaret Brown, the Denver mining heiress who'd been traveling with the Astors in Egypt, also came on board with their party. She was a larger than life figure, tall, powerfully built and with a natural charisma that some people possess through no effort on their part. It didn't take much telepathy to pick up on some of the more unpleasant thoughts and even whispered comments about the woman, who was not considered to be polished. From what I read, she managed to pursue knowledge, had mastered more than one language, and probably was much more educated than many of the women who stood looking down their collective noses at her. With my love of the underdog, I took to her immediately, although I suspected she didn't need my help.

As we stood on the Boat Deck while the tender relieved herself of the precious burden she carried, Peter propped his elbows on the railing, watching the smaller boat sway in the slight swells that surged against the black hull of the *Titanic*. "I located Littleton's room," he said. "Charles told me he is on C Deck in cabin 83." He started to say more, but a tall, handsome man with the most amazing, sweeping full mustache I'd seen in some time, approached, hat in hand. Of course, I knew him from pictures but meeting him was interesting, nonetheless.

"I'm Bruce Ismay." His voice was deep, his manners impeccable, and it was apparent that he'd been "finished" as far as secondary education went. "I understand you are the special guests of Mr. Morgan." I quietly admired the perfect tailoring of his fashionable wool coat and the gleam of dark hair swept into place by delicately scented pomade.

As Peter stepped up and did the manly thing by acting obsequious, Kipp studied Ismay intently, doing what Kipp could do and the rest of us couldn't. With his curious telepathic mind, he pushed past the superficial thoughts and feelings available to us and dug down into Ismay's mind to see what made him tick. The story of how he managed to survive the sinking would be debated until the end of time, and the fact he did live when so many others perished managed to follow him for the remainder of his life. In many ways, his choice to not stay on board with a stiff upper lip, listening to the orchestra play as the ship slipped beneath the frigid water, ruined an otherwise charmed life. After exchanging a few pleasantries, he departed, leaving us to stare after him.

"Well, he is a little resentful we took the parlor suite from him, but he's not too bothered," Kipp remarked. "All things considered, he'd rather be seen in a positive light by Morgan than to cause a fuss over a room. And he figures he can get it back on the return trip." Taking a seat on the deck, Kipp glanced up at me. "He carries feelings of responsibility shoved on him from the time he was young. His father, who was rigid and controlling, piled a burden of responsibilities on his shoulders, and he never could meet his father's standards. None of this," Kipp said, moving his head to indicate the ship, "would have been his, uh, cup of tea. But he's not a bad man, despite what history might show. He's a weak man, in many ways, defensive and on guard."

"There are a lot of interesting thoughts and feelings that I've detected," Elani said. I was glad she was contributing, since it was easy to get lost in Kipp's effortless ease of just being a superior symbiont. "When we were on the Promenade Deck near the bridge, I realized that some of the crew–specifically Chief Officer Wilde and Second Officer Lightoller–did, indeed, have what they might call bad feelings about this ship and having been transferred to her." She looked up at me, blinking her eyes against the glare of the sun. "Is that some kind of precognition or just superstition?" Her thick fur rippled as it was snagged by the ocean breeze; a stray ray of sunlight caught itself in the reflecting pool of her dark eyes. "Lightoller thought he'd be First Officer until the captain insisted that Wilde bump Murdock from the Chief Officer spot. There's some mild resentment against the captain but nothing serious...kind of what you might expect with the competitive nature of some humans."

I didn't have a good answer. History told of more than just those two who had anxiety about being on board the *Titanic*. There was at least one passenger cancellation due to a "bad feeling" and some fortunate abandonments by crew and passengers alike.

We were on day two of the voyage; it was Thursday, April 11, 1912. The previous night, dinner was served in the First Class Dining Room, and it was, per tradition, casual wear. But even at that, it didn't meet my idea of casual since there was not a pair of blue jeans or a sweatshirt in sight. Their idea of casual made me frown and worry over having to get dressed up in my finery. After that first night, first class passengers would be expected to dress in formal clothing for dinner and the activities that would stretch late into the night. Because of the lupines, we ate in our rooms. But we did, at some point, walk close enough to hear the music concert by the ship's orchestra and hid out, for a while, on the C Deck just off the landing of the Grand Staircase, listening to the strains of popular ragtime as well as classical music drift up to our ears as if it were lifted on wings. There was a part of me that wanted to go to steerage and enjoy the excitement of a multitude of people from different cultures mixing in music and dance, but I knew we had a specific mission and our man was in first class, as were we. But, hopefully we'd get a chance to see other parts of the ship as the days passed.

As we waited in Queenstown's harbor for the tenders to again ferry passengers to and from the waiting *Titanic*, I noted John Astor purchasing a piece of Irish fine lace work for his young wife. The times were odd and very hypocritical. It was well known that wealthy men could be permitted to be married and have a mistress; such behavior was acceptable and didn't affect one's social standing. But Astor had divorced his wife and later married his teenage love interest. The divorce ruined him socially, and he'd finally fled to Europe and the Middle East for a long period abroad, hoping when he got home all would be forgiven. It was characteristic of Molly Brown that she would travel with the couple, despite the disapprobation of society.

After procuring the lace cape, he walked towards us, tipping his hat as he passed. He had a long, narrow face and sad, dark eyes; his build was slight, topped off by narrow, sloping shoulders. There was nothing about his presence that spoke of charisma or energy. At least with Morgan, I knew there was some fire within his soul. I didn't bother to ask Kipp to do a deep dive but privately wondered if Astor was another one propelled by family to become this man who passed us on the Promenade Deck. His pretty Airedale, Kitty, walked politely at his side; her hackles rose at the sight of the lupines, but she was too well mannered to engage in a rumble.

"And I thought she'd like me," Kipp whined, disappointed, since he'd been eager to meet the famous Kitty. "What is it with the dogs?" he asked. "And Astor is a bit of a, uh, hound dog," he added unnecessarily. "Did you follow his thoughts about you, Petra?" Peter was grinning as I tried to keep my face from turning red. Yes, it appeared that John Jacob Astor had a full and vigorous appreciation of what he thought to be the opposite sex.

Standing at the rail, I turned my face towards the breeze, which threatened to pop my hat off of my head. With one hand on the crown to steady the hat, lest it become an airborne missile, I gazed at the steep Irish hillsides where green grass covered the curving slopes, only to be broken by the gleam of rocks beaten white by centuries of wind and water. The thick grass glistened in the light where the sun teased dew drops tangled in the dense growth. There was one lonely white house perched on a cliff, a monument to isolation. I could live like that, just me and Kipp, away from the busy world. Feeling a rumble beneath my feet, I realized the three massive propellers were turning, and the ship began to move forward, surging against the gray water. The *Titanic* pushed her nose towards the deepening Atlantic, and we were underway again.

"I hear a sad song," Kipp commented, tilting his head to one side. With the superior lupine ability to discriminate sound, both he and Elani picked up on the notes drifting from the aft section of the ship. I listened in to his thoughts and perceptions, and I could, also, hear the soulful sound of uillean pipes. An Irishman was giving his own private sendoff to his homeland; the wailing sound pulled at the heart and left me feeling pensive and somewhat empty.

We decided to break up, and I was reasonably okay with letting Peter freewheel. After all, how much trouble could he cause on a ship? As I asked myself that question, I tried to not recall what had happened in regards to the *General*. There were only so many places he could go, I figured. But we needed to expand our opportunities to run into Littleton, so off he and Elani went with heads up, searching for history and adventure. I was so busy watching them while walking in the opposite direction—never a good idea—that I stumbled over the leg of a deck chair, and before I could catch my balance, I went flying to the deck, hitting with that nauseating jolt that one experiences with the sudden and unexpected cessation of locomotion.

"Oh, my goodness!" a man's voice exclaimed. "Let me help you, my dear," he offered in a pleasing baritone. A strong hand gently reached underneath my arm, while the other lightly touched my back as he helped me prepare to stand. Kipp hovered, his face full of concern, amber eyes wide.

"Petra, are you okay?" Kipp asked, leaving wet nose prints on my cheek.

"Yeah," I replied in our private manner of speech. "Just feel like a stupid clodhopper."

"I'm Archibald Gracie," the man said, and I couldn't have been happier. Here was a man I'd hoped to meet and engage. "Are you injured? May I go fetch the doctor?" His eyes stared intently at my face.

"Thank you, Mr. Gracie," I replied, wanting to draw him out. From my knowledge of him, it would not be difficult since he was a garrulous man. "I am unhurt," I added, smiling at him. I took a moment to introduce myself before, with a little coquettish tilt of my head, adding dramatically, "Don't tell me that you are the Colonel Gracie who wrote *The Truth About Chickamauga.*!"

"Why indeed, ma'am, I am that person," he replied, a slight flush appearing on his cheekbones, pleased at his notoriety. "And how would it be that a gentle lady such as yourself would be familiar with my work about the war?" He smiled down at me, enjoying the moment and his fleeting fame. With a flourish of his hand, he indicated we should occupy a couple of deck chairs.

"Well, Colonel, I'm an avid student of the war," I replied truthfully, "and found your book to be filled with delightfully meticulous details." His gold stick pin was set with what appeared to be a fine sapphire that caught the light and winked at me; the ocean breeze carried with it the scent of expensive cologne that hinted of amber, woods and spices. The Colonel was well dressed in a fashionable Norfolk tweed jacket, similar to the one Peter wore. He had a handsome face and remarkable eyes that met my curious gaze as the wind teased a lock of hair free from the confinement of the bowler he wore. He was just old fashioned enough to not be certain he approved of a woman being so heavily invested in war trivia, but his need to be appreciated won the day, and he beamed at me.

"I will present you with a signed copy," he announced as I almost clapped my hands with delight. If there was any opportunity for me to return to contemporary times with that book tucked securely beneath my arm, I would give it a try.

Colonel Gracie would go on to write another book, *The Truth about the Titanic*, in his role as one of the survivors. His story was remarkable since he actually went down with the ship and managed to find his way to an overturned lifeboat. Sadly, he wouldn't live to see his last book published as his health failed before the tome was released.

I found myself liking this man as he began to ramble on about his book on the war, since he'd found a fan in me, despite my sex. Too many people found his stories to be filled with excessively eye popping details, but his ebullient nature could not be ignored. Per stories that emerged after the sinking, he served as an escort for several unaccompanied ladies on board and almost ran himself ragged making certain their needs were met, offering a strong arm to propel them along as needed. Kipp was gazing at him, head tilted to the side as he figured out what made Gracie, well, uh, Gracie. In the past, Kipp only did a deep dive when we were encountering a difficult person with a complex history, but now he almost did such a thing reflexively, and I suddenly realized it was instinctual on his part and that I shouldn't discourage him. Silently, I made a mental note to self to give Kipp a wider berth.

"And I note you are without an escort Miss Keaton," Gracie was saying, shaking me from my reverie about Kipp. This very nice man was preparing to add me to his little collection of women to place under a protective arm. He was sweet and exceedingly likeable, despite his tedious rambling on about the war that would make the faint of heart crave a stiff drink of some alcoholic beverage. I was the exception to the rule, and in me he'd found his soul mate, since I knew as many details as did he and maybe a few more that had escaped his notice.

"Oh, no, Colonel," I replied, trying not to flutter my eyelashes as Kipp rolled his eyes at me in disgust. "My brother, Peter, is elsewhere on board. And in any case, I have my Kipp." I reached over to stroke Kipp's broad back, his auburn fur bristling in the cool Atlantic breeze. Off in the distance what seemed to be a cloud dispersed before I realized it was a flock of gulls caught in midflight, their wings reflecting both the blue sky as well as the gray of the ocean.

"And a fine dog he is," Gracie replied, reaching over to thump Kipp's sides so vigorously that Kipp's teeth chattered slightly. "I have a dog at home named Buster," he added wistfully. "He's an old hound that I used to take hunting, but unfortunately he no longer can go the distance." He sighed, his face growing sad. "He has the will but not the legs."

"Why do humans think we like our sides pounded?" Kipp grumbled, rolling his shoulders to stretch out accumulated tension. "How would he like it if I grabbed him and shook him until he fell over?" Kipp glanced up at me. "And if I ever have a son, I won't call him Buster."

Ignoring Kipp's whine fest, I remained quiet, giving Gracie the opportunity to reflect over lost times. He, too, was growing older, just like his beloved hound. We actually spent quite a while there, resting in the deck chairs, watching people stroll past as well as gazing at the white tops of small waves created by the dark waters of the Atlantic, only to dissipate into fading patches of foam. Colonel Gracie rose once to carefully place a rug across my lap for warmth before allowing himself to be still. A steward brought us a couple of hot lemonades as Gracie plucked details about the war from my head. He wouldn't have admitted it, but he'd only found a few men who could match his knowledge, and here was I, a member of the fair and delicate sex, who could ramble on about the wisdom of certain artillery placements with confidence. His curiosity and delight at discovering a fellow student of the American Civil War over rode his chauvinism. And as to the latter, I held no grudge. He was an example of the culture of the day, and I made it a practice to avoid judging people by the contemporary mores with which I lived. It goes without saying to mention I'd seen a lot of change in the world since 1604. After our little break with Gracie ended, Kipp and I managed to find our way back to the parlor suite. Peter and Elani had arrived before us and were bursting with interesting observations.

"We actually ran into Littleton in the library," Peter began, his eyes rounded with excitement. For a moment his voice sounded oddly high pitched before he cleared his throat and continued with his tale. "I managed to engage him, just for a few minutes, over a book he selected." I tried not to smile at his intensity as Peter glanced at Elani. "At first the steward didn't seem to want to let Elani in, but I mentioned we were special guests of Mr. Morgan and had been led to believe it would be permitted, so she got to stay with me."

"So, what did you get from Littleton?" Kipp asked.

"He's not very sociable...somehow he is simultaneously angry and depressed," Elani replied. "I wonder if the death of his wife was the critical factor that propelled him to consider placing a bomb, hoping to cause such a tragedy." She shook her head. "He has managed to let long standing anger over inequities in the social system convince him that he's right and the system is wrong."

Peter nodded his head at Elani's assessment. "He probably won't allow us to engage with him to any degree, given his insular temperament. So we will watch him from a distance and monitor his thoughts. In any case, he won't do anything until the sinking, so we will ramp up our surveillance at that time.

"Littleton wants to explode the bomb on the last day of the voyage, within sight of New York," Peter continued. "It will be a symbolic gesture in his eyes. Actually, I don't think he really wants to kill a bunch of innocent people, although he finds the first class passengers to be wealthy degenerates. But he realizes any bomb explosion will affect the steerage folks, and he doesn't want that on his conscience. He's hoping to sink her close enough that there can be a rescue of the passengers."

"What was he reading?" I asked, not certain why I was curious.

"*The Moonstone*, by Wilkie Collins," Peter replied. "Why?"

"Just wondering." I shrugged my shoulders. "It's a complex book with lots of moving parts."

Beckoning at Peter and Elani to follow, I retreated to the red bedroom so plush and opulent that I felt a slight pang of guilt as I sat at the vanity to work on my hair which had become windswept after my time on deck with the Colonel. We only had a few minutes to prepare before tea with Thomas Andrews. Yes, obviously meeting these historical figures changed the timeline of history to a degree, but that was always the case. Leave as little a footprint as possible was our doctrine.

"I'm planning on going to the First Class Smoking Lounge tonight after dinner, hoping I can catch Littleton there," Peter remarked as he leaned over my shoulder to check his reflection as he straightened his tie. Our initial hesitancy and discomfort with one another had diminished, and he was more like a kid brother than a work acquaintance. I wish I could have said the same for poor Kipp and Elani...the tension between those two never let up. "In his thoughts, I caught the notion that he, perversely, wants to observe the most decadent part of the ship, and he believes that to be the First Class Smoking Lounge where all the rich men gather to play cards, smoke and drink as they manipulate the world like a gigantic chessboard." Peter stood straight and lightly fingered the watch chain that stretched across his weskit. "I think he is trying to justify his impending actions."

"Good plan," I agreed. "Hopefully, Elani can stay with you." I looked at her and winked.

"Oh, he won't get away from me easily," she assured me with a wag of her brush-like tail.

My hair was contained, Peter's tie was straight; however, Kipp's fur had become windblown from our time outside on deck, so I held up the comb with a mock threatening gesture. Despite my caution, the comb tangled in a knot on Kipp's back, and, in turn, he showed every tooth in his head in a mock growl.

"Oh, cut it out, Kipp," I said, working more gently with the comb. "We're going to have tea with Thomas Andrews, and we must look our best!"

Glancing up at the mirror, I caught a glimpse of the treasured pearl necklace bestowed upon me by Harrow; the patina of the strand reflected the warmth of my skin tone. My fingers lightly grazed the round objects, savoring the cool, organic sensation against my flesh, as I treated them like worry beads to soothe my soul. As I stared at my image, I realized there was no time for self-indulgent reflection.

It was time for tea.

CHAPTER 20

"Mr. Andrews, I cannot even feel the motion of the ship!" I exclaimed, honestly delighted with the effortless labor of the enormous ocean liner. She moved with the grace of a whale, cutting through the water with such streamlined ease that she left an almost imperceptible wake trailing behind, highlighted by the colors of the evening sun settling into the dips and curves of the water. It seemed as if an artist had taken a paint brush and filled the troughs and crests in the dark water with the hues of twilight.

At thirty nine, Andrews had accomplished much more than others his age and had done so by learning the jobs of everyone involved in the construction of a ship. Smart, I thought...his approach and attitude earned the respect of the laborers and thus ensured a superior outcome. His state room on the A Deck was comfortable but not excessively opulent in the style of our parlor suite. Fortunately, Andrews liked dogs and had extended the tea invitation to Kipp and Elani as well as Peter and me.

Andrews smiled, pleased at my compliment as to the steadiness of the *Titanic*. She was the culmination of all his knowledge and teased the problem solving side of his nature. His mind, although curious and open to us, was spinning with ideas he'd gathered during less than two days voyage. Next on the drawing board was the *Gigantic*, which would take the information gained from the *Oceanic* and *Titanic* and create a vessel even more spectacular, if that were possible.

"I already see room for improvements," he finally confessed, ducking his head as he made the admission. "I think that perhaps we could use part of the Reading and Writing Lounge on this deck and convert the space into more first class staterooms," he said, casually floating the idea to see what I would say since the change would affect the ladies on board. I noticed he had an endearing habit of tapping his right forefinger on the top of the table as his mind was busy problem solving and creating.

"I haven't actually been in that room," I confessed, taking care to replace the china cup on the plate where a sugar dusted tea cake rested. The tea service, white with the red White Star Line logo, filled me with bittersweet feelings. Some of that china would be recovered intact from the ocean floor one day for modern day morbid curiosity to be served by its display. At his raised eyebrows, I continued and explained, "Kipp was with me, and I didn't think he would be permitted. But I did take a peek inside from the doorway, and it is a lovely room." As I chatted I recalled women sitting in upholstered chairs casually placed around tables; the windows, stretching from floor to ceiling, were filled with panes set in a checkerboard pattern, and the flavor was of a pleasant country sitting room. Huge palms were nestled in the corners while ornate cornice work decorated the walls and ceiling from which crystal light fixtures imperceptibly swayed with the motion of the ship. "It seemed well utilized and popular," I added hopefully. For some reason that eluded me, I wanted Andrews to be completely happy with his creation.

"Well, I thought that since the Palm Courts seems to already be well frequented and there also is the Library for gathering, that the Reading and Writing Lounge would not be missed." Andrews smiled at me. "But, since you seem so fond of it, Miss Keaton, I may have to reconsider and not make any rash choices." I appreciated his gentle play as he delicately spared my feelings, none of which was necessary. He was truly a gentleman of the times.

As Peter led Andrews into a long, exhaustive interrogation about the engines, both the two reciprocating and the center low pressure turbine, I glanced at Kipp, who was resting in his Sphinx pose, eyes closed, head nodding as if he were asleep. But he wasn't.

"A remarkable man," Kipp observed. "Very confident but lacking arrogance, which is an interesting combination. He likes people and is gratified when people enjoy and appreciate his creation." Kipp's eyes snapped open. "But nothing is good enough, and he will make changes until he finds perfection."

"You know, you aren't the only people on board with dogs," Andrews was saying. "Several dogs are housed in the kennel, and I have it by solid sources that some of the other first class passengers keep their dogs in their rooms." He laughed. "I know Mr. Astor will not be parted from his dear Kitty. The story is that she became lost while he was traveling in Egypt, and he was frantic to find her. He almost lost his connection to get to Cherbourg in time to sail over the loss of Kitty." He leaned forward, eyebrows arched, to offer me more tea, which I politely declined. "And near the galley, there is a cat named Jenny who was brought aboard with her litter of kittens so they can chase the invisible rats that are supposed to inhabit all ships." Andrews' lips drew down at the thought of vermin on his ship. There were stories of rats on the *Titanic*, but Andrews wouldn't accept that notion unless one ran up and bit him. "And Mrs. Wright purchased some prize roosters and hens during her trip abroad. So if you hear crowing, you'll know the source and not question your hearing or your sanity."

"And who do you leave behind, sir, during this voyage?" I asked, my query probably too bold for the day but not caring.

"My wife, Helen, and our lovely daughter who is only a little tot," he replied, his voice softening. A shadow passed over his face as his large hands fumbled with the delicate tea cup. "I miss Elba already, although it has only been a few days," he added, using his nickname for Elizabeth, his only child. Glancing at me, his lips tightened for a second; he was not a man given to emotional outbursts.

I'd seen a picture of him and his family standing outdoors in front of a long, framed window. He was dressed in a suit, holding Elba, who looked as if her hair had been slicked down with a dampened comb for the photograph. His wife was smiling, her shoulder politely nestled against the body of her husband. I had to wonder, despite the brave smile on her face, if she was as unhappy with the size of her hat as was I with mine.

We managed to pass the time pleasantly, chatting mostly about our observations of the ship. He did seem curious as to how we became acquainted with Morgan, so we explained the web of lies that passed as our story. I, on occasion, felt a pang of guilt over the deceptive nature of my relationship with humans, and I did so with Andrews. A steward discretely peeked in to make certain there were adequate refreshments before disappearing again like a phantom in the mist.

"Mr. Morgan is an interesting man," Andrews remarked in the manner of someone making a carefully neutral comment. "He is very bright, and although not brought up around the ship building business, he catches on effortlessly."

"I'm led to understand his businesses are quite diverse," Peter replied. "To be honest, Mr. Morgan was doing a favor for our uncle, who is a friend of his. We barely made his acquaintance, and he was merely trying to help us get home."

Andrews' shoulders relaxed a little as he realized he didn't need to be so guarded with us. For all he knew, we didn't care for Morgan and had no dog in the hunt. Andrews' main beef was that the people who controlled the purse strings would often manipulate the budget in such a way that went against the grain of the designer. But to date his worries had been unfounded, and his reality with Morgan was that the ship pretty much had come together as envisioned. There was the redesign of the bulkheads to accommodate additional passenger space, but that would not affect the ship, from his way of thinking, since there were watertight doors in case of emergency. The changes were approved by Ismay, and Andrews' feeble attempts to dissuade him were not effective.

"And I'm afraid we might have displaced Mr. Ismay," Peter added, hoping to pull out Andrews in some discrete gossip. Of course, we could follow his thoughts, unexpressed or not, so he could hide nothing.

"I shouldn't fret over that," he said, smiling broadly. "Mr. Ismay would want any passengers to be well treated, so I'm certain he welcomes you aboard."

That wasn't exactly what he was thinking, but he was trying to be personable and diplomatic. He understood the way of the world, and there was always a bigger, badder dog in the yard. Andrews was evolved sufficiently to be happy with his place in life and just focus on his job. True, when others made changes to his vision, it rankled, but it was the same with most businesses that such might occur. In the end, his worst enemy was neither Ismay nor Morgan…it was his own unrelenting perfectionism.

After tea was concluded, we decided to once again prowl the Boat Deck as well as the Promenade Deck and make our way from one end of the first class promenade to the other. Honestly, we needed the physical exertion, especially the lupines. Their metabolism was notched at a higher rate than ours, and their need for exercise was greater. The brightness of the sun outside caused us to take a minute for our eyes to adjust, and we stood blinking, like moles exposed to the light for the first time. Kipp and Elani, although not on leashes, stuck to our sides like leeches, so as not to incur the criticism of any passengers or crew. A man was walking towards us, his stride long and purposeful; it was not difficult to recognize Captain Smith. As he approached, he glanced at our odd party and paused, nodding his head. At just over medium height with a barrel chest across which his white uniform jacket was neatly buttoned, he had a carefully trimmed white beard, eyes that squinted half shut against the sun, and a naturally booming voice that he had to restrain for polite conversation.

"I haven't made your acquaintance," he said, nodding his head. Smith glanced at the lupines, who both sat politely, smiling up at him. He liked dogs and even had one of his own at home. In general, if they were well behaved and, uh, continent, he had no objection to people hiding them out in their cabins. As the captain, he had to enforce rules but chose which ones were more important than others. His mind revealed he already knew we were friends of Morgan, and like most people, he was prepared to be annoyed at our special designation. But so far, reports had shown us to be quiet, well mannered, and asking for almost nothing from our kind steward, Charles. So, Smith had no issue with us.

As Peter went through the routine of introductions coupled with marveling over the beauty of the ship and professionalism of the crew, I stared out at the ocean. Having Peter along fed my lazy side, and it was nice to let him ramble on, seducing Smith in the manner of our kind, with gentle and interesting discourse. While they chatted, I could let my mind wander to other subjects. I'd been on ships in my long life, but never had I been on a vessel as large or with anything close to the opulence offered on the *Titanic*. I hadn't been idly flattering Andrews when I told him I couldn't feel any roll or movement of the ship. Yes, the sea was calm, but there were always waves that pushed against the hull as we plowed towards the west. It was getting late in the day, and the sun began to sink towards the horizon, becoming deeper orange as it drifted down to kiss the edge of the ocean. The reluctant light became entrapped in the water, and as I gazed back at the direction from which we'd traveled, the fire from the sun flickered, caught in the disruption the ship had made to the water, leaving a path of red and yellow streaking towards the east. One of the second class passengers, Lawrence Beesley, had described this phenomenon in the book he wrote after the sinking. His words were elegant, painting the perfect picture, while my feeble ones seemed awkward and clumsy in the back of my mind. All I knew was that it was beautiful. There was no land mass visible; I caught my breath at the isolation and loneliness. Kipp, sensing my mood, pushed closer, the warmth of his shoulder against my thigh.

"I love you," he reminded me.

I knew he was pulling me from having thoughts that were counterproductive to our mission. It was all too easy to let one's mind drift to what would occur in a few days, and meeting people such as Andrews and Smith only compounded those notions fraught with emotion. I looked down at Elani as she sat politely next to Peter, who was engaged, once again, in a discussion over the innovative low pressure turbine engine. Turning her head, she smiled at me, as only a lupine can do.

"I love you, too," she directed at me.

"Ditto back to both you guys," I finally replied with a lopsided smile.

"And Petra just loves our suite, Captain," Peter was saying. "So very kind for us to be treated in such a fabulous manner," he added.

Smith didn't care that we'd displaced Ismay and actually thought it all rather funny. He had no need for people to monitor his job performance, which he knew quite well after so many years of experience. In addition, Peter's humble expressions of gratitude were refreshing. Many of the elites expected excellence and were apt to pick out tiny flaws over which to obsess. Smith was another one who would inspire speculation that was endless, although he did go down with the ship, in the tradition of past captains. Was he intoxicated on the night of the sinking? Or did he, perhaps, allow Ismay to influence his decisions in order to break speed records and ignore the warnings about icebergs ahead? The competition between the White Star Line and Cunard was intense and unrelenting. We might pick up on some of the truth behind the speculations, but I wasn't overly confident. On the night of the accident there would be so many distressed thoughts, it might be difficult to tweak out those of a single individual. But we would try.

Our tour complete, we returned to our cabin. The steward had promised to bring us some dinner later, and Peter and Elani were planning to go to the men's after dinner lounge in hopes that Littleton would appear. As we rested on our personal promenade deck, I sat back, my eyes half shuttered closed, while enjoying the ocean air that streamed the length of the room, mildly hypnotized by the sway of the potted palms as the breeze touched them. The air carried with it the scent of the sea…organic, complex, and a little alien.

"Why would Smith have not slowed down?" Elani asked. She'd picked out a pleasant place on the floor and was lying on her side. Her neck was arched in a modified U so that she could see us.

"Who knows?" Kipp replied. "From my studies, his contemporaries followed a similar practice, which was to go full speed and just rely upon lookouts as well as warnings from other ships in the vicinity to spot for danger. So, he may have just been following the standard routine in place at that time. And based upon the hearings that were conducted to analyze the event, icebergs were not something that deterred ships; the crews merely watched for them and avoided them."

"But in April, 1912, the climate was different, and the air was colder than usual. As result, the icebergs drifted farther into the shipping lanes than was typical," Peter opined. "You'd think that everyone would have been more cautious. Or, at the very least, post more lookouts."

"But there was something else at play on that night," Elani said as she shifted from one side of her body to the other. "Because of the cold air temperature, there was the phenomenon of super refraction—which has been documented by ship captains for quite some time—where the light waves are bent due to cold air. The survivors described a flat calm, so there would be no water breaking on an iceberg, and the sea was close to freezing, the air was dense. With the refraction greater than usual, it created mirages, and possibly explained why the lookouts couldn't see the iceberg as well as why the people on board thought the *California* was closer than it was in actuality."

Kipp glanced at her and thumped his tail. She and Peter were the youngest of our quartet, but Elani was obviously determined to make her mark. It was good to see her speak up with such confidence. She'd obviously been studying to nail the atmospheric conditions and resulting issues. I wasn't smart enough to figure out about refraction, super or not, and was happy Elani's intellect was superior to my own. Kipp would have simply passed such things off as being due to my laziness, but perhaps I just wasn't the sharpest tool in the shed. I happily accepted my limitations.

"Well, all of those elements contribute as to why the *Titanic* has lingered with people as a mystery that just can't be solved," I said, sighing. "It's in the nature of humans to assign blame. Maybe there is no one factor, and it was the perfect storm of events that came together at that one pivotal moment."

The steward, after knocking politely, rolled in a little caddy that was piled with dinner fare. I had no interest in the meat selections, which seemed opulent, but there were sufficient vegetables for me to pick out enough for satiation. Kipp, initially, pulled back his lips over the scent of pickled herring, but after sampling one, wolfed down several more. I think he would have eaten an old shoe if it were boiled long enough to soften the leather.

"Good stuff," he remarked, nodding his head as Peter piled more on his plate. Elani tried to be polite and not stare.

We subsequently retired to our rooms and rested for a few hours until after the late formal dinner was served and first class passengers were free to meander and hobnob. I helped Peter don his tuxedo and watched fondly as he and Elani exited to make their way to the First Class Smoking Lounge. Peter's excitement, although tamped down to a manageable level, was balanced by Elani's calm confidence. It was the way of our kind.

"Kipp, I'll need your help so that I can focus on Peter, Elani and Littleton amidst all the activity," I requested. It was true we could pick up on thoughts over a reasonable distance, but it became more difficult with many people present. Peter and Elani would ping on our symbiont radar, but, frankly, I wasn't good enough to get the job done. Kipp was my superior, and I was glad to have him.

From the back of Kipp's mind, it seemed, I followed him as he connected with Peter and Elani; the sensation was odd, almost as if I was a voyeur, staring at the tableau from their eyes. They entered the smoking room from the glass revolving door that softly thumped as it turned; the air was already thick with cigar smoke, and I felt Peter suppress a sneeze as the sharp odor tickled the back of his throat. I could visualize the dark, mahogany paneled walls and deep leather chairs that invited one to sink in comfort and read or enjoy a brandy amidst talk of wealth and power. There were lead glass panels that allowed the glow of soft, amber light into the room as well as small, marble topped tables scattered across the fine carpet. Everything mimicked the best men's club amenities that society could offer. At several green baize covered tables, men were hunched over cards, playing bridge as well as poker. The emotions of the humans ran the gamut from pleasure and contentment to jealousy and competitiveness. A couple of men were sunk in the leather arm chairs, reading, their thoughts immersed in the books being consumed. They, perhaps, were the happiest, lost as they were in their own worlds and the ones created by the minds of authors.

"There's more than one man in this room who's a card sharp, looking to get easy money from rich men who think they are clever and unbeatable," Elani remarked, her thoughts merging with ours. I glanced at Kipp in the semidarkness of our room. We were nestled together on the bed, enjoying the coolness and silky feel of the red bed cover that draped over the sides of the frame. Kipp pushed closer, his chin buried on my chest. In moments of quiet, I fancied I could hear the ocean outside as it scraped along the side of the ship. I could have easily gone to sleep except Kipp would use the point of his chin to rouse me from time to time.

"Not our problem," I remarked, yawning, in response to Elani's thoughts of disapprobation. "Stay focused," I added unnecessarily.

That room contained some of the most famous men in the world confined in one small area, drinking brandy, laughing, and puffing on expensive cigars, as the air became heavy with big talk full of polite braggadocio circling amidst blue gray clouds of smoke. More than one of the men turned to glance disapprovingly at Elani, who took her cue and left Peter's side to curl up unobtrusively in a far corner behind a leather arm chair. It only took a second for her to be lost, as the men returned to their cigars and brandy. Peter wisely avoided the spirits and, instead, took a hot lemonade while accepting a fine cigar offered by an impeccably dressed steward who, in different times, could have passed as one of the swells in the room.

"I didn't know you smoke!" I hissed in the back of Peter's head. I had valid concern that he might become nauseated at the taste of the cigar, and all we needed was for Peter to vomit on the fine woven carpet in the middle of the smoking lounge.

"You don't have to know everything," he replied tartly and with more than a little indignant attitude. "I took up the cigar before we time shifted so that I could tolerate this. And, no, I don't care for it and plan on dropping the habit as soon as I get home." After a pause, he pleaded, "Please don't tell my mother."

Kipp giggled, and I had to shush him. We didn't need Peter to lose his focus. The next moment, I felt a pleased "aha" moment as Peter spied Littleton, who was sitting off to the side of the action, pretending to read a book. Peter actually negotiated the room quite well, managing to reply to queries from some of the men present, before casually approaching Littleton, who glanced up, glasses perched on the end of his nose. He nodded, recognizing Peter from the earlier encounter in the library.

"Not really my cup of tea," Peter remarked softly. When Littleton didn't answer, Peter added, "I don't fit in with this crowd and never had much of anything until as of late." He managed to convey the manner of an uncouth young man, awkward in his new found wealth. "Do you mind if I join you in this quiet corner?"

Littleton really didn't want his company but nodded his head and placed the book he was reading across his lap. Reaching to the marble topped round table, he picked up his half finished brandy and took a sip. Good, I thought. Maybe a little alcohol would loosen him up.

"I see you're reading Owen Wister's biography of Ulysses S. Grant," Peter remarked. "An amazing man," he added.

"Yes, he was unassuming, and people who didn't know him often failed to recognize his potential," Littleton replied. As he said it, he smiled inwardly, thinking the statement also fit him. "It is a shame his presidency was marred by scandal."

"What do you think President Lincoln saw in him?" Peter asked, sitting back comfortably now that he had Littleton engaged. He was feeling pleased that he had managed an initial hurdle with little effort. Elani, from her vantage point, quietly applauded her man.

"Well, if you read the accounts, Lincoln went through a succession of generals who he just could not motivate to engage the enemy. In Grant, he found an aggressive bulldog who was not afraid of battle." Littleton took another sip of brandy. His face was slightly flushed from the effects of the alcohol as well as from the heat of the only functioning fireplace on board the *Titanic*. "American history is interesting to me as a man from England," he added. "You are our cousins who started out a bit rough but have managed to finish nicely," he said, raising his brandy in a mock toast. His controlled voice veiled the sarcasm behind the remark.

"Well, I just took my first trip to England, and it is a beautiful country," Peter replied, trying to nudge Littleton to reveal his political ideation. "The people seemed very happy and prosperous," he added cleverly, just to push the emotional envelope.

Littleton, who was more guarded than most, found his lips loosened from stress and liquor and took the bait. "It may appear beautiful, but like all other societies, there are flaws." He glanced around the room, his mouth tightening as his brows drew together in a dark line. "The wealth is in the hand of a few while others suffer." He glanced at Peter, his eyes slightly unfocused. "There is no social mobility, nor is there fairness." Although he kept his words and attitude mild on the surface, his thoughts were roiling with anger and agitation. This was a very angry man.

"Yes, I quite agree with you, Mr. Littleton. My family, although not poor, struggled for years with a small business." Peter managed to convey a conspiratorial attitude as he glanced around the room at the world's elite while lowering his voice and tilting his head towards Littleton. "This travel is only by a fluke and certainly won't ever be repeated. I'll return home to take my place behind the counter of our store and try and sell dry goods." He laughed softly. "I think I'll enjoy this cigar while I can."

Littleton believed Peter since there was no need not to. His plans had been revealed to no one, and there would be no reason for anyone on board the *Titanic* to be suspicious of him. Soft laughter, cultured and restrained, echoed in the room. There was no boisterous display as the men were on their best high society behavior with one another.

"Perhaps you might like to join me and my sister for tea?" Peter asked. "We feel so uncomfortable on board with no friends."

Littleton squirmed, not wanting to accept but also trying very hard to fit in and not pull attention his way. Finally, he blurted out a lame excuse that he'd not been feeling well and stood, preparing to leave. He'd had more than enough of Peter's society at that point and pardoned himself, walking to the revolving door, his gait slightly unsteady, where he disappeared, moving towards the Grand Staircase.

"Petra, he left his book behind! This gives me an opportunity to return it to him," Peter said, excitement in his thoughts.

"Nicely done," I replied, meaning it. Peter obviously had learned restraint and subtlety, two sterling–and necessary–qualities for a symbiont. My hands found Kipp's large, upright ears, which I gently tugged before kissing the side of his furry face. He was tired after having to act as an amplifier for us. His eyes were shut, thoughts guarded. I realized he did that when he needed to regenerate and rest, so I let his mind drift from mine. Actually, we both fell asleep before Peter and Elani returned, triumphant, from their evening with the elite of society.

CHAPTER 21

"I still smell like smoke," Elani complained, crinkling her nose and baring her teeth as she touched her gray fur with delicate nostrils flared in displeasure.

"Yeah, you stink," Kipp replied undiplomatically, pretending not to notice when her ears drooped at his abruptness. "Peter, you stink, too."

Peter laughed softly at Kipp's unsolicited assessment and retreated, without a word, to the bathroom to freshen up. He'd fallen into bed the previous night–no, make that early morning–after a night of smoking and trying to engage Littleton. He did smell like the burnt out end of a stale cigar. As the lupines feasted on breakfast, I nibbled on some thick toast, upon which I'd smeared fresh butter that was of just the right spreading consistency. A tiny crock pot of jam with beads of condensation trickling down the smooth sides of the glazed pottery rested on the table top. The scent of fresh roses, brought by Charles that morning, filled the private promenade deck with a sweet fragrance that offset the sharp saltiness of the ocean.

"Pear preserves," I said, almost moaning. Not caring that I looked like an uncouth heathen, I licked the spoon clean.

"Hey, let me try some of that stuff," Kipp demanded, sticking his big head up into my face. I complied, balancing a sizeable wad of preserves on a crust of bread and holding it out. Carefully, he pulled his lips back from his teeth and took the morsel. He smiled inwardly as the sweetness hit the back of his tongue. "We need to get some of that stuff for the house when we get home." His tail wagged at the thought of food.

Peter rejoined us, his hair still damp from a bath. He'd shaved, tidying up his facial hair, and his cheeks had the look of smooth baby's flesh, all clean shorn and gleaming. Sitting at the table, he nodded as I poured him some coffee from the carafe. Charles, thinking we Americans would prefer coffee to tea in the morning, was doing his best to please. I missed Fitzhugh's Earl Grey, but that was in another time, another place.

"I plan on going to the smoking lounge again tonight and return Littleton's book, if he shows," Peter remarked. Standing, he walked to one of the windows that opened out to the Atlantic; he was restless and pensive. I saw his thick forelock of hair stir as the gusts of wind grazed his face. It was almost too cool to sit on the deck with the windows opened, but the lupines enjoyed the feel of the cleansing air tunneling through their fur; I pulled the collar of my dressing gown closer around my neck.

Elani glanced up at me and wagged her tail. "I thought it went well," she said, referring to the evening spent in the smoking lounge. "Peter was comfortable and confident," she added, looking over to him. It was clear she thought he needed some boot applied to nudge him out of his somber mood.

"It's difficult, is it not, to be around these people, make acquaintances and realize in a few days all of this will end in tragedy?" Peter asked, as he stared at the ocean. "What I find is that it disrupts my focus." He had obviously hesitated in his confession, not wanting any of us to think he'd lost any of his gameness for the experience. After a moment, he turned, his eyes meeting mine.

"I think we all feel that way, Peter," I replied, watching as his face relaxed at my admission.

"And there are so many things that we'll not be able to prove or disprove," he added, frowning.

"Such as?"

"The rivets in the bow of the ship were of a lesser grade wrought iron than those used elsewhere during construction," Peter replied. "How will we know if a higher grade material had been used would it have made a difference?"

"We won't know that," I replied. "It's tempting to look at all things with the gift of foresight and retrospection and ask questions. In the case of the *Titanic*, it was said later that she should have been moving at a slower rate of speed considering the condition of the ocean. However, Captain Smith seems, from what we studied, to have been following the usual protocol for ships crossing the Atlantic. Remember, too, he even changed the course of the ship southward to avoid icebergs, thinking that being in the Gulf Stream would save him. But it didn't." I sighed. "So many intersecting lines," I added, looking at the crust of bread resting forlornly on my plate. A smear of pear preserves half covered the brave White Star Line logo imprinted on the porcelain. I wanted more buttered bread and pear preserves but didn't want to be a total hog. Glancing over at Kipp, who shared my thoughts, I smiled as he winked at me, our private moment enjoyed.

We split up again, since moving separately allowed us to meet more passengers and continue to assess the feel of the ship. As I walked outside, the sun had brought its warmth, and the air felt pleasantly mild. The ship's orchestra was playing after having split into two groups, so that one was in the lounge while the other was set up on the Boat Deck, where upbeat ragtime songs echoed across the smooth, gray ocean. I drifted close enough to the bridge to eavesdrop, with Kipp's help to assist me to focus, on some of the dialog ongoing between members of the crew. The ship's chief engineer was on the bridge with Captain Smith.

"They're talking about the coal fires in boiler room five and six," Kipp said, tilting his head as if he was using his large ears rather than his excellent telepathy to listen in on their conversations. "The engineer is not overly worried and thinks by the time we get to New York the coal bins will be depleted enough to allow the remaining burning coal to be extinguished."

"I know some contemporary researchers have speculated that the coal fires could have weakened the hull and subsequent metal failure contributed to the sinking," I said, pausing to rest my elbows on the railing of the Promenade Deck. "But unless one could have inspected the hull in real time, there will be no way to prove that theory."

"Maybe that's the essential mystery of the *Titanic*," Kipp remarked, folding his haunches to sit at my side. "There's too much speculation and few enough provable facts." The breeze that skimmed over the surface of the water brought with it the smell of the ocean. Kipp's burnished fur was caught up by the wind and rippled, like a field of uncut grass before a storm.

Reaching up, I straightened my hat while bemoaning the fact I never seemed to have quite enough hat pins to do the proper job. I began to walk aft; Kipp stayed glued to my leg so that no one would issue a complaint about unleashed large dogs rampaging on the Promenade Deck. As we passed a grouping of deck chairs, I noticed a woman who was reclining, a book open across her lap. She perked up, obviously intrigued more by Kipp than me.

"Hello, fellow traveler!" The woman greeted me with a smile. I paused, nodding at her cheerful salutation as she indicated the empty deck chair next to hers. "Please join me," she invited. "I'm Helen Candee." Her pretty, oval face was an open window to her effortless charm, and it was easy to see why the men on the ship catered to her every whim. Even now, though there were no male heroes standing by with hot lemonades and woolen throws for warmth against the air, she was covered with a soft rug and had some type of beverage resting on a low mahogany table. I guess she could take care of herself. I introduced myself in kind as well as Kipp, who had really drawn her attention. As I sat on the closest deck chair, a steward appeared as if summoned by a magician and offered to bring me a drink. As he zoomed off to fetch a hot lemonade, I settled in to act out my role.

"I don't know when I've seen a more interesting looking dog," Mrs. Candee remarked. "I actually saw you earlier with a man, and he was likewise accompanied by another lovely animal."

I laughed softly, trying to act a smidgen cultured for a change by avoiding braying like a donkey. For reasons I didn't understand, Helen Candee's opinion of me mattered in that moment. "That's my brother,

Peter, and we are fortunate to have Kipp and Elani as our companions." Before she could ask, since I knew the question formed in her mind, I added, "Kipp is a Chinese Red Crested Mastiff."

"Oh, what a bother, Petra!" Kipp whined. "You promised you'd come up with some other name for me, and once again you stick to the same old worn out one."

"Shut up, Kipp," I murmured, squinting one eye half shut at him.

Mrs. Candee was a tiny little thing with a face that could have been copied from the mold for a perfect porcelain doll. Although I was not particularly large, I felt clumsy and oversized in her presence. As we chatted and I sipped on my hot lemonade, she mentioned she was traveling home to see to her son, who had been injured in an accident. Her thoughts betrayed her intense anxiety, but her face remained composed in the stoic way expected of her by her peers. I found myself immediately liking her and knew why others did, too. She was bright, clever and actually quite nice.

"Don't tell me that you are the author of *How Women May Earn a Living*?" I asked, smiling at her.

"Why, yes, I am. And how kind of you to remark upon it," she said, her cheeks flushing prettily.

"I found it to be a very bold and ambitious work," I replied, meaning it. I'd read the tome when it was originally published, and it was leaps and bounds ahead of its time. The fact she'd authored that novel, coupled with the rebellious lock of hair escaping her carefully coiffed style, told me more about her inner self than would any prolonged association.

At that moment, Colonel Gracie ambled up and stood, his head slightly tilted to one side, beaming as he beheld us. Mrs. Candee was one of the women under his "protection", since she was a female traveling alone. He playfully referred to the group of five men who took turns toting and fetching as well as serving as escort for the widow as "Our Coterie".

"I've never drawn that degree of male attention," I remarked to Kipp as Colonel Gracie waxed eloquent on the weather as well as the excellent service to be found on board the *Titanic*.

"You have me," Kipp replied confidently. "You don't need any other guys in your life." Turning his head, he winked slyly, slowly closing one amber eye at me.

I knew that Colonel Gracie had hoped to find Mrs. Candee unoccupied so he could score some time with her. None of it was nefarious in nature; he just liked being of assistance and fell sway to her effortless magnetism. The men who catered to her needs were all behaving as gentlemen, but there was an unspoken, subtle competition to be chosen as her favorite.

"What's that about?" Kipp asked, after I'd excused myself, saying that I had to meet Peter. As we walked away, Colonel Gracie, after claiming my vacant deck chair, signaled to a steward. More hot lemonades were obviously in order.

"Just an odd aspect of human nature. Some people need to be needed," I replied. "People become competitive for many reasons... some good and some bad. It's what drives the best and worst in humanity."

We continued our review of the ship and eventually made our way down the Grand Staircase to the Saloon Deck where we had begun our journey on the *Titanic*. From the Reception Room, which was amidships, we walked aft until we approached the kitchen galley. The smell of food being prepared wafted down the corridor, hinting at something spectacular on the horizon. Even in steerage, where the food served was a little less fancy than in first class, the fare was still wholesome and often much more nutritious and plentiful than what had been available at home. We turned a corner and startled the ship's cat, Jenny, who was chasing one of her kittens who had gone off unaccompanied on a bold adventure. The kitten, a little yellow ball of fur, dashed right at Kipp, who loved all creatures great and small. The kitten, seeing the huge lupine, skidded to a halt and puffed up, crab walking sideways while spitting and hissing at Kipp, whose ears drooped in disappointment. I was forced to admire the moxie of the tiny creature who was about the size of one of Kipp's paws.

"But I like cats," Kipp whined.

"Well, other than Lily, they don't care for you," I replied firmly.

Jenny also blew up like a puffer fish but showed the inherent bravery of a mother as she stalked forward, growling, to retrieve her little baby. This time, he returned to her side, and they skulked, low crawling, down the hall to disappear around a corner. To add to the general barnyard atmosphere, the roosters we'd heard about begin to crow; the lack of natural light had thrown off their timing, no doubt.

We kept walking and finally climbed back up the staircase, returning the way we'd come. On the B Deck, where our suite was located, we traveled aft until we approached the A la Carte Restaurant. We couldn't enter, since I had Kipp at my side, but we took a moment to inspect the room as best we could, through the entrance, while trying not to crane our necks like the curious onlookers that we were. The room was lovely, with fawn colored paneling of pale walnut, carpet the color of a pink blush rose, and small tables with lamps topped with shades that matched the hue of the carpet. Crystal chandeliers dangled from the ceiling, casting a soft, delicate light in the room. Many of the elite dined here, since it was more intimate than the large First Class Dining Room on the D Deck. It must have been near lunch time, because a woman approached the entrance as if to enter. Realizing I was blocking the doorway, I quit gawking and moved out of her way.

"I'm Margaret Brown," she said, holding out her hand to grasp mine in a strong grip. The fragrance of lavender teased me, probably the result of some scented lotion or sachets placed in her trunk amidst folds of clothing. "Are you dining?" she inquired, tilting her head to the side. The mischievous part of her wanted me to enter the room with Kipp at my side. At her core was a sassy rebelliousness that was infectious and definitely not typical for women during that time in history.

She was much taller than I, and her large hat only added more inches. A formidable presence, she knew that her status as being of humble beginnings and new money made her a bit of an outsider. Something in her nature made her push harder to enter the exclusive club versus retreating. She, like Mrs. Candee, had a charisma that was undeniable, as well as unbounded self confidence.

"I'm Petra Keaton," I replied. "And this is Kipp." Smiling, I gestured at my companion, who sat on cue and gave a soft bark just to amuse

Margaret Brown. "And I don't think he will be admitted, so, no, I usually eat in my cabin."

"Oh, you're the one," Margaret remarked, squinting her eyes as she peered at me a little more closely. "You're in the parlor suite and displaced Bruce Ismay." Subtlety was not one of her qualities. Throwing back her head, she laughed, enjoying the moment. "You know, it's good to shake up the establishment from time to time," she said, smiling at me. "And I should know since I've made a business out of doing just that."

I started to reply in the expected manner and tell her that I regretted Ismay's discomfiture as well as any inconvenience, but then I understood she really didn't care. Yes, she'd gone to college after gaining wealth and could probably put some of those people who looked down upon her to shame with her knowledge, but she had no need to brag. Margaret Brown knew exactly who she was.

"Well, I like dogs and they usually like me," she was saying, leaning forward to scratch Kipp's auburn head. "So, why don't you plan on meeting me in my cabin for tea later today? I'll introduce you to a few people."

Unable to turn down an invitation to peek into the inner thoughts of Margaret Brown, I accepted. Not exactly knowing why, I wanted to look reasonably well dressed, so when I returned to our cabin, I pulled out the gown I'd worn to meet J.P. Morgan–the pretty green frock that Kipp liked so much–and began to dress.

"Darn it," I fussed. "Where's Peter?" I asked, as I struggled to get the last two buttons fastened. "I'm not a contortionist!"

Kipp closed his eyes and concentrated, pushing aside the human thoughts milling about the enormous ship. "He's down at the squash court, setting up a time to play with Colonel Gracie." Opening his amber colored eyes, he glanced up at me. "And can you explain squash, please?"

"You hit a little ball with a racquet," I replied.

"Where's the fun in that?" Kipp grumbled. "I can see the fun in chasing a ball but hitting it...you humanoids have some odd things that you find amusing."

"I thought Gracie didn't play during the voyage until the morning of the accident," I replied, determined to not let Kipp divert my train of thoughts.

"Well, you know, history will be changed to some degree by our being here," Kipp replied, sounding for a moment like an elderly sage lecturing a class of eager youths. Stretching out on his side on the floor, he thumped his tail lazily. "Why are you so on edge?" he asked.

I'd finally managed to get the last button fastened and sat down in front of the dresser mirror; my cheeks were bright pink with the exertion of simply getting dressed. With relief, I recognized that humanity would make the transition, in most cultures, for simpler clothing. Why one needed multiple layers was beyond me. All I knew was that I appreciated the brassiere I wore versus a traditional corset. I didn't think Peter would help snug me into one of those, his knee in the middle of my back as he pulled the laces tighter and tighter!

"I'm not sure, Kipp." I sighed as I released my hair from the mussed French braid and began to brush through the dark mass. "No matter what I do, every time I meet someone new, I think of what will happen in a few days, and I feel sad. I try to push my feelings to the back of my head, but they linger there." As I rewound my hair on top of my head, I glanced in the mirror at Kipp, who watched with his usual curiosity and fascination over the lengths humanoids must go to simply get prepared for the day. He thumped his tail again.

"We'll make it, Petra. And I've been thinking about something," he added.

"What?"

"When we get close to the end, I want to remain as long as is possible. We'll need to send Peter and Elani off earlier, rather than later, if you get my meaning." His eyes met mine in the mirror.

"Yes, I agree," I replied.

"We don't want them getting so distracted by the chaos, fear and negative energy that they can't concentrate and time shift." Kipp sighed, his sides heaving. "I know you and I can do it, since we've shifted in the midst of extreme stress before."

"Only because you are so wonderful," I said, smiling at him.

"Yeah, that sounds about right," he replied with a yawn.

CHAPTER 22

I was pretty confident that the tea held by Mrs. Brown in her stateroom went far astray from the historical timeline. She, no doubt, might have sat with the assembled ladies in one of the common rooms to meet, sip tea and gossip, but the change of location to her cabin was made purely to accommodate Kipp. She'd invited Madeline Astor, the Countess of Rothes–who preferred to be called Noel—as well as the sweet natured Helen Candee. So, Kipp and I, the outsiders in all ways possible, settled in for a three hour session, since the tea stretched on into the late afternoon.

Never the one to stick by the standard of the day, I'd decided it was acceptable, since I was indoors and visiting another cabin, to not wear a hat. The hats were heavy, unpleasant and left me with hat hair which resulted in a sore scalp and a bad attitude. However, to my dismay, the other ladies were perfectly coiffed, with large hats carefully balanced on top of improbably fluffy layers of hair. Margaret Brown seemed to take notice of my blushed cheeks as I realized my error; with a grand gesture, she pulled the hat pins free and removed hers, tossing it carelessly to land upon a lovely settee.

"I've waited all day to do that," she said, laughing, running her fingers lightly along her hair line. Her behavior was quickly modeled by the others who rather impishly, I thought, removed theirs in quick succession. Their actions told me more about their character than I'd learn in a day of gentle discourse. And I knew they were relieved to rid themselves of the buckets on their heads, too, even if they usually tolerated their burdens with stoic reserve.

There was a distinct but not overpowering floral scent wafting about the stateroom. Of course, as was true in my suite, fresh flowers were artfully bunched in glass vases for visual appeal. And I detected, once again, the earthy smell of lavender as well as a gentle undercurrent of rose. Perhaps one of the ladies had bathed in rose water?

"Mrs. Brown is fluent in several languages," Madeline Astor was saying, as I snapped to attention to keep my focus. "Her proficiency came in handy as Mr. Astor and I traveled abroad," she added, her face flushing a little as her eyes dropped down to the table top where the tea service rested along with a plate of sweets. Madeline was rather quiet and definitely uncertain of her place with the older women. The divorce of her husband before their marriage, as well as the age difference that existed, made for an awkward social setting, and only Margaret Brown was unconcerned with such things. Madeline was a pretty girl with the glowing, smooth skin of a teenager; the determined set of her chin was offset by a soft cleft that made her seem even younger than her years. A large brooch set with fashionable jet nestled at her throat, the dark stones shining as the light reflected off of them. I noticed she was almost too careful in her handling of the tea cup.

"What an odd experience," Kipp murmured to me. "I've never had this happen, but I'm close enough to Madeline that I can feel the essence of her unborn baby." I wanted to hear more but was drawn into the conversation at that point.

"And, Miss Keaton, how is it you are traveling in such fine company?" the Countess asked, smiling, nodding at Kipp who tilted his head at her, wagging his tail as was expected.

As I launched into my fabricated story, I focused on her. What a fascinating woman, I thought. Beautiful on the surface as well as beneath...her dark eyes were soulful, depthless, her mouth a perfect bow shape with delicately rouged lips. As history would reflect, she was a stalwart member of Lifeboat 8, where she was put in charge of the tiller. She would be thought of as determined and courageous, giving hope to others when perhaps she had lost it for herself. Although a member of the peerage, she was genuinely humble.

"I have been working with William Harrow to raise funds for the women's hospital in Chelsea," she was saying. My head jerked at her words, and I came perilously close to spilling my cup of tea. "He, of course, is the founder and benefactor of the boys' home and school in Whitechapel," she remarked, looking at Margaret Brown. "Such a fine man, as is his nephew, Daniel."

I glanced at Kipp, who had closed his eyes. But he thumped his tail on the floor to give me his support. He was still engaged in his fascinated exploration of Madeline's baby.

"He can hear the words being spoken and doesn't understand, of course, but he reacts to the sounds by moving." Kipp glanced up to watch as Madeline's hand drifted to her belly as the baby shifted to get more comfortable. "What was your telepathy like with baby George?"

I wanted to answer, but it was too complex to manage that discussion with Kipp while attending to the ongoing one with the ladies. "I'll tell you sometime," I promised.

"Oh, yes, I was fortunate to meet him while in London," Helen remarked. "And so well favored, too," she added, almost giggling.

Mrs. Brown, since she was the hostess, warmed everyone's tea from the fresh pot a steward delivered. Holding up the plate of frosted cakes, she encouraged me to take another one. "Well, there's nothing wrong with a handsome man," she said. "A good heart with a nice face is something to appreciate. Now Mr. Brown, he is nothing to look at, but he's held my interest for all our years together," she added with a loud laugh.

It was interesting that perhaps the only women on board in first class who would not have been offended by the presence of Mrs. Astor, given the jaded reputation of her husband, were present in that room. The Countess of Rothes—Noel—was simply a fine human being and looked at people, despite their class, in the same fashion. The same could be said for Mrs. Candee. It didn't require much delving into Margaret's mind to recognize she picked our group for tea time specifically to help Madeline Astor gain some acceptance. She liked the woman–no make that girl–and didn't care for the disapprobation heaped upon her by others.

I confess I was mildly distracted as I surreptitiously looked around Margaret Brown's state room, while not as opulent as my accommodations, was lovely nonetheless. As I gazed at a watercolor on the far wall, my attention was snapped back to where it should be by a few spoken words.

"You know, in regards to Mr. Harrow," Noel was saying, "they say he fell in love many years ago and never found anyone to match her after she left him." She took a sip of tea and sighed. "That speaks of a loyal heart." Smiling, she glanced at me. "I was made to think of it because of your dog. It was said the woman he loved traveled with a large dog, as do you."

I darted a glance at Kipp, who met my eyes and understood how my heart was both lifted and injured by the words. Yes, it selfishly fed my soul to hear of Harrow's love for me, but the fact he'd never allowed himself to love again was sad. The three women were gazing at me, waiting for something; my face felt hot, and I could only hope the flesh hadn't turned beet red.

"So, maybe he is fond of dogs, too?" I felt clumsy in my response, laughing softly to cover that fact, hoping my voice sounded unconcerned with the topic.

"Yes, perhaps," Noel replied.

I was praying the talk of Harrow would move forward so that we could cheerfully gossip about other things. My wish was granted, and the more mature ladies delicately chatted about Bruce Ismay's family and his connections, as well as making a light pass over the fact Benjamin Guggenheim was traveling with his mistress while his wife waited for him at home. The women knew the score...rich men could have a wife at home and another woman, or two, on the side as long as they were relatively discrete. I guess it said something about John Astor that he actually got a divorce and remarried, despite the damage it did to his reputation. He must have loved Madeline or else he would have been content to keep the social status quo with a wife and a mistress or two. I was curious if Madeline Astor would be uncomfortable with the flow of conversation, but the fact the others included her oddly made her feel more accepted.

"Why do humans lack loyalty?" Kipp asked.

"It's more complicated than that, Kipp, and doesn't just boil down to loyalty," I responded. "Human hearts are one thing, but you combine that with the working of the brain, and people can be easily led astray...even when they know better."

Kipp sighed deeply and pushed his jaw deeper into the carpet upon which he lay. Closing his eyes, his thoughts drifted up to me. "All I know is I will always be completely yours, Petra, and there is no other for me."

In our manner, we continued to chat while I responded to the human dialog in the room. "Kipp, I've told you before that you may one day fall in love with another lupine and want to start a family. You really shouldn't allow yourself to not consider those options." I broke off some teacake and, with Margaret Brown's nod, held it out for Kipp to nibble. "It would be selfish for me to bind you to me in that way."

"You've done both, having a career and a family," he replied, his voice a little pouty.

"And both are wonderful," I said. "You know, Tula and I were together for a long time before we mutually agreed to retire from traveling to build families. I found someone I loved, had baby George, and, well, you know the rest. Tula's relationship ended, too, for various reasons, so we eventually resumed traveling. Kipp, I just want you to experience all you can in your lifetime."

"And I plan on it," he said. "Just drop it for now, okay?" His tone was irritated, his mood grumpy, so I let go of it, per his request.

The tea drew to a close, and I realized the ladies needed time to prepare for the evening meal, since formal wear was involved. In my contemporary world, I might have thrown on a pair of jeans, pulled a wrinkled t-shirt out of the dryer and popped into a local deli, but that wouldn't be happening on the *Titanic*. Kipp and I would be excluded from the dinner party, which was fine with me. I really had no interest and planned on prowling about third class while Peter once again made his way, with Elani at his side, to the smoking lounge in the hope Littleton would show up again. After all, Peter had his book to return.

Returning to the parlor suite, I realized I was tired. Peter and Elani were missing, no doubt wandering about the ship, displaying the curiosity and energy of the young. Once I'd been like that, and even though I was still relatively young for my kind, I felt like an old codger next to Peter. Cursing softly, I managed to unfasten the buttons from hell and slipped out of the tea gown, leaving only my chemise. Pulling the heavy red drapes to obscure any light, I climbed into the magnificent bed, waiting for Kipp to hop up and take his place next to me. "I need a nap," I said. "Wake me up in a couple of hours."

Kipp nestled closer. Our time on the ocean had caused his fur to pick up the scent of saltwater and ocean breeze, the smell of him tickling my nose. "I need a nap, too." His working overtime to amplify thoughts for the rest of us was no doubt fatiguing.

I woke suddenly, with that sense of disorientation one has when dreams have been deep and complex. Taking a deep breath, I exhaled out my nose, the sound loud in the room where only the ticking of a clock was audible. As my head cleared, I could hear muffled sounds of people on board, and I fancied I could actually detect the rumble of the engines that labored without rest. Kipp lifted his head and touched his damp nose to my cheek.

"I thought you'd never wake. It's been four hours."

"Are Peter and Elani back?"

"Yes, and Peter dressed to return to the smoking lounge. They left early to do some more wandering while waiting for the formal dinner to end."

"Well, let's do a little investigation of our own," I said, struggling to make my body work. "I want to go to steerage."

I decided to dress in my blouse and tweed traveling skirt since it was the least opulent of my clothing choices. I had no desire to stand out like a sore thumb in steerage and wished to be an unobtrusive observer. While gazing at my reflection in the dresser mirror, I completed a neat French braid of my hair, coiling the rope and securing it with hair pins. I planned on leaving the hats behind and for some reason didn't think they'd be missed below where the dress code might be a little more relaxed. Quietly, Kipp and I slipped out of the parlor suite and made our way down to F Deck, where the Third Class Dining Salon was located. I made certain one of the stewards recognized me so that I'd be allowed to depart when I was ready, since the areas of the ship where third class passengers could wander was limited. The noise itself could have drawn us, and before I realized it, we were swept up into the vortex of energy from different cultures mingling, driven by the excitement of adventure and new horizons. Kipp looked up at me, his eyes bright, tail waving.

"Now we're talking," he commented with satisfaction.

Music from groups of players echoed across the room, the tempos and strains familiar to me from my long life of travel. In a center clearing, there was a dance in progress that had origins predating an American style square dance, with a man calling out the steps. Different cultures had their own variations of the same basic dance pattern. I'd edged closer to watch when unexpectedly a man grabbed my hand and pulled me into the swirling mass of couples who somehow managed to not bang into one another. Kipp, delighted at my unexpected initiation, began to bark, bowing his body low as he shouted his encouragement.

There was a reason I rarely danced...I possessed the same skill level with dancing that I displayed with pouring tea. And that amounted to little or none. So, it was only through the grace and patience of my kind partner that I didn't stumble over my own two feet, and I know I stomped his a time or two. When I became breathless, I begged to be released, and he did so, leading me in the manner of a gentleman, with my hand neatly tucked in the crook of his arm, to the place from where he'd claimed me. Huffing and puffing, I found a bench populated by other ladies and plopped down to rest. A young woman next to me turned to regard me with curiosity since she'd not seen me before, and the fact I was accompanied by what appeared to be a large dog caused me to diverge from the expected norm.

"I'm Katie," she said, nodding her head, her tone pleasant and inviting. She had a plain, broad face with a nose that was too long to be considered conventionally attractive and pale blue eyes set just a notch too close to one another for comfort. But I liked her immediately, drawn by her inner self versus the cosmetic. "And who might you be?" she asked, directing her inquiry to Kipp, who barked in response. "I've not seen the likes of you before." Her accent hinted at rural England, somewhere in the north, I thought.

"I'm Petra and this is Kipp," I replied, resting my hand lightly on his head. "We're from upstairs," I added with a little mock grimace. "Kipp can't go into most places with me, and I thought we'd be welcomed here."

Katie laughed in response. "Yes, the fancy folks might be worried about dog hair in their fine food," she agreed. "You're more than welcome to visit with us." I shook away her offer of refreshment as we observed the ongoing festivities, laughing at some of the acrobatic antics of a few of the men who obviously wanted to show off for the ladies.

"And how are things upstairs?" Katie asked, trying to be heard over the din.

"Very nice," I replied. "I'm honestly not accustomed to such splendor, and it is just luck and a little inherited money that got me here." I hoped I didn't sound falsely modest, but based on Katie's thoughts, she was accepting of my story and didn't begrudge me my alleged windfall.

"From the way you talk, I don't think you're from England," she said, peering at me more closely.

"America," I replied.

"I was raised on a farm," Katie remarked. "Life was hard, scrabbling for food for too many of us to feed." She waved her arms at the steerage public room. "This seems pretty fine to me."

"Life is that way, isn't it? It's all in your perspective." My eyes met hers, and reluctantly my thoughts began to drift as I realized that poor Katie probably didn't make it as a survivor. There was a chance but statistically not a good one.

"Stop it, Petra!" Kipp ordered, his harsh voice almost a growl in the back of my head. Walking forward, he shoved his head in Katie's lap, allowing her to gently finger comb his thick fur and rub his upright ears.

"Such a fine beastie," she remarked, tilting her head to inspect him. "I had a little dog that I had to leave behind. My sister promised to take care of him, so he'll be fine." She gently bit her bottom lip, which was threatening to tremble. With another stroke of Kipp's ears, Katie added wistfully, "But I do miss him."

I admired her audacity at leaving her home, which despite its drawbacks was familiar to her, and striking out on her own in a new county. My life had been full of travel by my very nature, but I always could return home as long as I had a traveling partner. Katie's journey was more complicated and hazardous.

The night was growing long, I was tired, and with a murmured thank you to Katie for her hospitality, I managed to leave without being pulled into another dance. One of the Swedish men, who was involved in the genesis of an industrious polka, tried to catch my eye and that made me hurry my departure since I knew any degree of polka would tax my depleted energy levels. Because my brain felt overly stimulated, I led Kipp back to the top deck where the bracing cold of the night air could clear my senses. It was quiet up there, and if I'd felt the sense of isolation before in the midst of the ocean, nothing compared to that experience of floating in the middle of the Atlantic when all was dark. There was no moon, but there was an arching canopy of stars. The *Titanic* was steaming steadily towards the west, her lights reflecting off the black water. I could hear the strains of the ship's orchestra playing a ragtime tune, probably from the A la Carte Restaurant where women lingered to chat and gossip. The first class men, for the most part, would be gathered in the smoking lounge. Kipp focused and found Peter and Elani, the latter of whom acknowledged his ping with a forceful one of her own. It took little imagination on my part to visualize her sassy expression, her jaw dropping in a smile. Yeah, Kipp was good at his craft, but Elani was no slouch. Peter was engrossed in a discussion with someone, and Kipp didn't push far enough for details, lest he distract the young one from his purpose.

I was leaning against the railing, staring down into the hypnotic swirl of water as we passed, when a man paused and, after a moment's hesitation, approached. It was Thomas Andrews, who was wearing his heavy coat and hat against the chill of the nighttime air.

"Why Miss Keaton and Master Kipp," he remarked playfully, removing his hat. The slight breeze snagged his brown hair and softly teased it into a tangle across his broad forehead. "Is it not too chilly for you?" he asked me, his face creasing with concern. His thoughts betrayed his urge to remove his coat and offer it to me as a courtesy, but I forestalled him.

"Oh, no, not at all! I was down below where it was quite warm, so this feels good."

"You were in steerage?" he asked, a smile tugging at the corners of his lips.

"Oh, yes." I laughed. "It was one place I thought Kipp could fit in."

Andrews nodded his head. "Yes, I see your point. And how did you find steerage?" He was curious, hoping all classes of people would enjoy his creation.

"The people seemed happy, well fed and content, from my limited observation," I replied. The ocean breeze as well as the antics of the dance marathon down in third class had left me disheveled and struggling to regain my composure. Andrews' eyes glanced at my hair, the loosened strands of which were waving gaily in the breeze. "Somehow, I got nabbed and was made to dance way beyond my skill level," I added in explanation, my mouth twisting in a wry smile.

Andrews was forced to laugh in reply. Even though he'd been raised with more amenities than most, he was comfortable with all classes of people and lacked a judgmental gene. He might not have been able to visualize his own wife capering about steerage while dancing with unfamiliar men, but he was quietly amused that I had done so. And he didn't hold it against me.

"I like him more and more," Kipp remarked. He'd folded his haunches and was sitting politely, looking up at Andrews. In the background, the orchestra had changed to classical, and my eyelids drifted shut to the sound of Debussy. A couple of crew members walked past, their voices unexpectedly loud, echoing against the wall of the sea as one laughed at something said by the other.

"Clair de Lune," Andrews remarked, as he named the music. "I've always thought it sounds sad." After a pause, he added, "It's lonely here, isn't it? I mean, being in the midst of the ocean."

"Yes, it is," I replied simply.

Andrews looked down at Kipp, who brushed the deck with his tail he wagged in response to Andrews' smile. Leaning forward, the man tickled Kipp's ears, sighing as he stared at what to him was a big, handsome dog. "Kipp doesn't have to worry about such."

"No, his life is uncomplicated," I said, trying not to look at Kipp who was growling at me in the back of my head.

Andrews seemed to visually shake himself out of his somber mood and made his excuses, after I assured him I didn't need an escort back to my parlor suite. Looking back, many years later, I wondered if on some level Andrews had a premonition of danger ahead that night as we stood together at the railing watching the black water glide with a soft whisper past the metal hull of the *Titanic*.

Peter and Elani beat us back to the cabin and were waiting for our arrival so we could share stories. Elani, who missed Kipp when he was out of her view, danced lightly on her paws as she greeted him with a touch of noses. Peter gazed at me in curiosity since I looked mussed, my cheeks still reddened from the cold air above deck.

"How were things in the smoking lounge?" I asked, sitting on the comfortable settee in the middle of the sitting room. Peter had left the lighting minimal, and I was grateful, needing less stimulation and more quiet in my life at that moment.

"Good," he replied, taking a seat across from me. "Littleton was there again, and I managed to return his book. He was a little more conversant, since he allowed himself a liberal dose of brandy." Peter lifted the lapel of his formal jacket. "Gee, I smell like smoke again."

"We'll hang it out on the promenade deck to air overnight," I suggested, trying to suppress a yawn.

"Littleton has a strategy on how he will change identities when he bombs the ship," Peter went on. "There is a man in second class with the surname of Little. Littleton just plans on claiming he was that man and hope in the confusion there will be such chaos that he will pass, unnoticed. Remember, his plan is to wait until the ship is in sight of the New York harbor before the bomb detonates. The bomb is in his second trunk he brought on board, which is currently in his room. When we get fairly close to New York, he will set up the timer and ask to have the trunk removed to the Orlop Deck below the water line in one of the cargo holds. His reason is that the trunk is to be shipped, and he won't be taking it with him upon arrival in New York. Littleton thinks that his cachet as a first class passenger will compel the bell boy to help him do something that sounds unnecessary. A little coin in the palm of the bell boy might help, too. He plans on accompanying the trunk to make certain it is placed as near the wall of the hold as possible. His hope is the explosion will cause enough damage to rupture the outer hull. Littleton realizes the ship will probably be able to keep steaming, but the explosion will be a literal blow against the elitist structure that exists."

"A symbolic strike at the establishment," Kipp remarked, resting his head on his large paws. Elani lay close by his side, her eyes closed.

"How did you get access to all those details?" I asked.

"He, although trying to converse with me, was mentally rehearsing his plans over and over again." Peter glanced at me. "I think he is trying to keep his confidence up by talking internally to himself." Peter darted a look at Elani, who remained still. "To be honest, I was getting tangled up in his thoughts, which were somewhat disorganized. Elani stayed on target and kept everything clear."

Elani, with her eyes still closed, thumped her tail on the carpet, in response to the unsolicited accolade.

From outside our rooms, I heard the murmur of voices and soft laughter as people walked past, heading to their own accommodations. Keeping late hours for both men and women seemed routine aboard the *Titanic*. I wondered when the poor stewards got any sleep at all. The door to the promenade deck had been left ajar, and initially I was grateful, needing the bracing cool of the night air to help energize me. Peter, after getting my nod, crossed the room to close the door, since the dropping temperature was making the sitting parlor uncomfortable, even for the lupines. Peter loosened the tie at his throat, grimacing slightly as he tugged at it.

"I don't care for this formal wear any more than do you," he said, smiling at me. "And the cigars are getting old. I thought my face was turning green at one point tonight."

"It was," Elani remarked, her jaws opening wide in a maw revealing yawn.

"Peter, you're doing a remarkable job," I said, returning the smile. "I guess I'll be forced to take back all the bad things I've said about you."

"Really?" he asked, his face taking on the innocent expression of a child for a moment.

"Well, most of them," I replied.

CHAPTER 23

Day four had arrived, and it was Saturday, April 13, the day before the *Titanic* would confront her fate. The temperature had dropped precipitously, and the Library as well as other common areas was crowded. Only the most intrepid adventurers braved the bracing cold of the ocean air. From the protected view of the windows, the sky was a flawless blue with no clouds to break the perfect canopy, and it looked like any other spring day full of promise. After our breakfast in the parlor, since the promenade deck was a little too chilly for my likes, I decided to wander to the Library, since I thought Kipp could go with me and curl up, unobtrusively, by the door. We planned to meet Peter and Elani at the squash court where he had a game scheduled later that morning with Colonel Gracie. The visual impact of Kipp and Elani had lessened by familiarity, and the people I met in the hallways nodded, smiling at us. From recorded history, Colonel Gracie had not played squash until the morning of the fourteenth, which would be Sunday, but I suppose the little extra exercise he would get from Peter's challenge didn't cause any harm.

The Library was popular that day, due to the chill that forced people away from deck strolling to seek out warmer environments. On the *Titanic*, the Library was unusual in that it was available to both first and second class passengers. As I entered, I tried to open the door as narrowly as possible for me and Kipp to pass, not wishing to make a splash with our entrance; he immediately dropped to the floor and curled up in a ball to the side of the aperture. The steward who oversaw the room glanced my way, a slight frown creasing his face. I held up my hands in a little prayer gesture, tilting my head in what I hoped was a beguiling appeal. He tried not to smile and merely turned his head towards the stack of books he was sorting. I guess if he didn't see it, it didn't happen.

The room was interesting to me, book lover that I was and still am. I know Kipp enjoyed the use of a Kindle, and the variety of choices available for electronic books was massive, but I harbored a private passion for the feel and even smell of a bound book. I was being nudged into the electronic age dragging my feet. The Library had one wall of windows so that the patrons were treated to an unobstructed view of the harsh isolation that defined our journey. Taking a peek, I observed the far horizon where the sky and water met in a poorly defined line of demarcation between the sultry gray of the Atlantic and the brilliance of the blue sky. There were glass-cased shelves on one side of the room; the exposed paneling was a rich mahogany that gleamed in the natural light. In fact, all the surfaces on the ship seemed to be immaculate and dirt free, while I couldn't manage to keep ahead of the dust bunnies that proliferated in my own small house back in North Carolina. White fluted columns were spaced at even intervals, while little nooks made for snug places to read or, perhaps, draft a letter or telegram.

A man caught my attention, and it took me several seconds to recognize his face from the pictures I'd viewed when studying for the time shift. It was undoubtedly Lawrence Beesley, the school teacher from second class who managed to survive the sinking. I'd read his *The Loss of the S.S. Titanic*, and the room was captured perfectly by his descriptions, even down to the writing bureaus that were scattered along the walls. Unexpectedly his eyes met mine, and he smiled, nodding as his gaze darted toward Kipp, who was pretending to be asleep. There was an unspoken message that somehow related to his traveling second class and me showing up with a big dog, going where

I shouldn't have gone. His thoughts betrayed his amusement over my breaking a few rules in an age when proper women should be towing the line.

I moved on towards the book shelves and perused the volumes until I located Collins' *The Moonstone*. Smiling, I realized that Littleton had returned the book. Had he finished it, I wondered, or just given up when he became lost in the maze of too many complex characters? I confess, I found myself hopelessly mired in the book's multiplicity of plots and never had completed my read.

"Why don't you read it when we get home?" Kipp asked. His remark was grounding...we would survive this experience, and he would have it no other way.

"Good idea," I replied. Too distracted to concentrate on a book, I took a chair near the windows and watched the ripples and motion of the cold, remote Atlantic as we passed. Occasionally, a small white capped wave would make an appearance before being absorbed back into the uniform gray water. Despite the size and power of the ship upon which we traveled, it seemed as if we were a tiny, insignificant speck in the midst of jarring isolation. The *Titanic* was touted to be a safe mode of travel, but even if I had not known of the future of the ship, I would still have felt vulnerable. My mood, despite my attempts to stay focused, drifted, and it was impossible to not think of what would happen the following evening. Kipp's query was comforting in its casual certainty—we would get home again.

"Let's go down and watch Peter play squash," Kipp suggested, and it was not an invitation, it was an order. It didn't take much to recognize his attempts to lure me from my pensive thoughts.

With the *Titanic* being as large as she was, it took us more than a few minutes to find the Lower G deck where the squash court was located in the aft section. By the time we settled in the observation gallery where Elani greeted us with a toothy smile, Peter had paid his two shillings to the professional who was on board to provide lessons, and he and Gracie began to warm up. With a cheerful wave at me, Peter twirled his racquet, unable to stop from showing off a little. Gracie, too, lifted his hand in a greeting. Nice man that he was, he'd not forgotten his promise to give me a signed copy of his book, which had been delivered to our parlor suite the previous evening by a fresh faced teenage bell boy. As I'd thanked the youth, I recalled that none of the bell boys survived the sinking. Closing my eyes, I thought of the boy's family and the loss they'd suffer in less than two days.

Gracie, obviously, had played before. I'd not thought Peter much of an athlete, so I admit he surprised me by playing hard and rather viciously. Gracie was no slacker, and his pleasant exterior concealed a fiercely competitive nature. In the end, they evened out the scoring, and neither one had a clear victory. I met Peter in the hallway, where he was covered in sweat, his dark hair plastered down to his forehead.

"Miss Keaton, your brother really put me through my paces!" Gracie exclaimed, slapping Peter on his shoulder. "We're off now, to the Turkish bath."

I had to smile as the two of them tried not to limp as they walked away. They both must have been tired and stiff but were too proud to show it.

"I'll take Elani with me," I called after Peter, who waved in acknowledgement.

Since it was warm in the Lower G, I decided to brave the open deck. The lupines were panting, and I knew they would benefit from some cool air. Using the elevators, we made a rapid ascent and found our way to the Boat Deck, walking unmolested, since most sensible people had sought comfort over freezing off their behinds on an open deck. Resting my hand on the railing, I glanced down at the lupines, who had their feet planted, braced, against the breeze created by the speed of the *Titanic*, since she was traveling at over twenty knots. The wind was tunneling into their thick hair, brushing it up from the roots. The fresh, cleansing air with the sharp bite of salt would find its way down to their flesh.

"I think I'm finally getting the rest of the cigar smoke out of my hair," Elani remarked, glancing over her shoulder at me. She wagged her plumed tail, waiting, since she knew I had something else on my mind.

"You and Peter will need to leave the ship before us," I said. It seemed to be the right time to bring it up, and I needed to depend upon her good judgment to keep Peter's impulsivity in check.

"Why?" she asked, turning to face me as she sat. Kipp stared resolutely at an imaginary point on the horizon, his thoughts guarded.

"Littleton will probably blow the explosives sooner rather than later, once he realizes the *Titanic* is doomed. All of the witnesses seem to indicate possible explosions after the sinking is well underway, and the tilt of the ship is almost unmanageable. Kipp and I must stay as long as possible to determine what happens."

"And you trust you and Kipp but not us," Elani concluded, her voice quiet.

"It's not that, Elani. I know our capabilities—mine and Kipp's—but I don't know what will happen with your bond under so much emotional stress. You must trust me on this," I added.

"Peter is going to be upset," she began before Kipp cut her off.

"And you need to help him see the reason behind this and encourage him to do the correct thing. We can't have our concentration disturbed by having to take care of you two," he added savagely, his tone biting and cruel.

Elani almost winced at his abrasiveness but not quite. She was a tough lupine, despite her appearance. "I see," she replied. "I'm sure you're right." Turning her head, she stared off at the water as she composed her thoughts.

Glaring at the back of Kipp's head, I tried to soften his words. "Elani, this will be the greatest challenge I've ever taken. The slightest distraction could be disastrous for all of us."

She took a deep breath, her fur shimmering in the bright sunlight as her muscles rippled along her sleek sides. "Actually, I do understand, although, Kipp, you didn't have to be so rough. We are still learning and could make errors, just because we're young. I certainly don't want to go down with the ship, but I need you to promise we can stay as long as you think is safe." She was directing her words at me since Kipp's tone had stung her.

"You and Peter have the makings of a great team, Elani. But just as I did when I was younger, you need to grow into this. I wouldn't have suggested this trip for a young couple, but this is what we were given." My words drifted off.

"And you promised Peter's mother?" Elani asked, her tone light and teasing.

"And, yes, I did. Oh, yes, I did!"

I thought Kipp might apologize, but he didn't, and Elani and I ignored him as we walked along the deck. We met only a few passengers, their red-cheeked, chapped faces almost obscured from view due to being muffled up against the cold. By the time we returned to the parlor suite, I was uncomfortably chilled. Peter had arrived before us and was neatly dressed after his experience in the Turkish bath, his damp hair curling up against the white collar of his shirt. We decided, collectively, to rest in our respective rooms in order to prepare for the evening ahead. In retrospect, I believe our stress was increasing incrementally as we gained personal knowledge of the people we met. This was what I'd feared most…we get attached to humans, and it becomes difficult to let go of them to follow their natural destiny. As I stood to go to my room, Elani stopped me.

"Petra, may I speak with you a moment…alone?" she asked.

Peter raised his eyebrows but smiled and retreated. Kipp, after huffing through his nostrils, trotted off. He wouldn't admit it, but he was unsettled after his earlier caustic exchange with Elani. As he left, he departed my mind to give Elani privacy as she spoke with me. Even when grumpy, Kipp maintained his ethics.

"What is it, sweetheart?" I asked. Elani sat close, her jaw resting on my knees. Outside the room, some people passed, their voices a soft murmur. When she didn't answer immediately, I added, "Kipp didn't really mean what he said." It sounded lame even to me.

"Yes, he did. And even though his attitude was unpleasant, I realize he was trying to keep us safe." She glanced up at me. "But this isn't about Kipp, although he can be a total booger sometimes."

I tried not to smile at her use of "booger" which seemed like something a teenager might throw at another one in a fit of agitation.

"I want what you and Kipp have," she said. "You have managed to achieve what's natural for our kind. Kipp is always present to the point you two are almost inseparable. I have to believe it adds to greater trust and more strength as a team." She grew tired of sitting and lay down, copying Kipp's Sphinx pose, her head tilted up so that her dark eyes met mine. "And I know there are other things, too, but you don't talk about them."

"Like what?"

"I just get a feeling there are other skills that we symbionts possess that have been lost with time. Kipp is too effortless with his behavior." She blinked her eyes at me.

There were abilities that Kipp had demonstrated that were, well, unheard of except in history. For one, he could implant thoughts. We'd found references to that talent in old documents, but to date I'd not been able to mimic it. Of course, I'd not really tried, either. Kipp also could enter my dreams and manipulate the outcome. In that case, I'd found I could do the same, much to my surprise. Only Fitzhugh and Philo knew the full extent of Kipp's abilities, and we'd privately stretched some boundaries to see where we could go. Maybe it was time to share more of these things? But it wasn't my call alone.

"Elani, there are things that we–Kipp and I–are learning about our species." She wagged her tail. "When we get back, there needs to be a discussion between all of us–including Fitzhugh and Philo—about where to go with some of our knowledge." I shrugged my shoulders. "It's not my decision to make to share, one way or the other."

Elani smiled, as lupines do. "That's fair enough, just knowing we can have the discussion. But in the meantime, is there something Peter and I can do that will expand our relationship?"

"Yes, I think so. Tell Peter you want to drop some of the polite boundaries and move towards the type of bond that Kipp and I share. If you do that, you will be reversing some of the arbitrary rules and move towards a natural, unfettered style of communication."

She wagged her tail again. "I like the sound of that."

"Go get some rest, sweetheart." Leaning forward, I kissed her on the top of her furry head. "And you're right...sometimes Kipp can be a booger," I whispered, as she giggled in response.

Kipp was waiting for me in our room, which was darkened with curtains drawn. As I stripped down to my chemise, I glanced at Kipp, who still looked irritable, like a cranky old codger. He'd jumped up on the bed, sighing mightily as he made a big production of getting comfortable.

"And what's eating you, might I ask?" I inquired, arching an eyebrow.

"I'm not sure," he replied, staring at the wall.

"Well, you were pretty rough with Elani, Kipp, and that's not like you."

"She's such a kid and I, well, I don't know," he answered, grumbling again.

"You're worried about her," I said, trying not to smile but failing miserably. "You should be and that's okay." At least I had the good sense to not tease him. "Peter and Elani are more than friends to us, now. I feel like they are part of our family, just like Fitzhugh, Juno and Philo."

"Don't forget Lily," Kipp replied, licking his paw as if to indicate he was bored with the discussion.

I knew by his tone that he was relaxing. After a moment, I joined him, stretching out on top of the luxurious red brocade spread that covered the large bed. It was difficult to image in less than forty eight hours, this room in which we rested would be at the bottom of the Atlantic.

"It's tempting, isn't it, to want to change the time line and save these people as well as this ship." Kipp's moist nose brushed the side of my face.

Yes, it was. And years later, it still feels that way to me.

Our steward, Charles, delivered a note sent by Margaret Brown, inviting me to join some of the other ladies after dinner in the Reading and Writing Room on the Promenade Deck. The note made certain to invite Kipp, who had not crossed that threshold before. Peter would be with Elani in the lounge with the gents, so it seemed a good time for me to venture out. I'd thought of visiting steerage again, but since Margaret Brown broke the timeline and ship's rules to make the invite, I felt compelled to go. Since the ladies would be dressed in their finest, post dinner, I pulled out the watered blue silk gown that would pass as the fanciest thing I had. Managing to get it buttoned, fastened and settled appropriately was a two person job, so after cursing and muttering to myself, I called for Peter. Kipp stared up at me, his eyes bright. I glared back at him, knowing he was enjoying the moment.

"Hey, can you lend me a hand?" I called out.

"With what?" he yelled back.

"Just come here."

He knew I was getting dressed, so he cautiously tapped on the half closed door to the red room. At my invite, he slowly pushed the door open; I tried to not giggle at the apprehensive look on his face. Really, where had his mother been hiding him all these years? Kipp, in the meantime, was not helping by laughing softly in the back of my mind.

Peter's face turned a lovely shade of pale crimson as he approached. "Uh, what do you need?"

"I can't get the back fastened." I raised my eyebrows at him. "I'm not that flexible," I added, smiling.

He reached forward and, after fumbling for a moment, managed to get started. The dress was made to fit close to the body, and he was forced to grab both edges of the fabric and pull while I sucked in my breath.

"For goodness sake!" he finally exclaimed. "How do you stand this?"

"And you get my point," I replied. "This is why I don't wear corsets. The fit of this dress is bad enough as it is."

"I understand now, more than ever, why you dressed as a man during our trip to the *General*," Peter muttered.

After he finished, I guess he was feeling very familiar and comfortable since he'd helped to dress me, so he went over and sat on the edge of my bed upon which Kipp was resting. Casually, he scratched the top of Kipp's broad head, finding that favorite spot between Kipp's ears.

"Tomorrow, I think we need to hang out near the bridge and see if we can pick up on the crew's discussions about iceberg warnings," Peter remarked. "There has been much said over the years about Captain Smith's response to notifications, so I'd like to know what the crew was thinking."

"Good idea," I replied.

"We haven't really talked about what will happen after we hit the iceberg," Peter said, as he studiously examined his fingernails. "I just want you to know you can trust me to do whatever you tell me to do." He glanced up. "It won't be like it was on the *General*."

Our eyes met. I realized he meant what he said and smiled. "I know, Peter. I trust you." I was somewhat surprised to find that I did.

I'm not sure how Margaret Brown managed for Kipp to get a pass into the Reading and Writing Room, but she had, and the steward at the door looked away, humming a soft tune while pretending not to see the massive lupine glide past the aperture. Margaret, dressed in her post dinner finery, came to greet us, towering over me, making me feel tiny and dull in the midst of her charismatic lure. With a hand at my elbow, she pulled me to a far nook where she had a table prepared. I was pleased to see the Countess of Rothes, Madeline Astor, and Helen Candee, all of whom I'd met before. This time, Madame Aubert, the mistress of Benjamin Guggenheim was present, also.

"We enjoyed our visit with you the other day," Margaret was saying. "And we realize you're pretty much stuck in your cabin because of Kipp, so we planned an evening here," she added, pleased with herself and her generous gesture of inclusion.

"How kind," I responded, meaning it.

The steward rolled in a caddy that carried a large, insulated container filled with hot lemonade. Since the other ladies had just finished dinner, there was no need for food, but the steward brought a platter of after meal treats.

"So, Miss Keaton, how are you finding your accommodations?" Noel—the Countess—asked, smiling.

I, of course, was reading her underlying meaning, and she had no intent to be snarky. For a moment I envied her perfect oval of a face, with its blemish free complexion and dark eyes that invited trust and the sharing of confidences.

"Why, to be honest, it is a little embarrassing," I responded. As nice as the ladies were, and they really were kind to me, I realized they enjoyed taking care of the American bumpkin who had inherited some money but didn't know which fork to use at a fancy dinner. Yes, symbionts play a role, much like an actor. We don't find such deception to be a character defect but rather a necessary part of our existence. My acting innocent and humble invited them to want to watch over me. "My brother and I are not accustomed to such finery," I added, my eyes rounding shamelessly.

"Well, it's good to shake up the establishment," Margaret Brown remarked. "Look at me," she added, laughing loudly and not too ladylike. Leaning down, she gently rubbed her hand along Kipp's back. She liked dogs.

Helen Candee hid a smile behind her napkin. She found Margaret to be a bit uncouth but at the same time admired how she pushed and shoved her way to the top of society. Helen pushed, too, but with a different style and in a much less noticeable manner.

I glanced at Madame Aubert, who sat quietly. Despite all my research, I never followed what happened to her after Benjamin Guggenheim died during the tragedy. He famously went below, when he realized he could not be saved, dressed in his finest wear, and was reported to be drinking brandy and smoking a cigar, alongside his valet, who I suppose had no say so in the matter, as the ship sank. He uttered brave last words but had to have been terrified as the water began lapping at his feet.

As the ladies chatted about societal functions and gently gossiped about people they knew, I listened and nodded my head politely when anything remotely came my way. Finally, Helen mentioned Colonel Gracie, who was her self appointed caretaker while she was on board.

"The Colonel mentioned that he played squash with your brother this morning," she said, picking up the goody tray to offer me a taste of something sweet.

I selected a tiny tea cake frosted with confectioner's sugar and placed it on the small plate I'd been given. It was probably a bad choice since I'd end up with sugar all over my lips, chin and the front of my fine dress. Kipp giggled, knowing I'd make a predictable mess.

"Yes, he did. And he sent me a copy of his wonderful book, too," I replied. "Such a very nice man."

"But, my, how he goes on about the war, if you get him started," Helen remarked. "I am not versed on such things and usually ladies really don't engage in discussions about war."

Kipp glanced up at me, wagging his tail as Margaret handed him another tea cake. "I guess we know where you stand," he said, rolling his eyes. "You're not a lady."

"Nope, I guess not."

In the manner of our kind, I engaged in the gentle flow of conversation, occasionally spiked with some sassy gossip that was considered discrete and high brow, as I simultaneously monitored the thoughts of the other patrons. The general discussion surrounded the cold weather which precluded outdoor walking, as well as the excellent time that the *Titanic* was making as she steamed at maximum speed towards New York.

"I have it directly from Bruce," Margaret said, as she sipped her hot lemonade, "that Captain Smith thinks we might make it to New York early. He is hopeful, of course, since it will profile the ship to people put off by worry that she is not fast enough to compete with the Cunard ships."

My ears perked up. Of course, that statement did nothing to advance the oft repeated theory that Ismay had forced Smith to take unnecessary chances in an ocean dotted with icebergs. To get to the truth, we'd have to be focused on the bridge during the hours before the actual collision to determine the facts. Perhaps Ismay was just showing off by talking large to Margaret Brown?

"Tomorrow will be our critical day," I remarked to Kipp. "And a difficult one," I added.

Kipp gazed up at me and blinked his eyes, once.

"We'll face it together," he replied.

CHAPTER 24

Sunday arrived, and while Peter joined Colonel Gracie to play an early morning game of squash, I decided to prowl about the ship once again. I'd only made the one trip to steerage, and after breakfast had been served, I wandered down to the great common room in the hopes of finding Katie. Sadly, I didn't see her, but a group of small children who were playing with a ball were attracted to Kipp, who dutifully chased the ball and returned it to them, much to their delight. The children didn't speak English–or any of the other languages in which I was fluent—but since I knew their thoughts, it didn't matter, and I enjoyed watching their expressions as Kipp did his dog routine, making them laugh. The probability was that those children didn't survive; I forced my thoughts elsewhere.

"Why did I let Philo and Fitzhugh talk us into this?" I asked, feeling my mood drop down somewhere dark and low, as I watched the children run their fingers through Kipp's thick fur. His eyes closed as he enjoyed the touch of the small fingers scratching his pelt. Although I'd agreed to come, I obviously wanted to find someone to blame for my choices. It was not an attractive quality, I admit.

"You could have declined," he replied sensibly. "Isn't it too late to worry about it?"

"No, it isn't. We could leave right now and miss the last moments," I said, feeling my bottom lip poke out. His attempt to be reasonable and shift the impact for my decisions back on me was, well, irritating.

"But we won't, Petra. We've come too far." Kipp opened one eye to stare at me. "Let's go to the Boat Deck. Being around these children is making you moody."

There was one little blonde girl with bright eyes the color of the blooms on a stalk of delphinium who reluctantly let Kipp leave. I still see her, in my mind's eye, sometimes at night when I'm trying to drift off to sleep. Her clothing was not fine, but her mother had taken pride in the neatly braided hair and freshly washed skin that was pink and clean. She looked like a little doll.

Taking our time, we made our way upward, stopping on the D Deck, where Captain Smith was conducting a service since it was Sunday. The First Class Dining Room was full and the sounds of people singing a hymn rang out to us. Kipp cocked his head as he paid attention to the words, since he'd not heard a religious song before. I knew he was still working out his thoughts on a higher power and didn't weigh in.

"I like the lyrics," he remarked. "They sound hopeful."

"I think they are meant to be so," I replied simply.

Taking the Grand Staircase, we emerged on the Promenade Deck and walked aft, so that we wouldn't be protected by the steel and glass barrier erected on the forward section. I wanted to feel the cold and experience the pain of having the freezing air strike my face in all its brutality, hoping the image of the happy children in steerage would be forced from my mind. We walked until I felt tears burning my skin as the dropping temperatures caused my eyes to water unrelentingly. After I felt I'd tolerated enough of the harshness, we retreated forward, seeking respite in the enclosed section of the Promenade Deck and paused, near the bridge, so that Kipp could eavesdrop. Yes, I was close enough that I could do the same but felt lazy and still irritable and more than a little willing to let Kipp do the heavy lifting.

"Well, there's discussion among the bridge crew about icebergs. There have been more than one warning sent by wireless from other ships, describing sightings of bergs as well as flow ice. But no one seems extremely concerned, since visibility is good and there should be plenty of time to avoid a collision." Kipp looked up at me. "From the perspective of the crew, who are experienced, continuing to steam at full speed is not unusual."

"Future analysts fault Smith for not moving more slowly at this point. But as we know, since we shift through different periods in time, you can't take a perspective a hundred years after an event and apply it to the standard of the day." I nodded as Second Officer Lightoller passed me, tipping his hat as he did so. He was a serious man dedicated to his craft, but he managed to smile at Kipp. I took a deep breath. "So at this point, we don't get the impression that Smith is acting outside of what is customary or that Ismay has forced the issue." Shrugging my shoulders, I added, "We'll continue to watch and listen."

"Ismay's name didn't come up," Kipp said. "Captain Smith is making remarks that he'd like to get to New York early, just to show the Cunard folks that the White Star Line has created something amazing in the *Titanic*. It seems to be a matter of personal pride with him."

It was early afternoon by the time we returned to our parlor suite. Peter and Elani were already there and showed great patience and self control by waiting for us, since the steward had rolled in a cart with luncheon for our pleasure. The minute we hit the door, Elani started to eat, her muzzle deep in the bowl Peter had prepared. Smiling at Kipp, who began to drool, Peter set one down for him, too.

"Colonel Gracie beat my butt in squash," Peter admitted, his shoulders slumping sheepishly. "I'm glad you missed my humiliation."

"While you were receiving your lesson in the art of losing gracefully, we went to steerage again where Kipp played with a group of children before we hung out near the bridge," I replied, keeping my tone neutral. There was really no need for Peter and Elani to know the degree to which my exposure to the children had affected me. After all, it was my job to be the steady, mature symbiont in the room...if I could manage it. As we ate–I really nibbled, not having any appetite–I shared Kipp's impressions from eavesdropping on the bridge crew.

"So far, we don't find anyone who committed a gross error in judgment, do we?" Peter asked. Not a vegetarian like me, he was busy cutting apart a chicken breast covered in a delicate white sauce. Only the best for the *Titanic*, I thought wryly.

After the meal, we decided to rest, since we'd have to be in top condition to deal with the emotional stress created once the disaster began. I gripped Peter's forearm lightly, squeezing it gently. "Get some sleep," I advised. He knew better than to argue, and he and Elani both prepared to lie down, while Kipp and I retired to the red room for the last time.

Kipp hopped up on the bed, his thoughts quiet and guarded from me. After I'd stripped down to my chemise, I curled up next to him, using his warmth against the temperature in the room, which was slightly cool. He put his muzzle against my shoulder, his breath caressing the side of my face. Pulling him closer, I buried my face in his fur, smelling his lupine wildness, so foreign to me but yet a part of my existence.

"Oh, Kipp," I said softly, as he pushed closer. It was going to be a long night.

Kipp possessed an internal clock superior to any mechanical one, and at promptly seven pm, he awakened me with a mental knock at the doorway to my brain. I sat up suddenly, my face flushed from a dream, my skin covered in sweat. I dreamt we didn't get off in time, and I watched, horrified, as Peter and Elani slid down the steep angle of the deck to disappear into the black water. Peter's face, pale against the darkness, turned up towards me, his features twisted in agony. Then Kipp began to slide, his paws scrabbling against the wooden planking of the deck…that is when I awoke, my heart pounding, my stomach twisted in a knot.

"Gee, you could have taken care of that one," I whined.

"I figured it was good for you to confront your fears," he replied, licking my face for good measure, his raspy tongue warm against my cheek.

Peter was already dressed in his evening wear, since he planned on joining the first class men in the smoking room in his now usual routine. We could only hope Littleton would gather there, as he had the previous nights, lurking in a darkened corner like a malignant creature from a sad, twisted tale of mythology. The four of us stood awkwardly, not sure what to say.

Finally, Kipp moved forward and touched noses with Elani.

"Good luck," he said, his voice soft. He'd wanted to address her as "kid" but bit back the words at the last minute. She was no longer the kid in the room.

"You, too," she replied, blinking her eyes.

Peter and I stared at one another before he reached forward and pulled me into a surprisingly close hug. I finally relaxed and let him hold me for a moment. Inhaling, I caught the scent of his cologne which made him seem more mature than his young years. I felt proud of his accomplishment on this journey. He'd managed to insert himself into a difficult aspect of society and did so quite well for someone with limited experience.

"It will all be okay," I offered lamely, feeling the need, as the elder, to be reassuring. "You must listen to me and go when I say to go, no matter what." I was speaking to Peter and, to a lesser degree, Elani.

"I promise," he replied, his dark eyes sober, his face rigid.

"Your hair is getting a little long." I reached up to touch the edge of the dark mop that was curling against his white collar. It took some self restraint to not push his bangs away from his forehead.

"Yeah, off to get a trim when I get home tomorrow," he replied nonchalantly.

With that final remark and a lopsided cocky grin, Peter beckoned to Elani, and the pair departed to make their way to the First Class Smoking Lounge. Kipp and I had another destination in mind—we'd be on the forward deck watching, searching the darkness for what the crew saw on that fateful night just before the collision occurred. I'd dressed in my warmest clothes, even down to woolen underwear. Peter had handed me his heavy overcoat since Kipp and I planned on being outside for an extended period of time. My lightweight traveling jacket would have been woefully inadequate against the falling temperatures. And even though it was breaking time shift rules, I tucked the signed copy of Colonel Gracie's book in the inner deep pocket of the coat. Smiling, I recalled that I'd violated those rules before, my hand reaching up to touch Harrow's pearls. We weren't supposed to return with trophies, but I'd always felt life was full of exceptions. As I passed people, some of whom were on their way to their cabins, others who were heading to one of the various post dinner locations on board, it was impossible to meet their eyes. Keeping my head down, my chin tucked on my chest, I moved on, feeling resolute and single minded. There was no other choice...we were committed and would see this out as long as possible.

Kipp and I made our way forward on the Promenade Deck until we were located beneath the Bridge Deck and the wheel house. Kipp looked up at me and nodded. "This is good," he said, nuzzling my hand for comfort. Sitting, he closed his eyes, tilting his head slightly. We were alone; the blackness of the seemingly endless expanse of water stretched ahead of the *Titanic*. It looked benign, even welcoming to the humans on board who lacked our regrettable vision which gave us foresight but no authority to act.

"First Officer Murdock is on duty," Kipp said. "His thoughts are generally calm and confident but with mild concern over the number of iceberg warnings. They started receiving them early this morning from the *Caronia* and since then have received messages from several other vessels noting field ice, icebergs and growlers." Kipp looked up at me. "I know that a short time ago, McBride in the Radio Room was supposed to have received some type of warning from the *Californian*, but there is too much, uh, static for me to find him in all these people," Kipp concluded, his tone apologetic. "He's unfamiliar to me and that makes it difficult."

"It's okay, Kipp. Don't worry about it. You're doing great."

"But Murdock, like the captain, has steamed through similar conditions—or at least he thinks they are similar—before and believes that the necessary caution is applied." Kipp took a deep breath and stood, shaking himself from nose to tail, before seating himself again. "This deck is a little cold on my backside," he grumbled.

I didn't know how to reply since I thought my nose would freeze and fall off any moment. A man passed, tipping his hat, as he went aft towards more pleasant environs. He paused to give me the accurate time from his watch before departing again. It was 11:25 pm. The iceberg was fifteen minutes away.

"I want to go forward as far as we can to the open bow, so I can see what the crew are seeing," Kipp demanded. With that, we hustled back to the stairs taking us down to B Deck, where we moved quickly forward, ignoring the stares of people as we hurried along. The outside air was harsh, cutting into my skin like shards of glass. I'd left my hat in the suite, thinking it would be an encumbrance; for a moment I missed the clumsy warmth it provided. Normally the forward part of the deck that led to the sharp point of the bow was not for casual strolling, but there was no crew member lurking to politely redirect us, and we made our way past the upright support holding the crow's nest and the two men who were watching the black water until we had a clear view, my hands gripping the railing. Although I was wearing gloves, the cold from the metal was not put off by the thin barrier; my fingers throbbed and ached.

Borrowing Lightoller's description, there was a flat calm on that fateful night. The blackened sky stretched from horizon to horizon with no moon suspended in the darkness. The sole illumination came from an unusually vivid canopy of stars, which seemed almost artificial and out of place. I've rarely seen anything to match in the brilliance and clarity...it was as if someone had taken a length of black velvet cloth, punched holes in it from one end to the other, and shone a bright light on the other side of the fabric. The effect was disorienting, at least for me. Kipp's feet were planted wide, his eyes blinking against the numbing cold as he strained to see what lay ahead.

"I see it!" he exclaimed, his thought hitting the back of my head like a hammer. Kipp turned, looking at me. "Can't you see it?"

I couldn't, and neither could the two men in the crow's nest. Maybe it had to do with lupine vision, which was superior to mine, as well as humans, but all I could see was the depthless void ahead as I strained to find the massive object bobbing directly in front of us.

"The speculation about a mirage must be correct," Kipp said, his sides heaving; his breath was visible as clouds of white mist eerily visible in the darkness. "The cold, dense air has created a situation such that something that large and apparent has melted into an optical illusion and has been rendered invisible. And the flat calm doesn't help matters since there are no breakers visible against the berg."

"Why can you see it and the rest of us can't?"

"I guess my eyes are different, as well as my instincts," he replied. "But we are headed straight for it!" As he spoke, I saw his muscles bunch as if he was preparing for an impact.

The horizon was neither soft nor was there haze. It was a sharp horizon, and the stars seemed cut in two by the definition, their radiance shining onto the water, causing pinpoint spots of iridescent sheen on the ocean.

A minute later, I heard the thoughts of Fleet in the crow's nest as he recognized the danger, finally, first ringing the alarm bell three times, before calling the bridge to alert the crew. Turning, I stared up at the bridge and saw Murdock peering forward, his face pale from cold and shock. The fear he felt as he, too, finally saw the enormous iceberg floating heavily in the water, flooded over me in a nauseous wave. Swallowing hard, I twisted around to watch the iceberg ahead. As Murdock gave orders in quick succession, turning the ship as well as closing the watertight doors below decks to seal off compartments, there was a flurry of activity in the wheelhouse.

The looming iceberg, which had picked up a soft glow of light from the stars above, looked like a small mountain rocking gently in the water. My numb fingers tightened around the railing from where we stood on the side of the vessel that the iceberg would hit, as the bow of the ship began to swing away, slowly, but it was turning. Irrationally, I beat my fist on the cold metal of the railing, hoping that maybe this time something different would happen. After all, we'd disrupted the time continuum from our trip and maybe that would extend to a different outcome for the ship.

"It won't," Kipp said, pushing his heavy body against my legs. I felt his warmth through the thick fabric of the tweed traveling skirt that Suzanne had carefully crafted for me. It seemed I'd first tried on that skirt years ago as time ground to a halt as the iceberg drew closer.

"Petra, uh, let's move back a little," Kipp suggested, using his furry shoulder to prod me away from the railing. I'd become almost hypnotized by the iceberg, which was blocking the star filled night sky...we were almost upon it.

I hurried back several feet and waited, picking up on Murdock's fervent hope that he'd done enough to save the ship. But I felt his gut wrenching horror as the ship made contact with the berg. From beneath the soles of my shoes, I could feel the deck tremble and shudder, albeit slightly, as large chunks of ice detached from the berg to thud heavily on the deck. The top of the berg looked like the sail of a schooner, triangular and ghostly white, as the *Titanic* skimmed past it.

Kipp refocused on the bridge crew and noted the arrival of Captain Smith, who seemed sober and appropriate. "Well, there's another story debunked," Kipp remarked. "Smith was not under the influence of anything, as far as I can tell. He's alert and coherent, asking the right questions and taking action."

Thirty seven seconds elapsed from the moment the lookout spotted the iceberg, which lay malignantly in wait, and the collision. Somehow, that didn't seem possible to me. It felt as if minutes had passed as I waited for something to happen. And something had happened—the ship had been dealt a death blow, and very soon the crew would be forced to acknowledge that fact. The next moment, Kipp's ears went flat and he cringed, tying not to yelp in pain, as the engineers began to vent pressure from the boilers since the engines had stopped. Not to do so invited an explosion of the boilers. The noise was piercing and forced the humans around us to shout at one another to be heard.

Since the crew was not yet aware of the extent of the damage, the ship resumed her forward motion but at a greatly reduced speed while Captain Smith sent the ship's carpenter off to sound the ship. It was not long before the ship coasted to a halt–that time for good —lying quietly in the water like a child's toy left floating, unattended, on the surface of a still pond. Future analysts would postulate that the restarting of the engines for those few minutes hastened an already dire situation. Kipp and I drew closer to the bridge as passengers, who were unaware of the critical circumstances, arrived on the forward well deck to examine the chunks of ice that had fallen to the deck. There was general laughter and hilarity and no concern. After all, the *Titanic* was unsinkable, was it not?

"We need to find Peter and Elani," I said. "If we get separated when the agitation starts, we'll never be reunited." I glanced at Kipp. "I have to get them off in time." Even though we were early into the incident, I felt my throat tighten with anxiety. Curving my neck back, I stared up at the sky, which would have been lovely in any other circumstance, and took a deep breath, knowing I was no help to anyone if I let the stress I was feeling consume me and control my decisions.

As Kipp turned his massive head, his profile was captured by the light, and it almost appeared as if it were carved from a piece of granite, and the softness and vulnerability of his corporeal body melted away; he glanced at me and nodded. His actions might have seemed odd to any watching humans, but everyone was too preoccupied with their thoughts and perceptions to notice my "dog" nodding at me in agreement. "Peter will be in the smoking lounge," he said, using a logical assumption.

We began to thread our way back to the first class area, finally arriving at the smoking lounge, which was aft on the Promenade Deck. Not caring about propriety, I pushed past the revolving door, taking care to accommodate Kipp, and entered the no female zone. Several men were playing cards and none bothered to stand in courtesy, since I'd broken the house rule and gone past the impregnable barrier. My lack of couth was received by theirs in kind, so I claimed no foul. The steward anxiously approached, a worried furrow on his brow.

"May I help you?" he asked, trying to not stare at Kipp. Hovering anxiously, he stilled his hand which ached to take my elbow and propel me from the room. His lips were slightly pursed from agitation since the responsibility fell upon him to control the room's milieu.

"I need my brother," I replied. "Peter Keaton," I added.

"He left a few minutes ago," the steward answered. "I'm not sure where he went." His voice was dismissive, hurried and with a hopeful note that I'd take the proffered cue and depart.

I glanced around the room and realized Littleton was not there, either. Clenching my fists, I retreated, followed by Kipp.

"Don't get upset," Kipp advised. "He and Elani probably followed Littleton at a safe distance to see what he's going to do."

Kipp was right, of course. It was all too easy for me to lose confidence in Peter, and he was actually following the correct action for a curious symbiont to pursue the trail of the explosives. We knew Littleton's cabin was on C Deck, so we pushed our way down the staircase, ignoring curious people who were walking up; it was only a short time before Elani pinged for Kipp. "They're okay, just hanging out close enough to Littleton to follow his thoughts." Kipp paused, his jaw dropping for a moment as he panted. "They will meet us back at the smoking lounge as soon as they determine his plans." After a pause, he added, "The ship is beginning to flood, and the captain has ordered the wire operator to send out a distress call." Kipp's mouth opened again as he panted harder, the exertion almost overwhelming to tease out specific thoughts amidst the milling activity. "They will have started uncovering the lifeboats by now," he added.

"Let's go back upstairs to observe what happens on deck," I said, knowing it was the right course of action but not keen on having to do it.

Even though only a relatively short time had passed since the actual collision, the boat began to list, although it was very slight and only noticeable to a few people. I knew because I was looking for it. As we passed the Gymnasium, I peered inside...Madeline Astor and her husband, John, were sitting on the mechanical horses, sheltered from the bitter cold outside. Madeline's head lifted as she saw me staring at her, and a wan smile crossed her face. At that point, there was little excitement because none of the passengers thought the ship was in danger of sinking. Madeline was wearing a black coat with a soft sable collar that draped across her shoulders, framing the softness of her young face; a diamond necklace close to her slender throat flashed in the light. Ironic, I thought...John Astor was fabulously wealthy and a member of the elite of society, but none of that would save him. As if to reassure his wife, Astor had taken out a pen knife and was cutting into his flotation device, showing her how it was made.

Kipp closed his eyes, concentrating. "Elani says they are back in the smoking room. Frank Millet, Arthur Ryerson, Archie Butt and Clarence Moore are playing bridge, ignoring everything else going on. Another man is reading and likewise seems so absorbed in his book that he is unconcerned with his surroundings."

We were making slow circuits of the upper decks; as we moved forward, we noticed the men from steerage had begun a soccer match in the forward well deck, kicking the large chunks of ice as if they were balls in play. The cheers and loud yelling reverberated out across the black water that surrounded the ship. Nearby, Colonel Gracie was speaking with the squash pro who stood staring at the ocean, blinking his eyes as if he couldn't believe what he was seeing. The man's face was pale and rigid as if he had a pretty good idea of what lay ahead.

"Miss Keaton!" Gracie called out to me. "You must get in from this cold and wait until we get instructions." He lightly touched my elbow, preparing to prod me back inside. Lifting his head, he glanced around the immediate area. "Where's Peter?" he asked.

"Oh, he'll be along," I replied, smiling. I definitely didn't want to influence Gracie in any way or alter his time line, since his survival was nothing short of miraculous.

Second Officer Lightoller passed by, his shoulder lightly brushing mine as he made his way to the port side of the ship where the lifeboats were located; he was too preoccupied to beg pardon at the inadvertent contact. It was obvious he was angry, his face red with agitation, jaws clenched, and I heard muttering as he passed. His thoughts were less than noble but understandable.

"He finally had to ask Captain Smith for direction since Chief Officer Wilde isn't responding to him," Kipp said. "He's very agitated, thinking things are not being handled correctly." Kipp sighed. "But he got permission to swing the boats out, and he's full of motivation now, wanting to save as many people as possible." Kipp looked up at me. "He doesn't expect he will live past this night."

"But he does," I replied. "Improbable, just like Gracie, but he makes it and goes on to live a long life. Those two men literally went down with the ship, ended up in the freezing water and swam to the over-turned collapsible lifeboat." I shook my head in wonder. "They must have the quality found in some humans that makes them incapable of surrender."

We drew back close to the foyer of the Promenade Deck where the Grand Staircase spiraled gracefully down through several levels of the ship. The band was assembled there and started up an energetic "Great Big Beautiful Doll" that had people laughing and singing along, tapping their feet. A few couples began to dance, their movements as much a testament to the lilting music as it was to the freezing temperatures. People were clothed in a variety of attire, from formal evening wear to pajamas and dressing gowns. Bruce Ismay pushed past us, his face drawn and tense, robe cinched tightly about his narrow waist, leather slippers flapping loudly on the deck.

Murdock was busy loading women, children and men into the lifeboats, taking position on the opposite side of the ship from Lightoller. His worried thoughts were clear: Murdoch was concerned that the boats, if filled to capacity, would not hold up to the weight, and he feared they'd collapse, dumping passengers out into the Atlantic on the way down. He planned on loading additional people from a gangway hatch later on and had no way of knowing that hatch would be submerged before it could be used. Thomas Andrews was threading his way through the crowds, encouraging people to get in the lifeboats; his desperation was heart wrenching. Even though the passengers were not overly concerned, Andrews knew the ship was doomed. He glanced up and saw me, huddled in Peter's coat, my hand resting lightly on Kipp's broad head. Andrews shook his head from side to side but didn't approach, his mouth twisted in an apologetic smile. I guess he figured I'd refuse to leave Kipp. Turning away, he began to aggressively hustle a couple of hesitant women to get into Lifeboat 5.

It must have been almost 1 a.m., because the first of the emergency rockets was fired. And that's when things started to change. As the people stared up to watch the white flash pop against the dark sky, their faces were illuminated with a ghostly pallor that seemed horribly prophetic. I suppose the act of a ship advertising she was in distress caused the collective mood to become agitated. A crowd near me panicked and rushed towards a lifeboat as a group of men took up position, defending the lifeboat from being swamped and restricting entry. There were some elbows thrown and a few bursts of threatening language, but other than that, control was quickly asserted.

The fear from the assembled people escalated and intensified at that point. Many were still convinced the *Titanic* would not sink, and the thought of being lowered, in a comparatively small wooden boat, down the towering metal side of the huge liner, was a more terrifying prospect than staying aboard. Men began to prod their wives to take the children and board for safety sake. As I watched Murdock prepare to lower away, I clenched my fists, wanting to shout at him to put more people in the boat so more lives could be saved. However, he was fighting against people who didn't want to leave the *Titanic* as well as his own concern that lowering a full lifeboat could be dangerous. As a woman's husband insisted that she take her seat leaving him behind, I was unable to watch the tearful goodbyes, and Kipp and I walked away, trying to determine who was being seated and if the stories of steerage passengers deliberately obstructed from their place in a lifeboat were true. There did seem to be a higher concentration of first class passengers, but as I watched, I realized they had the quickest access to the decks where the lifeboats were kept. So, as Lightoller and Murdock began seating people, they just pulled from whoever was standing close by. Closing my eyes, I read the thoughts of the two men and understood there was no ill intent to prefer one class of people over another. They just wanted people–any people—to take a seat. The launching of the half empty lifeboats would be a source of endless criticism as well as speculation. I guess one had to be present, as was I, to understand how all the elements combined to make a looming disaster even worse.

Margaret Brown, dressed in a black and white traveling suit, was waiting patiently to be seated in Lifeboat 6. Turning her head, she saw me and waved me towards her so that she could secure me a spot. Knowing her strong personality and resolve, I was fearful she might try and pursue me and thus endanger herself. I shook my head, backing away as I quickly melted into the crowd. Kipp closed his eyes, concentrating.

"She's in the lifeboat now," he said, as I relaxed my tense shoulders.

"But it wasn't pretty, and she used some, uh, rude language as she was roughly shoved in to fall several feet until she landed hard in the bottom of the boat."

I think, in retrospect, the rigid thinking characteristic of that era is what doomed the steerage passengers, many of whom never even had a chance to leave the lower levels. In 1912, immigration regulations kept the steerage passengers segregated for one reason...the fear of communicable diseases. In many places the entryways were barricaded while some were eventually breached. Also, many steerage passengers didn't speak English and, no doubt, became hopelessly lost as they followed the confusing maze of hallways. I'd found navigating the decks a challenge, and I'd studied the plans before I'd arrived. I did note a steward, and I'd not seen him before, dutifully trundling small convoys of steerage passengers to the upper deck so they'd have a chance to get in a lifeboat. He was one of the quiet, unsung heroes of the night, carrying out his responsibilities until the end. Another aspect of a tiered society was the reality that many of the third class passengers were willing to wait patiently for their turn, which would never come. Yes, there were those aboard who viewed the steerage passengers with a falsely superior attitude as well as some outright loathing of particular ethnic groups, but I didn't encounter a wholesale conspiracy to purposely deny them salvation.

The massive liner was sinking by the bow as more and more water rushed in, causing spill over due to the poorly designed bulkheads. As the tilt of the deck began to increase, people became more eager to secure a spot in a lifeboat, space came at a premium...and that's when the agitation amongst the people escalated to hysteria.

CHAPTER 25

Kipp remained focused on the activity on the bridge, ears pricked forward, his expression intense. "I'm listening to Captain Smith," he said, as we both moved quickly aside as a quartet of people rushed past us, their faces pale and drawn from the cold; uncertainty bred fear as they raced down the deck. "I'm not sure what has happened to him, but he can't think what to do. It's almost as if he is frozen, unable to take any action. He's just standing on the bridge, staring at all the people milling around." Kipp twisted his head to look at me. "It's obvious that the other officers took control to try and save people. What's happened to him?"

"I don't know, Kipp. People can have emotional breakdowns, and I guess he has. Their anxiety can become so great they become paralyzed." I paused to watch a determined Murdock, assisted by a male passenger, force a screaming middle aged woman into a lifeboat. She was modestly dressed, lacking a coat and would no doubt suffer as result of the exposure. I wanted to offer her my heavy coat, but even a gesture that minor could change the arc of her life and was too risky. Murdock was handling her by the cumbersome life preserver she wore, grabbing the straps to maneuver her about; his anxiety made him less than gentle. Even though the air temperature was below freezing, sweat covered his face in small beads. I guess the warmth of his skin kept the sweat from freezing, too. "Smith will go down in history being criticized for not having taken more action during all of this, but I guess he was crippled and just couldn't."

Someone with a sympathetic heart had released the dogs from the kennel, and the beasts must have followed their instinct for freedom and seemed startled to find themselves on the upper deck running frantically in pack formation, their paws scrabbling on the wood surface, dodging people as they swerved around a corner to disappear from view. Kipp looked up at me, his expressive face sad. "They don't understand. The noise combined with the anxiety of the people is terrifying to them." He sighed and gazed off into the night. "They think they can run away from this and find a safe harbor."

Pulling off my gloves, I reached down to gently caress his ears. I needed to touch him without the barrier of fabric between us. We were on the move again, making our circuits, noting the increasing elevation of the deck as we drew near Lightoller's station. A young woman, the one we'd seen when we first boarded, approached him with her Great Dane, which seemed calm and well behaved, as opposed to the other dogs that raced past us at high speed. There was too much noise to hear the conversation, and I lacked the heart to listen in telepathically. I knew what happened without having to eavesdrop...the dog was too large and would not be permitted to board with his mistress. Actually, only a couple of dogs survived, small things hidden by their mistresses in folds of clothing. The young woman nodded her head and walked away, the dog at her side. The massive beast glanced up at her worried face a time or two, wagging his tail as if to comfort her. As she drew near me, her head lifted; she smiled–I noticed her lips were trembling—and raised an eyebrow. I couldn't meet her even gaze and stared, instead, at the malignant ocean, watching a lifeboat that had been lowered earlier bob lightly in the water, small waves beating at its wooden sides, as it became enveloped by the darkness and was lost to sight. Kipp and I both knew the destiny of the woman who would not go without her faithful companion.

"I love you," Kipp said, his soft words welcomed in the back of my mind.

"Ditto, kid," I replied.

"Maybe you were right." His voice seemed small and quiet against the surrounding chaos. "This is terrible to watch, the anguish of so many minds, families ripped apart...I should have listened to you, Petra. I'm sorry." Kipp's ears drooped as did his normally perky tail that was usually held high like a proud flag.

"We're not going there," I replied, my voice firm. "I agreed to this, and you should know by now that you can't make me do anything I don't want to do–despite the fact I whine about having done so." As a small crowd of people hurried towards us, Kipp and I jumped back to avoid being trampled. The ship settled more deeply in the water, as the bow took on the weight of the ocean; the *Titanic's* frame groaned from the burden on the metal. "When you look at all of this, remember these people will all be dead by the time we get home, even the youngest survivor." I made my voice deliberately harsh. "This is just history, and that's all it is."

"Yeah, right," Kipp replied. He recognized my tough, uncaring voice for what it was–false bravado.

I paused to ask another man for the time while regretting the fact I'd not thought of having a time piece of my own. It was almost a quarter after one, and people were becoming increasingly agitated as time passed. Our path took us back by Lightoller, who was stationed at Lifeboat 8. Despite the extreme cold, his face was red and wet with sweat, like Murdock's. Colonel Gracie and another man I'd not met were trying to persuade an older woman to get in the boat. She refused to leave her husband. I knew she must be Mrs. Straus who would linger famously in history as the one who chose to die with her husband. Watching, I saw the couple walk towards a line of deck chairs, struggling a little against the cold that made it difficult to breathe. Mr. Straus made certain his wife was comfortable, tucking her coat about her and fussing over her before he took his place. Their faces were relaxed since their choice had been made to remain together. Kipp tilted his head to the side as they stretched out their arms so that they could hold hands.

"That is love, isn't it?" he asked, looking up at me.

"Yes, Kipp. That is love."

We approached Lifeboat 14 when several men rushed the officer who was stationed there. Fifth Officer Lowe, as a warning, pulled out his firearm and fired a round into the night sky, the sound echoing across the water. His action seemed to restore order for the moment, although one would wonder if it was preferable to be shot versus falling into the freezing water. Overall, despite the fact people were fearful and desperate, there was no wholesale mutiny as in groups of people attempting to commandeer the small lifeboats. Maybe it was another indicator of the times that people would wait until they were told what they should do. Ismay and the governing board had decided to have the minimum number of lifeboats required by law, since more would have left the boat deck cluttered and the aesthetics of the graceful lines of the ship would have been diminished. In each of the officers was the nagging thought that surely a ship would be along soon to start removing the passengers before the *Titanic* sank. After all, the shipping lane was busy and well populated by other vessels, and the *Titanic* had been sending distress signals for some time.

Kipp pinged Elani and received one in response. She and Peter were in the smoking lounge again, marveling over the fact the same quartet of men were playing bridge, despite the alarming angle of the deck.

A few minutes later, the ship lurched, taking a severe list to port. The officers ordered everyone to run over to the starboard side to try and correct the issue as the bow of the liner dipped further under the water. Amazingly, the tilt began to slowly balance for the time being. People tend to sometimes think of ships as living creatures, and I almost thought I felt the *Titanic* shudder, as if she was trying to avoid the inevitable.

I decided to return to the smoking lounge and pick up Peter and Elani. As I did, I passed John Astor, who was standing with his hands on the railing, staring into the darkness, his face a pallid mask. Madeline, pregnant with his child, was off in one of the lifeboats, lost to her husband in the void. His Airedale, Kitty, moved restlessly at his feet, her anxiety clear as she whined, staring up at Astor, who was oblivious to her distress. I guess he had too much worry of his own to share hers. Benjamin Guggenheim, good to his promise, was dressed in his white tails and waited, a brandy sniffer in hand, to go down in style. His poor valet stood next to him in his best attire, having no choice in the matter. The valet's worried eyes caught mine, and I tried to smile, but my face felt frozen from the cold. The best I could manage was a tightening of my lips.

The *Titanic* dipped further by the bow, the metal superstructure moaning again in protest, and I heard the crash of things falling, probably nick knacks from table tops as well as chairs toppling. It was now becoming more of a challenge to walk uphill, but we arrived at the smoking lounge, where the few last holdouts were finishing their card game, seemingly unconcerned with the fact the ship was sinking beneath their feet. I peeked inside and almost swore...no Peter and Elani!

"When I find them..." I began but didn't need to finish my threat because at that moment they arrived.

"Tell me fast," I ordered. There was no time for embellishments or anything else. The *Titanic* lurched again, settling more deeply in the water, as I grabbed at a door facing. That last jolt seemed to awaken the card players, who glanced around with startled expressions. With nods at one another and murmured words, they rose and left, leaving us symbionts alone for a moment.

"Littleton, when he realized the ship is sinking, set the bomb timer in his room. He has no idea what type of damage he can do due to the location of his room, but he will detonate it if he can." Peter glanced over his shoulder, as if he was afraid someone might be listening. "He's already left C Deck and is up on the Boat Deck trying to get a spot in a lifeboat."

I stared at Peter and Elani, my mind working fast. Within a half hour, the Promenade Deck would be flooded, along with the First Class Smoking Lounge and the Reading and Writing room on the A Deck. We were running out of time.

"Petra?" Kipp's voice was heard only by me. "I want to find Thomas Andrews and stay with him until we have to leave," he said.

"Have you lost your mind?" I glared at him. "Kipp, we really don't have time to indulge your fancy," I added, my voice harsh.

"He comes to the smoking lounge and was last seen there by members of the crew," Kipp replied, ignoring my unkind comments. "I want to spend our last moments with him." He shrugged his massive shoulders, rolling his head to dispel built up tension. "Let's get Peter and Elani off the ship, and then you and I will go say goodbye to Andrews." He stared at me. "It's something I need to do."

"Why?" I asked staring at him, my mouth hanging inelegantly open.

"History would suggest he was alone at the end. I want to change that," Kipp replied, staring defiantly at me. He braced himself as the deck tilted a degree more, his paws finding traction in the fine carpet.

Not having time to argue with him, I walked ahead, followed by the others until I found a cabin, empty, its door hanging open, the interior lit dimly by the gimbal lamp. Hurrying, I pushed Peter and Elani inside, followed by Kipp.

"Okay, you two need to leave now," I ordered. Peter opened his mouth to argue but realized this was one time he needed to listen and be wise. Kipp and I moved back, remaining quiet, so as to allow the youngsters to focus. Peter sat on the floor, his legs crossed under him; Elani pushed close as Peter looped his arm around her neck. The last thing I saw were her beautiful dark eyes glancing up at me before they lost their piercing clarity as the margins of her and Peter's bodies gracefully blended into the surroundings of the room and soundlessly disappeared.

"It'd be nice if there was a lightning bolt or something dramatic when that happens," Kipp remarked. "Shazam!"

Despite the harsh reality of our current situation, I had to laugh, keeping my voice soft. The same thought had occurred to me on many occasions.

"We're not going to know if Littleton's explosive contributed to the sinking, are we?" Kipp asked, becoming serious again.

"I'm afraid by the time the explosions are heard, the ship will be at too great an angle for us to remain." I stared ahead, looking at the hallway which was elevated at a crazy incline, like a bizarre fun house in a carnival. "But, looking at things as they are evolving so rapidly, I can't image anything he'd set off in an interior cabin would make any difference. He didn't get the explosive device down to the hold, where it might have made considerable damage." We were hurrying, struggling against the angle of the deck, making our way back to the smoking lounge. At times, people would rush past, terror in their eyes as they realized there was no way off for them. As we paused at the entrance to the smoking lounge, I heard the soft strains of music and realized at least one mystery had been solved. The band that remained famously on deck until they could play no more had chosen "Nearer My God To Thee" as their final song. I pushed past the door, Kipp close behind; Thomas Andrews stood alone in the lounge, staring up at the painting which hung over the fire place mantle–*The Approach to Plymouth Harbor*. He turned, confusion on his face, to see us standing there.

"Miss Keaton," he said. "You must get to a lifeboat." His face was drawn, anxious and discouraged. I noticed his dark hair was mussed, as if he'd pushed fingers through it in agitation; his tie was loose at this throat.

"It's a little too late for that, don't you think?" I replied, smiling. "No, Mr. Andrews," I responded. "Kipp insisted we come see you, and I've learned to not resist his will."

Andrews looked distressed, confused, but generally calm. He knew his fate as he'd not chosen the way of Bruce Ismay. Like the captain, Andrews would go down with his ship.

"I never thought this would happen," he began, almost as if it was a relief to talk with someone. "True, I didn't want the changes in the bulkhead design to be made, but I never thought this would occur."

"Of course not," I responded. Kipp was nudging me to say more.

"Where's your brother?" Andrews asked.

"He left already."

"So, he made it to a lifeboat without you?" Andrews looked mildly horrified.

"No, he left another way," I replied.

Andrews' brow creased at my words, which was understandable. "I don't get your meaning," he said. The ship lurched, and Andrews automatically held out his hand as if to assist me. His innate gentility over-rode the emotions driven by his imminent demise. For a fleeting moment, I followed his thoughts of his wife as well as his daughter, Elba, before pulling back lest I get mired in his grief.

"Kipp insists I tell you some things that we hope will bring you some comfort," I said, struggling with my words. "We, Kipp and I, have traveled from the future to come back in time to examine what happened during the sinking of the *Titanic*." Andrews' face darkened as he stared at me, irritated at having to deal with a lunatic in his last moments. "I know you don't believe me, but you will have proof of what I say in just a few minutes," I added, spreading my hands, which were trembling, to indicate my need for him to listen. The engineers remained below, sacrificing themselves to ensure electricity and heat for as long as possible. Despite their efforts, the lounge had become uncomfortably cold. I felt a trickle of sweat roll down my back despite the falling temperature in the room.

His hand reached for the carved mantle; almost idly and in tune with his perfectionist nature, his finger tips found a place where the carving had not been sanded to complete smoothness. He frowned, staring at the imperceptible marring of the surface.

"Go on," he said, figuring he had no way to make me stop talking at that point.

"Kipp and I are telepathically connected," I said, "as are Peter and Elani. We can travel back in time to discover truths."

"And what did you discover here?" he asked, the corners of his mouth turning down.

"That there was an improbable sequence of events that led to this disaster. I didn't find any evil intent or villains, just flawed people who made some bad decisions. And there was also the fact you were working against very unusual natural events that contributed to this perfect storm." I struggled to keep my balance as the ship shifted again. "People in the future have the foresight to examine this event knowing things that you couldn't. Many years from now, the wreckage will be discovered on the ocean floor by a persistent man in a submersible, and the beauty of your ship will be shown, once again, to the world. It will reopen the endless fascination with this story."

He stared up at the ceiling, his eyes tracking the lovely molding as well as the overhead light fixture which was dangling at an odd angle. At that moment, I heard an enormous explosion, followed by screams of people, startled by the sound. Kipp looked up at me. "Was that Littleton's bomb?"

"I would think there is a high probability, since it sounded too close to have been one of the boilers in the bottom of the ship. But the C Deck is flooded by now, and we can't go check on the damage. Littleton is on the Boat Deck, trying to find a place in a lifeboat, which he will, since he survives this tragedy." I shrugged my shoulders at Kipp's frustration. We'd gone through a lot to prove nothing about the explosion except that maybe it happened, and, if so, it didn't seem to hasten the sinking, as far as we could determine.

"You, Mr. Andrews, will be well regarded by historians," I said. He frowned at me and started to speak but didn't. I knew his thoughts, however, and he personally felt the weight of responsibility for what was happening. "Your daughter, Elba, will go on to live a long and amazing life." At my words, his dark head lifted and a shadow of a smile touched his face. "She will become the first woman in Ireland to receive a license to pilot a flying machine," I remarked, deliberately using an old term for an airplane. "Elba will have a life full of helping others and making a difference that impacts the future in good way." Pulling up my skirt slightly, I sat on the floor, since standing was becoming too difficult. In an unladylike pose, I crossed my knees yoga style and used my hands to brace myself. "Your legacy, along with Elba, will be that other ship builders will learn from this moment and make sailing safer for future passengers."

"Well, I haven't decided yet if you've just gone crazy and are telling me things you think I want to hear," he replied. At that point, he was having to grip the carved fireplace mantle since he was unwilling to drop to the floor as had I. Chairs, one by one, were threatening to topple, their legs held fast in the beautiful carpet that stretched across the floor. Some of the smaller, marble top tables did crash over, rolling to come to a final rest against the inner wall of the room. The metal joints of the ship began to loudly protest, threatening to break under the stress that they physically could not bear. The groaning of the dying *Titanic* became almost unbearable. "You said you have proof of what you say," Andrews said, planting his feet more widely.

"Yes, I do."

Andrews was frowning at me, certain I'd gone bonkers. I waited for Kipp who, after balancing himself, walked towards Andrews. His natural four wheel drive gave him more stability than us upright creatures. With a wan smile, the man reached out, his fingers finding the top of Kipp's broad head. Gently, he scratched between Kipp's upright ears. Kipp returned to me and, after circling a time or two in the manner of wolves, he plopped down on the floor. As the ship shifted once again, Andrews gripped the mantle tighter as I curled my fingers into the nap of the carpet to get more traction. Kipp placed his head in my lap and together we concentrated on home and the time we'd left behind. The room darkened, and I heard a great rushing sound, as if wind was blowing past us, driven by a mighty storm. Looking up, the last thing I saw was Andrew's face, his features filled with amazement as Kipp and I vanished from sight.

CHAPTER 26

"Petra, get up. You've been asleep for four days."

Fitzhugh's voice was followed by a boney finger poking sharply into my shoulder; it was insistent and annoying, as was the sound of his voice, which was more than a little grating. Moaning, I tried to pull the covers over my head so that I could disappear, but Fitzhugh yanked the sheets back with a surprisingly strong hand. Finally, when I realized he wouldn't leave, I opened one eye. Fitzhugh and Juno were both staring at me. As I shifted in the bed, I heard a soft meow of protest and realized that Lily had bunked in and was curled up somewhere between me and Kipp, who radiated enough heat that I was damp from perspiration. However, it wasn't just his big, furry body that caused me to sweat. The nightmares had been endless.

"I've been hibernating," I finally replied, my tone gruff. "You've obviously forgotten what it's like to take a difficult trip since you've gotten old," I added, feeling mean, since I knew Fitzhugh never forgot anything.

"You've hibernated long enough," he replied, my words falling off his shoulders as if they'd not been spoken. "And since I'm old and with that comes experience, I know what I'm talking about."

I realized he was not going to leave me alone and finally sat up. My hair, after several days of being subjected to the pillow, was in disarray, and I had the sore scalp associated with bed head. Ruefully, knowing I looked a mess, I tried to push the stray strands from my face and finger comb them into submission.

"And what are you doing in my room?" I asked, my tone cross. "This is my room, you know, in case you forgot."

"Well, desperate times call for desperate measures," he replied lightly.

"Hi, Petra," Juno said, her tail wagging in greeting. "I missed you."

I couldn't be unkind to her so I managed a crooked smile. Kipp shifted slightly and planted his chin on my knee. His thoughts were guarded, and I felt alone since he'd left my mind. I knew he'd done it deliberately so that I could hibernate and rejuvenate, but I missed him all the same. It's that way with our kind.

"What's the date?" I asked.

"April 18," Fitzhugh replied, lifting his eyebrows. "Pretty good timing," he added. "You actually got back on the fourteenth."

"When did Peter and Elani return?"

"Three days ago before you, so they were off but not by much."

"How are they?"

Fitzhugh sighed and made himself comfortable by sitting on the edge of my bed. Juno decided to hop up, too. I was pleased to note her improving mobility.

"The doctor put me on glucosamine, and it's helping," she replied, giving the lupine equivalent of a nonchalant shrug. By nature, she was not a complainer.

"Peter and Elani are showing the remarkable, uh, elasticity of the young," Fitzhugh commented, struggling with his choice of words. "They didn't require hibernation, as you seem to," he added, his brows drawing together in a gray flecked line. "Maybe you're the one who's too old for this sort of nonsense."

"Whatever," I replied, yawning. My room was still dark, since the shutters were closed; I felt disoriented and more than a little confused. "What time is it?"

"It is nine o'clock," he replied. "Morning...and I'll have a pot of Earl Grey waiting for you once you've showered and dressed."

I looked around the room and realized my traveling clothes were tossed carelessly on the floor; I was clad in the chemise I'd been wearing when I left the *Titanic*. Inhaling, I could still smell and almost taste the salty tang from having been at sea. Oddly, I couldn't seem to recall anything once I arrived home and hit the bed. My lack of brain acuity resembled one becoming intoxicated, having memory loss and developing a hangover. Kipp licked my face, his warm breath caressing my cheek.

"Okay, I'm up."

As Fitzhugh hustled Juno and Lily out of the room, I staggered to the bathroom and flipped on the light, where the harshness of the bulbs did no favor to my appearance. My cheeks looked surprisingly hollow, my flesh pale and definitely not flushed with any sort of healthy color. Kipp followed me lazily, blinking his eyes at the bright light as he circled before plopping down on the bath mat.

"I still feel cold, Kipp," I remarked looking at him.

"Get a hot shower and have some tea," he advised, licking his paw as he conducted some minor ablutions of his own.

The hot water running through my hair did much to revive me, and by the time I toweled off and found a pair of sweat pants and one of my favorite soon–to–be worn out sweatshirts, I was feeling more like the old, familiar Petra. As I combed the tangles from my hair, I idly walked over to the pile of traveling clothes that would have to be returned to Technicorps, since they were company property. Picking up Peter's coat, I held it to my face...the scent of his aftershave from that final night remained trapped in the wool fibers. Shaking my head, I tried to rid myself of the thought since it was accompanied by a wave of sadness. Pushing my hand into the inner deep pocket, I was delighted to find the copy of Colonel Gracie's book which he signed. Opening the front cover, I bit my lip as I saw his bold scrawl proclaiming that I was his friend.

With the book in hand, I walked down the hallway, my eyes enjoying the familiarity of the wooden floor, worn in predictable places; I crossed the squeaky board that I knew like the back of my hand. Directly overhead was the light fixture I'd rescued from a junk store, magnificent except for the tiny flaw that had disqualified it from finding its way to an antique emporium and on to some foyer in a person's fine home. Kipp's toenails ticked softly against the hard surface of the floor.

The kitchen smelled of bergamot and faintly of Fitzhugh's dinner from the previous night, which must have involved abundant amounts of garlic. Light streamed in from the row of windows over-looking the back yard, and everything was just as I'd remembered it. The trip to the *Titanic* had not been a dream; I felt my head begin to clear. Fitzhugh waited for me at the dinette table, his favorite tea service carefully laid out.

Without speaking, I handed him the book as I took my seat. He opened it and smiled. "To my friend, Petra Keaton....Colonel Archibald Gracie," he read. "What a treasure!"

I was relieved he didn't reprimand me for the purloined book, since my possession of it broke the rules. Automatically, my hand moved to my throat before I remembered I'd taken off Harrow's pearls before showering. The precious strand lay on my dresser, waiting for me.

"So, you're not going to fuss at me for bringing it back?"

"Well, I was tempted," he began, before laughing. "No, I'm not going to fuss, and it will be our little secret." Once, we had no secrets between us, and now we seemed to be accumulating them quite regu-larly. He poured my tea and, without asking, added the local honey I enjoyed so much. "Peter and Elani have been showering praise on your and Kipp's leadership. Although you might not share, they told, vividly, of the harrowing conditions and how difficult it was to continue to observe and not intervene. From their perspectives, you two are super heroes."

Sipping my tea, I smiled wryly at him. "All I need is a pair of spandex tights and a cape," I replied. Glancing around the room, I remarked, "I think you are the true super hero, Fitzhugh. The kitchen seems neater than when I'm here taking care of things."

"What's a super hero?" Kipp asked, tilting his massive head to the side. He was resting on the floor where he'd found a warming patch of sunlight.

"Either humans or non humans with unusual powers, like extra strength, the ability to fly, or that sort of nonsense," I said, my voice flat. The hibernation following such a stressful time shift had dulled me, and I didn't bother to dig deeper for a clever response.

"I like the sound of that," Kipp responded, his tail thumping the floor. "Sign me up for extra powers, and I'd love to fly."

"Kipp, I'm sure there are no boundaries to your capabilities," Fitzhugh remarked lightly, laughing, as he held up his tea cup in mock salute. "Oh, and by the way, Philo is dropping by in an hour to take you two out to Duke Forest for a ramble in the woods."

"And I suppose I have no say so," I began, feeling the corners of my mouth turn down.

"Nope. And he said he'd bring breakfast, which is why I didn't fix your favorite strawberry Pop Tarts."

"Oh, good!" Kipp exclaimed. "That probably means Hardees biscuits."

With my tea cup in hand, I walked out on my back porch to gauge the temperature, since it appeared I'd be going for an outdoors excursion whether I wanted to or not. From my position as an amateur meteorologist, I speculated that a pleasant spring was upon us. The trees were filling their canopies, although the leaves were still a pale, almost translucent green, with an unspoken promise to deepen in hue as the weeks wore on. My azaleas were in bloom; the coral one Kipp and I had planted was obviously happy and thriving. My eyes wandered until I found the white azalea that marked the place where we'd buried my dear Tula's blanket in remembrance of her life. I was way too sentimental, and that fact hit me squarely between the eyes despite my protests. From the dinette set with the burned top, to the creamer I'd found with the broken handle —and the white azalea —I was surrounded with reminders of my connections to the past. Not just mine, but the histories of countless humans who were long gone from existence. Turning, I saw Kipp sitting on the other side of the door, watching me. He'd vacated his comfortable spot in my head to let me meander without his presence, but now he returned with a vengeance, filling every corner of my skull with Kipp. I smiled at him and lifted my hand in a little wave.

I was finishing braiding my hair when I heard Philo's voice. Odd,

I'd not paid attention to his arrival, which usually I felt due to my long standing connection with him. Grabbing a light jacket, I walked to the living room where Kipp was greeting Philo.

"So, what's keeping you?" Philo barked. It was grounding and comforting to be reacquainted with his brusqueness.

"I'm ready," I replied, my voice mild. "Kipp's only glad to see you because he thinks you come bearing biscuits."

Philo raised his eyebrows and glared at me. "Let's go."

During the drive to Duke Forest, Philo showed unusual restraint, driving almost carefully. At one point, a car passed us, the impatient driver honking his horn as he did so. He also gave Philo the standard middle finger salute known to all drivers.

"What did that mean?" Kipp asked.

"The driver was critiquing Philo's driving style," I replied.

"Oh, that's nice," Kipp replied as he started on his second egg and cheese biscuit.

Philo didn't speak, neither did I, during the drive. The countryside was damp with moisture that had collected overnight to coat the grass covered low hills. Patches of light mist rose from the ground where the sun began to burn off the beads of iridescent dew. To my right, a gathering of gold finches took flight, their bright yellow color startling against the pale, cloudless sky. Sighing, I nestled down in the seat after squirming a minute to get comfortable, and sat with my head tilted so I could allow myself to be hypnotized by the passing tableau. I think at some point, I began to drift off, pulled by the seductive allure of my recent hibernation. Perhaps I'd not been allowed sufficient time to recover thanks to Philo and Fitzhugh who seemed to think they knew what was better for me than did I.

"Wake up!" Philo dug his finger into my back, prodding me without mercy.

Grumbling, I sat up straighter. We were at our destination, so I had to rouse myself. Philo stopped the car with a jerk that made my neck pop. The sun, by then, was bringing enough warmth that I tossed my jacket onto the car seat. Kipp had hopped out and was prancing playfully, bowing his body as if teasing Philo to catch him. Within a minute, we disappeared as the forest swallowed us into its maw.

Wildflowers in a dense forest are an unexpected example of tenacity. Despite the struggle for sunlight to find its way through vegetation and tree limbs to the forest floor, little flowers abounded, their bright color unexpected against the dull wash of browns and greens. Leaning down, I inspected one, wishing I knew the botanical name, but I'd always been lazy that way. You'd think after living over four hundred years that I would have applied myself to acquiring more actual knowledge versus just experiencing things.

"It's like Thomas Andrews," I remarked out of nowhere, expecting Philo to immediately follow my lopsided train of thought. "He spent his life focusing on ship building and was an expert." Sighing, I spied another pale pink flower safely nestled like a precious gem amidst some early ferns. "I think I just bounce from place to place, learning just enough to get by but not enough to qualify as an expert on anything." I wasn't sure where that thought originated, but it defined part of my discontent.

Following my proclamation, we walked in silence for several minutes, before branching off of a well traveled trail to find a seldom used one that was partially grown over. Cars in the parking area indicated other patrons sharing the forest, but we had seen no one yet. The trail curved around the edge of a noisy stream which gurgled as the shallow water glided over a bed of polished rocks. Unexpectedly, Philo reached down and grabbed my hand; we continued, hand in hand, for a while.

Eventually we came upon a downed tree that invited us to sit and reflect. Kipp nosed around the floor of the woods until he found a comfortable place, padded with old leaves and free of sticks and rocks. After circling, he dropped down with a big grunt.

"How's Claire?" I asked, feeling it was polite to make inquiries. After all, we'd been friends for years.

"During the short time you've been away, she flew out to California to visit Silas." Philo was staring at a greening thicket across the stream. Overhead, there was a blur of bright blue as a jay, heading for home, cawed at us, seemingly irritated by our intrusion into his little world. "I'm not sure she'll come back," he added, his voice emotionless.

"I'm sorry."

Kipp twisted his head and gazed at us. "I don't understand how you can leave someone you love," he said, his words audible to me only. "I'll never leave you, Petra."

"I know, Kipp."

I'm not sure how long we sat like that before Philo seemed to shake himself out of his pensive mood. "So was it terrible?" He turned at looked at me. I saw, for the first time, new lines of worry on his face. And it seemed he'd acquired more gray hair overnight.

"I'm not convinced that being the leader of the Twelve is good for you," I answered, ignoring his question. "That plus your stress with Claire is taking a toll."

"Yes, I know I look old," he replied, his mouth twisting with displeasure. "How about not avoiding my question to you...how was the trip, and Kipp, I'm asking you, too."

Folding my hands in my lap, I waited for Kipp who, after nodding to me, decided to take the lead.

"Philo, it was fascinating, terrifying and tragic. It left me feeling, well, sad. I've never felt so pushed to intervene and do something to save so many lives but knew I couldn't." Kipp paused, and his tail began to wag, clearing a place in the leaves. "But the magic of meeting people we'd only read about in history was compelling. I'm almost ashamed to admit I'd go again."

Philo smiled, the first I'd seen on his face for a while, it seemed. "You are a true traveler, Kipp, with the needed attitude."

I watched a beetle, who seemed a rather early and intrepid explorer, make his way up a small mountain of leaves, only to have to carefully pick a safe path down the other side. He seemed determined to be about his business. Philo and Kipp were waiting, so I finally turned to Philo. "I wouldn't go again, unlike Kipp, who must be tougher than I am." Looking down I saw my hands were clenched into fists in my lap. Rolling my shoulders, I willed the knotted muscles to relax. "I can't get their faces out of my head...and when I dream..."

Philo put a hand on my shoulder and began to knead out the tension. "I've never traveled, so I can't imagine. But I admire you more than you know, Petra. You're one tough cookie."

"Maybe I don't want to be tough...maybe I want to be soft and squishy," I replied, trying to smile.

"Too late," he replied.

"And I need to tell you–since you're my boss–that we broke some rules while we were gone."

"Such as?"

"Well, while we were in London, we went to find Harrow and did so, from a distance. He didn't know we were there, observing him."

"And how did that leave you feeling?"

"Sad, empty, yearning...I don't know," I said. "And I brought back a book given to me by Archibald Gracie."

"Well, we will try and overlook your numerous faults," he replied, laughing softly.

"How are things at work, since I'll eventually have to return?" I asked, needing to change the subject.

"Oh, okay I think. Mark Elliott and Suzanne continue to be infatuated with one another." He rolled his eyes. "Fitzhugh hopes that they will marry and go off somewhere else to live."

"I thought he liked Mark. Or at least that's what he's said."

"Oh, you know Fitzhugh. If he's not in control, he's not truly happy." Philo sighed. "But I don't want to lose Suzanne because she's too valuable. I might look at reassigning Mark unless Fitzhugh can act reasonable."

"I'll talk with Fitzhugh," I offered.

"Well, if you think that will help."

"No, but I'll talk with him."

The End

NOTE FROM THE AUTHOR:

This story is a work of fiction, but many of the characters were indeed passengers and crew on board the *Titanic*. Captain Smith and First Officer Murdock went down with the ship, as did the designer, Thomas Andrews. The bodies of those men were never recovered. Bruce Ismay, as noted in the story, took a place in a lifeboat and survived. He was regarded as cowardly and lived much of the remainder of his life as a recluse. His part in the tragedy has been endlessly debated over the years. Second Officer Lightoller and Colonel Gracie actually went down with the ship but with remarkable luck and tenacity managed to find an overturned lifeboat and were eventually rescued. John Jacob Astor and Benjamin Guggenheim, two of the wealthiest men in the world, died during the accident. Astor's wife, Madeline, as well as Margaret Brown, the Countess of Rothes, and Helen Churchill Candee, were rescued and eventually resumed their previous lives. Margaret Brown and the Countess were highly regarded as heroines as they used their charisma and strength of will to motivate and direct their fellow passengers. Statistically, the greatest loss of life among the passengers was for men in second class.

The author, in writing about the loss of the *Titanic*, found the subject matter to be, well, titanic. She acknowledges the following sources for factual accounts of the tragic sinking in order to do honor to the people and their stories while crafting a tale of pure fiction:

Titanic: Those in Peril on the Sea, Steve Orlandella

The Sinking of the RMS Titanic, Charles River Editors

The Truth About the Titanic, Archibald Gracie

The Loss of the S.S. Titanic, Lawrence Beasley

The Night Lives On, Walter Lord

Gilded Lives, Fatal Voyage, Hugh Brewster

A Night to Remember, Walter Lord

Unsinkable, Daniel Allen Butler

The Last Log of the Titanic, David G. Brown

Inside the Titanic, Ken Marschall

ACKNOWLEDGMENTS

The author would like to express her gratitude towards some of the people who have been instrumental in the creation of this book. As always, she values the ongoing advocacy of her husband who never complains to find her hunched over the keyboard, a cup of coffee in hand. She is fortunate to work with the publishing team at *EPublishing Works!* and appreciates the guidance of Brian Paules. The author has worked for several years with Nina Paules and, as always, enjoys her cover designs as well as her support. Amy and Bobbi, you know who you are. It helps, always, to have friends for encouragement. And last, a special thank you to Nicholas Colvert, who helped her see the forest for the trees and who has never met a symbiont that he didn't like.

A CONSPIRACY TO MURDER, 1865

A SYMBIONT TIME TRAVEL ADVENTURES
SERIES, BOOK SIX

A trio of young women passed us, and my attention was drawn when I heard one refer to the middle girl as "Polly", since, if the old news accounts were accurate, the attack would be made on a girl named Polly Adams. She stood out from her companions, with a shorter, slighter silhouette. Without being overly conspicuous, we made a subtle loop around some large, dense shrubs and began to follow at a distance. The road, which was a packed mixture of dirt and rock, led down a gentle incline before a sharp right turn curved behind a copse of trees that seemed darker than the night itself. The women disappeared from our view when they took that turn, the trees and underbrush concealing them. Not unexpectedly, we heard a series of high pitched screams and darted forward, Kipp just a little ahead of me, his natural speed a distinct advantage, as usual. The other two girls who'd been accompanying Polly almost knocked us down as they raced past, retreating in the direction from which they'd come. It was clear, in their terror, they had abandoned the girl to her fate. Then we saw Polly, who'd been accosted by the man we sought. He was tall, much taller than was she, dressed as before in black clothing, and he bent over her, using one hand to hold her while he used the other to tear at her blouse. Even though our purpose was observational and to gain knowledge—which prevented our intervention during an attack—Kipp was caught up in his outrage over the mistreatment of a lady and gave voice to his disapprobation with a loud, aggressive bark. The man glanced up, and recognition of us flooded his thoughts, as he stared through the darkness in our direction.

We huddled in the shadows as I peered through the gloaming to try and better see the man's features, which were somewhat hidden under the brim of the hat that dipped deeply over his brow. I was convinced he wore a half mask on the top part of his face, leaving his mouth and chin uncovered. Spring-heeled Jack had been rumored to breathe blue fire, and I was waiting for such a display so that I could determine the mechanism, since it was clear this was a human man with no more powers than the rest of the species. As the man's eyes from behind the mask met mine, he lifted his right hand up to his mouth, and a moment later, a flame of blue fire shot out, about a foot in length, only serving to terrify poor Polly even more, if possible, as she slumped in a swoon. I could have been wrong, but I got the distinct impression he was showing off his prowess just to impress me.

The man dropped her abruptly and roughly to the ground and began to run, with Kipp in hot pursuit, Kipp's frenzied barking echoing against the emptiness of the park. There was a long, uninterrupted fence ahead, and the man took one amazing bound to clear the fence, as Kipp pulled up short with no route to follow. Dashing forward, I bent over the distraught Polly, who was babbling hysterically. As I helped her to her feet, she tried to pull together the remnants of her blouse, which had been shredded. The soft skin of her belly was scored and blood began to well along the cuts.

As others began to gather, drawn by the commotion, I quietly allowed myself to be absorbed by the crowd, and signaling Kipp, we faded into the darkness before a constable could arrive. I didn't need an interview of one Petra Goodgame to be recorded in the annals of history.

"He has a gas cylinder hidden beneath his sleeve, attached to his forearm." In my mind, I formed a diagram so Kipp could follow my thoughts. Yes, being a telepath has certain advantages. "Then, he uses a fire starter with a flint to get a spark and, whoosh, he creates the blue flame that we just saw." I felt satisfied I'd figured out the mechanics of one part of the theatre. Now we were left with the why behind it all.

A CONSPIRACY TO MURDER, 1865
Available in eBook and Print

ALSO BY T.L.B. WOOD

The Symbiont Time Travel Adventures Series

The Symbiont

Tombstone, 1881

Whitechapel, 1888

The Great Locomotive Chase, 1862

Titanic, 1912

A Conspiracy to Murder, 1865

ABOUT THE AUTHOR

T.L.B. Wood began her love of literature at an early age, encouraged by her mother who was an English teacher. She and her husband share a love of nature and animals, and more than one rescued dog or cat has found a forever home with the Wood family.

T.L.B. is an author in many genres: the inspirational romance *In the Eye of Hugo*, a paranormal history *The Way of Telitha*, the science fiction novels *The Last Child of Tole* and *The Ambassador from Tole*, and the epic fantasy *The Eagles of Arundell*.

She is best known for her young adult Symbiont Time Travel Adventure Series, which includes the books *The Symbiont, Tombstone, 1881, Whitechapel, 1888, The Great Locomotive Chase, 1862, Titanic, 1912.* and the forthcoming *A Conspiracy To Murder, 1865.*

In that series, time travelers with an eye for detail and a nose for trouble travel from the present era to investigate history's great mysteries. Humans think Petra is one of their own, a young woman accompanied by Kipp, her seemingly canine companion. But the reality is that Kipp and Petra are a bonded pair of telepaths in search of adventure.

T.L.B. has been described by reviewers as writing characters that "feel like old friends" with her "intelligent writing and research," and "improves with every book she writes."

Join the adventure!

www.ingramcontent.com/pod-product-compliance
Lightning Source LLC
Chambersburg PA
CBHW030957260626
47169CB00002B/576